Always a
Bridesmaid

LIZZIE SHANE

ISBN: 1537501216
ISBN-13: 978-1537501215

DEDICATION

For Leigh—thank you for being the best friend I could ever ask for and never turning Bridezilla, even in the face of thunderstorms and other minor catastrophes.

CHAPTER ONE

The death knell of Parvati Jai's professional hopes and dreams came on a Saturday morning in September, in the innocuous form of a phone call from her assistant manager.

"Sorry to bug you on your day off," Anna said by way of greeting, "but we're out of the Jamaican Blue Mountain."

The Jamaican Blue Mountain. The most expensive and exclusive coffee bean they offered—and the product with the least forgiving supplier.

With her cell phone pressed to her ear since the ancient Jetta pre-dated Bluetooth by about a decade, Parvati pulled into a nearby parking lot to avoid unintentional off-roading and a ticket she couldn't afford for distracted driving.

Her assistant manager's voice sounded more and more like the Voice of Doom as she went on. "We were supposed to get a delivery last Thursday, but there's nothing in the storeroom and when I called the supplier to confirm they sent it, they said our last check bounced. I know that's not even *possible*," Anna insisted with a touching—and delusional—faith in Parvati's solvency, "but they're dicking me around and refusing to expedite the shipment even though we've been one of their best customers for like five *years*."

A confession pressed up against the back of Parv's throat. She really should just tell Anna everything. From the truth that for every single one of those five years Common Grounds had been teetering on the edge of bankruptcy to the revelation of the elaborate shell game she'd been playing to keep things going for the last several months—borrowing from Peter to pay Paul until there was no one left to borrow from.

"Madison said I shouldn't bother you since you, like, *never* take a day off," Anna went on, her habitual irritation with the coffee shop's most popular barista tightening her voice. "But we're *totally* out of the Blue Mountain and some of our regulars are going to bitch."

"Don't worry," Parv said, finding her voice. "Offer ten percent off the Honduran blend instead—we have lots of that one. I'll straighten things out with the supplier when I get back from Monterey tonight. Everything will be great."

She hung up after a couple more minutes reassuring Anna with that lie lingering in the air.

Everything will be great.

She would need to tell them soon. Anna and Madison were going to lose their jobs when the shop went under, and she wanted to make sure they had plenty of time to look for other work. She could only put off the inevitable for so long.

Parvati knew she shouldn't have started paying for the coffee orders out of her personal account last spring, but Common Grounds simply didn't have the money and she'd been so sure if she could just hold on until summer that things would get better. Business always picked up during the tourist season.

But then Starbucks had opened on the edge of town, right off the Pacific Coast Highway—the same Starbucks whose very convenient parking lot she had swerved into when Anna called—and the tourists had proved to be much more drawn to familiar and convenient than they were to small town charm off the beaten path.

Even so, things had been a little better. The summer surge had been small, but noticeable. Just enough to give her hope.

Until she got the notice that the rent was going up. Again.

The cute little Main Street section of Eden was prospering, so her landlords felt justified in jacking up the rent accordingly—and the lease agreement she'd signed when she fell in love with the location didn't protect her against the rate hikes. If the camel's back hadn't already been broken in three places by then, that straw would have done it.

The personal check to her Blue Mountain supplier wouldn't have bounced—she was always so careful. But she'd had to replace the brakes on the Jetta—lest she go careening off the PCH and into the ocean—and she'd accidentally put the repairs on her debit card rather than the credit card with the identical logo.

The blow was one more than her checking account could handle.

By the time she realized what she'd done, the overdraft charges were just the icing on the cake. She had to appreciate the irony in being fined for not having any money, but it had forced her to face facts. Common Grounds wasn't just failing, it was dragging her down with it.

But even as she scrambled to find the money *somewhere* to cover the shipment, she kept smiling, kept hoping it would get better, kept promising that everything was going to be great, long after she knew it was a lie.

Parv tossed her cell phone onto the passenger seat and stared up at the Big Green Mermaid of Doom.

She loved Starbucks. It had been one of her favorite late night study locales during college and her soul deep affection for their dark roast blend had been a contributing factor in her decision to open Common Grounds in the first place.

It was a crying shame she'd never be able to look at one of them again without feeling a crushing sense of failure.

They were doing good business for a sunny Saturday morning after the tourist season tailed off—far better than Common Grounds was doubtless doing without its signature Jamaican Blue Mountain.

The front door opened and Parvati watched a Starbucks patron emerge with a grande cup clasped in one hand.

A very *familiar* Starbucks patron.

Parvati was out of her car before her brain caught up with her body, charging across the parking lot on a tide of righteous—and wildly irrational—indignation. "Traitor!"

Max looked up, a smile of greeting freezing on his face as his gaze flicked guiltily to the cup in his hand. "Parv. Hey. What are you doing here?"

"I could ask you the same thing, traitor. Since when is my coffee not good enough for you?"

She wasn't in the habit of bullying her customers into buying from her, but Max wasn't just a customer. He'd known her since she was six years old, ever since she became best friends with his sister Sidney. He'd been one of her first and most loyal customers since she opened Common Grounds and the last person she'd expect to defect to Starbucks.

God knew he could afford her prices—the man was holding the keys to a shiny new Tesla, for crying out loud.

He glanced at the car now, as if wondering if he could make a break for it before she tackled him and doused him with his own latte. "I was in a hurry and there was no parking at Common Grounds," he admitted. "For the record, your coffee is infinitely better."

It had better be, for what she paid for those damn beans. Parv had tried to make a niche for herself in high-end Eden, California by offering the luxury coffees her customers couldn't get anywhere else. It had made her clientele loyal—but limited. Even Parv couldn't afford to drink her own premium blend.

"Where are you going so dressed up?" Max asked.

Parv went along with his unsubtle attempt to change the subject from his espresso betrayal, eager for the distraction from all things Common Grounds.

"It's my parents' fortieth anniversary." She smoothed her skirt, the cocktail dress and heels she wore a far cry from her usual comfy casual flip-flops and maxi skirts. "My sisters are throwing them a big bash at their place in Monterey. Command performance." She'd put particular effort into her appearance today, taking the time to wrestle her thick hair into a classy chignon and slap on some makeup. Normally she would have been flattered Max noticed—especially since she'd had the Mount Everest of crushes on him ever since she'd figured out what boys were good for—but she was too nervous about facing her family and the inevitable questions they would ask. "Where are you off to in such a hurry you didn't have time for the best coffee in southern California?"

"Work." He snuck a glance at the massive diver's watch on his wrist. "New client wants us to upgrade the security at his estate."

"New client I've heard of?" she asked, shamelessly curious about Max's glamorous life. Growing up just up the road from Malibu, she'd had her fair share of celebrity sightings over the years, but Max owned and ran a company that provided bodyguards and security systems for the stars themselves. There was no competing with that.

She should have known he was headed to a work thing because of the flawlessly tailored suit. If left to his own devices, Max was more a T-shirt and jeans guy, but he certainly looked good in a suit. Of course, Parvati always thought he looked good.

Max Dewitt was tall and muscular enough that he should have looked like a wrestler in a monkey suit, but instead he looked like James Bond—a sexy, super ripped James Bond with perfectly styled dark brown hair and steely grey eyes that somehow managed to be warm when he smiled at her.

Which he did now, revealing perfectly straight, perfectly white teeth. And the dimple…really the dimple was just unfair. Sex appeal overkill.

He shook his head, still smiling. "Even if it was someone you'd heard of I wouldn't tell you who."

Parv made a face. "Your ethics are seriously interfering with my ability to live vicariously through you."

"You know I hate to disappoint you…"

"But you aren't going to tell me squat. I get it. Go on. Go be important with your fancy celebrity while my family spends the rest of the day giving me concerned looks and speculating on my sexuality because I haven't managed to find a nice man and give him babies yet."

He arched a single brow. "You're what? Twenty-eight?"

"Twenty-nine." *Closing in on thirty.*

"Then you're too young to get married. Twenty-nine is the new nineteen."

"My sister got married at nineteen. In fact, so did my parents."

Max tilted his head to the side. "Cultural thing?"

Her sister Devi would probably eviscerate him for assuming it had anything to do with being Indian American, but Parv had always liked that Max didn't dance around their differences and just asked. "You might think so, but my family is thoroughly Americanized. They just believe in marrying young."

Her parents had met as freshmen at Stanford and married immediately before the term began their sophomore year. Forty years ago today. And they were still nuts about each other.

"I think I saw your parents once," Max commented, "when you and Sidney graduated high school—but I don't think I ever met your sisters."

"They're all older. I was the surprise baby. By the time I was in high school, my sisters were all off curing cancer and revolutionizing the tech world." And generally making the rest of humanity feel inferior.

"I take it you aren't close."

Parv shrugged. "Angie's geographically close. She's just up in Santa Barbara with her perfect house, perfect husband, perfect job and perfect kids." She caught him glancing at his watch again and waved him toward his Tesla. "Sorry. Go make the world safe for celebrities. I can be insecure on my own time."

He started moving toward the driver's side of his car, but he did give her one last devastating smile, dimple flashing. "Chin up, Parv. You're pretty damn perfect yourself."

There was a time not so long ago when that compliment would have made her melt into a happy puddle of feminine hormones at his feet, but she'd learned not to take his compliments too seriously. He was only being nice to his little sister's best friend. Nothing more.

So she smiled and bantered back, keeping it light. "You'd know all about perfection."

He laughed and slid into his car, zipping out of the parking lot a moment later.

Max Dewitt. Her first and most devastating crush. And he still didn't have a clue.

Thank God. The last thing she needed was for him to figure out she'd pined for him for ten solid years between the ages of fourteen and twenty-four. She'd only begun to be able to talk to him without her tongue swelling up in the last five years. He was comfortable with her now. If he found out she'd once doodled *Mrs. Parvati Dewitt* on everything she owned, he'd probably be kind and sympathetic and look at her with the same barely-veiled pity that her aunts had been sending her way for the last several years.

Poor spinster Parvati.

Poor *broke* spinster Parvati.

Poor broke *failure* spinster Parvati.

Her family was going to be asking her today, over and over and over again, how the business was going. If she was dating anyone.

She could handle the dating question—she'd been handling that one for years—but when they asked her about Common Grounds…

She was going to have to lie.

Soon enough the truth would come out. When she closed Common Grounds, everyone would know that she had failed, but this was her parents' day. She refused to be the one less-than-perfect aspect of their legacy. If she told the truth, it would spread through the party like wildfire, carried on a wave of well-intentioned concern—which just made it that much worse. They all wanted the best for her, so it was that much more painful when she disappointed them. Her parents would worry. Her sisters would be annoyed with her for ruining the big day.

As lies went, it was a small one.

And maybe when she was forced to admit defeat and close Common Grounds for good, she could claim she just wanted a change. That she wasn't in debt up to her eyeballs. Better they think she was too flighty to stick with it than that she was a failure. If they believed it.

Parvati turned away from the Big Green Mermaid of Doom and pulled out onto the Pacific Coast Highway, headed north toward an afternoon of lies, starting with the one she told herself as she drove.

"Everything will be great."

CHAPTER TWO

Max zipped south on the Pacific Coast Highway, relieved that he seemed to have beaten the Saturday morning sightseers that could turn this fifteen mile stretch of highway into a two hour odyssey. Southern California traffic was always an unpredictable pain in his ass, but he might make it to his meeting on time after all—even with Parvati's little delay.

He took a sip of his dark roast—which really wasn't as good as the gourmet stuff at Common Grounds—and squashed the lingering flicker of guilt. He wasn't sorry that he'd stopped for coffee—he would never apologize for his daily caffeine regimen—but he did feel bad that Parv had caught him.

He knew she'd just been giving him shit with that traitor business, but he'd seen the tension in her face before she'd hidden it, the fear. All was not well in Parvati's world and he had a hunch it had more to do with Common Grounds than she was ready to admit. He'd always had a natural eye for business—and businesses in trouble. He'd been amazed Parv had managed to keep her shop open for as long as she had— Starbucks opening two miles away had to be the final nail in the coffin—but she obviously wasn't ready to face facts yet.

It was a shame really. She did make the best cup of

coffee in Southern California—and he was hopelessly addicted to those little fancy pastries she was always slipping him on the sly. She would always be Sidney's BFF first and foremost, but she'd also become part of his life, part of his morning routine, like his day didn't begin until Parv shoved an éclair on him, insisting she was trying out a new recipe and needed his critique.

He would miss seeing her every day if her shop closed—almost as much as he would miss her astronomically expensive premium blend coffees.

His phone rang a mile south of Malibu, distracting him from his musings on how he could keep Common Grounds afloat. His father's name popped up on the car's central computer console, all in caps, just like he'd entered it into his phone. Titus Dewitt didn't do anything in a small way.

Max considered ignoring his father's call—he could shoot him a text saying he was working and Titus would respect that, but he'd pay for it later. No one said no to Titus Dewitt.

Max hit the button on his steering wheel to connect the call, taking a deep breath—telling himself he was just waiting for the Bluetooth connection to complete—before speaking. "Hello, sir."

"Maximus." His father's gruff voice was as harsh and businesslike as it had been since Max was old enough to remember. Neither of his parents had been what could be considered nurturing. They were breeding success and they'd made sure their children had known it from the cradle. It was a minor miracle Sidney was as well adjusted as she was. God knew Max hadn't come away unscathed.

"I don't have long to talk. I'm on my way to a business meeting."

"I won't keep you," Titus replied quickly, not seeming to notice anything odd about the fact that Max was working on a Saturday morning. But then he wouldn't. "I wanted to confirm you were going to be present on Monday."

The slight Swiss accent his father had recently adopted colored the words, but other than that there was no inflection, no emotion to indicate that *Monday* was the preliminary meeting to hammer out the legal details for the dissolution of his parents' thirty-four year marriage.

The lawyers seemed more passionate about the proceedings than any of the parties involved. But that made sense, considering the parties involved were his parents and neither of them wanted sloppy divorce proceedings to threaten investor confidence in the pharmaceutical company his mother represented as CEO or the trillion-dollar multinational conglomerate his father had founded. They were trying to keep the entire thing under wraps for as long as possible, but after Monday the papers would be filed and the separation of one of America's premier power couples would go public.

"I'll be there."

He didn't know why his father had insisted on his presence—watching his parents' marriage be dismantled was hardly his idea of a good time—but when Titus Dewitt insisted, even world leaders listened.

"Good. I look forward to seeing you, son."

"You too, sir," Max replied, the words automatic. He wasn't sure he was looking forward to clapping eyes on his father for the first time in six months.

They'd never been the kind of family that spent much time together or indulged in public displays of affection, but in the last few months their mother had been making an effort with both Sidney and Max to have more of a relationship with them. She'd started having weekly lunches with them whenever their schedules allowed—which wasn't often, but it was downright maternal for the Dewitt family.

Titus, on the other hand, still seemed most devoted to his favorite child—Titacorp.

He didn't blame either of his parents for their divorce—it wasn't like he'd ever had any romantic notions about marriage. The only thing that surprised him about the situation was that either of them cared enough about their marital state to go the trouble of legally extricating themselves from the alliance. His mother still lived at the Eden estate, but his father had spent most of his time over the last decade in Bern, Switzerland where he'd relocated the Titacorp headquarters to facilitate doing business in Europe. Though born in New York with a silver spoon in his mouth, Titus Dewitt had gone to boarding school in Switzerland and bonded with the future finance ministers of several European countries before he inherited his father's modest millions and turned them into the thriving multi-national corporation that was his only pride and joy.

Max pulled up to the gatehouse at the entrance to Hank "the Hammer" Hudson's Pacific Palisades neighborhood, rolling down his window to greet the guard, grateful for the distraction from thoughts of his father. "Hey, James."

"Good morning, Mr. Dewitt," James answered crisply, tapping his name into the computer in front of him. Max had installed security systems for three other residents in the gated community, but he was pleased to see James still checked his name against the approved visitors list for the day and logged him into the system. Some gated communities had security that was laughable at best, but this was a decent starting point to the security network Elite Protection would be setting up for Hudson's family.

Decent, but not failsafe.

The kids who had ripped off Paris Hilton a few years back had just climbed a hill to bypass the gatehouse. A guard kept out the amateurs and tourists, but stars had people after them who were motivated and determined. They couldn't afford to assume a gate guard was all it took to keep them safe.

Max waved to James as he rolled through the gate, following his GPS's instructions through the complex.

The house itself was massive—a sprawling showplace—and Max immediately began cataloguing the security upgrades they would need to make as he parked behind his electronics specialist on the street in front of the mansion. Candy leaned against the bumper of her new car—the one she'd no doubt purchased as soon as she sold him her old Tesla because she wanted to drive the absolute *latest* technology. Max didn't recognize the manufacturer's sigil, but knowing Candy it was probably a one-of-a-kind prototype of some kind.

His tech specialist changed her appearance even more frequently than she changed cars and today she'd gone for spy chic—tight-fitting black-on-black with her hair blonde and slicked back and a pair of sunglasses wrapping around the front of her face and completely hiding her eyes.

"He doesn't even have exterior lights," she said, disgust plain in her voice as he joined her at her car.

He studied her for a moment until he identified the

look. "*Leverage*?"

"Parker's my girl," she confirmed. "I would have made a kickass thief if I hadn't decided to give Elite Protection the benefit of my genius."

"And Elite Protection thanks you for choosing us over a life of crime." He turned his attention back to the job. "We'll need to install security cameras, motion sensors, lights, perimeter beams—he wants the full treatment."

Candy arched one platinum brow. "Don't tell me someone's threatening the Hammer?"

"He was very interested in telling me that none of the security is for him. The Hammer fears no man. But apparently his ex is in rehab for the foreseeable future and he suddenly has full custody of a teenage daughter and he wants to make sure she's safe."

"He thinks someone is going to be dumb enough to come after the baby girl of a three-hundred pound mass of muscle with neck tattoos and a reputation for putting grown men into traction?"

Max shrugged. "Ours is not to question why—"

"Ours is but to install the freaking security," Candy finished for him and they started up the driveway.

Max took an instant dislike to Hank "Call me the Hammer" Hudson as soon as the pro-wrestler-turned-action-star opened his front door and began leering down at Candy—but he didn't have to like his clients to protect their sorry asses.

Candy could have taken the asshole apart, even if she was half his size, but Max made sure he kept himself between his tech guru and their client as they did a walk-through of the house, discussing the security options Elite Protection could provide.

"It's all for Cherish," the Hammer insisted for the

third time as they wrapped up the tour by inspecting the access points to the house from the back yard and pool deck. "Do you think we could get one of those biometric locks? I want to know every time someone enters or exits the house, whether I'm here or not. You can't be too careful."

"Cameras would be much cheaper to install and give you the same ability to see everyone who entered and exited the property," Candy commented.

"I'm not worried about the money." The Hammer puffed up to his full six and half feet. "I keep my women safe."

"We can install biometrics later if you feel the cameras aren't doing the job, but why don't we start there," Max intervened before Candy could react to Hudson's commentary on *his women*.

"That sounds good. But what about one of those tracking bracelets? Something could happen to Cherish when she isn't at the house."

"There are apps you can use to track her phone and we can get you set up with one of those," Max explained, having met enough overprotective celebrity parents that he didn't even blink at those requests anymore.

"In our experience, trying to put a teenager in a house-arrest ankle bracelet doesn't usually work out very well," Candy added helpfully.

"And will you be responding *personally* to any security calls?" Hudson asked her with a leer.

Max's calm, easy demeanor didn't falter for a second even as he smothered the urge to see if the Hammer had a glass jaw. "Any calls will go to police dispatch as well as a local emergency response firm we have an agreement with. That way we can guarantee a rapid response for each of our clients regardless of their distance from our main offices."

He kept his relaxed smile in place until he and Candy were on their way back down the driveway with a signed contract in hand and a plan for her to return on Monday for installation.

"Bring Tank when you come back," Max instructed, his shoulders rigid and hands tight in his pockets. The former NFL lineman was the one man on his payroll who would dwarf the Hammer.

"I was thinking I'd bring Pretty Boy." Candy swung along at his side, every muscle loose.

Half Tank's size, which still made him a reasonably big guy, Pretty Boy was one of his most requested bodyguards. He moonlighted as a male model, picked up new martial arts styles as a hobby, and had an amazing ability to never lose his lazy smile, no matter the provocation—except where Candy was concerned.

"You think he won't kill the Hammer if he comes on to you again?"

Candy's expression turned thoughtful for a moment. "Tank's probably a better choice."

Max had no idea what was or wasn't going on between Candy and Pretty Boy, and he didn't particularly want to know. He didn't interfere in the personal lives of his employees. But he'd just as soon Pretty Boy didn't get arraigned for assaulting a potential client who couldn't keep his mouth shut around Candy.

Tank—a wall of former-NFL muscle with a teddy bear's heart—would be just as protective of Candy and even more of a deterrent since he *looked* like the biggest badass on the Elite Protection payroll. He was actually among the least trained when it came to hand-to-hand combat and martial arts, but sometimes just looking like a scary motherfucker was enough.

Which was part of why Candy so rarely went into the field. She might be able to take out all the boys on the Elite Protection team with one arm tied behind her back, but she looked like a pixie, even when she was at her most badass, and that was only desirable in close protection soft work where the security team needed to blend in as a friend or family member.

Most of the Elite Protection jobs were about a *show* of possible force, rather than the more covert techniques involved in government protection. Celebrities wanted people to be able to see their bodyguards were the biggest, strongest—and sexiest.

Which was why Elite Protection was such a success.

Pretty Boy wasn't the only one on the payroll who could have been on the cover of a magazine. EP was about giving celebrities bodyguards everyone else would envy. They had become personal protection status symbols.

If Max knew one thing, it was how to turn anything into a luxury item—even a bodyguard. It was part of why Forbes magazine had done a feature on him after he'd sold his first company for millions at twenty-three. Prince Maximus, they'd called him, claiming he'd inherited King Titus's Midas touch.

He'd never wanted to be his father—there was a reason he'd turned down his father's every offer to come work at Titacorp—but no one in the business world ever looked at him without seeing Titus Dewitt's son first and what he'd built second.

"Take it easy, Boss," Candy called cheerfully as she hopped into her car and sped off to enjoy the rest of her Saturday.

Max climbed into the Tesla and pushed the button to

start it. It was still early—he could take the rest of the day off, try to remember what it felt like to relax, but instead he pointed the car toward the Elite Protection offices in Beverly Hills. There was work to be done. And he was his father's son.

CHAPTER THREE

Parvati's parents' place in Monterey was even bigger than the showplace where she'd grown up in Eden, easily accommodating the one-hundred-and-twenty guests that mingled on the back lawn. They'd moved up here to be closer to their grandchildren, since three of Parv's four sisters lived between Palo Alto and San Francisco, and they'd wanted to have plenty of room for the whole family to visit without feeling crowded.

The driveway was long and wide enough to accommodate half a dozen cars, but Parv still had to park halfway down the street, wedge her feet into the heels she'd kicked off during the drive, and trot half a mile balancing the oversized handbag she never went anywhere without, her parents' present, and the his-and-hers Godiva cupcakes she'd made specially for them.

The stupid heels were already pinching by the time she reached the front step and began carefully rearranging the items in her arms so she could open the door. It swung open before she could get a hand free, revealing her sister Angie and Angie's familiar frown.

"You're late."

"The invitation said twelve-thirty." Parv awkwardly caught the cupcakes when Angie plucked the present out of her hands, upsetting her balancing act.

Angie looked pointedly at the grandfather clock to one side of the foyer as she set the gift on top of a pastel-wrapped mountain of them, her lips pursed in disapproval. "It's twelve-forty. And the rest of us arrived early to help direct the caterers so Mom and Dad wouldn't have to worry about setting up."

"If you wanted me here earlier, you should have said earlier." Though she wasn't surprised the others had come. Angie would probably show up at dawn if it meant she got to dictate hors d'oeuvres placement. Her oldest sister had always had a hard-on for bossing people around.

Parv was saved from whatever Angie would have said next as one of her aunts rushed into the foyer, her sari rustling. "Parvati, Angira, there you are. Come now. Your father is going to say a few words."

"Coming, auntie," they replied in unison, hurrying in her wake out to the back terrace where the guests were gathered.

It was an eclectic group, three generations of the Jai family mingled with a Who's Who of Northern California in a broad mix of ages and ethnicities. Her parents stood near the gazebo on the most elevated part of the terrace, their arms linked around one another's waists as they smiled out over their assembled loved ones.

Parv's heart double-clutched a little at the sight. They looked so happy.

Forty years and they still woke up every morning wanting to see the same face looking back at them. Her parents were partners in the truest sense of the world. Since they were both nineteen years old, they'd never had to deal with a success or a failure alone.

She wanted that.

She wanted it with an ache in her chest that never seemed to go away, even when she managed to ignore it for days or weeks or even months at a time. But how did you get that when you weren't nineteen anymore? When every man you met seemed to either be taken or have made the decision *not* to want that kind of a partnership?

Her father raised his glass and quiet spread over the terrace, distracting Parvati from her morose musings.

"Thank you all for being here today to celebrate with us," he began, his voice ringing clearly over the crowd and carrying to every corner of the yard. Dr. Arjun Jai had always been good at making speeches. It was part of what had made him not just one of the premiere researchers at the pharmaceutical company run by Sidney and Max's mother, but also one of its primary spokespeople—though he mainly worked from home since his semi-retirement, cutting back his hours and guiding research studies from his personal computer so he could spend more time with his family.

"We are so honored and so fortunate to be able to share this day with so many people we love. Sunny and I have always considered ourselves lucky to have each other, and especially blessed by our five beautiful, intelligent, successful daughters—of whom we couldn't be more proud and who have given us nine brilliant, talented grandchildren to dote on. We could not ask for more than we have been given in this life, but you have spoiled us with one additional thing—the opportunity to celebrate our blessings with you." He lifted his glass higher. "To you, our friends and family."

On the steps leading up to the gazebo another of her aunts lifted her own glass, calling out, "To Arjun and Sunny!" which the rest of the guests echoed en masse.

Her parents descended and the jazz band began a light familiar melody—something that tickled at the edge of Parvati's memory with lyrics she couldn't quite remember about fairy tales coming true. Parv wove through the crowd, holding the cupcake case protectively so it didn't get jostled and ruin the icing she'd redone five times to get it just right. She smiled at her parents' friends, avoiding getting waylaid by relatives by nodding toward her parents and murmuring, "Just on my way to say hello," but she didn't make it all the way to her parents before the crowd of well-wishers around them stopped her progress.

She bumped shoulders with one of her female cousins, also trying to wedge her way through the crowd to offer her greetings and congratulations—and also with the hunted look of a young, single female at a family gathering that was all about love and marriages, though Lolly was five years younger than Parv and hadn't yet reached the pitying sighs stage.

"Hey, cuz. Haven't seen you up here in a while." In a nod to the occasion, Lolly wore a pink-and-white floral sundress that perfectly complemented the hot pink streaks in her hair and the garnet stud in her left nostril. She worked as a singer in a San Francisco night club when she wasn't going to grad school to get her PhD in compositional theory.

"Haven't been up in a while," Parv admitted. "The shop keeps me busy." She nodded toward the band in an attempt to distract her cousin from further questioning. "Do you know this song?"

"*Young at Heart*," Lolly answered instantly. "Popularized by Frank Sinatra."

"That's it. I knew I knew it."

The crowd around her parents shifted then and she was saved from further small talk when her father spotted her.

"Parvati! There you are!"

She didn't have to force the smile that covered her face as the crowd parted to make way for her. "Happy Anniversary." She stepped up to give her parents each a one armed hug before handing them the cupcake case. "I made these for you. Your favorite Godiva with raspberry ganache."

"Oh, how decadent." Her mother clutched the case greedily. "Thank you, baby." Though fifty-nine, she could easily have passed for a decade younger, especially when she smiled. Once a developmental psychologist and educational advisor to the governor of California, she had taken advantage of her own quasi-retirement to write a book on the psychology of highly successful individuals and had become the darling of the motivational speaking circuit.

Her mother had *literally* written the book on success and Parv was a giant failure. There really should be awards given for that kind of irony.

Their hugs were warm, swallowing her up with acceptance and pride and making her feel like even more of a fraud.

"How was your drive?" her father asked. "Good?"

"It was great." The desire to spill the entire truth rose up in her throat but she swallowed it down. "Gorgeous day for it."

"You should move closer," her mother urged, in a familiar refrain. "Expand north. Monterey needs premium coffee too. Or Cupertino. All those programmers keeping their long hours."

"I'm busy enough with the one shop. I can't imagine

opening another." Especially since the first was about to go down in a blaze of debt.

What were they going to say when they found out the truth? She knew they would always adore her, but she couldn't stand the idea of disappointing them.

"Arjun, Sunila, come take a picture with the Lieutenant Governor before he has to go."

Her parents each squeezed her hands affectionately before allowing themselves to be ushered off for a photo op. Parv hated the little flicker of relief she felt when they walked away. Relief that she wouldn't have to lie to their faces anymore. As crowded as the terrace was, she might not even see them again before the party ended.

She drifted off in search of a cocktail, determined to lay low, but she'd only made it three feet before a firm hand gripped her arm hard and the harried, permanently exhausted face of her middle sister appeared in front of her. "Asha."

"Have you seen Hunter?"

Parv automatically looked down, checking around Asha's legs by habit. "You've lost one of your sons?"

"Lost is a strong word." Asha's anxious gaze continued to scan the crowds. A muckety-muck at a Silicon Valley powerhouse, Asha had married at twenty-two—downright late for Parv's family—but waited until her thirties to start having children, so the twin terrors were now only five. Parv could only imagine the destruction they would wreak once they hit puberty.

"Did you try the pool shed? That's where Dad keeps the water pistols when the kids aren't playing with them."

"Pool toys. Of course. I knew you'd know how to think like a child."

Asha darted off in the direction of the pool shed and

Parv made a conscious effort not to be bothered by her last comment—that was just Asha, thoughtlessly insensitive. And yes, Parv was the fun aunt. That was a compliment, damn it. She wasn't going to give herself a complex just because her four perfect sisters seemed convinced she'd never grown up past the age of eight.

"Auntie Parv!"

A slim form slammed into her side and Parvati's arms closed automatically around her eldest niece in a hug. "Katie!" She squeezed, rocking Katie in a hug. "How's my favorite soon-to-be USC freshman?"

"Ah-*may*-zing," Katie gushed, bouncing back to stand at arm's length. "New student orientation starts next week and Jonah and I already moved into our new place. It's so *gorge*, Aunt Parv. You'll just die when you see it."

Parv felt a little flicker of concern. "You decided not to live in the dorms?"

Katie made a face. "They wouldn't let Jonah and me live together and I can't imagine having a roommate that isn't him."

"But living together, that's...big."

"We have two bedrooms. Mom insisted. Though I'm sure she knows we're, you know, but this way she and Dad can pretend we aren't."

"It's good that you have your own space. Going away to college...a lot can change." Though living with her high school boyfriend off campus, Parvati had to wonder how much of a college experience Katie was going to give herself. It seemed like she was closing off her options just when the world was opening up for her. "So you and Jonah are still good?"

Angie appeared at Katie's side before she could respond, her Bossy Mom persona in full effect. "Kateri, where's Jonah?"

"Around somewhere," Katie said with the concern of a girl who had brought her boyfriend to so many Jai family gatherings he was practically a member of the family now.

"Well, find him and go pay your respects to your grandparents. This is an important day." Angie gave her a significant look and Katie's grin grew suspiciously broad before she bounded off to do her mother's bidding.

Parv wondered if she could escape into the crowd before Angie noticed, but her oldest sister was already sending a piercing stare her way. "How are you, Parvati?"

"I'm great." She plastered a fake smile on her face—hoping to blind Angie with sheer brightness if she couldn't muster up authenticity.

Angie looked unconvinced by the high-beam attempt. "We worry about you."

Parv knew the "we" in this case referred to her sisters. Her four perfect sisters with their four perfect lives who could never quite figure out why Parvati couldn't seem to float through life on a similar cloud of perfection.

Angie, Ranee, Asha and Devi had each been born a year apart—in that order—and had ranged in age from ten to seven when Parvati made her unexpected appearance.

Angie—as a typical firstborn—came into the world believing she was the boss of everything and everyone she surveyed. She met a boy who seemed perfectly content to agree with that assessment when she was seventeen and married him less than two years later. Parv had always suspected that Angie most likely

31

proposed to Kevin herself, but since she was only a child at the time she'd been shut out of the sisterly gossip and could only speculate.

Katie came along when Angie was a junior at the University of California at Santa Barbara, but Angie had still managed to graduate summa cum laude. She worked in local government—some sort of city planning thing that let her boss people around all day—and had produced three more Mensa babies, each more perfectly well behaved than the last. Her husband adored her—whisking her off for anniversary weekends in Paris—and her Santa Barbara home was always meticulously tidy.

Some days it was hard not to hate Angie.

Calm, unflappable Ranee was the doctor of the family and at thirty-eight had already developed one of the most promising gene-therapy based treatments for cancer currently going through experimental trials. Married to a fellow M.D.—though the two had only been pre-med when they tied the knot—she lived and worked in San Francisco and had two children with such bright, inquisitive minds that they had made Parv feel a little slow since they were in kindergarten. Now twelve and thirteen respectively, they'd just returned from a summer trip to Africa for a clean water project.

Tech-genius Asha and her husband both worked in Silicon Valley, at one of those massive tech campuses with private chefs and full-time onsite day care for the Twin Terrors, though they would be starting kindergarten soon.

And then there was Devi. Closest to Parv in age, sometimes it felt like they were farthest apart in temperament. A self-described rabid feminist, Devi had made a career out of being militantly politically correct and taking offense at *everything*. A professor of sociology at Stanford, she'd recently published a book about race relations in America that had surpassed their mother's on the nonfiction bestseller lists and was currently working on a manifesto about identity in the twenty-first century.

Devi had married a man as politically and socially conscious as she was and their only child was a thin, intense nine-year-old girl with long black hair who used words like *disenfranchisement* and *perspective bias* in everyday conversation. Parvati considered it her personal mission to remind somber little Aya that she was, in fact, a child, and make her giggle as often as possible. A duty Parvati never shirked with any of her nieces and nephews.

She loved the lot of them to distraction. She just wished her entire family didn't make her feel so constantly inferior.

Sadly, the genius gene appeared to have skipped Parv. While they were all busy curing cancer and changing the world, she was running her cute little coffee shop in Eden—running it straight into the ground.

"What's to worry about?" Parv asked Angie cheerfully—then immediately regretted phrasing it as a question to give her such an easy opening. Not that Angie needed an opening. She probably would have bulldozed right through regardless of how Parv responded.

"We just want you to be happy. Don't you want more? A family? A home of your own rather than renting an apartment over someone else's garage? A husband?"

She wanted all those things. She wanted them with

that same ache in her chest that kept making it hard for her to breathe today, but if she told Angie how much she wanted them then she'd have to admit how inept she was at getting the things she wanted. "Sure I do. Eventually. And I am dating. It's not like I'm not looking."

"But what are you looking for? If you've been looking this long and you haven't found the right guy, maybe you're being too picky. Or focusing on the wrong things. I can't help feeling you're missing real opportunities at happiness."

"You're going to give me dating advice? You haven't had to try to meet a guy since you were seventeen and all you had to do then was bat your eyelashes in chemistry class."

Angie ceded that point for the moment. "At least think about your career. A coffee place is a cute hobby, but don't you think it's time for something more permanent?" She seemed to see the way Parv's face was tightening with irritation, because she held up a hand. "Just promise me the next time you get a real job with a real employer that you'll make sure it's someone with a good 401(k) matching program. We worry about your future."

You worry about having to support me if I'm broke and alone when I'm seventy. Parvati bit back the words, knowing they were unfair—but Angie's words were unfair too. How dare she assume Common Grounds was just a hobby?

The fact that it hadn't made a substantial profit in the last three years and was about to go out of business might support that belief, but Angie's lack of faith that she could make something of herself made her want to scream—right there in the middle of her parents' garden party.

She'd always been the baby. Always the one who was patted on the head and left behind. Always the one they talked about rather than talking *to*. And they were still doing it. Worrying about her en masse when she wasn't around. Discussing all the ways she was screwing up her life.

Wouldn't they just love it when Common Grounds went under and proved them all right?

But even as she had the thought, she knew it was unfair. They didn't want her to fail. They really did worry about her. Even if they never understood her. Or what it must be like *not* to meet the love of your life in high school or college. To actually have to look for him. To have to *wait* for Prince Charming to find you for an entire freaking decade.

Though if she was one hundred percent honest with herself, she had thought she fell for the man of her dreams when she was fourteen. He just hadn't fallen back. A concept Angie probably couldn't begin to comprehend.

"We're just worried that—"

Thankfully a fork striking a glass repeatedly interrupted whatever worry Angie was about to add to the pile. Parv turned gratefully toward the gazebo steps where her father stood, flanked by her mother on one side and Katie on the other.

"Oh jeez, *now*?" Angie grumbled.

Her father waited for a hush to spread over the guests before he raised his voice, smiling broadly. "I thought we were done with speeches for the day, but our eldest granddaughter has just given us some news. We could imagine no better gift for our fortieth anniversary than that she share it now with all our family and friends."

He turned to Katie, who moved up a step, tugging Jonah up with her by their joined hands.

Parv's gaze fell to those linked hands, a sudden gaping sense of dread opening up inside her. She knew all of Katie's news. Katie told her everything. It was something to do with USC. Or moving in together. It couldn't be—

"Jonah and I are engaged!"

That.

A gasp and cheer rose in quick succession and the floor dropped out from under Parv.

CHAPTER FOUR

She hadn't fainted.

So that was good. In retrospect, it felt like quite an accomplishment, staying on her feet with her blood rushing in her ears—though her sisters would have certainly rolled their eyes and declared it a melodramatic overreaction if she'd collapsed in a heap at Katie's announcement.

She remembered when Katie was born.

Remembered being taken to the hospital when she was eleven years old and having that tiny little person placed into her arms. Remembered the feeling—the massive, awe-inspiring feeling of loving someone she'd just met more completely than she'd ever loved another being in her life.

From that moment on, Katie had been special.

And now she was engaged. Eighteen, about to start college, with her parents still paying her share of the rent for the apartment she was living in with Jonah, and getting married.

And no one else seemed to see the wrongness of that.

They'd cheered. They'd toasted. They'd hugged the happy couple and teased them about their own fortieth wedding anniversary. They'd asked when the wedding would be—and Parv hadn't been able to think past scheduling a honeymoon around a semester break.

Did no one else see that they were babies? Yes, the Jai family had made a tradition out of teenage marriages, but Katie was different, wasn't she? And times had changed in the last twenty years, hadn't they?

Or was Parvati only reacting to the fact that Katie had proven, once and for all, that she wasn't like Parv.

The aunties had swarmed around Parv for the rest of the party, clucking and tsking and patting her on the hand like she was in mourning. Parv had kept a smile on her face and even managed to hug Katie and squeak, "Congratulations!" with an admirable degree of sincerity. She posed for family pictures with her sisters, her parents, and the cast of thousands that was her extended family, and never once did her cheerful *Everything is going to be great* attitude waver.

Until she was driving home and finally had a chance to process the day.

No one had tried to set her up.

She didn't know why those words seemed to echo in her mind like the Gong of Doom, but they were the first thing to penetrate her determined good cheer as she headed toward the 101, taking the fast route and forgoing the pretty coastal highway.

No one mentioned a nice boy they knew. No one threatened to introduce her to a coworker who had just gotten divorced.

Her family had officially written her off.

Katie was getting married and Parvati was a lost cause. An old maid. A spinster.

She hated those words. Words that didn't even exist for men because no one judged *them* for remaining unmarried past the age of twenty-five, but Parv had apparently missed her one chance at happiness by not locking someone down before high school graduation.

Angie's well-intentioned words came back to her—along with the bite of them. Her sisters worried about her. Worried that she was going about her life all wrong and was going to end up miserable and alone. Of course they did. She was the failure sister. The one who couldn't land a man—and whose single focus in the last five years was about to go out of business.

Parv fumbled with her cell at a stoplight while she waited for the green, punching in Sidney's number by heart even though it was programmed in. She put the phone on speaker in her lap as the light turned green and listened to it ringing. And ringing.

She knew even before she heard that familiar click-pause of the voicemail taking over that she wasn't going to reach Sidney. She rarely did these days. She waited through the familiar message—*you've reached Sidney Dewitt of Once Upon a Bride. I'm sorry I'm not available to take your call at this time, but please leave a detailed message…*

"Hey, Sid—" Parv broke off, suddenly unsure what to say. If Sidney had answered, she could have vented. She could have babbled. But somehow everything she wanted to complain about didn't seem important enough for a voicemail message. It wasn't urgent—it was just the slow crumbling of her life. It would still be crumbling tomorrow. "Just headed back from my parents' thing," she said, hearing the slight waver in her own voice and replacing it with an upbeat note. "I'll be driving for a while so give me a call if you have a chance to talk. 'Kay. Bye."

She considered calling Victoria, but it was Saturday and she would be with her family—and Parv had never been as close to Tori in their little friendship triumvirate as she had been to Sidney. Sidney was the glue that had made them the Three Musketeers. Back when they were all single.

Back before Sidney fell in love with Josh and the two of them started filming a reality television show about dream weddings for deserving couples that took up all of their time.

Back before Tori reunited with her daughter's father and the three of them became an instant family, wholly focused on making up for the time they'd lost.

Back when there had been Tuesday Girls' Nights and she'd never felt like a leper because she hadn't been The Single One, she'd just been one of the girls.

Now she didn't even have anyone she could talk to about how things were changing because Sid and Tori were the ones she would normally talk to and if she let on that she was anything other than blindingly happy for them, then she would be the awful, selfish friend who couldn't be happy for her friends' happiness because she missed who the three of them had been before.

She'd always been single, but she hadn't felt alone. They'd always been there for her. But things changed—and she was the one who hadn't changed with them.

It was almost nine when she arrived home—and remembered that she was going to have to do something about the Blue Mountain shipment. The day already felt like a never-ending shit-storm, but as exhausted as she was she knew she wouldn't be able to sleep yet anyway, so she slipped inside just long enough to exchange the Torture Heels for a pair of flip flops and began the walk down the hill of her neighborhood toward the Main Street area of town and Common Grounds.

It was full dark, but she knew every pebble along the way, having walked this path nearly every day for the last five years—most days in the dark, since she was often baking before dawn and doing orders and payroll long after the shop closed.

It was a long-ish walk—thirty minutes downhill and longer going up at the end of the day when she was exhausted, but it was worth it to spare an extra parking space for a customer in their tiny lot. And in daylight, the view was spectacular—vineyards in the hills behind her, the glittering blue sprawl of the Pacific Ocean in front. There was a reason Eden, California was so popular with the ridiculously wealthy who wanted more of a small town, community feel in the stretch of land between Malibu and Santa Barbara.

The adorable little Main Street area was a tourist attraction, but also a draw for the locals who were rabid about preserving the character of the town.

The *character* of the town was the excuse the council had given her for the city ordinances that dictated the business hours of any shop along the Main Street stretch—making it impossible for Parvati to stay open long enough to compete with the Big Green Mermaid of Doom just outside the city limits.

The *character* of the town was why they raised property taxes to pay for the new lamp posts lining the street—and Parv's landlord had responded by raising her rent.

She loved Main Street. The character of it. The atmosphere was a large part of her decision to open her shop there. She just hadn't realized how much that feel was going to cost her.

She'd always known the first couple years were going to be hard. She'd gone to business school. She knew all about start-up costs and operating losses.

Don't worry. Things are always rough at first. That was

her mantra for the first two years. Then the mantra had changed. *Don't worry. I'll take care of it. Everything's great.* As if by saying it over and over again she could make it true.

Parv unlocked the door, stepping inside and breathing in the smell that always soothed her nerves — coffee beans, polished wood, and pastry crust. She loved this place.

She flipped on the light to see it all. The comfy sitting area, the high top tables, the gorgeous pastry display case. She'd made this.

And now it was going away.

Parv sniffled, indulging in a maudlin moment as she made her way through the gorgeous gleaming stainless steel of her kitchen to the tiny box of an office, cluttered with everything she'd just as soon ignore. The detritus of running a business.

The records were here. Payroll. Suppliers. Rent. Utilities —

She should probably turn off the light she'd left on out front. She couldn't afford the electricity.

She opened the five-year-old laptop and fired up the bookkeeping program, listening to it whirr softly as it chugged through the software's start-up process. And then there they were. A neat little march of red numbers across the page.

She'd already known. She didn't know why she'd felt the need to come here and stare at the numbers as if that would change something. There wasn't any money to pay the suppliers. Common Grounds was done.

"Parvati?"

Her chair legs scraped loudly in the silence as she came to her feet at the voice calling from the front of house. She sniffled and scrubbed away the wetness on her face, rushing out of the office, through her gorgeous kitchen. "I'm sorry—we're closed," she called before she even reached the swinging door that opened behind the counter—though whoever was out there had to know that. They had called for her specifically.

Then she stepped out into the warm light of the front and saw the man standing with one hand resting on her display case—like the physical embodiment of everything she'd ever wanted but couldn't have.

Max.

"Of course it would be you." Of course *he* would be the one to see her when she was having a little private breakdown.

"Your door was unlocked." Max nodded toward the door in question and Parv followed his gaze. "What do you mean of course?"

That brought her gaze back to his—and to the wrinkle of concern between his brows.

"Parv? You okay?"

"What are you doing here?"

"I was driving by on my way home and saw the lights on. Wanted to make sure everything was okay—and to apologize again for my coffee betrayal this morning. Thought maybe you'd let me buy a make-up latte."

* * * * *

As lies went, it was a small one. He had been driving by. And he had wanted to make up for that morning—but Eden's Main Street wasn't on his drive home. He'd just wanted to see her.

Max had worked later than he expected—pacifying clients, adjusting schedules, and considering various marketing proposals for the new celebrity self-defense classes Elite Protection was going to begin offering in the spring. The hours had slipped away from him, as they always seemed to, and it was after nine before he got to the turn-off for his house—and kept driving.

It was impulse to zip up to Eden. He'd kept thinking about Parv throughout the day and the excuse of an apology latte had seemed a good one—until he pulled off the PCH into the Main Street district and saw a row of darkened windows. He'd forgotten everything would be closed.

Then he'd turned the corner onto Main Street itself and seen her shop, a beacon of golden light spilling out the windows, inviting him in.

When he'd seen the deserted interior and found the door unlocked, it had roused his security-focused instincts. His relief when she'd appeared out of the back room had been acute—because she was Sidney's best friend and his sister would be destroyed if anything happened to her—but then he'd noticed her red nose. Her pale face. Her damp eyes.

There was something unnatural about seeing Parv upset. She was Sidney's sunny friend. Always smiling. Wise-cracking with him over his morning latte. She was the exuberant, vivacious one. When Sidney would freak out, it was Parv's voice he would hear—encouraging her, cheerleading, saying everything was going to be great.

But who cheered up Parv?

"What's wrong?" he asked, coming around the counter.

"You're not allowed back here," she said, but the words were defeated and completely lacked the authority to shoo him back around the barrier.

"Don't worry. I know the owner."

She gave a half-hearted little sniff-laugh and a tear slipped from her eye, rolling down her cheek.

"Hey." He closed the last of the distance between them, tugging her into his arms. Her resistance was token at best and she let him tuck her against his chest. It wasn't until his arms settled around her that he realized he'd never hugged Parvati before.

They were friendly—he'd slung his arm over her shoulder when they posed for group photos over the years—but now with her tucked against his chest, he realized how much smaller than him she was. The top of her head came to his collarbone, her cheek resting against his pecs. She smelled of sugar—doubtless from all the baking magic she performed in the kitchen of Common Grounds—and was soft and curved in his arms. Parv had never been waiflike, but he'd always preferred a figure with a little lushness to it—

Not that it mattered what he preferred. This was Parvati. Sidney's best friend. The word *lush* should never be in the same sentence with her.

She hadn't fallen apart in his arms, he realized. There were no sobs, just the occasional sniffle, but she held onto him tightly, like he was her anchor.

Too tightly. He could feel every inch of her, pressed against every inch of him. And any second now she was going to notice that his body was very happy with their current situation.

Max gently set her away from him. "How about some tea?" he asked, scrambling for something neutral and comforting. People drank tea when they were upset, didn't they?

Parv sniffled, her dark eyes seeming larger and more compelling with moisture clumping her eyelashes. "Did you just offer me my own tea?"

He glanced at the tea display next to him. "I did. But at least you know it's the good stuff."

She snorted, grabbing two mugs. Max had never been a tea drinker—triple shot lattes were his drink of choice—but he didn't stop her as she measured loose grounds into some kind of sieve ball, something about the action seeming to calm her as much as his hug had.

He watched silently as she filled a small teapot with hot water, bent to retrieve a bottle of Sweet Tea Vodka from a hidden cupboard, and put the entire collection on a tray, carrying it over to the sitting area by the gas fireplace. The fireplace was dark now, but somehow that added to the after-hours feel of the shop, making the setting even more intimate.

Not *intimate* intimate. She was his sister's best friend.

But as he settled down opposite her in one of the comfy armchairs, something felt different. He'd always been comfortable around Parvati—they'd known one another forever—but it was the distant comfort of easy banter and surface chatter. Tonight was something else entirely.

"You wanna tell me what's going on?" he asked, keeping his tone light, as if there was a chance in hell he was leaving here without finding out exactly what was bothering Parvati.

"What isn't going on?" she countered, filling the mugs and handing him one as she lifted her own to inhale the steam. Max mirrored her action and was surprised how much he enjoyed the sweet scent. Parv lifted her mug in a mocking toast. "Here's to me. I'm officially failing in every aspect of my life."

"I'm not drinking to that. I'm sure it isn't true."

"You're sure?" Irritation snapped in her eyes.

"You're an expert on my life, are you?"

Max bit his tongue. He didn't know this unfamiliar Parvati, vibrating with anger at his attempt to comfort her. Sidney liked to tell him he was useless at women, but he'd always thought he was rather good with them—he'd certainly never had any complaints—but now he was starting to realize his little sister may have had a point. He had no idea what to say to Parv.

Luckily, she seemed perfectly willing to fill the silence.

"My eighteen-year-old niece got engaged today, but I can't even find someone I want to go on a second date with. My sisters are worried about me because I couldn't land the love of my life when I was sixteen, but the only person I wanted then was you and we all know how well *that* turned out—"

Max choked on the sip of tea in his throat. "Wait. What?"

"Don't pretend you didn't know I had a crush on you."

She kept speaking, but Max's ears shut off.

He remembered her at sixteen. Mostly he remembered the string of inappropriate teenage fantasies he'd had about her mouth before he'd grown up enough to get his hormones under control. Or somewhat under control. She still had the same mouth. But he hadn't thought about it that way in years. She was Parv. She was Sidney's best friend. She was entirely off limits. He hadn't even *considered* thinking of her that way.

And he sure as hell hadn't known she'd had a crush on him.

Had. Past tense.

She'd obviously grown out of it. She'd talked about it

like it was nothing. A harmless little teenage crush. Totally natural. He was two years older. Her friendship with Sidney made him close enough to her and off-limits enough to be the perfect mix of attainable and unattainable. He was the natural choice for a crush. It was nothing personal.

But something felt like it had shifted. Something subtle and small. Inconsequential.

He tuned back into her diatribe, hoping she hadn't noticed his distraction.

"—and I just hate it. I hate that nothing in my life is going the way I thought it would. I hate that I spent five years trying to make this place fly and now I'm going to have nothing to show for it. I hate that everyone is going to know that I failed as soon as I announce we're closing. And I hate lying to my parents about how bad things are."

"How bad are they?"

She sank into the depths of her chair, cradling her mug between both hands. "I need to tell my employees, but that will make it real. So I keep putting it off. I thought summer would be better—and I'm discovering I have a heretofore unexplored gift for denial." Her gaze moved around the shop, taking it all in. "I talked to a small business advisor about selling the business as a whole, but apparently it's worth more piecemeal. If I sell off all the assets, that should be almost enough to pay everyone off. A premium espresso machine is worth something—even used. The display cases, the dishes, the furniture…" She traced a finger along the arm of her chair. "Everything will have to go. The kitchen will be the hardest. My parents gave me the oven as a present when I first opened. It's so gorgeous—and even if I get what it's worth, I'll just barely get enough to walk away with nothing." She lifted her mug again in a toast. "So here's to me. Turning thirty with nothing but failure to show for the last decade."

"I'm still not drinking to that. You'll bounce back. This doesn't have to be the end of the world."

"Everything will be great?" She snorted, but he didn't get the joke. "I'm good at saying that. *Everything will be great. I'll take care of it. Don't worry.*" She breathed out a soft, huffing laugh. "No one else has to worry because I do enough of that for everyone." She shook her head. "I don't know how you do it."

"Do what?"

"Run a business. Five years of constant stress and I'm falling apart, but you make it look so easy."

"It isn't easy, but I don't get stressed out." He shrugged. He just wasn't built that way. He was a Dewitt. And Dewitts created businesses. It was who he was. "Sidney tells me I need to stop and smell the roses sometimes, but I think the fact that I never stop working is why I never have time to stop and feel the stress."

He'd never been able to slow down. To stop pushing for even a second. Max was always working. Which was why he'd been able to take an idea, turn it into a successful business and sell it off by the time he was twenty-three.

"You smell the roses," Parv insisted. "You took three years off to travel the world after you sold your first business." There was envy in her tone.

He didn't want to dissuade her from her idea of him as someone who actually knew how to enjoy life, though he couldn't say why.

He hadn't smelled the roses on his trip. Backpacking across Thailand. Doing charity work in the Sahara. Climbing Mount Fuji. Getting his third black-belt in

China. He'd always been moving. Always working. Competitive tourism.

But he liked Parvati's idea of him. He would have liked to be that guy. The one who could slow down.

Parv slumped down in her chair and Max realized how late it had gotten—and she'd driven to Monterey and back today. He rose, setting aside his cup and taking hers out of her hands. "Come on. Let's get you home."

CHAPTER FIVE

There was something surreal about walking into her kitchen and finding Max Dewitt standing at her sink with his shirtsleeves rolled up doing dishes. Parvati paused on the threshold, watching him. He'd taken his jacket off and left it neatly folded on the pristine counter behind him as he scrubbed clean the mugs and teapot they'd used.

She'd slipped away to shut off the computer in the back office—reminded again that she had no idea what she was going to do about the Blue Mountain shipment because there was simply no money left—and when she returned he was making himself useful, erasing any work she might have had to do. Taking care of her.

The sight tugged at something inside her and she had to remind herself that this was just Max. He was protective. He took care of people. It was in his DNA. But he didn't get attached. Not to things and certainly not to people.

She'd seen him go through girlfriends at a rate that would have made some of his celebrity clients blink. She knew he wasn't Mister Forever. But that didn't stop a weak part inside her from wishing that he could have been.

He looked up as he set the dishes on the drying rack, finding her watching him. His eyes crinkled as he gave her a little half-smile of welcome and Parv's ovaries lurched. He'd always been her fantasy —

And she'd had to go and tell him that.

Brilliant.

She couldn't even blame the vodka because she hadn't had that much. Just a tiny splash. Her only excuse was that the pressure of the day had built up on her and she'd needed the release valve of spilling all her deepest darkest secrets to Max Dewitt.

Including the fact that she'd been secretly in love with him for over a decade.

At least he hadn't run screaming into the night. Though neither had he jumped her bones — so there was one fantasy crushed.

She'd known he wouldn't gasp, "But I've always loved you too!" and make mad passionate love to her right there on the floor of Common Grounds, but it had been a nice little daydream while it lasted.

No, there was no passionate obsession in his eyes. Only friendship. Concern. And if she was honest with herself, she needed that more than she needed a mad, passionate embrace from a man who'd never been able to take a relationship past the three week mark.

He collected his coat. "Shall we?"

She nodded and he held the door for her while she flipped off the lights, leaving the kitchen in that lovely, peaceful quiet of the middle of the night that she'd always loved.

Sadly, lovely peaceful quiet didn't pay the bills.

He shrugged into his coat on the sidewalk while she locked up. "I didn't see your car."

"I walked."

He nodded and moved to the passenger door of his Tesla, opening it for her. She wondered if the move was bodyguard training or gentlemanly courtesy as she slid into the plush grey leather interior. He closed the door and she watched him round the hood—he would be so many women's fantasy. Right up until they realized that he wouldn't stay. Parv was lucky that she already knew that little fact. Lucky that they were just friends—or at least that's what she told herself as he climbed into the driver's seat and started the car.

"When did you buy this one?" she asked, petting the leather, making conversation so she wouldn't have to think about how amazing he smelled. "Last I saw you were driving...a Corvette?" He'd gone through a series of muscle cars in the last few years—clearly a man who enjoyed power—and she'd always had trouble keeping up.

"Eco-friendly is in," he commented, taking the turn up the hill. "My clients like this. The image it projects. And Candy was looking to sell, so I took it off her hands."

"Your tech wizard?" A little flare of jealousy kicked up at the name. She'd met all of Max's employees over the years at Christmas parties and Labor Day picnics and she'd never seen any sort of sparks flying between Max and Candy, but she knew firsthand that the woman was brilliant. And beautiful.

"Yeah."

She listened carefully, but couldn't hear any trace of unrequited love in the one syllable answer. "It's nice," she commented in a gross understatement. She didn't know much about cars, but she knew this one screamed wealth and luxury.

"Thanks," Max said, already pulling into her driveway since the two mile walk took less than five minutes to drive. He parked his shiny new car behind her dilapidated Jetta and cut the engine.

"Do you want to come in?" She unfastened her seat belt. "The owners are out of town so we won't disturb anyone."

The house was a typical Eden estate—a gorgeous, sprawling Mediterranean style mansion with exquisite views. Parvati had an apartment over the three car garage—a converted in-law suite with private access— and could only afford the rent because the Marquez family gave her a break on the rent in exchange for her keeping an eye on the main house and watering their plants whenever they were on their yacht in the Mediterranean, which tended to be more than half the year.

"I should get home," Max said in reply to her invitation, but neither of them moved to get out of the car.

There was something different about tonight—all the usual barriers of cheerful, distant friendliness were down. She could be honest with him in this moment, but she knew as soon as she went inside it would be over. They would revert back to who they'd been to one another before—Sidney's brother and Sidney's friend. And she wasn't ready for that yet. She liked the unexpected closeness too much.

"You knew, didn't you?" she asked softly. "That we're going under."

"I had a hunch."

She twisted to face him. "Please don't tell anyone."

She just needed to keep this secret a little while longer. Until she could feel like she knew what she was doing. Until she had a plan and could brace herself for the fallout.

"Hey." He put his hand over hers where she'd placed

it on the center console when she turned. "You're gonna be okay. It's just business."

"No," she whispered, feeling those awful tears building again. "It isn't."

It was easy for him to say that, but it wasn't just business. It was every corner of her life. It was Katie and her family. Their expectations. All of it.

Maybe she lacked perspective. Maybe it was a case of first-world problems and she needed to be grateful for the amazing family she had. The roof over her head—even if she was going to have to go live with her parents when she couldn't pay her rent anymore. Maybe none of her problems mattered in the long run, but they were *her* problems and right now, in the middle of the night, closed in the front seat of Max's car with him and her honesty, they didn't feel like nothing.

She looked up at the house again—someone else's beautiful house. It had been supposed to be a temporary measure. She'd thought, when she moved in after grad school, that it would be a short-term situation. She'd intentionally picked something that wasn't designed to be permanent because she'd thought she would meet her Mister Right any day and she wouldn't want a long-term lease keeping her from starting a life with him.

Now…

"I'm so tired of dating." Max didn't even blink at the sudden change of topic. "I think that's part of why I loved the idea of going on *Marrying Mister Perfect* so much. Sidney didn't even want to audition. I talked her into it—and then watched her get picked to fall in love on national television while I stayed home."

It would have been crazy—she knew that—but it could also have been *it* for her. The love story that made her years of singleness and struggle worth it. And the exposure of the show could only have been good for the shop. It had certainly catapulted Sidney's career into the stratosphere.

She'd had to fight her jealousy the entire time Sidney was on the show. Had to fight to be happy for her friend and not let anyone see how badly she'd wanted it for herself.

Devi would doubtless have told her that she didn't get it because they'd already picked out a token ethnic girl in Elena Suarez—if Devi had known about the audition. Parv had never admitted to her family that she'd tried out.

Sidney hadn't liked the idea of being on camera. Parv and Tori had to talk her into doing it, convincing her it would be good for the wedding planning business she and Tori ran together.

Then, of course, she'd gone on the show and fallen in love not with the man she was *supposed* to love, but with the host—whom Parv had always shamelessly crushed on when they watched MMP on their Girls' Nights.

So Sidney got her happily ever after and Parv was happy for her. Really really really happy. So happy her friend was happy...even as she tried to squash the little voice inside her screaming that she was supposed to get a happily ever after too.

She'd wanted it, when Sidney wasn't sure. She'd dated enough men to populate the casts of a dozen dating shows. She'd *tried* to find love, damn it. She wasn't supposed to be the charity case that everyone else was trying to fix up with the single guys who were left over.

Maybe she was too picky—her sisters certainly thought so. Maybe she'd been comparing everyone to Max, hoping to feel that awed, swept away feeling she'd felt when he'd slow danced with her at Sidney's sweet sixteen. A pity dance.

The only relationship she would ever have with Max Dewitt would be a pity one and she knew that, knew she needed to put aside the fantasy of him and look at real men, but she wanted that magic. She wanted it so badly.

"You would have hated being on *Marrying Mister Perfect*," he said, interrupting her longing.

She frowned at him. "No, I wouldn't."

"I watched a few seasons when Sidney was picked to go on it. They pick party girls."

"I can be a party girl."

His eyebrows lifted skeptically. "Day drinking and cat fights? That's your new thing?"

"Not everyone they pick is a party girl. Sidney isn't like that."

"Sidney's an exception."

Because she was so gorgeous the producers hadn't cared. The California blond with legs for days and a cute little wedding planning business.

"You're an introvert," Max reminded her. "Tell me you aren't happiest when you're hiding in the kitchen by yourself."

"I'm not hiding. I just like to bake. And plenty of introverts go on the show. Look at Caitlyn. She *won*."

"Yeah, but they can only have so many sane girls on a show like that or it falls apart. They need big drama. Big personalities. Crazies."

"I am dramatic!"

"Tonight you are. But how many years have you repressed this? And tomorrow you'll be back to keeping it together."

He thought she was repressed. Brilliant. This day just kept getting better.

She reached for the door handle. "Good night, Max."

"Parv." He stopped her with a hand on her arm, the touch so light she barely felt it. "You're too good for that show."

"Yeah." She opened the door. "That must be why they rejected me."

CHAPTER SIX

Max was right about one thing. The next day she was back to keeping things together.

Parv flipped on the lights in Common Grounds' kitchen at five-thirty the next morning. She turned on the ovens, letting her fingers linger over the controls. Sunday was one of her usual baking days. Madison would be in later to open the front of house and Parv would jump on the register to help her if they had a rush, but most of the morning she'd be left alone with her batters and doughs. And her thoughts.

Baking days were usually her favorite days of the week, when she could commune with the stainless steel perfection of her kitchen and think through solutions to the shop's problems, but she was out of ideas now. And starting to feel like she was dragging out the inevitable.

The shop was usually quiet in the afternoons, after Madison left, with just a few of their regulars lingering over their coffee refills, and Parv would restock the front of house, getting ready for the Monday morning rush as she chatted with the regulars and filled the occasional order.

It was a good day, Sunday. But even getting out the ingredients for a batch of cinnamon pecan rolls didn't brighten her spirits.

She wanted to go into every day bright and cheerful

and believing that things would turn around—she'd done that for years—but she couldn't seem to get there anymore. Her optimism was busted. It kept her going through the motions, but she no longer believed everything would be great. And she missed believing. She felt like she'd been trying to force a square peg into a round hole for the last five years and she didn't know how long she could go on trying now that she could see it would never fit.

Sweet scents filled the kitchen and she was elbow deep in a batch of savory bacon-gruyere muffins when Madison came in two hours later.

They exchanged good mornings and Madison disappeared through the door to the front of house to open the shop—and Parv had a guilty moment of acute relief that Anna wasn't working today.

She adored both of her employees, but they couldn't have been more different. While Madison would quietly go about her duties and maintain a sweet, smiling attitude, Anna was abrasive, invasive, and never let anything go. Madison was a doe-eyed Kansas country-girl who never had a harsh word for anyone and always kept her corn-silk hair in a low ponytail, while Anna was a bossy Bronx smart-ass with heavy black eyeliner, neon streaks in her jet black hair, and a line of silver earrings marching up the shell of her left ear.

They'd both come to California for college—Madison now a sophomore and Anna just entering her senior year—and they were both popular with her customers, in spite of the drastic differences in their personalities and the fact that their oil-and-water personalities had them at each other's throats on the rare occasions when Parv scheduled them to work the same shifts. Anna seemed to be the one person who could get a rise out of sweet, pliable Madison. And Madison knew exactly how to get under Anna's skin.

But Parv didn't mind having to do the occasional contortions with the schedule to keep them separated. She adored both young women.

She was going to have to tell them soon.

They wouldn't have trouble finding new jobs, but she needed to give them warning. She owed them that for their loyalty over the last few years. She'd had other baristas. Some had graduated—either from high school or college—and moved on with their lives. Others had left to go to Starbucks when they opened—and Parv couldn't begrudge them that. She couldn't compete with their benefits or offer full time.

She hadn't bothered replacing the last few employees she'd lost when Starbucks opened at the beginning of the summer. She'd made it work with her skeleton crew for the last four months—for once grateful for that stupid city ordinance that restricted their hours of operation.

The timer went off and she moved to the oven, focusing only on the flakiness of her pastries and whether the cream for the fruit tarts was too sweet for the next couple hours, losing herself in the familiar actions.

It wasn't until Madison poked her head around the door at quarter to eleven that Parv realized they hadn't had a morning rush today.

"We sold out of the bacon-gruyere muffins and the quiche," Madison reported. "And that sexy Max is asking for you out front."

Parv felt her face heat and focused on the less disturbing part of Madison's news as she dusted flour off her hands. "The bacon muffins are gone already?"

"Mrs. Kenney took half a dozen home for her boys. And she asked if you were going to make any more of the spinach-feta ones. She said her husband loves those."

Any reply she might have made slipped out of her mind when she stepped into the front of house and saw the man examining the contents of the pastry case. Madison moved to the far end of the counter to tidy up the tea display, giving them the illusion of privacy.

Though they were pretty damn private. The seating areas were almost empty—just law student Corey hunched over her laptop at the window and retired Mr. Nunoz reading his tablet near the fire. This was even quieter than usual.

From the school year starting? The Green Mermaid Effect? Or were her customers subconsciously picking up on the scent of impending failure in the air and staying away?

She forced herself to stop stalling and look at Max, dreading meeting his eyes. She'd told him she had a crush on him last night, but not just that. Things had been almost *intimate* between them—and if there was one thing she knew about Max it was that he didn't do intimate. He was king of the three-week relationship, all the fun, none of the deep stuff.

She'd worried this morning—between the quiche Lorraine and the double-fudge brownies—that things were going to be weird between them in the light of day.

But there was nothing uncomfortable or awkward in his gaze as he smiled at her, dimple flashing, one of her to-go cups in hand. "Hey. Sorry to drag you out of your kitchen. I wanted to know how you were doing this morning and Madison wouldn't let me sneak back there."

"You're not allowed back there. I know you. You'd

eat all my stock."

"Probably," he admitted, unabashed. He tapped the case. "Can I get a cherry-orange scone for the road?"

Her hands automatically went through the motions of pulling out a bag and a sheet of the pastry tissue to package the scone for him. She eyed his crisp button down shirt and slacks—he'd probably left his suit jacket in the car. "Don't tell me you're going into work on a Sunday?"

"People need protection seven days a week."

"You need to seriously reconsider your work-life balance, Maximus."

He arched a brow. "And how many hours have you already put in this morning? Do you want to be the pot or the kettle?"

"That's different," she argued, the words automatic.

"Really. How?"

She opened her mouth but no words came out. It was different—because she had different rules for herself than for everyone else. Because she'd stopped thinking of having a work-life balance. Because her life *was* her work. Every morning. Every afternoon.

And she was miserable.

Maybe it would be a good thing to let the shop go. But what would she do? Who would she be then?

Max took his scone from her lax grip, setting a five on the counter. "Don't work too hard, Parv."

He started toward the door. "Your change…"

"Keep it."

She watched him go, the easy, athletic way he moved giving a hint of his martial arts training, but it was his confidence that bled through every movement, drawing her eye. She'd been worried after telling him about her crush, but nothing had changed. He was still just Max with her.

If anything, this had made things easier between them. She used to hold on to the idea that someday he might look at her differently, that he would pick up his coffee one morning, look over at her and *wham*. Love. Or that she would get brave enough to confess her crush one day and they would just sort of fall into one another's arms like something out of a bad romantic comedy.

Now there was no chance of them magically hooking up and that lingering weight of futile hope had lifted. This was better. They could just be friends.

She should have told him years ago.

* * * * *

Why hadn't she told him years ago?

Max strode down the sidewalk toward the parking spot he'd snagged at the end of Main, but his thoughts were firmly back in Common Grounds. He'd stopped in to make sure she was all right after the night before. He'd never seen Parvati so pessimistic, but this morning everything had been fine. She was the same old Parvati.

He was the one who had changed.

Something had shifted. Some subtle little mechanism inside him that kept her safely inside the Friend Zone.

He hadn't really *looked* at Parvati in years. She was a fixture in his life. Sidney's best friend. Off-limits. But did she have to be? It made sense for him to keep his distance when they were younger, but they were both adults now. Capable of making their own decisions— and when she'd said she had a crush on him it had planted the seed that had taken root in his brain while he slept last night.

She had referred to the crush in the past tense. She might not even be interested. Hell, she might be seeing someone. Though she'd said she couldn't find anyone she wanted to go on a second date with—which was insane. Were all the men in California blind? How the hell was she still single?

Max wasn't winning any medals for relationship longevity, and God knew she could do better than his sorry, commitment-averse ass, but he couldn't seem to get the idea out of his head. Maybe all she wanted was a fling.

A fling with Parvati. The idea was interesting. Very interesting.

CHAPTER SEVEN

Taunted by Max's words about working too hard, Parvati left Common Grounds ten minutes after closing time. Trying to remember who she was before she became work obsessed, she put on workout clothes and sneakers and headed down to the marina park.

The park, with miles of landscaped paths overlooking the Pacific, had always been one of her favorite places in Eden, but she couldn't remember the last time she'd been down here. Certainly long enough that after five minutes of torturous jogging she slowed to a walk.

She'd never been much of a runner. Running was Sidney's drug of choice and Parv had only come along for the company and the views—and to combat the inevitable expansion of her thighs when she sampled her own recipes a little too frequently.

It was a magnificent afternoon, even by California standards, as if the universe had decided to reward her for her decision to take some time for herself. The sun glittered on the ocean, but a light breeze off the water kept it from feeling too hot.

Parv passed families picnicking and a bridal couple posing for wedding photos. The happy couple beamed at one another, capturing this moment of blissful happiness for the rest of their lives, neither of them looking old enough to vote—which only reminded her of Katie. Just a baby and already engaged.

She rounded a corner and saw another bridal pair—much more elaborately dressed than the casual, beachy look of the previous couple—and looking even younger. Parvati moved more quickly, practically power-walking down the path until she rounded another bend.

Another gorgeous vista. Another pair of bridal babies.

What the hell? Eden had always been a popular spot for destination weddings and she'd seen her fair share of bridal parties taking photos at the marina park before, but this was ridiculous. Everywhere she looked she kept seeing more of them—and none of them could be older than twenty-five.

She knew the popularity of Sidney's new wedding planning show had turned Eden into even more of a wedding hot spot, but she hadn't been prepared to be bombarded with baby brides.

Maybe one of the couples was working with Sidney and Tori at Once Upon a Bride. Maybe Sidney was even here.

Parv pulled out her cell phone, dialing by heart, but the phone didn't even ring before it went through to voicemail. At least in the past she would have been able to commiserate with Sidney. They would have been walking together. Sidney would have been making mental notes about which photographers seemed to be the best with the couples.

High-pitched laughter drew her eye to a craggy outcropping where a petite and perfect bride was being thrown over the shoulder of her manly groom, much to the delight of the photographer.

Parv looked away on a jab of jealousy. Damn it.

How had she suddenly become old for a bride? She wasn't even *thirty*, damn it. People were getting married and starting families into their forties now. She had time—but the universe seemed to be conspiring to tell her she was over the hill, matrimonially.

Or maybe it was just telling her that it was time. Time to move on with her life. Time to stop comparing every man she met to Max. Time to stop relying on her friends to make her feel complete.

Time to find a date for Katie's wedding.

And time to close Common Grounds.

This was it.

She was going to do it. Close the shop. Start new. Maybe even start e-dating again. It was time.

* * * * *

"Max. What are you doing here?"

The first person Max saw when he walked into the lawyers' office on Monday was his mother, frowning at him in confusion. "Dad seemed to think I needed to be present. Didn't he tell you?"

"We're communicating exclusively through lawyers these days," Marguerite Dewitt replied, without a trace of emotion. But then, there had never been much emotion involved in the alliance between his parents.

Max had always figured there must have been some heat, some passion in the beginning, some spark that drew them together in the first place, but by the time he was old enough to remember, his parents' marriage had been clinical. Businesslike.

Their divorce was apparently going to be the same.

"We'll get started as soon as your father and his team arrive. Would you like anything?" His mother guided him to a sideboard set up with coffee, tea, bottled water and various crackers and cheeses.

"I'm fine."

It was disconcerting, seeing her so calm. He didn't know why he'd expected anything different. When she'd informed him six months ago that she was divorcing his father, she'd been cool as the proverbial cucumber. The most shocking thing about the entire thing was that either of them wanted to bother with a divorce. They'd pretty much lived their own lives for the last decade, coming together only when holidays demanded it or work schedules permitted. He couldn't imagine either of them was unhappy with the situation—they were too detached from one another for that much emotion.

"This is just a formality," his mother explained. "We've already negotiated the settlement. Today we'll just be reading over everything one last time and signing. Then there will be a hearing in a few weeks to finalize things. Barring any unforeseen legal obstacles, the entire thing should be resolved before Halloween."

"Great," Max said, since she seemed to want him to say something.

Thankfully his father arrived before he had to get any more enthusiastic about his parents' divorce.

"Max. So glad you could make it." His father clapped him on the shoulder before turning to his soon-to-be-ex wife. "Marguerite. You look well."

"Thank you, Titus. You as well." Perfectly civil.

Max wanted to shake them both.

"Shall we get started?" his father asked as the lawyers filed in around the giant conference table.

Max held back. "Isn't Sidney coming?"

"She couldn't make it." His father explained. "Filming today, apparently. You'll be representing both your interests today. Sidney was never particularly interested in the business anyway."

Max didn't argue—he didn't know whether his father was right or not about Sidney's disinterest, but arguing with Titus Dewitt was about as effective as trying to empty the desert of sand one handful at a time—you could keep working at it for days and never make any noticeable progress.

His parents took their seats on either side of the table, flanked by what looked like twenty-seven lawyers each. Max hesitated, unsure where to sit, feeling a distinct jab of discomfort at the idea that he had to quite literally pick a side.

"Max." His father jerked his chin to the empty chair three down from his on the paternal side of the table.

Max's gaze flicked to his mother, who gave a slight nod to the chair as well, so he decided he was being ridiculous and took the empty space so they could begin.

It was all legalese, but everyone in the room was fluent in the language, so things moved quickly. Concerns were raised and dealt with in a brisk, businesslike manner. His parents had a prenup—not surprising, given their personalities and careers—but there were still details to work through and Max listened absently to the minutiae and the sound of several dozen lawyers turning pages in tandem.

The only part that seemed to impact him at all, or struck him as at all strange, was the language about current and future children. He and Sidney were listed by name in the section establishing a trust both of his parents agreed to pay into equally which they would inherit upon the death of one or both of them. But in the section negating Marguerite's claim on Titacorp holdings in the event of Titus's death, the language about Titus's heirs was suspiciously vague—referring to any current or future children of Titus Dewitt.

Max understood that the lawyers wanted to dot every I and cross every T, and Titus was still capable of fathering more children, but why wouldn't the lawyers refer to him and Sidney by name as the current children? Unless there were other Dewitts floating around that Titus already knew about. Was there more to this divorce than he'd suspected? A scandal behind the emotionless façade?

Now didn't seem to be the time to ask if Titus was fathering children all over the globe, so Max kept his mouth shut. Neither he nor Sidney had ever wanted a controlling share of Titacorp anyway. They'd been trained since birth to build something of their own and the lesson had clearly stuck.

Max listened to the rest of the reading of the settlement, watched his parents sign, and that was it. No fanfare. No drama. All business.

His parents and their lawyers stood, shaking hands all around. His father announced that he had an afternoon flight to catch and wove through his lawyers to clasp Max's shoulder. "Thank you for being here."

"I still don't see why it was necessary."

"It's important that you understand that regardless of what happens between your mother and me, you are my legacy."

What if I'm not sure I want to be?

His father and his entourage cleared out and Max fell in beside his mother on their way out of the building. "That was odd."

His mother didn't ask him what. "Your father's legacy is very important to him."

He almost asked then. Almost asked her if his father had other children Max didn't know about, but the last thing he wanted to do was upset her immediately after she'd signed her divorce settlement papers. If that would upset her. He wasn't sure he'd ever seen his mother upset.

"Sidney's coming up to the house for lunch on Saturday. Would you like to join us?"

"Sure. I hardly see her anymore since she's started filming the new show with Josh."

Her mother made an agreeable noise as they emerged into the parking lot. "She seems happy though. With him. With the show."

"I think she is." Max kept his tone as neutral as his mother's had been. "He's a good guy."

His mother's lips twitched. "Did you run a background check on him before or after they started dating?"

"Both." He grinned at his mother's short, rarely used laugh. "You can never be too careful."

"And you, Max? Are you seeing anyone?"

Parv's face flashed in his mind, but he just shook his head. "You know better than to start looking to me for grandchildren."

His mother pursed her lips, considering the comment. "I might like being a grandmother. And don't sell yourself short, Maximus. You could be a wonderful father."

"I'll stick to uncle, if you don't mind." Her driver pulled her car around and he stepped forward to open the door for her. "See you Saturday."

"Noon. Don't be late."

CHAPTER EIGHT

Parv sat across from her employees during the Monday afternoon lull, wishing she had a cup of coffee to hold so she would know what to do with her hands. Anna didn't work Mondays, but she'd made a special trip for this meeting and now looked as uncomfortable as Parv felt. It was only the thirteenth, but Parv had hidden in the office when Madison arrived for her shift and gotten their paychecks ready early, hoping that would soften the blow of what she had to tell them.

She hadn't really loved the people management aspect of owning her own business—she'd always figured during interviews that she was more nervous than the person applying and the one time in the last five years that she'd had to fire someone, a high school brat who showed up late and missed shifts, had practically given her an ulcer—but she loved these girls.

They were smart. They were hardworking. They were responsible and seemed to genuinely love working at Common Grounds.

They deserved better than to lose their jobs, but Parv consoled herself that they would get better ones. She would do everything in her power to make that happen.

She forced herself to meet their eyes and forced a smile—then wondered if smiling in this situation was inappropriate and let it fall from her face, trying to project an air of calm reassurance instead. Though she was pretty sure all she was projecting was seven different kinds of crazy since her face couldn't seem to decide which kind of expression to wear.

Madison's brow wrinkled in concern. Anna just began to look pissed—but then Anna generally looked angry whenever things surprised her. Parv glanced toward the front door—the most cowardly part of her wishing that a customer would come into the empty shop and force her to postpone the announcement—but all she saw was the sunshine outside. Another gorgeous day in Eden, California.

Not a bad day for the shop to die.

"So." Parv swallowed hard, looking back to her faithful duo. "Here's the situation. And I'd appreciate it if you can keep it to yourselves as much as you're able to. Obviously that won't be for long—" They'd need to start looking for other jobs. She'd give them glowing recommendations. Parv took a deep breath and forced herself to say it. "I'm closing Common Grounds."

Madison sucked in a sharp breath.

Anna just looked grim. "The Blue Mountain," she said.

Parv nodded. "That was the canary in the coal mine, but we've been struggling for a while now—" Or ever since they opened. "—and I've come to the decision that it's time to start winding things down. Our lease goes until the end of the year and nothing is going to change right away—though we'll have shortages in some of our usual products, like the Blue Mountain, as we start using up our stock."

Madison sniffed and Parv shot her a desperate look. "Please don't cry. If you cry, I'll cry. This is good for you guys. You're so much better than this. I'll give you the best recommendations you've ever seen and you'll get jobs that pay you what you deserve."

Anna's lips pursed tight, but she didn't say a word—which made Parv nervous. Anna never held back her opinions.

"You don't need to worry that I'm not going to be able to pay you." She retrieved the envelopes from the capacious pocket of her cardigan. "In fact, payday is a little early this month. I just want you both to feel very comfortable with everything that's happening. For now it's business as usual—we'll keep selling coffee, I'll keep making pastries, nothing has to change right away—but I felt you had the right to know."

"When?" Anna spoke, the single word rough.

"I'm not sure exactly. November, most likely. Six or seven weeks from now. Maybe less. And we may cut our hours back before then. So if you have a better offer before then you're under no obligation to stay."

"I'll stay."

Parv smiled, touched by the show of support from Anna, her least touchy-feely employee. "Keep your options open. You never know what the next few months will bring."

"I want to stay too," Madison added.

"No one is being laid off today. This is just so you can prepare yourselves."

"Isn't there any way we can save the shop?" Madison asked. "Some new promotion?"

"Jesus, Bambi, you think she hasn't thought of that?" Anna snapped.

"Hey," Parv intervened, waiting until the two of them stopped glowering at each other. "It's a nice thought, but the writing's been on the wall for a while now. It's time. Common Grounds is done."

* * * * *

She managed not to cry until she was alone in the back office and even then it was just a few quiet, dignified sniffles. Anna had snatched up her check and stalked out. Madison had returned behind the counter and begun cleaning things—as if she could polish Common Grounds into success. Parv had told her she didn't have to finish out her shift—she was only on for another half hour and there were no customers anyway, but Madison had given her such a look of betrayal that Parv had retreated back to the office to "take care of some paperwork" to give Madison time to process the news in her own way.

She barely cried. Her eyes were hardly even wet when she fished out her cell phone and dialed Sidney's number again—not expecting an answer since it was one thirty on a Monday afternoon and if she couldn't get Sidney during non-working hours she didn't have a snowball's chance right now.

"Hello?"

"Sid! I caught you."

Sidney's voice rushed out, impatient and frazzled. "Hey. Sorry. I saw you called this weekend, but it was an insane time. I think I was holding up one end of a couch when the phone rang."

"Redecorating?"

"No, we moved. Didn't I tell you? God, I don't know where my brain is these days. I can't keep track of who I've told what."

"You *moved*?" Parv echoed.

Sidney lived just down the street in the attic apartment two stories above the storefront for the wedding planning business she ran with Victoria—when she wasn't filming her new wedding reality TV show with Josh. Victoria lived in the apartment on the second floor of the building with her daughter Lorelei, where she'd hosted Girls' Nights and they'd spent countless hours commiserating over the sad state of the Dating World these days.

But now Tori's ex was back and Sidney had Josh and they hadn't had a Girls' Night in weeks.

"I've been sleeping at Josh's most nights anyway since he got the new condo. And with Nick living with Tori and Lorelei now they were tripping over each other. My place was too small for two people, but it's perfect as a suite for Lorelei, especially now that she's getting old enough to really want her own space. The two apartments were originally one two-story place so it was the obvious choice to combine them again—we'd been talking about it for weeks. When we realized we had a weekend without filming, we had to jump at it. Our schedule is insane for the next few weeks, but Nick and Josh called in some of their frat buddies and we were able to get my stuff moved over to Josh's and Lorelei's transferred upstairs all in two days."

"Why didn't you call me?" An irrational trickle of hurt threaded through the question. "I could have helped."

"We had it under control. And I figured you'd be working anyway."

"I could have made time. I can't believe you moved without even telling me."

"Why are you making a thing of this?" A hint of irritation sparked in Sidney's voice. "I was trying to be considerate. I didn't want you to feel like you had to take time off work to help when we didn't need you."

"I wasn't working. I had my parents' anniversary thing."

"So you *were* busy."

"That isn't the point."

"Well, can we get to the point?" Sidney asked. "I have about seven thousand things to do before we film tomorrow."

The sharpness in her voice sealed Parv's lips. She couldn't tell Sidney about Common Grounds closing now. The timing couldn't be more wrong. And she really should tell Tori and Sidney in person. "Are we doing Girls' Night tomorrow?"

"We can't this week," Sidney answered without hesitation—and Parv felt another irrational surge of hurt that Sidney hadn't even paused to consider.

She didn't know who the 'we' in Sid's sentence was—her and Tori and Lorelei? Her and Josh?—either way, it was obvious Parvati was no longer part of the we.

"I have another call coming in." Sidney's voice was abrupt, her attention already elsewhere. "We'll talk soon." She hung up before Parv could say another word, leaving her staring at the phone wondering what just happened.

* * * * *

Max could see Parv was pissed as soon as he walked through the door of Common Grounds that night five minutes before closing. The shop was empty and she stood in front of the counter, polishing the already-spotless pastry case with manic fervor—as if she could make it shine by sheer rpms.

She looked up when he entered, no smile of greeting

lighting her face, just a hint of a scowl. "If you want coffee it better be French press or drip. I already cleaned the espresso machine."

He crossed the shop to lean against the counter near her. "And if I just came to bask in your sparkling personality?"

"We're all out of sparkle today." She flung the Windex wipe into the garbage for a three-pointer and pivoted to face him, hands planted on her hips, her stance confrontational. "Did you know your sister moved?"

"Sidney?"

"Do you have another sister?"

"What, did she move in with Josh?"

Parvati rounded the counter and snatched up another cleaning product, attacking another already-gleaming surface. "Apparently while she was ignoring my calls all weekend, she was moving."

Max eyed her cautiously. "And we're angry about this."

As soon as he said the word angry, the fight seemed to drain out of her and she sagged against the counter. "I used to know everything. I was the one Sidney told about her day. I was the one she would bitch to when the cable guy was late or the florist for some wedding was jerking her around. I was her *best friend*. Now I don't even know that she's planning on moving in with her boyfriend, let alone that she already did it?"

"Hey." He came around the counter, ready to offer what comfort he could, but before he reached her she was back in motion, moving past him, flipping over the closed sign and locking the front door.

"I wasn't needed. I get that," Parv said as she moved, briskly going through the motions of closing with the inattention of years of experience. "But I wanted to be there for sentimental value, if nothing else. Josh's frat brothers helped them move out, but I helped her move *in*. Tori and Sidney and I wrestled that stupid couch up three flights of stairs all by ourselves, swearing and laughing the whole way. How could they not remember that? I used to be part of *everything*."

"If it's any consolation, they didn't call me either." And he could have been much more than just sentimental help. He could have shown up with a team of muscle and gotten it done in half the time.

"Of course they didn't," Parvati said, offhand. "Sidney knows better than to rely on you for stuff like that. But I'm always there to help. That's what I do."

Her analysis jarred him, the words hitting like an unexpected right hook to the jaw. "I'm reliable."

"Of course you are," Parv agreed. "But you're an island. You don't involve yourself in other people's lives."

"Sidney knows she can rely on me." He hated how defensive he sounded. Like he was afraid she was right. "I did all the security for her for that celebrity wedding in May."

"And she's grateful," Parv said quickly. "That isn't what I meant. It's just… It's the love languages."

"I don't know what that is."

"It's this book," Parv explained, finishing up with the front of house closing routine and waving him with her back to the kitchen. "My sister Asha used to be obsessed with it—I think because she's never been particularly good at dealing with feelings stuff and this was a way of approaching it analytically." She paused, seeming to remember that he hadn't just arrived to hear her vent. "Did you want coffee? Or a muffin?"

"I'm good." He really had come just because he wanted to see her—the fact that he could grab a late cup of coffee or a danish just a convenient excuse.

"Anyway, there are five love languages. The ways people show and receive love—and I'm probably going to get this wrong because I only heard about it from Asha—but they're physical touch, verbal praise, gift giving, the other one that I always forget, and acts of service. That's me. Acts of service. I do things for people to show them that I care. I want the people in my life to know that they can always call me, day or night, and I will move heaven and earth to help them. And Sidney didn't call."

And finally her tirade made sense. "That doesn't mean she's rejecting your friendship."

"I know." She sank onto a kitchen stool. "I'm sorry. I know I over-freaked, but it's been a day. I told Madison and Anna today that I'm closing Common Grounds."

Max hadn't realized she'd already gotten to that point. He'd been thinking about her situation for the last couple days, turning over options, his brain automatically churning away to fix the problem.

"What if you didn't have to?"

CHAPTER NINE

"What did you say?"

"The luxury coffee angle is a good one," he went on, oblivious to the dual spikes of hope and panic his words inspired. "But you need to work on broadening your market. People in Eden can afford to pay a ridiculous amount for a premium cup of coffee—you were right about that—but you need to attach a cachet to your product. Make it the kind of luxury item that even someone who can't really afford it would treat themselves to when they wanted to feel pampered. Something that the rich indulge in and the aspirational splurge on. Marketing is all about psychology. You need to drum up demand as a luxury brand and build a reputation as *the* elite coffee spot—and the best way to do that is getting celebrities involved. Your problem is you're too far north. People will travel for a luxury experience, but you have to get them hooked first and most of the stars live farther south—Mulholland, Pacific Palisades, the Hollywood Hills. There's a reason I have my offices in Beverly Hills even though the commute is a pain in my ass."

"I can't afford a storefront in Beverly Hills. I can't even afford one here."

"What if I invested?"

Her heart began hammering, distractingly loud—and

she couldn't tell whether it was from excitement or terror. She'd never realized how similar those two emotions could be.

"You have to admit I have an eye for business and I think you have something here. You could move the shop, but I'd recommend opening a second one. Keep this one as the flagship location." He looked around her kitchen, his gaze seeming to weigh and measure the value of everything it touched, and she had to resist the urge to smack him, suddenly defensive of her beautiful sparkling ovens. "You'd have to change the name," he went on relentlessly. "No one wants to pay exorbitantly for something Common. Why not Uncommon Grounds?"

"Because the whole idea was to create a place where different people from different perspectives and different walks of life could come together. To have a gathering place."

"Gathering places don't make money."

She grimaced. "So I've discovered."

"I know this is your comfort zone—Eden is home. It's familiar. But you need to think big." He thrust his hands into his pockets, finally looking at her rather than the potential investment around him. "I would probably be annoying to work with," he stated and she almost laughed at the understatement. "I'd be bossy and you'd want to kill me at least once a week, but if you trust me, Parv, I think we could have this place thriving in six months."

"Six months," she echoed, the words hitting her in the gut and she finally identified the chaotic emotion that had been sneaking around behind all the hope and fear.

Anger.

He was right. She'd failed abysmally in five years of trying, but Max could doubtless make Common Grounds—or *Un*common Grounds—successful in six months flat. Which just made her feel even more pathetic.

"I don't need you to save me, Max. I know you feel bad for me, but I don't need your pity."

He frowned. "I don't make investments out of pity."

"Maybe I don't want you swooping in and taking over."

"You'd rather go out of business than accept my help."

It wasn't a question, but she answered him anyway. "It doesn't sound like help. It sounds like it wouldn't be mine anymore. Win or lose, succeed or fail, at least Common Grounds is what I made it."

"You're being ridiculous." The dismissiveness in his voice made her want to throw her mixer at his head. "There's a time for pride—"

"And a time to butt the hell out. This isn't your business, Max."

"Don't you *want* your business to succeed?"

She couldn't think about that. All she could see was Max's perfect face, breezing through life without a single speed bump while she couldn't seem to make it five feet without falling flat on her face. "Right now I just want you to get out of my kitchen."

"This is ridiculous." His face tightened with irritation. "You're being irrational."

"Get. Out. Of. My. Kitchen."

"Fine." He started toward the back door. "I'm going. But the offer still stands."

She barely managed to keep from throwing things at him—the only thing stopping her the fact that the kitchen was already clean and tidy, everything put away.

Irrational!

As if anyone would be rational with the infallible Max Dewitt pointing out how *easy* it would be for him to succeed where she had failed. It was even worse because it was him—the man she'd admitted she had a crush on less than forty-eight hours earlier. As if this week could get any more demoralizing.

She didn't even have anyone she could vent to about his overbearing jackassery.

She grabbed her mixer and thunked it on the counter before stalking into the pantry, gathering ingredients and smacking them down on her pristine counters with a little more force than strictly necessary. She'd planned to go home early—as soon as she closed—but there was nothing waiting for her there but her Netflix queue, so she set out to mess up her spotless kitchen instead.

Twenty minutes of baking therapy later, she was ready to admit that Max might not, in fact, be the Antichrist. That he may have just been trying to help and that she may have overreacted a tiny bit.

By the time she had a beautiful batch of cake pops ready for sale, she'd rolled through a dozen options as to why the idea of keeping the shop open and even expanding had freaked her out so much—and she kept coming back to the same conclusion.

One that didn't sit particularly well.

She picked out five of the prettiest cake pops and bundled them in a little bouquet. She wrapped them in cellophane to protect them and put the rest in the pastry case, ready for the morning. By the time she had walked up to her place, collected her car, and driven out to Max's she'd rehearsed in her head fifty times exactly what she was going to say to him. The flowery words of her apology. But when he opened the front door of his gorgeous mountain retreat and she thrust the cake pop bouquet at him, the first words out of her mouth weren't what she'd planned at all.

"I don't want to own a coffee shop anymore."

* * * * *

Max blinked at the woman on his doorstep—the same women he'd been mentally, and sometimes verbally, swearing at for the last hour. He'd tried to help—without a single ulterior motive, thank you very much—and she'd thrown him out of her kitchen. What the hell kind of thank you was that? He'd been ready to ride to her rescue—and the damn irrational woman needed rescuing—and she'd spat in his face. Metaphorically speaking.

He'd been ready to continue their argument when he saw her car pull up out front. He'd stalked to the door, ready to whip it open and give her a piece of his mind as soon as she rang the bell—but the first words out of her mouth brought his tirade screeching to a halt before it even began.

He eyed the cake-pop bouquet at the end of her outstretched arm. "Okay…"

"I'm not sure I ever should have been a business-owner."

He took the cake-pops from her before her arm muscles gave out. "Do you want to come in?"

She moved past him into the house, still lost in her epiphany. "What I really love is the baking. I was never cut out to own a business."

"I don't think that's true. You're smart. You made a

few missteps, but if a few things had fallen your way you could have made it work even without my help." He dropped the cake pops into a glass—an edible bouquet in a make-shift vase.

"I made emotional decisions. I think intellectually I knew they were bad when I was making them because I always felt like I had to justify them. I fell in love with the Main Street location—the warmth and kitsch of it— so I signed the lease even though the terms were poor and the rent was too high. I ignored the fact that our parking situation was a total clusterfuck because there was nothing I could do to make it easier for customers to get to me without moving to a new location and I'd committed to the lease. I figured if I just worked harder, it wouldn't matter. I tried to get an exemption from the ordinance restricting our hours, but I could have fought harder. I'm not a hard ass. I'm a softy and everyone knows it. So I get screwed and tell myself it'll be okay because I'll work harder."

"Drink?" He was already pouring them both scotch, but Parv didn't seem to notice, even when he pressed it into her hand.

"The first time they raised the rent, I used it as an excuse to sell more baked goods. I brought in artists to sell their work on my walls for a small commission. I introduced new premium blends—but the freaking beans were so expensive our profit margins were pathetic. I brought in book club nights—when we weren't necessarily 'open' but I could still sell products. And I never once felt like I could relax. Five years of stress, Max. The only place I felt like myself was in my stainless steel palace of a kitchen. Which was too big, really, for a coffee house, but I indulged because it was the only place I could *breathe*."

She took a long swallow of her drink, but he knew she wasn't done by the way she was still pacing the floor. He waited—and her rant resumed. "I hate payroll and hiring and firing. I'm a people person. I wanted to create Common Grounds as a gathering place. A Mecca. Someplace warm and comfortable where people come to be together or to be alone but they always feel like they can be themselves. It was a stupid dream—I can see that now—but that's who I am. I'm acts of service. I want to do things for people. Create things for people. Which makes me the worst freaking small business owner on the planet."

"No, it doesn't."

"I never wanted the business owner side of things, but I couldn't get an expensive degree and then go to work for minimum wage icing cakes in a bakery. I had to make something of myself. And this was the only way I could think of to do that and still be me. But it wasn't me. It was me trying to live up to my sisters and be good enough to make my parents proud. It was five years of me trying to be something I'm not."

"I understand the pressure to live up to a family name," Max said, his voice dry enough to catch Parvati's attention.

She lifted her gaze to meet his, seeming to really see him for the first time since she'd come in, and sank down onto his living room sofa—a giant, overstuffed brown sectional that faced his giant screen TV and fireplace.

"I'm sorry," she groaned. "I came here to apologize and instead I ranted at you again. I just feel so *alone* sometimes. I know you probably don't get that. You're an island. But you know what's the one reason I wish I'd gotten married at nineteen like my sisters? So I would have a partner. Someone who would be in this with me so I wouldn't have to feel so freaking alone. I know it's anti-feminist to want someone to take care of me, but I do. It was different when we were the three musketeers, but now everything is different. Sidney doesn't need me anymore—and she seems to have forgotten that I might still need her."

He sat down at the other corner of the sectional—and her face suddenly contorted. "Oh God, please don't tell Sidney I said that."

"I won't. Cone of Silence."

She nodded, a shadow of a smile touching her lips as she sank deeper into his couch, the last of the tension she'd ridden through the door dissipating. "Can we just erase the last two hours? I'm sorry I was a basket case." She toed off her flip flops and lifted her bare feet to the ottoman. "Why did you come to the shop? It can't have been to listen to me have a nervous breakdown."

"Honestly, I just wanted to see you." He took a drink of his own scotch, enjoying the way the smoky flavor lingered on his palate. "I had a weird day too. My parents are getting divorced."

"Sidney told me. How are you doing with it?"

He frowned. No one had asked him that. His parents both told him what they wanted him to feel. Sidney assumed he was okay with everything, since he didn't let on that he wasn't. And no one asked.

Another sip of scotch. "It's...odd."

Parvati offered softly, "I can't imagine my parents apart."

"It isn't that. They were never a traditional couple. I think what's bothering me about the whole thing is not the divorce, it's that I can't figure out why it's happening. They both care more about business than anything else and they're going through backflips to ensure that the dissolution of their personal relationship doesn't impact either of their businesses—when they could just be staying together. Why go to the trouble?"

"Maybe they weren't happy."

"And after thirty-four years they finally decided to do something about it? No. It's something else. I keep feeling like they're keeping it from me. The real reason. And it's making me paranoid. Today at the settlement meeting, my father's lawyers had vague language about his present and future children and I got it into my head that he's had a secret family living in Switzerland this entire time."

"Seriously?"

"I know it's ridiculous. I *know* that. But it made a weird kind of sense. If he was trying to be with his other family, it would explain why all this was happening."

"Maybe it's an emotional decision. Not everyone in the world is as driven by logic as you are."

"My parents are." It was the one thing about which he was one hundred percent certain.

Parv shifted her bare feet on the ottoman and her long, loose skirt slid up, revealing the edge of the tattoo on her inner left ankle that he'd noticed for the first time on Saturday, when she was dressed up for her parents' party.

Max nodded to the ink, eager to change the subject. "When did you get that?"

She turned her ankle, drawing the hem of her skirt up to show off the design. It was a bird in flight, just a simple black graphic—and when she continued to pull her skirt toward her knee he realized it had two friends, winging up her calf. There was something free about the tattoo. Unfettered. And he wondered when was the last time Parv had felt unfettered.

"About two years ago," she said—and for a second he thought she was answering his unspoken question, until he remembered what he'd asked. "One of my employees—Anna—was going in to get her sleeve filled in and she talked me into going with her. I knew as soon as I saw this design that I wanted it—but the tattoo artist told me to go home and come back in a week if I was still sure."

"Sounds like he wasn't much a salesman."

"*She* thought it was better to have good word of mouth from happy customers than bad reviews from impulse shoppers. And I have recommended her to half a dozen other people, so obviously it was a good practice."

Max frowned, a stray thought rearing in his mind. "Does Sidney have tattoos?"

"Would it bother you if she did?"

It would bother me that I didn't know. "Of course not."

"She doesn't. Or at least she didn't last time I talked to her. For all I know she and Josh decided to get celebratory tattoos after they moved in together." She drained the rest of her scotch. "Don't mind me, I'm just bitter."

"Have you talked to her about it?"

"About my bitterness and envy? Who has the time?" Her joking tone faded quickly. "I feel like a terrible friend. Like I'm incapable of being happy for her because things are taking off for her right when they're falling apart for me."

"You aren't a terrible friend. And this, whatever it is that's going on with you two, is temporary. You've been friends since you were six. This is nothing."

"It doesn't feel like nothing. But I'm sure you're

91

right."

"Of course I am. The great Max Dewitt is never wrong."

She snorted. "Even when he's referring to himself in the third person?"

"Especially then." He stood, levering himself off the couch. "Come on. I skipped dinner and I'm betting you did too."

* * * * *

He was right. She was more in the habit of grabbing a snack when she had five minutes of free time than anything else. "Regular mealtimes are overrated," she argued, but she climbed off his couch and trailed him toward the kitchen, the hardwood floors smooth beneath her bare feet.

She'd been to Max's house before, always for an event of some kind—a Super Bowl party, a Labor Day picnic, a Christmas mixer—and the events had always been catered. Which meant the kitchens were taken over by the catering companies and essentially off limits for the guests.

So for all the times she'd sprawled on the overstuffed sectional or admired the mountain views from the back deck, she'd never before clapped eyes on the sprawling chef's kitchen.

She practically had a spontaneous orgasm on sight.

It was perfection. Vast expanses of cooking space. Double ovens—with a separate warming drawer. A professional grade cook top. And the refrigerator. Dear God, the refrigerator. It was large enough to hide the body of a WWE wrestler with room left over.

She could see the walk-in pantry through the open

door—the poor thing only half full.

"You know, sometimes I hate you a little bit," she commented as she ran a loving hand over the island, which was large enough to qualify as a continent. "It is an insult to this kitchen to be owned by a man who doesn't cook."

"I cook," Max said defensively, opening the fridge and letting out a puff of cold air. "I've been told my French toast is an erotic experience."

She groaned. "That's your go-to morning-after breakfast, isn't it? Let me give you a hint, honey. They weren't talking about your cooking abilities. They were just trying to flatter you enough to get you to invite them to move in."

"There isn't enough flattery in the world for that."

"Because you're an island."

He frowned. "I wish you'd stop saying that."

She spread her arms on his continent, bending over to press her cheek to the marble. "I don't blame your sleepover guests for wanting to stay. If I had this kitchen, I could cater out of it and die happy. I wouldn't need to worry about owning a fancy pants coffee shop or driving myself slowly into debt."

"I'd like to think my kitchen isn't the only reason they want to stay."

She looked up at him. There was a dangerous little quirk to the left side of his mouth. Dangerous because it was almost suggestive and invited her to think things she definitely should not be thinking. He was one of the most handsome men she'd ever seen with his dark hair, grey eyes, and muscular shoulders that made a girl wonder how it would feel to grab onto them when he was straining above her...or pinning her to a wall, because really muscles like those *should* be used for the greater good and she couldn't imagine a greater good than pinning her to the nearest flat surface.

"You should do it."

She blinked. What had they been talking about?

At her blank look, he explained, "Use my kitchen to cater out of. It *is* an insult that it doesn't get more use."

"I couldn't."

"Why not?"

Because there would be no way to repay that. She would owe him so big—and not just financially. And she'd be dependent on him. No. She couldn't.

But part of her loved the idea. It was seductive. The thought that she might not have to worry about anything for a while. That she could take a break to find her feet. After everything was over with Common Grounds.

"You could pay me in baked goods," Max suggested, pulling deli meats and mustard out of the fridge. "I'm always trying to seduce my mother's chefs away from her and you're better than all of them."

She got distracted watching his hands, the strong capable fingers going through the motions of slapping together a couple sandwiches. *Seduce away...*

When he looked up, their eyes met and she almost thought she saw a flash of heat kindle in the grey. But this was *Max*. She forced herself to respond normally. "At baking, maybe. I'm not a chef."

He shrugged, the heat falling away like a mirage of wishful thinking. "The offer stands."

"You're making me a lot of offers today." And none of them were the kind of propositions she'd fantasized about. The kind his eyes had seemed to promise for that all-too-brief moment.

He met her eyes, his own expression serious. "You

deserve better than what you're getting."

If only he'd meant that romantically. If only he'd wanted to show her what she really deserved.

But Parv was too worn down by dating realities to pin any hopes on *if onlys*. So she just smiled. "I'll think about it."

CHAPTER TEN

"Parvati. Is that friend of yours still a wedding planner?"

Parv knew better than to expect pleasantries from Angie, so when her eldest sister's name came up on the caller ID, she knew it was going to be a quick and businesslike conversation.

"Sidney and Tori still have their wedding planning business, though they're pretty hard to get since they were featured on that *Marrying Mister Perfect* wedding special. Why?" she asked, though she had a sinking feeling she knew.

"How hard to get?" Angie demanded. "So hard that they wouldn't do a favor for the niece of a friend? Kateri is talking about getting married at Christmas time and simply *will not* listen to me that it takes longer than that to plan a big wedding. I thought if a professional told her, she might hear it."

"Christmas?" Parv squeaked. "How is she even thinking about that? Aren't her classes starting this week?"

"Not until tomorrow. But if you think her classes are going to distract Kateri once she has an idea in her head, you don't know my daughter."

"I wonder where she got that pigheadedness," Parv drawled.

"I'm not pigheaded. I'm focused. Can you get Kateri in with your friends or not?"

"They're based out of Eden. I don't think they do house calls to LA."

"She'll drive up for the weekend," Angie said, as if it was already a fait accompli. "Week after next. Can you arrange it?"

"I don't know, Angie. Tori and Sidney are overrun right now—"

Angie made an irritable tsking noise. "Will you at least ask them and get back to me? Is that so much to ask for your firstborn niece?"

No one could guilt trip like a Jai—even one who had married and changed her name. "Do you want them to plan the wedding or just tell Katie that it's impossible on three months' notice?"

"Definitely the latter, but I'm open to the former. I'd love to plan the whole thing myself, but it's a lot of work and a smart woman knows when to delegate. You'll get back to me?"

"I'll ask. But don't hold your breath."

"Great. Thanks, Parv."

The line was dead before she could reply—or change her mind.

Not giving herself time to overthink it, she immediately pulled up the main office number for Once Upon a Bride—because with the way things had been lately she figured her odds of getting through on Sidney's private cell were slim to none. Which was a demoralizing commentary on the state of their friendship, but she wasn't going to stress about it. She was turning over a new leaf since last night, trying out the radical new idea of not stressing herself out about every little thing. Maybe tomorrow she'd take up meditation.

A crisp, businesslike voice answered on the third ring. "Once Upon a Bride. How can we help you?"

"Hey, Tori. It's Parv."

Victoria Jackson, the other half of Once Upon a Bride, was efficiency given physical form. When Sidney had first started working with her, Parv had found Tori's brisk, no-nonsense manner more than a little intimidating, but she was Sid's other best friend and after you'd cried through *The Notebook* with someone half a dozen times it was hard to feel awkward. When Sidney had gone away to film *Marrying Mister Perfect*, she and Tori had gotten closer, but they'd never be besties without Sid there as their link.

"Hey, Parv. What's up?"

Getting straight to the point was all Tori, so Parv didn't mind the abrupt tone—which would have set her teeth on edge coming from Sidney—with whom she'd had long, rambling, pointless conversations about everything since they were six years old. Maybe she needed to stop expecting things to stay the same—but that was a concern for another day.

"I have a favor to ask, actually. A business one. My niece Katie just got engaged—"

"Little Katie? Dear God. I remember when she was Lorelei's age."

"She's eighteen," Parv said—trying to keep the *she's just a baby* panic out of her voice. "And apparently she thinks she can plan a big wedding overnight. My sister was hoping you'd be willing to talk to her about how long it realistically takes to plan a big wedding."

"How big?"

"I'm not sure, but even if it's just our family we're probably looking at over a hundred."

"Indian ceremony? The whole multi-day event?"

"I don't know." She hadn't even considered that part. Jonah was Jewish and Katie's father was a blond-haired, blue-eyed Protestant, but who knew what Katie would want? Over the years the Jai family had developed an accepting amalgation of religions—only Devi was devoutly Hindi, though both she and Ranee had wanted traditional Indian ceremonies when they married. "Angie had a western wedding so I'm guessing that's what Katie will want, but she could surprise me. I don't know for sure if they're looking to hire a wedding planner too, but could you make time the weekend after next to talk to them for a few minutes if Katie drives up from school?"

"For you? Absolutely." She heard tapping and pictured Tori tabbing through her calendar. "How's Sunday at eleven?"

"Perfect." Especially because it meant she wouldn't have to explain to Angie why she couldn't have her way. "Thank you, Tori."

"Anytime. And pass along my congratulations."

"I will." Just as soon as she got over feeling like Katie was jumping off a bridge and everyone was standing around cheering when they should be putting her in a safety harness and advising her of the risks.

But what right did she have to give romantic advice? Waiting hadn't exactly led to her own happily ever after. Not that she'd ever had someone tempt her not to wait. Maybe she should be cheering with everyone else. Katie had found her person—even if they were both babies. And Jonah was a sweetheart.

Everything would be great.

* * * * *

Max pulled into his mother's driveway promptly at eleven-fifty-five on Saturday afternoon, but there was already another car waiting there. It wasn't the old SUV Sidney usually drove, but his mother always kept her cars neatly tucked away in one of the garages, so unless her mother was springing a secret lover on her children Sidney must have bought the shiny new BMW Crossover. Apparently hosting reality wedding shows paid well.

As he walked past the silver Beemer toward the door, he wondered if Parv knew about Sid's new purchase or if he was going to hear another edition of the Sid's-cut-me-out-of-the-loop refrain. Not that he blamed Parv for feeling jilted. The two of them had been joined at the hip for over twenty years. It had to be jarring when that kind of connection just vanished.

Not that he would know. He didn't have any friends he was that attached to. But that didn't make him an island. He was independent. That was a virtue. He liked being known as a person who could stand on his own two feet. Not just some spoiled rich kid parasite who was only successful because Daddy got him a job. And if that independence spilled over into other areas of his life...well. That was fine. It wasn't hurting anyone.

And now he sounded defensive even in his own mind.

He'd asked his parents for advice when he was making business decisions—because that was their specialty—or when he was buying a house—because it was a major investment. He'd always thought he had good relationships with them before the divorce stuff had blindsided him. So maybe they all kept one another at a distance—but was that so wrong? Not everyone was touchy feely all the time.

Max shook his head, trying to get Parvati out of it. He'd seen her off and on all week as he was getting his coffee at Common Grounds, but they hadn't really talked since that night in his kitchen.

The night when he'd almost kissed her.

She'd been standing there, petting the marble with her expression a mix of covetousness and awe—and he'd wanted her to look at him that way. Possessive and passionate. He'd wanted to round the island and take her face between his hands and kiss the mouth that had consumed him for the better part of his teenage years.

But she'd been in a vulnerable place and he didn't do that kind of thing. Especially because he didn't want her to think that his offers had come with strings attached. Not that she was going to take him up on either of his offers anyway. She'd said she would think about it, but he wasn't sure he believed her.

And he'd spent entirely too much time in the last week wondering what she would choose. It was probably better if she turned him down. If just the idea of working with Parvati was this distracting, he didn't want to consider what the reality would do to his focus. He needed to be focused on his own business.

The week had been busy at Elite Protection. Hank the Hammer continued to be a pain the ass, repeatedly requesting Candy return to "adjust" the system she and Tank had installed on Monday. His other bodyguards had been so overbooked on close protection details that Max had needed to step in and cover a couple jobs himself—though it had been good to remind himself that he wasn't just a pencil pusher.

And he wasn't unreliable. No matter what Parv said about him being an island. Protecting people was his job—and yes, his job was harder to do when he formed emotional attachments with his subjects, so he was very good at keeping his distance. Which made him a professional. Not an island, damn it.

He rang the bell, expecting his mother to open the door since her housekeeper took the weekends off, but when the door swung open it was Sidney glaring at him from the foyer.

"Did you tell Mom that Josh and I wanted to have kids right away?" She snapped, barring the way like she might not let him in the house. "We aren't even engaged."

"I didn't tell her anything," Max protested. "She may have said something about grandkids and I may have implied that she had a better shot with you than with me, but that's all."

"That was enough," Sidney grumbled, but she stepped back to let him across the threshold.

"Speaking of Josh," Max said as he strolled toward the living room, "I heard you guys were shacking up."

He threw himself onto one of the chairs and Sidney sank delicately down to the edge of the one facing his. Her brows drew together. "How did you hear that?"

"I ran into Parvati."

Sidney's expression tightened even further and Max felt a little stab of concern. He'd thought Parv was being overly sensitive where Sid was concerned, but maybe there was strife in their friendship after all.

"Don't tell me you wanted to help move furniture too."

Max shrugged. "I could have."

Sidney's brows arched high, telegraphing her skepticism—no wonder she was on television, her face was incredibly expressive. She could call him a moron without even opening her mouth—or maybe that was a particular skill of sisters. "You never wanted to before."

The truth was it never would have occurred to him that Sidney might want him to help her move until Parvati pointed it out. Sidney knew she could rely on him for the big things, but the little things had never been important enough to bother one another about. Maybe he was more of an island than he'd wanted to admit.

"I'm helpful." Max heard the defensiveness in his tone and intentionally leaned back in his chair, taking an even lazier, I-don't-give-a-damn pose. "I helped with security for that wedding."

Sidney rolled her eyes. "Fine. Next time I have more help than I need moving a couch down three flights of stairs, I'll be sure to call you so you can supervise."

"Why are we moving couches?" Their mother entered the room, tucking away her cell phone in a silent admission that she'd snuck off to take a work call in true Dewitt fashion.

"Sidney's living with Josh." Max grinned as he shamelessly ratted her out.

Her mother turned instantly to Sidney. "Oh, Sidney, that's wonderful. But why didn't you call me for help?"

Sidney shot him a death glare.

CHAPTER ELEVEN

Max pulled out of his mother's driveway a few hours later, intending to head home, but instead his car seemed to point toward the Main Street district and Common Grounds.

Lunch with his family had been good, but odd. The news of his parents' divorce had broken on Wednesday, but there was a political scandal taking up most of the airtime on the twenty-four hour news channels so the Dewitt story had been barely a sidebar on the financial news shows. Titacorp stock had wavered and rallied quickly, while their mother's company had leaked a projected earnings report and the stock price had gone through the roof.

"I don't know what I was so worried about," their mother had said, smiling at the head of the table as if the stock price were the only thing affected by her soon-to-be single state. "We could have done this years ago."

Max had almost asked why they hadn't, why now was suddenly the time for divorce, but Sidney had changed the subject and he'd held his tongue.

Sidney's relationship with their mother had been strained for years—his sister always convinced their mother was judging her and Marguerite not exactly being the touchy-feely type. Now they were making steady progress toward a good—if somewhat unconventional—mother-daughter relationship and he wasn't going to disrupt that by stirring things up over quinoa and farro.

The sunny Saturday afternoon had brought Edeners out in droves and Max had to park three blocks down from Common Grounds, but when he made it back to the shop on foot he found a new sign taped to the door with amended hours. It was only five past three, but she'd already closed for the day if the new sign and the locked door were to be believed.

But when Max peered through the window, he saw Parvati seated in front of the fireplace inside. He rapped on the glass and her head jerked toward the sound, their eyes connecting through the pane. She came to the door, unlocking it and opening it wide enough to peek out. "What are you doing here?"

"I was hoping for more cake pops," he said, keeping it light and easy. "But I see you've changed your hours."

"Economizing." She opened the door wider. "Come on in. I'll sneak you some cake pops if you promise not to tell anyone else you're getting special treatment."

"Deal."

He followed her into the shop, stopping to lock the door behind him. By the time he joined her at the counter, she'd already grabbed a pair of cake pops—one pink and one yellow and set them on a pair of plates. "Lemon or confetti?"

"Lemon."

They took their cake pops to the fireplace seating area where she'd been before and settled into the chairs there. He saw Parv surreptitiously tuck a tablet down between her leg and the arm of the chair, but he didn't comment on it—too busy going into silent raptures over the lemon heaven on his tongue.

They ate in silence until he was chasing the last crumbs across his plate with the pad of one finger. "I take it your shortened hours are a sign you aren't going to be expanding to Beverly Hills."

"No. But I appreciate the offer. And never in my life, not if I live to be a hundred, will I ever forget how you tried to stand me on my feet again."

He frowned. "Is that a quote?"

A shadow of a grin flitted across her mouth. "*The Philadelphia Story*. I love that movie."

"Old one, right? Cary Grant?"

"That's the one. They should remake old movies like that. We need more C.K. Dexter Haven more than a seventh remake of Spiderman."

"Hey. Don't knock Spiderman. I always connected with Peter Parker."

She tilted her head, studying him. "I figured you for more a Batman type. Or Tony Stark. Hot zillionaire protecting the weak. Isn't that more your shtick?"

With anyone else he would have thought she was flirting, but Parv was so matter of fact—as if his hotness was just a fact. And not one that affected her personally.

Her gaze tracked past him, toward the door over his shoulder. "I keep wondering if I should put up a sign saying we're closing. Do you think people would stop coming if they knew we were going to be shutting down in a couple months?"

"Some might. But it might rally support from some of your more loyal customers. You'll have to put up a sign eventually, but until you know your actual closing date it might be a little premature."

She nodded, her gaze still distant. "I'm going to have to tell my parents."

"At some point," Max agreed, but the look in her

eyes as she stared past his shoulder was so miserable he immediately sought to change the subject. "What are you working on?"

When she looked at him in confusion, he nodded to the tablet—and was fascinated to watch her cheeks darken with a subtle flush. He grinned. "Now you have to tell me."

"I was just...it's an online dating site, okay? I'm trying e-dating." She brandished the tablet. "And I'm sure my parents will be delighted that I'm using their Christmas gift in an attempt to finally land a man."

Max felt a strange, uncomfortable stirring in his gut at the idea. "Have you met someone?"

"Not yet. I just started trying." His stomach pitched again, until she continued, "And it's awful."

"Awful?" he asked, hoping he didn't sound too cheerful.

"The first guy who messaged me actually seemed determined to hook me up with his dad. He wouldn't stop talking about how his dad thought my profile picture was hot and how his father thought I was *too much woman* for him, so I should date him and his father back to back to see which one I liked better. And then when I said I wasn't into Daddy figures, he told me that high school guys would line up to date a girl like me. Which is both creepy and extremely illegal since I'm almost thirty."

"So not the best first impression."

"You could say that."

"Why do you need to date online? You must meet men here all the time. Guys drink coffee."

"They do. And then they go home to their wives." When he started to argue, she held up a hand. "I'm never going to be the sort of girl who writes her phone number on the side of a cardboard cup. And five minutes of friendly chit-chat over the pastry case isn't the same thing as really knowing someone—especially when not every married or taken guy wears a wedding ring and I could cross a line with someone else's man without even realizing it. No. The internet is safer." She glared at her tablet. "Unfortunately, it seems like the good guys never email you back."

"Hey. You said yourself you just started. Give it time."

She made a face. "I just worry about what they're going to think of me."

"They're going to think you're amazing. They'd be idiots not to."

"Really? A never-married nearly-thirty who's slowly going out of business? I felt like I was lying when I filled out my profile. I said I owned a coffee shop, but my true passion was baking."

"Isn't that your true passion?"

"It's the only time I don't feel like the weight of the shop is going to crush me. Does that count?"

"It wasn't a lie. And no one will judge you based on what you do." He'd kick the ass of anyone who tried.

She snorted. "Of course they will. Have you never been on a date? That's the first thing people ask. We're all defined by what we do and e-dating is all about judging people. You don't know anything about them— you have to judge them."

"I'm sure it isn't that bad."

"Are you?" Her look said he was pitiably naïve. "It isn't like dating someone you've known casually in another setting. You don't have that prolonged exposure to build on. Or the chemistry of being attracted to one another and one of you making a move. Instead you have to take every little tiny scrap of information you get about a person and use it to figure out if you're going to be a match. There's already the weird pressure put on it that you have to have romantic feelings for a person you're meeting for the first time."

"So why do it?"

"Because how else am I supposed to meet the man of my dreams? I used to be so proud of the fact that I didn't get married before I graduated college, but now it seems like the joke was on me because if you don't meet your husband in high school or college, you don't have the same chance to get to know one another without expectations and learn if you might like one another before you start dating. With e-dating you have to figure it all out based on a profile and a first date and everything is harder that way."

"Well, however you meet him, don't settle for less than someone fantastic. You deserve that."

She snorted. "Right now I'll settle for literate and breathing. And literate is optional."

* * * * *

After Parvati closed the door behind Max a little while later, she propped her shoulder against the glass, watching him walk down the street. It had been surprisingly easy to talk to him about her online dating crap. She'd never thought she would be that comfortable around Max, but something had shifted in their relationship in the last few weeks. He wasn't just Sidney's hot brother anymore. He was a friend.

A hot friend, yes, but she seemed to have finally gotten her stupid crush on him completely under control. If only she'd known that confessing it to him would quash it, she could have done that years ago.

She abandoned her post at the door, checking to make sure it was locked before heading to the back office. She'd run the numbers this morning, looking at which hours of the day were the most profitable, and come away with the decision to shorten the evening hours. Which would give her the time to start looking into selling off the furniture and equipment, when the time came.

Just part of the inevitable march toward closure.

She looked at her cell phone—another step on the march taunting her.

She had to tell her parents.

She brought up their number, but hesitated before hitting send, staring at the photo saved for their contact on her phone. Their reactions couldn't be any worse than the ones she was imagining.

But their confusion when she explained that she was going out of business an inch ahead of bankruptcy was almost as bad.

"I don't understand," her father's voice hesitated over the words. "Do you need money?"

"No. It doesn't make sense to pour any more money into Common Grounds. I've been avoiding the truth for a long time, but I've got to face facts now. We'll be closing soon."

"But what will you do?" her mother's voice, more puzzled than anything else. As if the idea of failure was a complex math equation she couldn't quite grasp.

"I'm not one hundred percent sure yet, but I think I might try to get a job in a bakery for a little while. Just until I figure some things out."

"A bakery?" her father repeated, as if the word were Swahili.

"Just for a while." She looked around her office, searching for some excuse to get off the phone before they could ask more questions she didn't have answers for yet, finally settling on the pathetic, "Look, I've gotta go. I'll see you soon."

"We love you, Parvati," her mother said hurriedly, squeezing the words in before she could hang up—and Parv could almost hear the word *still* inserted into the sentence.

She was lucky to have her family. She knew she was lucky. But somehow it was a small comfort. All she could feel was the acute guilt that she'd let them down.

CHAPTER TWELVE

She didn't end up hanging a sign—grateful for Max's advice to wait until she had more firm details—but word began to spread anyway. The shortened hours had launched a frenzy of whispered speculation among the customers and Parv had given Anna and Madison permission to answer honestly if any of the customers asked point blank—not wanting to put the girls in the position of having to lie for her.

By the next week when Angie and Katie arrived in town for their meeting at Once Upon a Bride, the closure of Common Grounds was the worst kept secret in Eden. But that wasn't what had her nervous as she walked Angie and Katie across the street.

She hadn't heard from Sidney or Tori since she set up the meeting with Tori. Normally she wouldn't worry that her friends would have double booked themselves or forgotten about her request—but normally she wouldn't go for almost two weeks without talking to them every day. Everything had changed in the last few months.

She listened absently to the rush of information Angie was pouring over Katie, her ears perking up when she heard the word caterer.

"We've got Montague's confirmed to cater, but the contracts the venue sent over were unacceptable—"

"You already booked a caterer for the wedding?" Parv interrupted, nearly giving herself whiplash when she jerked around to stare at Angie. Katie and Jonah had only been engaged for a few weeks. Things couldn't have progressed that far already.

"It's for the engagement party," Angie explained. "Katie and Jonah have a three day weekend at the end of October and we're going to have the party in Santa Barbara that Saturday so their local friends will be able to make it."

"The ones who aren't away at college?"

"That's why we need to get the venue pinned down so we can send out the invitations right away—to give people who want to attend time to arrange travel. Katie, you need to get me updated addresses."

"Why can't we just use email for the engagement party?"

Angie's eyebrows flew up and her mouth puckered lemon-tight. "If that's the kind of tone you want to set for your wedding."

Parv opened the frosted glass door to Once Upon a Bride and ushered them in before a full mother-daughter war could be declared over engagement party invitations.

Tori immediately appeared from a back room and approached them, her professional smile glued in place. She was still as tall, graceful, and meticulously put together as ever, but somewhere in the last few months since she'd gotten back together with Lorelei's father, something that had always seemed hard and guarded about her had softened into a subtle welcoming warmth.

She extended her hand to Angie first—accurately reading the power dynamics in the room. "Angie, it's so good to see you again. And Kateri—best wishes on your upcoming wedding. I understand you had a few logistical questions. Why don't we have a seat, take a look at some of our idea books and see what we can come up with for you?"

Parv trailed along uselessly and sat on an extra chair as Tori took control of the situation, easily diffusing any tension between Angie and Katie before it could pop up, even as she masterfully guided the pair toward a plan for the wedding that took into account Katie's impatience and her mother's grandiose ideas.

The one major battle was over the date. Tori agreed with Angie that planning a splashy wedding in two and a half months would be virtually impossible, but Katie insisted waiting until June would be torture. With a little gentle prodding from Tori, spring break emerged as the obvious compromise—especially as holding the wedding on the first weekend of the break would give them an entire week for their honeymoon before classes resumed.

No one else seemed to notice that they were planning a wedding for children, but Parv couldn't seem to get past it. Yes, her parents and all of her sisters had married young, but times were different now. People were waiting longer. And yes, she had just complained to Max about not finding her own Mr. Right while she was in school—but where Katie was concerned logic didn't apply.

"So. March twelfth," Tori said with brisk efficiency, making a note in her tablet. "An afternoon wedding. At a vineyard. That's all very do-able. Have you already started looking at dresses?"

"We have an appointment this afternoon in Santa Barbara," Angie answered before Katie could. "In fact, we should probably get on the road if we're going to make it in time."

They all stood, shaking hands and thanking one another. Tori wouldn't be officially planning the wedding, but Once Upon a Bride apparently now had a new Consultant service where they would be available as advisors throughout the process and Angie had signed up for that—so she could plan her dream wedding for her baby by herself, but have professionals on speed-dial.

They moved in a clump toward the front door, discussing colors, and Parv tuned out the discussion. She'd never been one of those girls who dreamed about her wedding, planning every detail before she even met Mr. Right. She just wanted to find her person. The rest of it was just window dressing.

The back door to the shop clanged open and Parv looked toward the sound in time to see Sidney emerge from the back hallway in a sundress and flip flops, shoving her sunglasses up to the top of her head as she moved. Her step hitched momentarily when she saw them, but she changed direction to move toward them, her own professional smile sliding into place. "Hello. What's this?"

"Kateri's getting married," Tori explained to her partner. "I thought you weren't getting back until tonight."

"I caught an earlier flight. We're shooting at some prospective venues up the coast tomorrow and Josh wanted to head up early and stay at some little B&B he knows about, but I left my tablet here at the office so I've just come to grab it. He's waiting out back—probably with the engine running." She grinned.

Katie bounced into the conversation, unable to contain herself any longer. "You're the one from

Marrying Mister Perfect."

Sidney smiled, the smooth, practiced smile of a woman who got that reaction a lot. "I am."

"Oh my gosh. I loved you on the show. You were so smart to ditch that Daniel. Are you really dating Josh Pendleton? I loved that wedding special you two did. Is it true that Caitlyn's pregnant?"

"It is. That's actually where I was this weekend. I just flew back from her baby shower."

Katie squealed.

Angie touched her daughter's arm. "Katie. Your appointment."

The thought of wedding dresses brought Katie back from Reality-TV-ville and they began moving toward the door again, Sidney now trailing along as Tori explained that they'd be consulting on the wedding.

Parv found herself next to Angie in the little pack as Katie begged Tori and Sidney for dress shopping tips.

"Mom told me you're closing your little shop."

Sidney swung around. "You're what?"

Parv cringed. Not exactly how she'd envisioned telling Sidney. "I'm closing Common Grounds. In a month or two."

"Mom didn't tell me what you were doing next," Angie asked, with her characteristic irritation over not knowing everything before anyone else.

"It's a work in progress," Parv admitted.

Angie's brows pinched. "You can tell me."

Of course Angie thought she was hiding something. Because in Angie's world the only reason a person closed a business was because you already had a bigger, better offer lined up. "You'll be the first to know," Parv promised—and Angie's look said both of them knew she was full of shit with that one.

"You should open a coffee shop near USC," Katie urged. "There are, like, two dozen of them, but none of them are as good as yours."

Parv didn't bother mentioning that the thought of opening another shop gave her hives; Katie was already off on another tangent—complaining about the lack of bridal boutiques within easy walking distance of the USC campus.

Parv walked them back to Angie's Mercedes and wished them good shopping karma—surprised when Sidney made the walk with them rather than rushing back to Josh and their romantic getaway.

She learned why as soon as Angie pulled away.

"Why didn't you tell me you were closing Common Grounds?" Irritation was vivid in the words. "I can't believe you told *Angie* before me. She drives you nuts."

"Technically I told my mother and my mother told Angie."

"Are you trying to get back at me for not telling you about moving in with Josh? Because that's just childish."

The unfairness of the accusation dug under her skin like nettles and she retorted, "Believe it or not, I didn't want to bare my soul to your voicemail and you and I haven't actually talked in weeks. When was I supposed to tell you?"

Sidney had the grace to flush. "I've been busy."

"I know. And I understand. I do. But you don't get to fuss at me about not knowing what's going on in my life when you never take five seconds to ask."

"You're right," Sidney admitted, though her expression remained tensely defensive. "We haven't talked in too long. Let's do Girls' Night this Tuesday. I'll check with Tori to see if she's free."

Parv was tempted to grumble that maybe *she* wasn't

free, that just because she wasn't in a relationship didn't mean she had no life—and in fact, she had her first internet date on Tuesday evening, but that *would* be childish. And it was just a coffee date and would be over before Girls' Night—and it might actually be good to have an excuse to leave the date if it got awkward. So she accepted Sidney's olive branch with as much grace as her current temper tantrum could muster. "Tuesday sounds great."

"Good." Sidney nodded—and then ruined it by looking over her shoulder back at Once Upon a Bride.

"Go. I know Josh is waiting."

Sidney was moving before Parv finished talking. "I'll see you Tuesday."

"Can't wait." She wanted the words to be true, but she'd gotten so annoyed with Sidney putting her last lately that it was hard for her to feel suitably grateful for the Girls' Night concession.

She pulled out her phone, calling Max as she walked back to Common Grounds. He answered on the second ring.

"Elite Protection." Strong. Firm. All business.

"Tell me to stop being a baby and holding a grudge."

"Who am I telling you to forgive?" Everything about his tone softened and warmed, triggering an answering softening in her.

"Irrelevant," Parv insisted, not wanting to drag sibling dynamics into things. "I'm being childish and I need someone to tell me to snap out of it."

"Snap out of it. But if this is one of those internet date snap judgment things, I am fully in favor of holding grudges—and restraining orders, if necessary."

She snorted, opening the door to Common Grounds and nodding to Anna where she manned the counter. "I haven't even had my first date yet. That's Tuesday. Coffee—at Starbucks, if I can cross the threshold without bursting into tears. His name is Tyler. If anything happens to me, I am entrusting it to you to track him down and avenge me."

"You want me to run a background check?"

"I don't know his last name yet." She waved to one of the regulars and ducked into the kitchen.

"Parv." Disapproval radiated through the phone. "Get his last name. And let me sic Candy on him. You at least need to know if he has a criminal record. Restraining orders against him. Domestic abuse charges."

"You're an extremely depressing dating coach."

"I'm not your dating coach. And Sidney would kill me if I let anything happen to you."

"It's coffee. In a public place. I'll keep an eye on my cup so he can't roofie me. That's going to have to be enough for you."

"Text me a picture when you meet him. And call me as soon as you leave."

"You're insane. You realize that, right?"

"I'm in personal security. This is my thing."

"For celebrities. No one cares about coffee shop owners."

"I care."

Her resistance melted a little at the stark words. "I'll call when the date is over, but I'm not forcing him to pose for a mug shot on sight. Deal?"

"Find out his last name."

She rolled her eyes even though he wasn't there to see it. "Goodbye, Max."

"Bye, Parv."

CHAPTER THIRTEEN

Parvati pulled into the Starbucks parking lot at five minutes to six on Tuesday evening, and cut the Jetta's engine. Since she had a couple minutes, she checked her makeup in the rearview mirror, adjusted her silk scarf, and gave herself a brief pep talk.

Tyler had seemed extremely sane in their initial emails. His profile said he was thirty-two, worked in "business administration" of some kind, didn't smoke, liked dogs and wanted kids. All marks in his favor. But Parv had been on this merry-go-round before. Her previous online dating experiences had taught her that she really knew *nothing* about a man until she met him face to face.

Still. He hadn't tried to pimp her out to his dad. She was willing to take that as a win today.

Parv climbed out of her car, automatically smoothing her maxi dress, and walked toward the Big Green Mermaid of Doom.

She'd told Tyler that she owned a coffee shop, but had wanted to meet on neutral territory — so he'd chosen her competitor for their first date. She opened the door, pausing just inside and scanning the dining area for any man of approximately the right age who looked vaguely like the profile picture. The pictures, she'd learned, could be wildly unreliable.

There weren't any thirty-somethings, so she decided to go ahead and get her coffee—if only to save them from the no-let-me-pay dance.

She hadn't been inside a Starbucks in years, but she still remembered her favorite order and it rolled easily off her tongue. She paid, waited for her drink, picked it up when the barista butchered her name, and looked around for a place to sit—cozy enough to be date-ish, but no loveseats or couches or anything that invited too much touching right off the bat.

She'd just started to wonder if she'd been stood up—and felt a little frisson of guilt at the relief she'd felt at the idea that she *wouldn't* have to go through all the first date stress—when her phone buzzed.

She fished it out, expecting to see a running-late text from Tyler, since she'd given him her number, but instead it was Max.

Proof of life.

She snorted and typed back. *Alive and kicking. He hasn't showed yet.*

His reply was almost instantaneous. *What kind of asshole is late for a first date?*

The kind who underestimates California traffic during Tuesday night rush hour?

Cut him loose. He isn't good enough for you.

Parv was smiling and trying to compose a suitably snarky comeback, when a hesitant voice said, "Parvati?"

He'd made the second a in her name long—the most common mispronunciation—but when she looked up, she found his profile pictures hadn't lied and she smiled at his sweet, eager face as she gently corrected, "It's Par-vuh-tee. Tyler?"

He grinned. "That's me. I see you already have your coffee. Sorry I'm late. I never seem to allow enough time for traffic. I wanted to text you, but I can't stand people who text and drive."

She smiled, heartened. "Me neither. Why don't you get your drink and I'll find us someplace to sit?"

"Perfect."

As soon as he turned to the cashier to order, she moved to the two arm chairs that had just opened up in one corner—and hurried to text Max before Tyler arrived.

He's here. It was *traffic. And he's cute!*

The reply was immediate. *So was Ted Bundy. Don't be drawn in.*

She snorted, blushing when she realized Tyler had arrived with his drink in time to hear the sound. "A friend checking up on me," she explained as she hurriedly stowed her phone. "So, Tyler, you're in business administration?"

"I'm office manager for my family business. Roofing contractors. Nothing like your family."

She blinked, thrown by the last addendum. Had one of her sisters somehow found her online profile and set this up? "You know my family?"

"Well, no, I don't. Just what I read."

"What you read?"

"I Googled you," Tyler explained, as if it were the most natural thing in the world.

"But we didn't exchange last names."

"I know, but you said you owned a coffee shop in Eden and I thought, how many people named Parvati can there be in Eden who own coffee shops."

He'd mispronounced her name again, but she barely noticed, unease slithering too loudly in her ears. "I'm at a disadvantage. I don't know anything about you." And now she was beginning to seriously regret not having

Max dig into his past.

"I'm nobody special. Did your mother really meet Oprah?"

* * * * *

"You know I hate you, right?"

Max grinned as soon as he heard Parvati's voice, even if she sounded mildly pissed when she called thirty minutes after her last text. "I may have heard that somewhere before," he said, unable to keep the laughter out of his voice. "Why do you hate me now?"

"It's so annoying when you're right."

"Your date started talking about his human thumb collection?"

"No. He wasn't a serial killer, and I'm not locked in his trunk, so if you have someone tailing his car home you can call off the dogs. It was just lousy."

He shouldn't be relieved. He wasn't going to be Parvati's Mr. Forever—though he wouldn't mind filling in as Mr. Right Now—so he shouldn't be rooting against her dates. But he was. He definitely was. "Lousy how?"

A knock on his office door brought Max back to the present as Cross poked his head in. Max held up two fingers, nodding toward the phone, and Cross nodded and hitched his thumb over his shoulder. Max would find him as soon as he was done with Parv.

"He Googled me."

"He what?" Max asked, jerking his attention back to the conversation. "Is that a euphemism now?"

"No. He actually Googled me. He used my first name, occupation, and zip code to find out who I was and then did extensive research on my family."

Warning bells rang in his head. "How sure are you

he isn't a stalker?"

"Very. He was just eager. He wanted to be prepared. He'd actually prepared talking points for our date—most having to do with my family history. I kept trying to convince him I was a nice normal girl on a nice normal first date really, really, really hoping to meet a nice normal guy, but once he found out my mom had been interviewed by Oprah, it was all over."

"Your mom was interviewed by Oprah?"

"Focus, Max."

"Sorry. But you have to admit that's pretty cool."

"I really hate you right now."

He smiled at her cheerful tone. "No, you don't. You love me. I'm irresistible."

"You just keep telling yourself that, buddy." He heard her car door bing over the speakerphone. "I've gotta go. I just got to Tori's for Girls' Night. See ya later, Max. And thanks for looking out for me."

"Anytime. And get the last name next time. Candy loves to do background checks. She gets to hack into all kinds of systems she isn't supposed to have access to."

"Bye, Max."

"G'night, Parv."

Max rose from his desk, shoving his cell phone in his pocket, and went in search of Cross. The retired NFL defensive back wasn't his newest employee, but he was the one with the least personal protection experience. A born perfectionist, Cross was constantly studying and training to be better, so Max wasn't surprised to find him in the weight room downstairs.

Cross immediately lowered the free weights when Max walked in, straightening to face him.

"Everything go okay this afternoon?" Max asked. Cross had been working with a new client, an A-list actress who wanted him to guard her decoy so the paparazzi would buy the ruse and she'd have some privacy.

"Smooth and easy," Cross replied. "She went shopping, and all I had to do was keep everyone from getting close enough to realize she's not really Maggie Tate. But the lookalike is incredible. Mannerisms. Speech patterns. She has Maggie down. And they look so much alike I would have thought I was guarding Maggie myself if not for the fact that I saw them standing next to one another. Do you think Maggie Tate has a secret twin?"

"Don't even think that. The tabloids would love it and suddenly they'd be dragging out all their photos and comparing every tiny detail—and we'd lose the decoy guard job because she wouldn't be able to use her decoy anymore."

"It's just weird." Cross shrugged. "I didn't realize how much of this job was acting."

"You should talk to Candy. She does all the hiding-in-plain-sight jobs we get since the rest of you are so busy. And recognizable." All of the other guards were minor celebrities in their own right. It was part of the cachet of being guarded by Elite Protection. Clients always knew their protection was going to be gorgeous and moderately famous.

"I actually wanted to talk to you about that." The subtle tinge of discomfort in the words alerted Max that this was Cross's real reason for seeking him out.

"Cover work?"

"No, the fact that we're busy. I know you want to start offering celebrity self-defense classes and we're getting so many clients we've had to start turning some down, and I thought you might want to hire some more people—"

"And you have someone in mind. Who is it?" He was always interested in referrals from his people—no one knew what the job required better than they did. Cross himself had been recommended by Tank. But Cross seemed uncomfortable, and it was setting off subtle warning bells.

"Elia Aiavao."

Max frowned. "Why is that name familiar?"

"MMA."

His head rocked back on a nod. "Wasn't he in a coma?"

"He's healthy now."

But Max heard what Cross wasn't saying. His career as a fighter was over.

"He doesn't have protection experience, but he could do the same training program you sent me to," Cross went on. "He's a smart guy. We played ball together in college and he was the guy who could always read the offense. It's part of what made him a great fighter."

Until a motorcycle accident had put an end to his career. "Give him my number and we'll set up an interview."

"Thank you."

His relief made Max uneasy. "No promises."

"I don't need any."

CHAPTER FOURTEEN

Girls' Night felt different.

Maybe it was the fact that Lorelei had retreated to her upstairs lair and wouldn't be joining them, or the fact that Nick and Tori were laughing in the kitchen when Parv came in, making her feel like she was interrupting their domestic ritual where she never had before.

Then Sidney and Josh arrived—Sidney for Girls' Night and Josh to pick up Nick since they were meeting some of his guy friends for a movie—and it only got worse. Parv hovered in the background, clutching the glass of wine Nick had poured for her, and watched the two couples go through their farewell dance.

None of them were making a show of it, but that almost made it worse somehow. The fact that they were all so comfortable with each other that the leave-taking was nothing special.

Parv had never felt like such an outsider with her friends before—and she wished she could crush the little spike of envy watching them inspired.

As soon as the door closed behind Josh and Nick, Sidney spun toward Parv, beaming. "We need champagne. We're celebrating."

And then she flashed her left hand, showing off the giant rock on her third finger.

The whooshing feeling was back, like the floor had

just dropped out from under her again. Even knowing it had been likely to happen eventually, the reality hit Parv hard—equal parts happiness for her friend and a disoriented feeling like nothing in her life was steady anymore and she needed to hold onto the nearest fixed object to keep from being flung off the merry-go-round.

"You're getting married!" she gasped, hoping she sounded more excited than breathless from the dizzy spinning feeling—and the two-ton weight suddenly pressing on her chest.

Sidney came to give her a closer look at the ring—all twenty-seven zillion karats of it. "It was this weekend— that little getaway to the B&B. He had it all planned— but it wasn't a cheesy *Marrying Mister Perfect* scene. It was so *us.* And I cried. I never thought I was a crier, but as soon as he pulled out that ring I started blubbering so hard he could barely understand my answer."

Parv felt tears pricking in her own eyes, but she noticed that Tori wasn't squealing and gushing over the ring. "You'd already heard?"

"I saw the ring this morning," Tori admitted. "And I actually have some news too—though no champagne for mine."

Sidney froze, then spun toward Tori with wide eyes. "*No.*"

"No?" Parv looked between the two of them trying to figure out what she'd missed. "Are you engaged too?"

"Well, yes," Tori said, as if it was nothing, "but Nick and I have been moving in that direction ever since we got back together. That isn't my news." She rested her hand over her abdomen—and the floor fell away beneath Parv's feet again even before she confirmed it with the words. "I'm pregnant."

"Oh, *Tori.*" And then Parv was tearing up—and

trying to convince herself that they were all happy tears. Everything seemed to be happening at light speed and she was still stuck in neutral, watching it all whiz by.

"Nick and I have decided to do a quick little wedding in a couple weeks," Tori went on. "Get it over with. Just a few people, but obviously we want you to be there."

"Of course. I wouldn't miss it," Parv promised.

"I'd wondered why you were suddenly in such a hurry!" Sidney exclaimed—and Parv realized they'd already started on the wedding plans. "When are you due?"

"May thirtieth. We only tested positive on Saturday. We aren't telling anyone yet—still first trimester—but I wanted you guys to know."

"That's incredible," Parv murmured.

Tori looked pointedly at Sidney. "Are you and Josh going to get started right away? We could be pregnant together."

"Oh no," Sidney insisted. "We're in no hurry. We can't even agree on a wedding date. I think kids are way off."

Tori waved them over to the island, pouring Sidney a glass of wine and getting water for herself as they gathered around. "Which dates were you considering?"

"Josh was thinking February—but anything even remotely Valentine's is way too cliché and that doesn't give us any time to plan, and you know people will be watching to see what we do with our wedding because of the show—though we've agreed we aren't going to feature our own wedding. It would be too weird. Though it would probably be great for ratings."

"You could get hitched on April Fool's," Parv suggested. "Like that actress who announced her wedding on Twitter and everyone was debating for months whether it was real or a hoax. *That'd* be great for ratings."

"My wedding isn't a publicity stunt." Sidney shot her a *look*—apparently forgetting she'd brought ratings into the conversation in the first place. "Besides, we always tell our brides you can't plan a showstopper wedding in less than six months so I was thinking maybe early June—but with you due at the end of May, Tori, that would probably be cutting it close."

"If I get a vote, I'd rather be pregnant than sleep deprived with a newborn for your wedding. With Lorelei I had a weird surge of energy in my last trimester but I remember almost nothing of her first six months beyond how tired I was all the time."

"This time will be different. This time you'll have Nick to help," Sidney reminded her. "But maybe we can do early May. I'll need to look at the filming schedule for *Once Upon a Bride*—especially if we get picked up for a second season. I talked to Caitlyn yesterday morning and that should be long enough after her baby is born that she's comfortable traveling with him—"

Caitlyn. Sidney's best friend from *Marrying Mister Perfect*.

Parvati barely heard her as she went on.

She knew Sidney had her show friends now, the other girls from her season of *MMP*. They'd been in the reality TV trenches together. They understood Sidney's life in ways that Parv didn't. But that didn't help the little ache in her chest that Sidney had already told Caitlyn, had called her the morning after the proposal, while telling Parv seemed like almost an afterthought. She'd been replaced.

But she refused to let her insecurity wreck this moment for Sidney. Parv took a long swallow of her wine, forced a smile, and lifted her glass. "I guess May it is. Here's to May. And to the luckiest guy I know and your future together."

Sidney beamed. "Thank you." She lifted her glass, taking a sip before her gaze flicked back to Parvati. "Speaking of the future I was thinking about your problem, with Common Grounds. Why don't you go on one of those Bake-Off shows? You'd have a great chance and even if you didn't win it would be great exposure."

"Sadly not everything can be solved by a reality television show. It'd be too little too late." Besides, she'd already auditioned and been turned down by half a dozen different baking shows.

"I'd feature you on *Once Upon a Bride*, but you don't do wedding cakes. Though I bet if you did they'd be amazing. You could probably give Lacey's Cakes a run for her money if you decided to open a bakery—"

Parv listened to her friends trying to help by listing all the ways she *would* be successful, if only she'd done everything differently, and took another healthy swallow of wine. It was going to be a long Girls' Night.

* * * * *

Max had only been home fifteen minutes before his doorbell rang. He smiled to himself when he pulled open the door to find Parvati on his doorstep again. But this time there were no cake pops. Just an irritable scowl.

"Did you hear?" she demanded.

He arched a brow. "Was there something I was supposed to hear?"

"Sidney? Ring a bell?"

"The wedding thing?"

Parv groaned, visibly deflating. "I can't believe she

told you before me."

"I am her brother."

"And I've been her best friend since we were six years old!" She glowered up at him. "When did she tell you?"

"Yesterday? She called while I was at work."

"I'm officially a pariah." She slumped against his doorjamb.

"Come here." He grabbed her wrist, tugging her across the threshold. He pulled her into the living room and shoved her toward the sofa as he went to mix drinks. "You aren't a pariah."

"No. I'm just broke and alone while everyone around me is coupling off and skyrocketing to success."

He paused with the scotch bottle poised over the glass. "If you're going to whine all night, I'm going to send you home."

"I'm allowed to whine. I just spent all night listening to my two best friends go on and on about weddings and pregnancies and double dates with their fiancés, while my life has become more pathetic every day. I'm the girl who invested all her energy in her career and failed. And I don't even have a good excuse! Tori's a single mom and *she* was able to make a success of herself. Other people have had to claw their way up from the bottom and they make it. I was just stupid. I just *failed*."

"So try again." He crossed the floor to her and pressed the glass into her hand.

"You make it sound so easy."

"And you make it sound harder than it has to be." He sank down onto the sofa beside her.

"Says the man to whom everything has always come easily. You don't even have to work for women to fall into your arms. You just dimple at them and it's Game Over, but I can't even make it to date three."

"I'm still willing to do background checks on anyone you want. Just saying." He took a sip, savoring the flavor, and propped his glass on his stomach.

"Don't you think that takes a little of the romance out of it?"

"Internet dating is romantic?"

"I'm trying to let it be. Lots of people meet that way these days. It's the new normal." She drained half her scotch in an impressive gulp. "Though I'm beginning to think that after a certain age all men fall into two categories: giant man-children who never grew up and never want to, and bitter divorcees with so much baggage they secretly hate all women. Luckily those ones are easy to spot. They're the ones who ask you weirdly specific questions about your shopping habits and how you feel about Honda Civics when they meet you, as if they're interviewing you to see if you're their ex in disguise."

"And which am I?" He rose to bring the bottle back to the couch, topping up her glass before he sat back down.

"Are you kidding?" Parv snorted. "Man-child all the way."

"Hey. Don't insult the purveyor of scotch."

"Is it an insult if it's true?"

Max frowned. "I'm not sure I like how you see me."

"Ha. Join the club." Another impressive gulp. "My sisters all think I'm still six years old. Irresponsible Parvati. Impulsive Parvati. Selfish Parvati. As if I am forever locked into the person I was when I was a child. *Everyone* is a brat at six." She eyed the cubes in her glass, swirling the liquor. "Though sometimes I do feel like I'm not really an adult. I'm the fun aunt. I never became the wife. I never became the mom. Life is different without kids. I get that. I never had to spend every hour of every day thinking about how my actions would affect someone else. But that doesn't mean I couldn't."

"Of course you could."

She didn't seem to hear him—Parvati had impressive powers of selective deafness. "Maybe my sister is right. Maybe I never did grow up. Maybe I am still waiting for the fairy tale. But is that so wrong?"

She was obviously waiting for an answer so he took a guess. "No?"

"No!" she agreed vehemently. "I'm not too picky just because I don't want to keep dating the Google Stalker or the patronizing asshole who tried to mansplain politics to me because I clearly must not understand the issues if I disagree with him or the one who insisted on paying for my latte only to have his credit card declined and wheedle me into paying for his."

Max frowned. "Where are you meeting these guys?"

"Online. That's where everyone is these days. Like the guy who tells me on our first date that he's going to be 'greedy with my time'—when he doesn't know me at all. Obviously, I'm awesome, but he doesn't know that yet so why does he want to get so insta-possessive? You can't trust that. And then there are the ones who seem promising, but abruptly stop talking to you after you've had sex—"

"Whoa. Hold on. You're having sex with them?" A fist wrapped around his stomach, squeezing hard. "I thought you just had your first date tonight."

She separated one finger from the glass to point at him. "This was my first date this go around, but this isn't my first rodeo. No sir. And I'm not admitting to you how many times I've tried this before because then you'll know exactly how much of a dating failure I am."

"You aren't a failure."

"No. Apparently I'm just so bad at sex that men have to run in the opposite direction without even a goodbye text."

"Men are assholes." And he wanted to break the kneecaps of anyone who treated her like that. "What are their names?"

"Yes, they are assholes and no, you can't kill them. Though I personally think if you've put your boy parts inside her girl parts then she at least merits a break-up text. That's just courtesy." She took a long swallow of scotch. "There's no courtesy left in the world."

He eyed her empty glass, measuring it against her apparent inebriation. "How much did you have to drink before you came over here?"

"A couple." Her head fell back against the couch. "Then there are the ones that I like a lot at first, the ones who seem so promising, but then they freak out at the waiter for no freaking reason and you realize you could deal with it, you could handle it but should you have to? Shouldn't it be magical? At least at first? At least for a little while?"

He eyed the way she'd started to list sideways. "I've never thought relationships were particularly magical."

She glared at him. "You're like my sisters. They say it's just a choice you make and then you stick with it and make the best of it. That there's no such thing as a perfect fit. That you use your head and not your heart, but I'm a romantic, thank you very much."

"I know," he murmured. "That's why I worry about you. Romantics have their hearts wide open and open hearts are open targets."

"So I'm supposed to close my heart?" She glowered at him. "That sounds like a great plan. I'll add that to my list of advice. So much freaking advice. Put yourself out there, Parv—but it will happen when you stop looking. So what am I supposed to do? Put myself out there, but not look?"

"I'm not the expert." What he was was completely out of his depth in this conversation. How had they gotten here?

"What am I asking you for anyway?" she grumbled. "You think I'm repressed."

He did a double take. "I what?"

Her full lips pursed in a pout. "You said I was repressed."

"No, I didn't." He would have remembered something like that. Parvati was the least repressed person he knew.

"That night when you drove me home. After my parents' party."

"I didn't say that, Parv," he insisted.

"Yes, you did. You said I was repressed."

"I wouldn't say that." She was fire and freedom and uninhibited pleasure in the little things in life. Just the way she nibbled on a cake pop was enough to make his entire body tense. That was *not* repressed.

"I'm not, you know," she insisted, tossing back the last of her scotch. "I can be impulsive. I can be wild. I have a *tattoo*."

She thrust her ankle at him and he caught it in self defense before it could connect with his stomach.

Her skin was soft beneath his fingers, silky smooth. The bones were more delicate than he expected. He'd never noticed how feminine an ankle could be. How erotic.

Shit. He needed to not be following that line of thinking when she was swaying beside him, drunk off her cute little ass. He put her foot back on the floor. "Did you eat anything before you started drinking?"

"I had a coffee date. I had coffee for dinner. And then Tori gave me wine."

"Did you drive yourself up here?" The idea of her on the road like this made his blood chill.

"I was fine to drive before you gave me a pint of scotch."

"It wasn't a pint." But it had been a very healthy pour. Two pours. And now she was too drunk to get herself home and if he drove her, her car would be stuck up here.

And if she stayed…

She was drunk. Way too drunk. And he was not that guy.

"Come on." He pulled her to her feet and began steering her toward his private wing of the house.

"Where are we going?" she asked, unresisting.

"You're going to sleep it off in the guest room."

His place was a sprawling single story ranch with sky-high ceilings. The entertaining areas—living room, kitchen, dining and game rooms—were all to the left while the master, office, and guest bedrooms all opened off a hall to the right. He walked her to that hall.

She twisted around, walking backwards so she could face him, completely trusting that he wasn't going to ram her into a wall. "I bet you have a great guest room. I bet it's decked out with gourmet mini soaps."

"Gourmet soap?"

"You know what I mean. Designer."

"Don't get your hopes up. I don't have many guests." But the interior decorator he'd had deck out the place had promised it would be so luxurious his guests would never want to leave, so for all he knew there were designer soaps.

"I bet you have a king bed, don't you?"

The muscles in his back tightened at the word *bed* coming out of Parvati's unfairly sexy mouth, but he opened the door to the guest room and gently shoved her inside. "This is you."

She caught the doorframe, looking up at him from beneath her lashes, and for a second he was sure she was going to invite him in. And equally sure he was going to turn her down and it was going to change everything.

Things he didn't want to change.

He liked Parvati. He liked having her in his life like this. Yes, she was hot as freaking hell, but his idea to have a fling with her was beyond stupid because this was *Parv.* She was permanent. And he didn't do permanent in relationships. He needed them to stay friends—

Which was why it made no sense whatsoever that he was *disappointed* when she mumbled, "G'night, Max. Thanks for listening," and retreated into the guest room, shutting the door.

He could want her, but that didn't change the fact that she was just as off limits as she'd always been. Parvati Jai was in the Friend Zone and that was where she needed to stay. Permanently.

CHAPTER FIFTEEN

The sun was streaming through floor-to-ceiling windows and painting the mountains gold when Parvati woke up the next morning. Which was her first hint that something wasn't right, because she didn't have floor-to-ceiling windows or a mountain view.

Her second hint was her headache. And her third was the vague way her entire body seemed to ache.

Nothing like a Wednesday morning hangover to make you feel like a real adult.

Thank God Madison had been scheduled to open Common Grounds this morning because by the look of it she'd already missed the beginning of the morning rush.

She rolled over and her first sliver of awkwardness worked its way into her hung-over brain.

She was at Max's. She remembered coming over last night after she'd left Tori's. Feeling lost and adrift and wanting to be with someone who wouldn't make her feel quite so alone. Then there was the scotch. And bitching about things she really shouldn't have been telling Max—

And Max shoving her into the guest room as soon as it became obvious she was two-scotches over the driving limit.

She didn't think she'd come on to him.

God, she hoped she hadn't come on to him.

She climbed out of bed—dreading facing him but needing to get on with her day. At least she didn't have to worry about spending time getting dressed, since she appeared to have slept in her clothes. She smoothed out the wrinkles as she crept down the hallway, her ears tuned for any hint of Max, but all she heard was silence.

She vaguely remembered dropping her purse beside the couch, but now it was neatly arranged on the coffee table. The little kitten heels she must have kicked off at some point were positioned side-by-side by the door.

But no Max.

She crept into the kitchen, half expecting to find him whipping up French toast, but instead she found a note propped up on the counter with her name on it.

Parv—

I had to get to the office, but make yourself at home. Especially in the kitchen. Any baked goods that just happen to appear here will be welcomed with open arms.

Max

She sank onto the nearest stool, relieved as soon as she read the first words. He wasn't here. She didn't have to face him. It would have been awkward, but he'd done the one thing guaranteed to put them back on comfortable ground. He'd gone about his life as if nothing had happened. And nothing had.

* * * * *

"Your two o'clock just pulled up on a gorgeous Harley and Hank the Hammer has now emailed me three times with different excuses why we need to hack into his daughter's phone for her own protection. He's threatening to sue."

Max looked up from the financials he'd been

reviewing when Candy appeared in his office. "Remind the Hammer he hired us to upgrade the security on his house, not stalk his daughter—" He broke off. "On second thought, don't. I'll tell him. He shouldn't even be contacting you. Has he been bothering you?"

"Not so you'd notice. You want me to show your two o'clock in?"

"If you don't mind." She usually didn't volunteer for guide duty—more right-hand-man than receptionist.

Candy smiled broadly. "Oh no. My *pleasure*."

The reason for her enthusiasm walked through the door three minutes later.

Elia Aiavao was six-foot-five with muscles everywhere—evidently his convalescence hadn't negatively impacted his conditioning. He wore a white button down shirt with the cuffs folded back open over a snug black t-shirt and black cargo pants. Tattoos crawled up the side of his neck and down his arms to the backs of his hands in thick, black tribal bands, but his hair was neatly trimmed and the grin he flashed Candy as she waved him through the door was easy-going—and proved why Aiavao had earned the nickname the Smiling Samoan during his Mixed Martial Arts career.

He was huge, but a friendlier looking badass Max had never seen. Though there was something less-than-happy in his eyes, hiding behind that ready smile. He put on a good show, but there was more to Elia Aiavao than a toothy grin.

"Mr. Aiavao. I'm Max Dewitt. Thank you for coming in today."

"Just Elia's good." He extended his hand and walked forward with only a slight hitch in his step.

Max let his gaze flick down, noting the matching

motorcycle boots. If he hadn't read up on the Smiling Samoan's infamous crash, he never would have known the left leg was a prosthesis below the knee.

Elia followed his gaze, his grin never wavering. "I'm getting better with it every day. Though I have to admit it's weird when I go to the beach and random strangers come up to me to thank me for my service. I might have to get a tattoo that reads, 'You're welcome, but I'm not a heroic war vet.'"

Max shook his hand, unsurprised by the strong grip, and waved him to a chair. Following Elia's lead, he didn't dance around the topic. "You still ride a Harley?"

Elia settled into the chair, stretching his left leg out in front of him in a way that made Max wonder if he was in pain. "Some of the cruisers come with a modified heel-shifter that I can work even with my robo-leg."

"I wouldn't think that would be the primary issue."

Elia shrugged. "If I'd lost my leg in a car accident, am I supposed to never ride in a car again? I *like* riding my bike. Fuck any drunk-driving asshole who thinks they're gonna take that away from me." He smiled. "Pardon the language."

Max smiled, liking Elia already. "Cross tells me you used to play football."

"A few years in college before I got into MMA and decided I'd rather get my concussions in octagons rather than on fields. I was a beast," he said with absolutely no modesty and a grin that took the arrogance out of the statement. "I could still probably do MMA—the rules about amputees are different from state to state—but I would know I wasn't as good and I don't want to be a novelty act. And this seems like an interesting gig."

"You'd still be a novelty act in some ways. Our clients don't just want protection, they want a bodyguard who is also a status symbol. You'd be exploited. On display."

"Then it's a good thing my helmet protected my money-maker," Elia said, flashing white even teeth that had to be veneers after all the times they'd been publicly knocked out. "Cross said it's all about pretty faces."

"That's part of it," Max admitted. "But you'd have to be able to physically remove the client from a bad situation as well. The training would be extensive and even then you might not be suited to the job."

Elia sobered, rubbing his thigh above his knee in a gesture Max would bet money he wasn't aware of. His hands were scarred in places and Max didn't know what other damage the accident had done, but his face was completely unmarked. And it was a pretty face. Elia certainly met that part of the Elite Protection criteria.

"Watch my fights," he said. "I don't give up. Even when I'm outmatched. I'm stubborn as fuck and I can do this job."

"You don't know Hank Hudson, do you?"

"The Hammer? Nah. He's one of those WWE pansies, isn't he?"

Max snorted. He was liking Elia more and more.

* * * * *

Twenty minutes later, Max walked Elia out, promising to be in touch soon, and headed up to the break room, finding Candy at the table with her tablet while Pretty Boy sprawled on the couch and played X-Box—his preferred method of keeping loose before a job.

"Can we keep him?" Candy asked when he walked in. "He's prettier than Pretty Boy."

"Hey," the model-slash-bodyguard protested

without looking up from the screen.

Max grabbed a Vitamin water and sat down opposite Candy. "What do you think? I know you've been hacking into his life since the second he arrived."

Candy shrugged, not bothering to deny it. Today she wore skinny jeans, flannel, and a pair of chunky glasses that kept sliding down her nose. Apparently hipster-lumberjack was her new look. "He was a badass." She turned her tablet so Max could see the video of an MMA fight playing on her screen. "And anyone called the Smiling Samoan probably wouldn't let diva clients rattle him or piss him off." She shrugged again. "I don't know. He could be good."

If he could do the job.

The addendum went unspoken, but they all heard it. Elite Protection was about luxury bodyguards, but they were still *bodyguards*, and some of the best in the business when it came to close protection. Max couldn't do anything to damage that reputation—no matter how much he liked a guy. Some of the clients would love the sexy MMA amputee, but the first priority was making sure the clients were safe and he didn't have any experience. And he was still learning how to go through life with one leg.

EP couldn't be his learning curve. But didn't he deserve a chance to prove that he could do it? There was no quit in Elia Aiavao.

Max watched the video and Aiavao moved with lethal grace, his body poetry in motion, every movement an extension of his will—and now all those instincts that had made him so lethal had to be modified to fit his new form.

Max wished he could talk it out with Parv. She had a way of clarifying things for him, but he hadn't seen her since the night she'd gotten drunk at his place.

Not that he was avoiding her. He was just avoiding the temptation—once he realized he wasn't sure he would keep resisting it.

He'd sent her a text thanking her for the cookies she'd left for him and she'd occasionally send him messages with snarky comments about her internet dates, but he was keeping his distance. It was better that way—and she hadn't shown up at his house again, which just indicated that she agreed.

They'd gotten a little too close to the fire. They wouldn't do that again.

CHAPTER SIXTEEN

"What are you doing here?"

Parv had no excuse for the tactless words that fell out of her mouth as soon as she clapped eyes on Max at the yacht club where Victoria and Nick were having their "tiny little thrown together wedding"—which appeared to mean only fifty-odd guests.

He looked good in his pale grey suit—but then Max always looked good.

His eyebrows popped up. "I wasn't expecting a parade, but I thought you might be a little happy to see me. I *was* invited."

"I didn't know you and Tori were that close," Parv explained, trying to pedal back her initial surprise.

She was lousy at weddings. She'd always been lousy at weddings. She'd hoped it was a phase—that the fact that she was a total wedding failure had to do with the fact that she'd been to most of the weddings between the ages of eight and fifteen—which were awkward years for everyone. But even though everything felt different now, she could still feel that familiar awkward discomfort rising up.

She fidgeted with her skirt until Max caught her hand and tucked it into the crook of his arm, walking them toward the chairs that had been set up in an arc around the trellis arch. "Tori and I get along fine though

146

I'm probably only here as unofficial security. But when someone invites me to a wedding, I go."

"Who knew you were so biddable?"

He found a pair of empty chairs for them and they settled in to wait for the ceremony. "Your cookies found a good home."

"What?"

"The cookies. The ones you left at the house. They were great."

"Oh. Right. You're welcome."

Max frowned at her. "You okay?"

"Sure. Of course. Great."

But she didn't feel great. She felt like she was two breaths away from a panic attack. And wouldn't that make Tori's big day that much more special?

"Parv?"

"Mm-hmm?"

"You're cutting off the circulation to my fingers."

She looked down at her hold on his hand—she hadn't even realized she'd taken it—and forced herself to release her death grip. "Oops."

"You sure you're okay?"

But then—*thank God, thank God, please let it start*—the string quartet began to play Pachebel's Canon, Nick took his place at the arch and Lorelei began a stately processional as the maid of honor.

Parv rose when the wedding march began and turned with everyone else to look back toward the head of the aisle where Tori appeared. She looked magnificent—but then Tori was always perfection. The dress was a silky ivory that looked like something out of nineteen twenties Hollywood, moving sinuously with her as she came down the aisle holding a simple bouquet of long stemmed calla lilies.

The ceremony was brief. A few words. Vows. And that was it.

They'd elected to go with the traditional vows, but instead of feeling rote there was something particularly powerful about hearing them repeat the familiar words. Parv's throat closed off as Nick promised to be there for Tori for better or for worse, envy pressing in on her so tight she lost her breath.

It was her first wedding in years. Tori and Sidney planned them all the time, so she seemed to always be hearing about weddings, but she hadn't even been to the *Marrying Mister Perfect* Wedding of the Century that had launched Sidney's career into the stratosphere last May.

She hadn't been to a wedding since she'd wanted one.

It was amazing how much that changed things.

The sight of them pledging themselves to one another was more beautiful, more poignant somehow. She sniffed, glad lots of people cried at weddings and no one would think she was anything other than choked up at the beauty of it. Which she was. But there was another layer beneath her happiness for Tori and Nick. And Sidney and Josh. And everyone who had found someone they wanted to spend the rest of their life with. Someone they *loved*.

God, she wanted it.

Max tried to give her a linen handkerchief when they stood to watch the recessional, but she couldn't imagine smudging her eye makeup all over that pristine white, so she shook her head, swiping at her eyes with her fingertips instead.

"Parv?" he murmured under his breath.

"I'm just so happy for them." She sniffled. "Let's go find Sidney and Josh. They must be around here somewhere."

But Sidney had shifted into planner mode and was ushering everyone into the reception hall to find their tables for dinner service while Tori and Nick had their first photos as bride and groom.

Max and Parv were seated at different tables—which was a relief since if he kept watching her like she was going to shatter, she might actually do it. They parted ways and Parv found her place—at a table in outer Siberia populated by other singles, all awkwardly alone.

Tori had said she wasn't planning to have a formal reception, but something must have changed her mind because Parv sat through a chicken course, toasts—including an adorable one by Lorelei—and the first dance before she felt like she could sneak out the side door without attracting attention to her exit.

She was happy for them.

So damn happy for them she could barely breathe for all the damn happiness.

She crossed the lawn, her heels squishing into the grass until she reached the more stable footing of the dock. Nick and Tori had reunited on that dock, under the gazebo on the end. Parv had heard the story a dozen times in the last few months. About the misunderstanding that kept them apart for ten years. About the chance encounter at a wedding that had brought them together again—and the way all those years had fallen away.

She'd been so happy for Tori. She still was. She just hadn't realized then how much things were going to change.

She gripped the railing, looking out over the gorgeous yachts lined up in neat little rows. It was a romantic spot. The perfect spot to reunite with an old flame.

Footsteps on the wooden planks directly behind her made Parv's spine stiffen. Until Max leaned over the rail at her side, his forearms propped on the wood. She forced herself to relax.

"You okay?" he asked, turning his head from the view. "I saw you sneak out."

"I'm great. I just needed some air."

"Parv."

Just that. Just her name in that soft, slightly scolding way.

When had he gotten to know her so well? When had he become the one person she could say absolutely anything to?

When had Max Dewitt become her best friend?

"It was different when my sisters got married," she whispered. "I didn't want it for myself then. I was eight and a half at Angie's wedding. I remember how itchy the crinoline on the flower girl dress was and how we had to stand out in the sun for hours smiling for the photographer. I'm sure I was obnoxious. My mother kept telling me that it was Angie's day and I needed to be good. So I stood where they put me and did what I was told—right up until she threw the bouquet." Parv cringed at the memory of that bunch of flowers flying at her chest like it was laser guided. "It was a low toss and they'd shoved me in the front, so of course I caught it. Devi was jealous. She'd wanted it for herself, and I didn't understand why, so she snapped at me that now I had to get married next, but I was eight and boys were gross, so I burst into tears. And to this day that's all my family will talk about when they talk about Angie's wedding. How I wouldn't stop crying."

"You were eight."

"I know. All my sisters were married by the time I was fifteen—and I tolerated every wedding, but I never wanted it for myself. I was proud of myself for waiting. But now it's different. I look at Tori and Sidney and they have it all. Successful careers, men who adore them and want to marry them. Now I want it—and it feels like I've already fallen so far behind it's never going to happen for me. Like all the dreams I denied I wanted for so long are slipping away. I've never even come close. And I feel horrible and selfish for standing out here feeling sorry for myself on Tori's day."

"Tori's day is going great. It's your day I'm worried about."

"It isn't my day. I just didn't realize I was going to become a puddle of sadness as soon as she walked down the aisle. I really am happy for her."

"I know you are."

"And the last thing I want to do is screw up someone else's big moment."

"I know that."

"And now I have to come up with a date for my niece's engagement party."

Max cocked his head at her. "You can't go alone?"

"I could have. But Angie was being so annoying, just *assuming* that I wouldn't have someone to bring so I told her I was bringing a plus one. And now when I show up alone she's going to be unbearable."

"Can't you take one of your online guys?"

"Are you kidding? A wedding function at which he meets my *entire* family? On a first date?"

"So no one's made it to date two, huh?"

"Not yet." But she kept trying. Because she was a glutton for punishment. Or a hopeless romantic. Sometimes it was hard to tell the difference.

"I could take you."

The words were so unexpected it took a moment for them to register. When they did, she turned to face him, skeptical. "You want to come to my niece's engagement party?"

"I want you to know that you aren't alone. That's what friends are for, right?"

Jesus. She almost burst into tears again right there.

How was she supposed to withstand Max Dewitt and his savior complex? Always swooping to the rescue. If he weren't also an unapologetic man-whore with the attention span of a fruit fly, she could really fall in love with him.

Though she hadn't heard about him with many women lately—not even his usual rotating cast of leggy brunettes.

"What have you been up to?" She leaned a hip against the rail. "I haven't seen you in a while."

"Work has been busy. I've actually been thinking about hiring a new guy to cover the extra work we've been getting."

"Oh yeah? Do you have a superstud in mind?"

He frowned. "*Superstud*?"

"You pick your bodyguards because they're hot. Did you think I hadn't noticed?" When he continued to frown down at her, she grinned. "So. The new guy is hot. Or you wouldn't even be considering him. So what's the problem?"

"I don't know whether it's a problem yet or not. He doesn't have any experience—but neither did Cross when I brought him on. He used to be a professional fighter, so I know he can handle himself, but he was recently in a motorcycle accident that took off his left leg below the knee."

"Whoa."

"You'd never know it to look at him. And he looks like Aquaman's hotter little brother."

"He gets my vote. I love Jason Mamoa." Parv sighed. "Which way are you leaning?"

"I don't know. I've always had a gut feeling when it came to hiring new people, but I really *like* him and I'm wondering if that's clouding my judgment. What if he isn't a good investment?"

"Then you fire him. At least you gave him a shot."

But Max wouldn't fire him. She knew him better than that.

He talked about Elite Protection like he was a ruthless businessman, making decisions with his head and damning his heart—but Parv had always seen his company as the island of misfit toys. His people were all distractingly good-looking, yes, but they were also dinged up by life and adrift until Max brought them together and gave them a home.

Max may not see it, but Elite Protection was a family and he was their heart. And she had a feeling they'd just found their newest member.

CHAPTER SEVENTEEN

Parvati was in her depressing shoebox of an office, writing out the sign announcing the final days of Common Grounds, when she realized she'd fallen stupidly in love with Max.

She'd already been thinking about him—remembering how nice it was to have him to bounce ideas off of when she was trying to decide how to announce the closure—when her phone rang and his name appeared on the screen.

She picked up the phone, grinning before she even heard his voice. "Hey."

"Hey back," he said. "What am I supposed to wear to this engagement party tomorrow?"

"A suit?" She barely stopped herself before suggesting the grey one that matched his eyes.

"So I don't need to go out and buy Indian clothes? Candy was just asking me if you were wearing a sari and I realized I don't think I've ever seen you in one."

"And you won't tomorrow. There will be a few people more traditionally dressed, but almost everyone will be in suits and dresses. You'll fit right in."

"Are you sure? Candy looks like she would love to play dress-up on me."

"Positive. Though if you decide to let Candy dress you some other time, promise me you'll take pictures."

"I never keep photographic evidence." She heard a sound like his desk chair squeaking. "What are you up to? Did I catch you at a busy time?"

"No, I'm just making a sign announcing the closure of Common Grounds." She doodled idly on a piece of scratch paper, enjoying the sound of his voice. "I talked to the property management company like you suggested and apparently there's another vendor who wants this space for the holidays, so if I can vacate by November 15th, I can get a break on my rent."

"That's fast."

"It is. But now that I've decided to close, I'm ready for it to be over. And I'd be closed for Thanksgiving anyway. And my employees will have finals then, so it makes sense to just bite the bullet."

"And the countdown begins."

"Two weeks until we close and one more to sell off the equipment," she agreed, the words surreal. What was she going to do with all her free time? "How's your work going? Did you decide to hire that guy?"

"I did," Max admitted, though he didn't sound certain. "Provisionally. I'm sending him to the next training session. We'll see how that goes."

"Maybe he'll be great."

She could almost hear him shrug. "We'll see."

They hung up a moment later and she went back to her sign—

And realized she was humming.

Writing up a sign announcing the demise of her business. Sitting in the little box of an office with the walls so steeped in stress over the last few years that she could barely walk through the door without slumping. And *humming*.

Happy because of Max.

She should have seen it coming. She should have known what was happening, but it wasn't until she caught herself humming that she knew.

She was in love with Max Dewitt.

Crap. Crap crap crap.

She wasn't supposed to be in love with him. They were friends. She needed him too much to ruin it by falling for him. Just because he was sexy and kind and amazing—damn it. She needed to get a hold of her heart. Rein it in.

Max was a bad bet. She knew that. She knew she wasn't his type—the leggy, exotic women with exciting, important lives who didn't mind relationships that only lasted a week or two. She may not have a mortgage and a picket fence and a dog, but she *wanted* those things. And Max seemed determined to avoid them at all cost.

Okay. So she was in love with him. She could handle that. She'd had a crush on him all through high school. She had experience suppressing her feelings for Max. She just needed to remember that nothing could ever happen between them.

* * * * *

In retrospect, taking a man she was head-over-heels in love with to her niece's engagement party when she'd shown up solo to every other family function over the last five years was probably not Parvati's best idea.

He picked her up at her place—*like a real date*, her stupid hormones whispered—and arched his brows appreciatively when he saw the maroon tea-length wrap dress she'd chosen for the night. Her hair was down—as it always was when she wasn't in the kitchen—but she'd fluffed it up and slapped on some makeup.

"Why, Miss Jai. You clean up nice."

"So do you." He'd worn the grey suit. The one that matched his eyes and made her girl parts swoon.

"Shall we?" He crooked his elbow for her and she tucked her hand on his arm, suddenly feeling much less steady on her heels.

He held her door for her, but his eyes danced and she knew he was only *playing* at being her date, not actually trying to impress her with his chivalry. She sank into the Tesla, nervously smoothing her skirt as he rounded the hood and started the engine. Her stomach was in knots and she just knew the drive to Santa Barbara was going to be excruciatingly awkward—but Max asked her about her customers' reactions to the sign and then about the family members he would be meeting that night and the drive passed without a single awkward silence.

Which was good, because when they arrived at the country club her sister had booked for the evening, there were plenty of awkward silences waiting for them.

Parvati had failed to adequately consider how her family would react to Max. Some were openly shocked. Others visibly confused until Parv explained that they were just friends. A couple even asking him who he was there with—while he was standing right next to Parvati. They just didn't know what to make of the Perfect Ten Max Dewitt with Spinster Parvati.

By the time Parv had run the gauntlet and was able to drag Max over to the buffet for the semi-privacy of grabbing something to eat, she was bristling with irritation. "I think half my family thought I was gay."

Max chuckled, but didn't refute the claim. "I take it you don't bring a lot of men to family functions."

"Try none. I wouldn't have worried about having a date for this party, but my sister said something about how I could always be relied on not to bring a plus one and my better judgment exploded."

"I think I like it when your better judgment explodes." He grinned when she glared at him. "I'm serious. I love this. It's a glimpse behind the curtain to the real Parvati Jai. You're different with your family."

"Insecure and neurotic, you mean?" She balanced one last appetizer on her plate and turned to search for an open table—little cocktail tables and high tops had been set up near the buffet, leaving most of the room open for the dance floor. A big band orchestra played jazz standards while Jonah and Katie—who had taken swing dance classes in high school—showed off their skills.

"Maybe," Max acknowledged. "You're definitely quieter. I'm so used to seeing you with Sidney when you're always bubbly and giggling. I guess I wasn't expecting you to be so much more subdued with your family. It's a new side to you."

"Welcome to the Dark Side."

"I don't think they're all judging you, if that's what you're worried about." He followed her to a nearby high top that had just opened up. "Drink?"

"Please."

He veered toward the bar with her order—being stopped twice by her curious family members before he made it across the room.

"Okay. Who is *that*?" Katie appeared at her side before Max made it to the bar, leaving Jonah waltzing his mother across the dance floor.

"Max. Just a friend. Are you enjoying your party?"

"It's the *best* night," Katie gushed, easily diverted. "Everyone I love is here—if we had someone to officiate we could get married right now and I'd be happy. Your friend isn't a minister, is he?"

"Sorry. To the best of my knowledge he has no power to perform weddings."

"That's okay. He's hot, so I won't hold his lack of ordination against him."

"How's USC?"

"Amazing. Jonah and I love our Intro to Psych professor so much we're both considering changing majors. Can you just see us as psychologists?"

Parv wondered if there was a psychological term for when the word *I* was completely swallowed up by *we*. "You'd be great. If that's what excites you."

"I don't know how anyone can decide what they want to do with the rest of their life when they're only eighteen."

And yet you're getting married. Parv bit her tongue. "You have time."

Katie rolled my eyes. "Tell that to my mother. Every other week she reminds me that she and my father are only paying for four years and I'd better have a degree at the end of them or I have to repay her every penny of my tuition."

An arm curved around Parv's side, setting a drink at her elbow. "Could be worse," Max said. "You could have to pay your own way through college."

"Oh, I'm not complaining!" Katie said quickly, her eyes wide as she stared up at Max, as dazzled as if she was trying to gaze straight into the sun. "I just mean that I don't have a lot of time to make up my mind on what I want my major to be."

Parv introduced Max and the bride-to-be, who continued to gaze up at him adoringly—it really wasn't fair that he had that effect on women.

"What did you study?" Max asked Parv, still

standing too close to her. Her entire family was going to get ideas at this rate.

She edged away from him an inch. "Business. You?"

"Same. With a psych minor. So I could learn how to mess with the minds of my competitors."

"Isn't psychology *fascinating*? Jonah and I—my mother is waving at me. I think she wants Grandpa to do some kind of speech. I'd better go find my fiancé."

Katie bounded off and Parv took a long swallow of her drink, lifting the glass to Max in a toast. "Thank you."

Max's gaze followed Katie across the room. "Has no one realized the bride is a baby and needs to be locked in her room until she's old enough to get married?"

"She's eighteen. It's legal. And her fiancé is just as young."

They watched as Jonah intercepted Katie and her niece twined both her arms around one of his, hanging onto him as they made their way toward the stage where her mother was now gesturing urgently.

"I can't imagine getting married at eighteen. Their brains are still developing."

"Weren't you running a business from your dorm room at that age?"

"That isn't the same thing. Though I might have been more successful if I had gotten married young—less time and mental energy spent trying to figure out how to get girls to sleep with me if I had a wife."

Parv cringed. "Can we please avoid implying that my baby niece is getting married for the access to regular sex?"

"Sorry."

They fell silent as Angie spoke into the microphone, calling their attention to the stage. After a volley of speeches by half a dozen family members on each side of the aisle, Angie turned the microphone back over to the band leader and the music started up again.

Max took Parv's empty glass from her hands and passed it to a waiter. "Come on. Let's dance."

"Of course you can dance. You can do everything," she grumbled as he led her to the floor.

He twirled her into his arms, and Parv was grateful for the few swing classes she'd taken with Katie so she didn't tromp all over his feet as he pulled her into an easy shuffle.

"Ballroom dance club was part of my elaborate plan to get girls to sleep with me in college," he admitted, smoothly guiding her through the steps. "Do you know what the ratio of women to straight men was in that club?"

"You aren't going to convince me you had a hard time getting girls in college." She remembered too well how insanely gorgeous he'd been, even when he was going through awkward growth spurts.

"Okay, fine. I just liked to dance." He spun her out and then reeled her back in, the move startling a laugh out of her.

"You should be a professional wedding date. That can be your next business. You'll make millions."

He arched his brows at her. "What makes you think I'm looking for a new business?"

"Aren't you? Sidney calls it your three year itch. Once a business is thriving, you have to sell it and run away to Thailand or Africa."

* * * * *

Max frowned, tucking Parv closer to avoid another

couple on the dance floor. The more he saw himself through Parv and Sidney's eyes, the more uncomfortable he became with their image of him. "I think my sister tells you too much."

Parv grimaced. "Not lately."

The song ended and the band segued into a slow, jazzy old ballad. Max drew Parv into the sway of the dance—and tried not to think about how she fit in his arms. She was off limits and he needed to remind himself of that.

"How goes the e-dating battle?" He pitched his voice just for her ears.

Parv groaned. "Don't ask."

"That bad?"

"I went out with a guy last week who kept insisting I was the spitting image of Priyanka Chopra—only he couldn't remember her name so he kept calling her 'Quantico Girl.'"

Max studied her. "I can see it."

Parv rolled her eyes, visibly unimpressed. "Please."

"No, I can. It's the mouth."

"He was trying to get laid. What's your excuse?"

"I'm serious," Max insisted. "I used to have fantasies about that mouth."

Parv missed a step. "What?"

It wasn't until he had to bring her back into the rhythm of the dance that he realized he'd said too much.

Parv was hot. He'd always thought she was hot. Insanely, holy shit, *hot*. And it was starting to bug the hell out of him that she didn't see how sexy she was.

Her mouth had made him insane for *years*. But she was his sister's best friend and he wasn't supposed to admit things like that about his sister's best friend. Not to himself and certainly not to her.

He forced his tone to be casual, blasé. As if he hadn't said anything out of the ordinary. "I was a horny teenager. And you have a hot mouth. Accept it."

She blinked, blushing. "Okay."

He needed to get them back on friendly terms. Brotherly terms. Even if the way he was feeling with her swaying so close to him was far from brotherly.

He'd forgotten how long this song was. *Bewitched, Bothered and Bewildered*. He was definitely that. And if there were another three verses he might lose his mind if he couldn't get things back on comfortable footing.

He wasn't possessive of her. He was protective. That was fine. Brotherly, damn it.

"I'm starting some new self-defense courses at Elite Protection. You should take some."

She frowned at the apparent non sequitur. "I thought those were for celebrities only."

"That's the idea—so they don't have to worry about fans or paparazzi sneaking into the classes—but you have an in with the owner." He steered her away from another couple. "I just don't like the idea of you going out with all these strangers and not knowing how to defend yourself."

"You could teach me yourself."

The image hit him in the gut—grappling with Parvati, putting his hands on her to teach her how to twist her way free. No. He most definitely could not teach her himself. Not without both of them ending up naked.

CHAPTER EIGHTEEN

He'd been silent for too long.

She didn't know what she'd said, but it felt like some line she hadn't even known was there had been crossed.

Max wasn't looking at her. He was making a point of looking everywhere else and as soon as the song ended he released her like she was radioactive.

"I need some air," he said abruptly. "Do you want some air?"

"Sure."

He gestured for her to precede him toward the door and fell into step behind her, one hand resting lightly on the small of her back. She wondered if he was even aware of the touch or if it was just instinctive—Max the protector, always with one hand on his subject, aware of her on an instinctual level that had nothing to do with attraction and everything to do with who he was.

She needed to remind herself of that. No matter what he might say about her mouth, Max saw her as someone to look after. His little sister's friend. His friend, perhaps. But just a friend.

She opened the door to the terrace overlooking the golf course. The tables and patio chairs that would be out here during the day were stacked to one side, leaving only a vast, unused space between them and the carved stone railing that wrapped around the perimeter of the terrace.

Max left the door open, the music drifting out after them as he thrust his hands into his pockets and walked out on the moonlit space. Parv watched him, uncertain what to make of his odd mood.

Things had seemed normal between them while they were dancing. Comfortable. But somehow a switch had flipped and she didn't know what had changed.

Had she somehow given away her feelings for him?

No. He would have run for the hills if he'd had a clue, not for the nearest balcony.

"Maybe I should try internet dating too," he said suddenly, still facing the golf course. "These days most of the people I meet are clients and that's just bad business."

"You'll be the toast of online dating." She came up beside him and boosted herself up on the railing. "Some of the sites are perfect for no strings hook-ups."

"What if I want strings?" He turned toward her suddenly and she was startled by the intensity on his face. "You think I can't want what Sidney and Josh have? That I can't commit to something real?"

Parv stared at him. Was he saying what she thought he was saying? That he wanted a real relationship? Or was it only a hallucination brought on by the romantic lyrics floating out of the ballroom?

Someday my happy arms will hold you…

"I thought you didn't want that. I guess I figured if you did, it would be easy for you."

And someday I'll know that moment divine…

"It's hard to imagine the great Max Dewitt lonely," she said, her voice strangely hoarse. "You can have anyone you want."

"Can I?"

He held her gaze—and the world fell away.

This was it. This was the moment when everything would change. His gaze dropped to her mouth and she remembered what he'd said earlier.

I used to have fantasies about that mouth.

God yes. She'd had fantasies about every part of him. The song continued to whisper seductively about *all the things you are* and she felt all of her doubts falling away one by one. This was it. Fate. Serendipity. The moment in her life that made all the waiting worth it.

Max Dewitt was going to kiss her.

Finally.

He leaned closer, one hand lifting toward her face.

"*Max.*" It was more exhale than speech, but he didn't seem to mind. Nothing broke his focus on her lips.

It was happening. It was really happening. He was so close now.

Parvati would have pinched herself if she didn't think she'd fall off the railing if she moved a single muscle. The universe was finally giving her the fairy tale—

"Parvati! There you are."

Max jerked back guiltily—and Parvati jumped in surprise, grabbing at the railing with both hands when she started to tip backward toward the golf course. Max reached out to steady her, but stopped before making contact when she regained her balance without his help.

Which was almost enough to make her let go again, just to see if he would touch her before she took a header toward the sidewalk below.

He wasn't looking at her lips now. He wasn't looking at any part of her.

Nearly moaning in frustration, Parv turned to glare at the intruder. Asha stood in the doorway, oblivious to the idea that she might have interrupted something—though, in her defense, Parv had introduced Max as just a friend earlier. "Did you need something, Asha?"

"Mom's looking for you. There's someone she wants you to meet who might have a job for you."

Parv groaned her parents' latest attempt to be supportive was to push networking introductions and job interviews on her. "Tell her I'll be right there."

"Her friend is leaving soon—"

"I'll be right there, Asha."

"No," Max said suddenly, reaching for her arm. "You should go now."

The Universe hated her.

The band began a frantic, up-tempo number—as if the mood wasn't already dead—and Parv took Max's hand, hopping down from the stone railing. As soon as her feet touched the ground, he let her go—and Parv somehow resisted the urge to cry. Was it really so much to ask that she get the fantasy? Just once?

But the Fates weren't with her.

For the rest of the night they never returned to the terrace, or to the dance floor. Max was always close, but always with a careful distance between them—too far to touch.

During that moment on the terrace she'd been *so sure* she was about to get everything she'd ever wanted in one delicious Max-sized package, but the moment was gone and they never came close again. By the time he was driving her home, she'd convinced herself that it was just a trick of the music and the moonlight, making her think things that weren't real. He hadn't really been fixated on her mouth. He hadn't really said he wanted a real relationship. She'd just wanted it so badly she'd convinced herself it was happening.

This was why she should never have let herself fall in love with him.

He'd probably thought they were having a perfectly normal conversation about their respective dating prospects and there she was mentally running away into happily-ever-after-ville. The radio played softly the entire ride home, saving her from having to talk to him, and Parv listened to one romantic song after the next, wondering if she would ever hear a love song without this wistful ache.

Max pulled up in front of her place. He always walked her to the door, always made sure everything was safe and secure before he left, but she still jumped a little when he put his hand on her back as they approached her door.

"I had fun tonight," he said casually.

"My family loved you." And why wouldn't they? He was one of them. The Success Elite.

Yet somehow he'd never made her feel inferior. How was that even possible? How was it Perfect Max never looked at her like she was less than perfect?

"They all adore you," he commented.

"I know. I'm lucky." Which just made her beat herself up that much more when she disappointed them. She unlocked her door and turned to face him. "Thank you for tonight, Max. I owe you."

At first she thought he was nodding, ducking his chin. Later, when she described the moment, she would say it was an accident. She hadn't expected anything. Frankly, she was still busy being frustrated by the anticlimactic moment on the terrace. She certainly didn't plan it. Max didn't give her any kind of look or signal.

It just sort of happened. She couldn't even be sure which one of them initiated it.

All she knew was one second she was saying goodnight to him and the next they were kissing.

It wasn't the sort of passionate embrace she'd fantasized about. It was a sweet kiss. A soft, quick brush of his mouth over hers—not a tentative first date kiss, but the kind of kiss two people who had been dating for years might give one another as a hello or goodbye. Absentminded. Automatic. A familiar kiss.

And right when she started to wonder if it was a friendly familiar kiss—if that was all they were, condemned forever as *just friends* with no chemistry, no heat—Max leaned back just enough to draw in a sharp breath, angled his head and everything changed.

It wasn't sweet anymore. His lips resettled on hers, coaxing and pressing as he deepened the kiss and her brain stuttered to comprehend what was happening—*how had they gotten here?*

But then, before she could react, before she could do more than part her lips, he broke away, putting three feet between them and dropping hands she hadn't even realized had taken hold of her shoulders.

"Goodnight, Parv." Casual. Collected.

"Goodnight, Max," she echoed automatically, her higher mental functions thrown offline by the last sixty seconds.

Dazed, she watched him walk to his car and open the driver's door before she snapped out of it and retreated quickly inside, slamming the door and leaning against it. One hand lifted to touch her lips.

What had just happened?

Well, obviously she knew *what* had happened, but… what the hell?

What did it mean? And—most importantly—was it going to happen again? Because she'd been so surprised she hadn't been able to enjoy it properly and if Max was going to start kissing her, she wanted to enjoy every second of it.

CHAPTER NINETEEN

Parv woke up the next morning and immediately plugged in and turned on her phone, which she'd forgotten to do the night before, so dazed by what she was starting to think of as the Accidental Kiss.

She wasn't *expecting* Max to call, but neither did she want to miss his call just in case he felt like calling and professing his undying love to her. But when she turned on her phone it was to find two missed calls from Sidney, not her brother.

Had Max told Sidney that they'd kissed? Could he have called her for permission to date Parv?

It was too early for civilized humans to be awake, so Parv shot Sidney a text apologizing for missing her calls and telling her to call as soon as she was awake. Then she bounced out of bed, trying not to obsess, and headed to Common Grounds to open it and bake away her confusion.

But two hours later she was still as confused as ever—though at least she had cranberry orange muffins to show for her angst. She kept her phone on her—and even took it out of her pocket roughly every sixty seconds to make sure she hadn't accidentally turned off the ringer and missed a call. From Sidney of course. Max wouldn't call. It hadn't even been a real kiss. He was probably as puzzled by it as she was.

But if he wasn't…

Her phone rang, mid-daydream, and Parv jumped, fishing it out of her pocket and scooching back farther behind the counter to answer it so she wouldn't disturb her lone Saturday morning customer. Sidney's name showed on the screen.

"Sid?"

"Hey. What happened to you last night?" Sidney asked. "I called you three times."

"It was Katie's engagement party and I forgot to turn my phone back on when I got home. What's up?" *Did Max call you? Do you* know?

"Oh, you know, the usual. My father hates my fiancé."

The words were so unexpected, it took Parv a full twenty seconds to process them. "What?"

"My father was in town last night—something to do with finalizing my parents' divorce—and since he's here so rarely, I thought it would be a good time for him to meet Josh. I should have waited for a night when Max was available because he's always a good buffer, but he had some *thing* last night that he couldn't get out of, though he refused to tell me what it was—"

"He didn't tell you?" Parv felt a flicker of unease. Why wouldn't he want Sidney to know he'd been with her?

"You know how Max gets. All mysterious. Probably a confidential work thing. Or a woman he doesn't want anyone to know he's seeing."

The words seared through Parv. "Probably," she echoed weakly.

"Anyway, he wasn't available and I stupidly went ahead with dinner anyway and without my mother or Max there to run interference it was a bloodbath."

"Your father really hates Josh? How is that possible? Everyone loves Josh."

"We've found the one person on the planet who doesn't love Josh. Lucky me."

"Why doesn't he like him?" Parv asked, still unable to process the idea of anyone hating Josh.

"You name it. He's divorced. He makes his living being charming on camera. He treats me like a princess and never makes me feel like I'm not good enough. Hell, I don't know. Since when does my father need a reason?"

"He said he doesn't like Josh because he treats you well?"

"No. That was just me being bitter. He said some shit about me being a *Dewitt* and lowering my standards—as if *I'm* the one who's settling with Josh."

"Neither of you are settling."

"He actually accused me of turning myself into a Kardashian because we're on reality TV. God, the engagement party is going to be a nightmare," Sidney groaned. "If there even is an engagement party. If there even is a wedding."

A traitorous little thought whispered in the back of her mind—that if there wasn't a wedding maybe she'd get her best friend back—but the guilt chaser that followed made her feel sick to her stomach for even letting something so horrible and petty slither through her brain. "Of course there will be a wedding," she insisted, firm and confident.

"Don't be so sure," Sidney grumbled. "He kept going on about how if this was what I wanted it was *fine*, but I was a Dewitt and I needed to think about what was important to me. He actually said I could do better *in front of Josh*. I wanted to punch him. I can only imagine how Josh felt."

"Have you talked to him about it?"

"He's pissed. But he keeps saying he sees my dad's side of it. That he just wants what's best for me. I'm terrified he's going to realize I'm not worth the trouble and bail."

"He isn't going to bail."

"You didn't see how awful my father was. I wouldn't want to have to put up with someone treating me like that at holidays. Let alone at the wedding! This is the man who's supposed to walk me down the aisle. What if he gets to the altar and refuses to give me away? What if he decides to take the *speak now* option rather than holding his peace?"

"He won't. Once he gets to know Josh, he'll love him. Everyone likes Josh. He's a prince among men."

"Sure, but how's he going to get to know him? He's already on a plane back to Switzerland and God only knows when he'll be back—and by 'God' I mean my father since he seems to think he's the Almighty."

"Maybe next time he's back you can get together with Josh and Max. You said Max is good at smoothing things over with your father."

"He is. That's true. When he isn't off banging models he refuses to bring home to meet my mother."

Parv cringed—even though there hadn't been any banging, she was hardly model material and she'd already met his mother. "Maybe he isn't doing that anymore. Maybe he's matured." She remembered his words the night before with aching detail. "Maybe he's thinking about settling down with someone special."

Sidney groaned. "Oh God, not this again. Parv, do me a favor and don't get all starry-eyed about my brother. The last thing I need right now is to be stuck in the middle when my brother and his fifteen second attention span break your heart."

Parv winced, reliving the accidental kiss that she could *not* tell Sidney about, even if she desperately wanted to ask what it meant. And why Max would have hidden from his sister the fact that he was with her—which was impossible since Sidney was the sister in question.

This was why Sidney didn't want them getting together. It blurred all sorts of lines that didn't need to be blurred.

But if Max wanted to be with her…

She wasn't going to say no. No matter how much Sidney might want to keep things easy between them. Some things were worth the complication.

That was what she told herself on Saturday, when she told Sidney everything was fine and got off the phone as quickly as possible. By the time Monday had rolled around and she still hadn't seen or heard from Max, her rational side had managed to overrule her heart—reminding her that Max wasn't known for his relationship longevity. For all she knew, he'd already lost interest. Or he regretted the kiss as much as she feared.

The more she thought about it, the more she couldn't remember how it had started. She thought it had just sort of happened, but what if she'd leaned in and made the connection without realizing it and he'd just been too much of a gentleman to push her away? What if the accidental kiss had really been her accidentally throwing herself at him?

Was he avoiding her because he felt so awkward about the fact that she'd made a pass at him and he didn't know how to let her down easy? If he'd *wanted* to kiss her, wouldn't he have at least called by now? They were in the habit of talking almost every day. Or at least texting. And suddenly all she heard were crickets—and not the kind that came as a text notification.

By Monday afternoon, she was convinced she'd thrown herself at him and completely destroyed their friendship. Things were going to be strained between them now. This was exactly what Sidney had feared. One little accidental kiss could ruin everything—Parv didn't even want to think about how much worse it would have been if she'd accidentally slept with him.

Though at least then she would have the memory of sleeping with him—and if the memory of the kiss was anything to go by, that might have been worth it.

But no. She'd stupidly fallen in love with him—or convinced herself that she had because he was a good friend with the body of a Greek god and she'd let herself over-rely on him because she was feeling lonely and lost. And then when she believed it was *true love*, she'd taken him to a family gathering designed to brainwash her into thinking romantically and then attacked him at the end of the night, ruining everything.

She needed distance. It was good that he'd been avoiding her for two days. She was never going to learn to stand on her own two feet if he was always there to support her. And she was a strong, independent woman. She was going to stand herself back up, damn it.

So she left the shop in Madison's capable hands and walked down the block, ringing the bell over the door of Lacey's Cakes.

Lacey stepped out of the back when she heard the bell, cleaning icing off her hands with the towel tucked into her apron, and stopped, frowning when she saw

Parv in her lobby. Lacey had none of the delicacy of her name. A large, middle-aged Germanic woman with a perpetual glower, she aimed it at Parv now. "Can I help you?" she asked skeptically.

Lacey was on the town council that had denied all of Parv's requests to extend Common Grounds' hours. She was also Parv's primary competitor for sweet treats on Main Street. Parv had always thought Lacey should have recused herself from those votes because of a potential conflict of interest, but Lacey hadn't shared her opinion—and their relationship had been strained at best ever since.

But Lacey's Cakes was also the best bakery in Eden and the only other one within walking distance of her place—which was a necessity considering how frequently the Jetta had taken to breaking down lately.

Parv straightened her spine and bit the bullet. "I'm sure you've heard Common Grounds is closing."

"I have," Lacey admitted—and at least she didn't look pleased. Parv wasn't sure she could have gone on if Lacey had done a victory lap.

"I was wondering if you needed some extra help over the holidays."

Lacey frowned. "Look, I know your counter girls are good, but I don't need someone on the cash register full time. What I need during the holiday rush is another baker."

"I know. I wasn't asking for Madison and Anna." The two of them had both sworn to her that they already had jobs lined up for the winter semester. "I was asking for me."

Lacey's grumpy expression didn't budge, but she did take a moment to consider it. "You wouldn't be allowed to change any of my recipes," she said finally. "I don't want creativity. I want a worker bee."

"I can do that."

Lacey eyed her, speculative through her perma-glower. "It would be part time. And only fifteen dollars an hour."

Parv resisted the urge to point out that after running a failing small business the money Lacey could pay her would actually be a raise. "I can work with that."

"And just for the holidays. I don't need help year round and I'm not going to keep you on for charity."

"I wouldn't expect you to."

Lacey continued to eye her. "Okay," she said finally. "But you'll have to sign a non-compete and if I catch you trying to poach any of my customers, I'll fire your ass in a second and make sure no one else in Eden will ever hire you."

"I'm not going to have a business, so I don't know what I would do with your customers if I could poach them. Though you might be able to pick up some of mine if you consider letting me make one or two of their favorites."

"I'll consider it," Lacey allowed grudgingly. "When can you start?"

"November sixteenth?" It was the day after her lease expired on Common Grounds. She would need to jump right in to keep herself from wallowing in depression anyway. And she would need the money if she wanted to keep eating and paying her rent.

Lacey nodded. "All right. The sixteenth."

Parv wasn't overly optimistic about the work environment at Lacey's Cakes, but Lacey did know her stuff. Her wedding cakes were works of art and Parv would be able to learn from her, if nothing else. And make some money without the stress of worrying about paying her employees or covering her overhead.

She crossed back to Common Grounds and Madison looked up from the milk she was frothing when Parv joined her behind the counter. "Your friend was just here."

"My friend?"

"The cute, flirty one. Max. You just missed him."

"Story of my life. Did he leave a message?"

"Nope. Just took his Americano to go." Madison eyed her, her baby blues concerned. "You okay, boss?"

"I'm great." For a woman who'd just realized her accidental kiss was never going to be repeated. He hadn't even said he'd be back or he'd see her soon. And apparently he'd flirted with Madison. Her love life just kept getting better and better.

CHAPTER TWENTY

Max made himself wait two days before he dropped by Common Grounds after The Kiss.

Then he had to wait another two days while she wasn't there when he dropped in for his coffee each morning, so it was Wednesday morning—during the busy morning rush which she was handling by herself—when he finally saw her for the first time since that night.

He'd given her space to think about things and decided he was going to take his cues from her. He hadn't planned on kissing her, but once it had happened he wasn't going to regret it. But he also wasn't going to push it if it wasn't something she wanted to repeat. He'd never really done the relationship thing—but he hadn't been lying when he said he might want that for himself. Someday. And Parv was the kind of person he would want it with. He'd give it a try, if that was what she wanted—because chances to be with a girl like her didn't come along every day—and Max was smart enough not to let good opportunities pass him by.

But when he walked into Common Grounds on Wednesday and she looked up at him, her expression frazzled and distant, he felt a distinct thud of disappointment when she didn't smile. "Max. What can I get you?"

No mention of the kiss. No smile. No wink. Not even a glimmer in the back of her eyes saying she remembered kissing him on Friday night.

Shit.

She regretted the kiss. He'd thought she'd wanted it as much as he had—that she'd leaned in at the exact same moment so it was impossible to tell which one of them had initiated it. But what if that had been wishful thinking on his part? Or what if it had been an impulse, a whim—one she'd been regretting ever since?

"Americano," he said through the dredge of disappointment. "Busy today."

She nodded, her attention on her hands as she prepared drinks. He didn't say anything until she'd handed off drinks to two other customers and he was the only one hovering near the counter waiting. This was her place of business. She was doing her job. Maybe he wasn't reading distance so much as professionalism.

But when it was just him at the counter, she still didn't look up. Still didn't smile. The awkwardness remained.

He searched for some way to bring up the kiss without bringing up the kiss. "Did your niece get back down to LA okay?"

"She did." Parv finally looked up, but her expression stayed blankly professional. "I really appreciate you being my plus one on Friday. I owe you one."

Her plus one. Not her date. And owing him one didn't exactly sound like a romantic overture. He shrugged. "It was nothing."

"Maybe." Was that relief in her eyes? "But thanks for coming with me anyway. Always a relief to have an ally at those things."

"Any time."

"Hopefully I won't have to bother you again."

Well. That was clear. He'd obviously read the situation wrong. He hadn't dated anyone in a while—too busy with his business—and his rusty radar was probably reading all the signals wrong. He'd misinterpreted her interest. Okay then.

He grabbed his Americano, sliding over a bill to pay for it. "See you round, Parv."

"See ya, Max."

* * * * *

Parv held it together as she watched Max leave. She held it together through the morning rush, busy hands keeping her tangled up feelings from rising up to the top of her thoughts.

It was nothing.

She leaned against the counter, breathing through emotions she couldn't quite identify. It was over. That was good. Anything with Max would have been too complicated. And it never would have lasted. And it would have hurt like a bitch when it ended.

Better to end it now. Before it took a hold of her heart. She'd had the fantasy—for about two-point-two seconds. Now she could move on with reality. A reality in which she and Max were friends and nothing more. And where her person was still out there, waiting for her to find him.

* * * * *

"I was wondering why you'd been such a grumpy

bastard lately, but now I get it."

Max looked up from his computer, frowning at Candy where she leaned against his doorjamb, dressed like something out of a Raymond Chandler novel today. "I've been a grumpy bastard?"

"Just for a couple weeks."

Since he'd kissed Parv and she'd put distance between them—she hadn't dropped by his house once since her niece's engagement party. No more cake pop deliveries. And he'd only seen her a couple of brief, rigidly awkward times at Common Grounds when he'd gone in to get his morning coffee.

Candy approached and lifted her cell phone, flashing the screen at Max too quickly for him to see what she was showing him. "Makes sense now."

Parv was on her phone? "What is that?"

"The news just broke. About your dad."

Panic spiked. Was his father okay? Was he sick? Dying? Was that why his parents had gotten divorced? But that didn't make any sense. And why wouldn't they have told him? Though the answer to that was obvious—his parents had always excelled at keeping things from their children in the name of protecting them.

"What about my father?"

Candy paled, her sympathetic expression falling into horror. "I thought you knew already."

"What happened to my father, Candy?"

"Nothing." She handed him the phone with the article brought up on the screen. "He got married."

It made so much sense Max felt like an idiot for feeling even a faint shimmer of surprise. "Of course he did."

She was twenty-five, the article said. Younger than

183

Sidney. His administrative assistant. His six month pregnant administrative assistant.

What a cliché. He'd been banging his secretary.

But the photo that accompanied the article made something angry clench in Max's stomach. His father looked smugly self-satisifed as he gazed at his blushing—and visibly pregnant—bride. So freaking proud of himself.

In a small ceremony with only family and close friends present…

No. No family could have been present. He hadn't known. Sidney hadn't known.

Had his mother known?

"I have to go out."

"Sure," Candy said, moving out of his way as he grabbed his keys and the suit jacket he'd thrown over the back of his chair. "We'll hold down the fort here."

"I know you will."

Candy could run Elite Protection without him if it came to it. And today she would have to. He had to see his mother.

* * * * *

Sidney's shiny new SUV was already in the driveway when Max pulled up. She must have seen the news as well—and if she'd been at the Once Upon a Bride office rather than filming her drive would have taken half the time his had. He'd had an hour to work up a dozen questions and replay all the possible answers in his mind, not calling, wanting to read his mother's face when he asked her.

He'd tried calling his father from the car—getting voicemail on every number he tried until he resorted to calling the Titacorp offices and was transferred through three different receptionists before being informed that Mr. Dewitt was unavailable as he was currently on his honeymoon.

His *honeymoon*. The man who hadn't even taken the time to fly home for birthdays or graduations had whisked his new wife off to some Mediterranean villa for the week.

"Why would you keep something like that from us?" Sidney was demanding—not quietly—when Max let himself in through the front door, in no mood to knock.

"It was your father's choice."

Max followed the sound of their voices into the living room, stopping in the archway opening. "So you did know."

"About Claudine?" His mother turned toward him, taking his arrival in stride. "Yes. I knew. But it wasn't my place to tell you. Your father had his reasons for wanting to keep it quiet and even if I disagreed with his choice, I had to respect his decision."

"He violated the prenup," Max reminded her. "You could have gone after him for millions."

"My lifestyle is perfectly comfortable without your father's money," Marguerite said, in what had to be the understatement of the century as she stood in the vaulted living room of her three million dollar mansion.

"Why aren't you angry?" Sidney demanded. "He *cheated* on you."

"I know. I've known for almost three years. And I think he genuinely loves her. Isn't that better than cheating for cheating's sake? He wasn't trying to hurt me. I'm not sure I ever entered into his decision to be with her."

"You're his wife," Max snapped. "Don't you think

you should have entered into the decision?"

"Oh God," Sidney groaned. "She was twenty-two when he started sleeping with her?"

"Our relationship hasn't been exclusive for years," Marguerite said, calm and cool as if she was facing her board. "Did you think it had been? We only see each other two or three times a year. Even old people have needs."

Max cringed. He'd thought more about his parents' sex life in the last two hours than he'd planned to for his entire life. "Why didn't you tell us this was why you were getting divorced? Don't you think we had a right to know?"

"This wasn't why we decided to get divorced. The divorce was my choice. Your father viewed his relationship with Claudine as a separate matter. I think he should have told you, but it wasn't my decision. And quite frankly it doesn't concern me anymore. I'm sorry that you're upset, but it wasn't my call. I recommend you speak to your father. I have a business to run." She pivoted on her heel and marched back to her home office—from which she worked most days so her commute didn't cut into her productive hours.

"Did you try calling him?" Sidney asked when their mother had made her exit.

"He's on his honeymoon, apparently."

Sidney grimaced. "They told me the same thing. Did you know?" Max hesitated long enough that Sidney whipped toward him. "Max? You knew?"

He shook his head. "There was a clause in the separation agreements. About future children. The wording struck me as oddly precise, but I told myself I was being paranoid. He's never made time for people—I couldn't imagine him taking the time to have an affair, let alone get married."

"The last time I saw him he was an ass to my fiancé, but he never said a word about his own. Mom said he was trying to be paternal. Trying to show he was protective of me, but I just wanted to scream, 'Now? Now you've decided to care about my life?'"

"Better late than never?" Max couldn't manage a drop of sincerity and Sidney grimaced.

"Do you think he really loves her?" A soft vulnerability hid in his sister's voice.

They were separated by the width of the room and Max couldn't tell if he was supposed to go to her. They weren't huggers, the Dewitts. She'd probably check him for a fever if he got all touchy-feely on her.

"We always thought he was incapable of caring about anyone," she went on. "What if he was just incapable of caring about us?"

"Hey." He did cross the room then, tugging her into his arms, Dewitt stoicism be damned. "He's the broken one. Not you."

"Not *us*," she insisted, hugging him back.

But Max wasn't so sure.

Sidney had always been different. She'd always cared about people. About romance and feelings. She created dream weddings for a living. Max was his father's son. He cared about being the best. About pushing himself farther and harder than anyone else was willing to go.

Even when he'd taken time off to travel, it hadn't been to unwind and relax. It hadn't been to find himself—unless the version of himself he'd been looking for was just as incapable of slowing down. He'd built himself in his father's image. And why? To get his approval? To be good enough? Only to have the old man

187

turn around and give the attention he'd been begging for all his life to his twenty-something secretary. *Claudine.*

He almost wished his mother hadn't told them the name. It made her real. The woman, born after he was, who was going to give birth to his half-sibling.

Max reached for the one aspect of his life that always made sense. "I need to get back to work."

CHAPTER TWENTY-ONE

Common Grounds closed without fanfare.

Her customers bought their last coffees, told her they were sorry to see her go, and went about their lives, resigned to going a few miles down the road for Starbucks in the future, the loss of Common Grounds a tiny blip in their lives.

Some asked her what she would be doing next, seeming relieved when she told them she'd be working down the street at Lacey's Cakes for a while and they wouldn't be completely losing her as a source of baked goods.

Others stocked up on the beans of their favorite coffees and got the supplier information from Parvati so they could support their expensive coffee habits without her as the go-between.

But no one cried. Not even Parv. In fact, she felt pretty good about the whole situation. It was a relief to pay the final bills—and know there wouldn't be another round coming. Every piece of furniture that was sold off after they were officially closed for business was another weight lifted off her back. She felt lighter every day— until she could almost float right through the ceiling with the freedom of it.

She wasn't a business owner anymore. And it felt incredible.

Her only regret in the whole thing was Madison and Anna.

Anna had landed an internship with an indie music label that started in January, so she'd found her feet, but Madison had been evasive about her future plans. The two had been even more snippy and contentious with one another over the final few weeks, but it wasn't until they showed up on the final day of the lease to pick up their checks that Parv got the first inkling why.

She didn't mean to eavesdrop. She wasn't used to Common Grounds being so quiet, to voices carrying so easily in the newly empty space. The door to the kitchen had been propped open by the movers who'd taken out the ovens. Parv came out of her office with their checks in her hand and froze in the kitchen when she heard the low, intense note in Madison's voice carrying from the front of house.

Madison who was always chirpy and happy and never said *anything* in that serious, intent way.

"I love Common Grounds, but maybe ultimately this is a good thing."

"How can this possibly be a good thing?" Anna snapped, true to form.

"I love you."

Parv had started to walk again, to intervene in the fight, but she went still at those words—and from the silence echoing from the front room, so did Anna—who had never been speechless a day in her life.

"I was never going to tell you that," Madison went on. "I was going to go on, coming to work every day because you were here. Even when you weren't on shift, there was always this feeling when I was here, like you might drop by to pick up a check or check your schedule. I love Common Grounds, but I came in every day to see you. And I know you don't feel the same way. I know you don't even really like me, but that's my truth and I wanted to be brave enough to tell you before I never see you again."

There was a pause, then the sound of footsteps carried clearly though the open door, but Parv was still surprised when Madison walked through.

"I'm sorry," Parv blurted, caught listening, but Madison smiled, head high.

"I'm not." She took her check from Parv's numb fingers, hugged her quick and hard and whispered, "Thank you for everything, Parv."

Then she was gone. Leaving two stunned women behind her.

Parv crossed into the front room to find Anna leaning against the counter—one of the few furniture pieces that remained—staring into space with a baffled expression. She looked up at the sound of Parv's footsteps, a frown pulling down between her pierced brows. "What the hell was that?"

"I take it you didn't suspect she had feelings for you."

"Hell no. Did you?"

Parv shook her head. "It's always the quiet ones."

Anna's face scrunched up. "She's just so…"

Wholesome? Innocent? "Not your type?"

"Bambi?" Anna snorted. "You could say that." She shook her head. "I thought she was straight. She flirts with the male customers. It used to make me crazy, watching her go all simpering and sweet."

Parv had never seen Madison flirt with anyone, but she kept her opinion to herself.

"I thought she hated me," Anna went on, bemused. "She *should* hate me. I'm awful to her."

"Don't shoot the messenger, but did you ever wonder *why* you're so awful to her?"

"She's so annoying," Anna said without hesitation. "Little Miss Kansas Perfect who everything always came easily to. She's one of those people who's just gonna float through life without any problems and I'm supposed to what? Cheer her on when she gets everything I want without even trying?"

"Okay…" Parv had thought Anna might have unrequited feelings for Madison too, but evidently that wasn't the case. "But maybe there's more to Madison than you thought."

"I guess," Anna acknowledged without enthusiasm.

"You could call her—"

"No." Anna picked up the check Parv had set on the counter beside her. "No offense, Boss, but I don't need you matchmaking for me. And Madison can make all the cute speeches she wants, but she's not my girl."

* * * * *

And so Common Grounds closed. Not with a bang, but with a whimper.

Sidney didn't come by—and Parv told herself that she understood. That Sid's schedule was crazy these days and if she'd been able to make it she would have.

Max didn't call—but Parv told herself that was for the best. Their relationship had gotten muddied by her over-reliance on him. It was good for them to take this space.

Every single member of her family called—and each of them seemed more baffled than the last by Parv's insistence that she really was going to work for barely more than minimum wage icing cakes for a few months while she decided what to do next.

It was a strange experience, working at Lacey's Cakes. She hadn't had a boss in five years, which took some getting used to. She wasn't used to having set hours—and for the expectation to be that she *wouldn't* work except during those hours. The sudden abundance of free time was disorienting.

She suddenly had time for books again. And movies. And binge-watching the shows she'd overheard her customers talking about for years.

But the best part was that she had time to go shopping with Katie when she came home for Thanksgiving.

She'd always made time for her family and friends, but it was a whole new feeling when she didn't have to *make* the time. When it was just there. Hers to do with what she would without the guilt that she really ought to be working if she was going to make her business a success.

The freedom was phenomenal.

"I thought you already bought a wedding dress," Parv asked as she held the door of the exclusive Eden bridal boutique for their Saturday appointment. One of Katie's brothers had a cross country meet that afternoon and Angie had pulled carpool duty so it was just the two of them at the store.

"I did," Katie admitted, "but what if it's the wrong dress? Everything hinges around the dress. I just want to try on two or three more and then I know I'll be sure. Besides, this way you can try on some of the bridesmaid dresses I've been considering. I made the appointment for both of us."

"You want me to be a bridesmaid?"

"Of course!" Katie blinked at her, startled. "Didn't I

ask you? God, I swear I have wedding brain. It will be a miracle if I pass any of my classes. I don't know how my mom did it. Though she says it was easier back then. All I know is I feel like my brains will leak out of my ears if I try to remember one more thing. But I couldn't get married without you in the wedding. You're my favorite aunt. Just don't tell the others I said that."

"You're my favorite too."

The sales clerk—who called herself a consultant—arrived then, saving Parv from tearing up all over Katie. When they were back in their dressing room, sipping champagne that Katie wasn't technically old enough for while the sales consultant darted off to collect an array of dresses, Parv found herself once again remembering the first time she held Katie.

"I never thought you'd be getting married before me."

"You just haven't found the right guy." Katie looked up from the wedding magazine she'd been flipping through. "What about that guy you brought to my engagement party? He's cute."

"He's a friend."

"So? Jonah was a friend."

Parvati resisted the urge to explain that it was a little different when you weren't in high school anymore. Though was it? Sometimes Max had her wishing she could pass him a note in study hall just to get some clarity. "It isn't like that."

"But you *want* to get married? Because my folks talk about you sometimes and my dad thinks you might be a feminist who doesn't think she needs a man—which is his code for lesbian."

Oh joy. Her family was talking about her. "I think a lot of people in our family thought that, but no. I'm not a lesbian. Or a man-hating feminist."

The sales consultant reappeared then and all further discussion of feminism was tabled in favor of trying on poofy dresses. And they were poofy. Katie seemed to have a bigger is better approach to bridal wear. The circumference of her skirts would have made Scarlet O'Hara proud.

Parv stood in her own poofy dress, eyeing the miles of fabric keeping a perimeter around Katie. "How is Jonah going to stand close enough to you for the first dance?"

Katie had been twirling on the pedestal and now frowned into the mirror. "That's just what my mother said. She likes the one we already have."

"Which is smaller?"

"It's an A-line. Classic, my mother called it. And it's nice. It's got some lace and some off-the-shoulder stuff going on, but it just doesn't make me feel like a princess."

"Wouldn't you rather feel like you?"

"I get to feel like me every day. I want to feel like a princess when I get married. But Mom thought the ball gowns were over the top."

Angie was one to talk. Her wedding dress had needed its own zipcode. "What does Jonah think? He's the one who has to dance with that skirt."

Katie gasped, horrified. "Jonah can't know anything about the dress! That's the one part of the wedding he is absolutely *not* allowed to have an opinion on. Not that he has opinions on any of it."

The edge of bitterness in Katie's voice set warning bells clamoring in Parv's mind, but the sales consultant swept in with a mermaid gown then and it was several minutes and two gowns later before she had a chance to bring it up again.

"Are you worried Jonah doesn't care about the wedding?"

"No, he cares," Kateri insisted, executing a tight turn on the pedestal and frowning. "I can't move my knees. I think we have to eliminate mermaid cuts. I am not waddling around on my wedding day. But I like yours." She waved Parv onto the pedestal in front of the mirror array.

Parv actually liked hers too. It was charcoal gray, long, and silky. The bodice gathered to one side just below the bust with a little pearl clasp. Classy and simple. The kind of thing Angie would approve of. "Does it go with the dress you already bought?"

Katie wrinkled her nose, considering. "It does, actually. But if I choose that bridesmaid dress am I admitting my mother was right about my wedding dress?"

"There are worse things than your mother being right."

Katie snorted. "Are there?"

The sales consultant reappeared with another dress— a designer number that cost more than Parv's car and was too wide to fit inside it. Katie sighed as she swished the skirts back and forth. "If a girl can't feel like a princess on her wedding day, when can she?"

"Prom?" Parv commented and watched Katie freeze.

"Oh God. It does look like my prom dress, doesn't it? My wedding pictures would look exactly like my prom photos. Damn it. I hate it when my mother's right."

"So no ball gown?"

"I don't know!" Katie wailed. "How do people make these decisions? It's like as soon as you decide to get married you have to make eleven million other decisions and everything matters and everyone is going to judge you for every little thing and no one can make the decision for you because it's *your* wedding and there's no right or wrong—at least that's what they tell you—but there is right or wrong because everyone is watching you to see what you decide. Even the *card stock* is important because the invitations *set the tone*. God, I am so sick of making decisions."

Katie sank onto the pedestal, swaths of expensive fabric billowing around her. "Do you have any idea how isolating it is to plan a wedding? It's supposed to be about bringing the two of you together, but that's a big fat lie. My mom wants to plan everything, but I still have to make all the decisions. She's always saying she can't choose for me. It isn't *her* wedding."

"Can't Jonah make some of the decisions?"

"Oh please. Jonah wants to get married. He wants a big wedding with all our friends and family. He wants it to be perfect for me. But the second I ask him what he thinks about invitations, or seating charts, or centerpieces, or colors, or venues, or even what kind of tuxedo he wants to wear, all he says is *whatever you want, sweetie* and *you know what's best, babe* and I just want to scream. It feels like I'm doing it all by myself."

Parv's heart ached at the panic and frustration in Katie's voice. She came to crouch as close as she could to Katie with the obstacle of the skirts, reaching out a hand to touch her niece's shoulder. "Maybe you're rushing into things. You're so young. You could take some time—"

"God, you sound just like my mother!" Katie shook her off.

"I do?"

Parv's genuine shock seemed to calm Katie down.

She caught Parv's hand, linking their fingers. "I'm sorry. I just love him, okay? And I've decided to marry him and I would love it if you guys could get behind me."

"We are behind you. All the way." And if it fell apart, they'd be there to pick up the pieces. Always.

"Good."

CHAPTER TWENTY-TWO

Parv was behind Katie all the way—but she still worried. Especially since it sounded like Jonah wasn't pulling his weight as the groom. But luckily she had access to a couple of experts and she brought up her concerns at the next Girls' Night with Tori and Sidney.

Sidney's show was taking a break from filming over the holidays, which meant she finally had time for regular Girls' Nights again—but since she was using the break to get a jump on her own wedding planning the only topics of conversation tended to be Sidney's wedding and Tori's morning sickness.

"It happens all the time," Sidney said when Parv brought up her concerns for Katie. "The grooms think they're giving you exactly what you want when really they're just delegating stress. Josh is doing it too. *You're so good at this, it's what you do, whatever you choose will be perfect, honey*—which means all the responsibility is on the bride. And all the stress is on the bride. Which is why women turn into Bridezillas and wedding planners can charge so much for their services."

"Hallelujah," Tori said, toasting with a glass of club soda she was trying to use to calm her stomach. "Speaking of which, we also pay our assistants very well—and now that Sidney's doing the show, I'm completely overworked. And I'm going to be going on maternity leave in a few months and we're *really* going to need more help then. Do you have any interest? It wouldn't be exotic, mostly answering phones and making appointments, at least for the first few months, but you could work your way up."

"I…"

She'd never seen herself as a wedding planner, but it was a good job. She could do it for a few months. Figure out what she really wanted to do.

But she'd be working for Tori and Sidney. Totally dependent on her friends. It would change things. And so many things were already changing.

"Take some time to think about it," Sidney recommended. "We didn't mean to just spring it on you. We've been discussing bringing on extra help for a while."

She'd be in the loop again if she worked at Once Upon a Bride. But was it what she wanted? "You know, I appreciate the offer, but I think I'm going to stay at the bakery. At least for now. But I think I know someone who might be just what you're looking for, if you're interested. Do you remember Madison? Who used to work at Common Grounds?"

"I'm sure she'd be great," Sidney said, quickly moving past any mention of Common Grounds like she was uncomfortable with the reminder of Parv's failure. "But don't decide right this second. Just give it some thought."

"Sure," Parv agreed, though she couldn't imagine changing her mind. If she hadn't wanted to be Max's personal baker, she wasn't likely to decide to be Sidney's personal slave. Speaking of… "What's Max up to these days? I never see him anymore since I'm no longer his caffeine source."

Sidney grimaced, propping her glass on her stomach where she was stretched out on Tori's sofa. "I haven't seen him either. He's sort of fallen off the grid since all that stuff with our dad. I think he's even started sleeping at his office."

"What stuff with your dad?" Parv asked, feeling completely out of the loop.

"Didn't I tell you? He got married. To a woman younger than me who's currently seven months pregnant which his child."

"Whoa."

"Yeah." Sidney lifted her glass in a mocking toast. "My father. Class act. He didn't even tell us. We found out about it when a tabloid broke the story."

"Damn." Poor Max. He had a strange enough relationship with his father already without this in the mix.

"I should be offended he didn't ask me to plan the wedding, but part of me was almost relieved he turned out to be such a cliché. I don't have to care about what he thinks anymore."

She said it, but Parv knew Sidney still cared what her father thought. No one could get rid of that programming so easily.

"On the plus side, her dress was gorgeous. Sort of Grecian and flowing. So at least he didn't embarrass us by marrying someone with no style."

"Have you thought about what kind of dress you want?" Parv asked, redirecting the conversation toward less turbulent waters.

"Oh my God, didn't I tell you?" Sidney gasped—a phrase that seemed to keep echoing around Parv everywhere she went. "Tori and I found the perfect dress last week. We weren't even looking, really. Not for me, anyway. Just some preliminary scouting of boutiques for the next season of *Once Upon a Bride* and there it was. Discontinued, but exactly my size, and *perfect*. Hang on, I have a picture."

Parv didn't move as Sidney scrambled to figure out where she'd left her phone.

She'd never been the kind of girl who dreamed about wedding dress shopping. She'd hated being dragged along to store after store when her sisters bought their dresses. She'd never wanted to play dress up.

So it was something of a surprise how disappointed she was that Sidney had bought her dress without her.

Girls' Nights may be back, but she was still out of the loop.

* * * * *

Parvati kept busy at the bakery as Christmas approached, but the hours were still so much shorter than she was used to that she didn't know what to do with herself. She spent more time with her family—which was actually less stressful than she'd anticipated—and threw herself into the holidays, as much as her limited budget allowed. She marathoned *Sex in the City*—and spent hours pondering whether she was a Charlotte or a Carrie and whether it was possible to turn herself into a Samantha by sheer force of will.

And she missed Max.

Sex in the City probably hadn't helped that. He reminded her of Mr. Big—even though she'd never actually dated him and his only physical similarity to Chris Noth was the dark hair.

She called him once, in a moment of weakness, missing the friendship they'd had before she'd screwed it up by accidentally kissing him. He didn't pick up—which was probably for the best—and she'd left a rambling message wishing him happy holidays.

Sidney and Josh were jetting off to the Christmas wedding of one of the other women from Sid's season of *Marrying Mister Perfect* and Parv would be heading up to Monterey for the holidays so they had their Girls' Christmas early—which only served to highlight for Parv how much life had changed in the last year.

Last year Sid had just gotten back from *Marrying Mister Perfect*, but the show hadn't aired yet. They hadn't yet known that she'd left the show because she'd fallen in love with Josh instead of Mr. Perfect Daniel. Nick hadn't yet come back into Tori's life. Once Upon a Bride had been struggling almost as much as Common Grounds, but they'd hung in there together. Just been three single girls, making it work.

And now everything had changed.

"Do you have plans for New Year's yet?" Sidney asked as they passed around presents. "Elena's throwing a party. You should come if you don't already have somewhere to be."

Elena. Another of the Suitorettes from Sidney's season of *Marrying Mister Perfect*. And another woman who'd recently met and married the love of her life. Though in this case the love of her life was one of Max's bodyguards.

"Will Max be there?"

"Probably not. He usually has to work New Year's. Lots of celebrities going to events and looking for extra security. I'm not sure how Adam managed to get the night off." Sidney looked up from the silver bow in her hands, frowning. "Why do you ask?"

"I haven't seen him in a while," Parv hedged. "And

somehow the idea of being with you and Josh and Tori and Nick and a bunch of other couples as everyone is kissing in the New Year without having anyone to kiss myself lacks appeal."

Sidney arched a brow. "You were planning to kiss Max?"

Parvati realized her mistake as soon as she saw Sidney's expression. "Of course not. But he has all those hot bodyguards. I figured one of them is bound to be single."

"I think half of them are single—but most of them will be working that night. Don't worry. We'll find you someone to kiss. What about one of Josh's frat brothers? They're going to be in the wedding party. I know at least a couple of them are single."

And now she was a charity case. Her friends were officially struggling to find people willing to kiss her.

"I don't need you to find someone to kiss me."

"What about one of your internet dates?" Tori suggested.

Parv cringed at the thought. "I don't do internet dating during the holidays. There's too much pressure. Everything is too loaded. Everyone's trying to force a love connection. When you take a first date to your office Christmas party or to a New Year's Eve bash there's an expectation. Everyone's desperate over the holidays. The family pressure, societal pressure, everyone taking stock and realizing that they're another year older and still haven't found the person they want to spend the rest of their life with…"

And for Parvati, it was a time for realizing that in the last year the last two single people in her life had paired off, leaving her more alone than ever.

She missed Max.

Which was her only excuse for trolling her online dating profile at three o'clock in the afternoon on New Year's Eve when she damn well knew better.

She was tired of another New Year's with no one to kiss.

She'd walked by Common Grounds earlier—or what had been Common Grounds and was now a Christmas ornament store for one more week. She hadn't gone to wallow. Just to remember. To put it to bed, in a way. To close the door on the last year of Common Grounds.

New Year. New beginnings.

This year she was going to be more than her work.

When she'd arrived home, it had been with new purpose—and even though she knew internet dating over the holidays was a minefield, she still wanted to go into the new year with new hope, so she began browsing.

She'd only been online for a couple of minutes when an invitation to chat icon popped up, pinging cheerfully. She hesitated—remembering with distinct unease the time she'd chatted with the man who'd wanted to fix her up with his dad *and* himself—but this year she wasn't going to let the past slow her down, so she tapped the accept button.

I normally don't send messages between Thanksgiving and New Year's, when everyone is so panicked by the holidays, but I just saw your profile today and I didn't want to miss my chance by waiting.

She smiled, feeling a sudden sense of connection with Parker299. Even if it was a line he'd used a dozen times before, it was working. *I usually avoid dating sites during the holidays too*, she typed back. *But something made me check my messages today.*

She clicked over to his profile as she waited for his

reply. The pictures left almost everything to the imagination—extreme close ups on smiling pale blue eyes behind a pair of black-rimmed glasses and distant, blurry shots of a largish man standing in front of a mountain—but there was something about the humor in his eyes that appealed to her.

Is it cheesy if I say it's Fate?

Parv grinned to herself. *Absolutely.*

Oh well. You may as well find out I'm cheesy right off the bat.

Her smile wouldn't seem to go away. What if this was her guy? Thirty-three. Wanted kids. Had a dog. With his occupation listed as manager. A regular, stable guy with a regular stable job.

Cheesy is a plus. She flexed her fingers, deciding it was time to start living for her future. *Got any big plans for the New Year?*

CHAPTER TWENTY-THREE

Max walked into the Beverly Hills bistro his mother had chosen for their lunch, smiling to the hostess as he gave his name and explained he was meeting someone. The girl directed him to the table where his mother waited and hovered as he bent to drop a kiss in the air beside his mother's cheek.

"Happy birthday," his mother said, sliding a neatly wrapped package across the tablecloth.

Max took the box, shaking it gently as he sank onto his chair. "Cufflinks?"

"Actually it's a certificate for a day at my spa. You've been working too much."

"And you thought a mud bath would help?"

"My masseuse is an artist. Say thank you, Maximus."

"Thank you, Mother."

"Enjoy your meal," the hostess murmured, handing over his menu before retreating to her post.

His mother sighed. "That poor girl. She was trying so hard and you didn't even give her a second glance."

"Who?" he asked, opening his menu.

"The hostess, dear."

He looked up, frowning. "Was she flirting?"

"That's it," his mother declared. "You're officially working too hard. I've never known you to be so exhausted that you couldn't notice when a woman was batting her eyes at you."

"I thought this was a birthday lunch, not an intervention."

"Can't it be both?"

Max frowned—and seriously considered getting up and walking out.

His mother wasn't in the habit of making a fuss over birthdays, but when she'd called him to invite him to a birthday lunch he'd agreed—in part because she'd chosen a restaurant that was only a mile away from the Elite Protection offices, and in larger part because Candy had overheard the invitation and threatened to lock him out of the EP computer system until he agreed.

He had been working a lot, but in his defense the holidays were award season in Hollywood and it was always a busy time for those employed by A-list celebrities. Luckily Elia had taken to his training and the Smiling Samoan had been able to join the security teams, though he was still learning on the job. Max had been interviewing additional candidates—he'd need at least two more bodyguards at the rate EP was growing—but he hadn't found anyone else yet that met his requirements.

With the Golden Globes last week and the Oscar nominations just revealed, they were approaching the end of awards season, but he'd planned the launch of the new self-defense program for the beginning of March, so now was not the time to be letting up.

"There's more to life than work, Max," his mother said.

He arched his brows skeptically. "You're the authority on work-life balance now?"

"I know your father and I didn't exactly set a good example on that front, but I don't want you to make the same mistakes we made."

"I wasn't aware you thought of work as a mistake. I thought that was the marriage." His mother's mouth tightened and he immediately regretted the words. "Sorry."

"We did love each other, you know." His mother lifted the glass of wine she must have ordered before he arrived. "I know you didn't see much of that by the time you were old enough to understand it, but it wasn't a cold business alliance right from the beginning, no matter what you and Sidney choose to think."

"We choose to think it because no one has ever let on that it was anything else. Why did you marry him?"

At first he didn't think she would answer, but then her gaze went distant though her mouth remained tight. "He understood me. And he wasn't intimidated by my ambition or my competence—which was saying something forty years ago. It was heady stuff, being with someone who accepted me and believed in me like that."

"So what happened?"

"Your father might have a different answer, but if you ask me we were too accommodating of each other."

The waiter finally arrived then, taking their orders and forcing Max to wait to ask the question pushing against the inside of his brain.

"How can you be too accommodating?" he asked as soon as they were alone again.

"We never made any demands on one another, but we also never relied on one another. We were both so completely independent we never really learned how to need each other. We always lived separate lives and now I have to wonder if that was our biggest mistake. We never had to let each other in. It can be intoxicating, being needed. Being relied on."

Max didn't ask if that was what *Claudine* had gotten out of her relationship with his father. He hadn't heard from his father beyond an email announcing the birth of his new half-sibling. A boy they'd decided to call Magnus.

He'd deleted the email, telling himself the news didn't affect him and focusing on his work. He could control his business, even when he couldn't control the people in his life. And if he wasn't happy by the strictest definition of the word, at least he wasn't miserable either.

"Did I tell you why I decided to divorce your father?"

His attention sharpened. "I assumed it had to do with the fact that both of you were sleeping around."

She smiled as if his presumption was adorably naïve. "No." She picked up her fork, idly spinning it on the tip of one tine. "I had a health scare last year."

"You what?"

"It wasn't cancer or anything like that. It wasn't anything, as it turns out, but there were a couple of tense days where I didn't know that. And I realized I didn't have anyone in my life beyond my stockholders who would care if something happened to me."

"*Mom.* I would care. Sidney would care." Something thick pressed against the back of his throat even as frustration burned in his chest. "Why didn't you tell us?"

"Like I said. It was nothing."

"But you didn't know that. You went through that alone."

"Exactly. And I don't want that for you. It was an important moment for me. It led me to make some changes—be better about spending time with you and

Sidney, dissolve my relationship with your father, I've even been cutting back on work a bit, though not too much." She set down her fork, aligning it deliberately beside the other cutlery. "Don't be like your father and me. You need to let people in, Maximus."

"I let people in," he insisted.

"Who?"

Parvati.

The answer was so instinctive he almost said her name aloud before he caught himself.

He hadn't seen Parv in months. Not since Common Grounds closed. But he'd kept the message she left for him over the holidays, *accidentally* replaying it every time he listened to his voicemail.

Parv had relied on him. And he'd let himself rely on her.

She'd burrowed into his life when he wasn't looking and become his best friend, and now there was a Parv shaped hole where she'd been.

He missed her. But how did he get her back after all this time? Could he just call her up and pick right up where they'd left off?

"Max?"

"I let Sidney in," he lied to his mother, grateful when their food arrived and he could change the topic, but Parvati stayed in his thoughts all through the afternoon and into the evening when he was shutting down his computer and driving home, earlier than the midnight commute that had become his habit lately.

Caught in the seven o'clock traffic heading north, his phone chimed a text alert as he was stopped in the gridlock behind an accident on the PCH. Max picked up his cell, his heart thudding hard at the sight of Parv's name on his screen.

Happy Birthday, Maximus!

It wasn't much, but she'd reopened the window of communication between them and he wasn't going to let it close again. His thumbs raced over the screen, typing back. *Is that all I get? One measly little birthday text?*

The chime came again after he'd inched forward two car lengths.

What else do you want?

Was she flirting with him? His heartbeat accelerated. Then the chime came again.

What do you get the man who has everything?

He didn't have everything. He didn't have her.

Holy shit. He was in love with Parvati. When the hell had that happened? And how had it taken him so long to realize it?

Max typed again, trying not to scare her off, but needing her so badly his heart pounded with it. *I expect at least a cake.*

His pulse drummed in his ears as he waited for her reply, driving north past the accident and into the regular evening congestion. It couldn't have been more than five minutes, but it felt like fifty before the chime came again.

Max held his phone in one hand, the urge to sneak a peek at the text killing him as he waited for the next stoppage. Why did the damn traffic have to flow so smoothly now? Finally, he pulled off into a turn-out, unable to wait any longer.

Deal. I'm at work now. Do you have plans later or should I bring your cake to your place after we close?

His heart drummed in his ears. *My place is perfect.*

Now he just had to keep from killing himself with his impatience to get home to her.

* * * * *

Max cleaned—not that he'd been home enough lately to get the house dirty. And he did have a cleaning service come in once a week to do the dusting and vacuuming, but he needed something to do with his hands while he was waiting for Parv.

He was nervous.

Max Dewitt didn't do nervous—even when he was jumping out of a plane or negotiating a three-million dollar deal—but Parv changed the rules.

She'd seemed to want to keep things on a Just Friends level lately, but she'd had a crush on him once. He could work with that. Max knew how to be persuasive. But Parv had always seen right through his bullshit. The usual game wouldn't work with her. Not that he wanted it to. He didn't want games. Not with her.

When the doorbell finally rang, he was ready to jump out of his skin. He threw open the door and there she was—the smile on her face easing the crazy agitation in his chest.

Her hair was loose around her shoulders in dark waves, though there was a kink in it just below her ears, like it had been yanked back in a tight ponytail all day and just released as she was walking up the driveway. Her eyes were dark and smiling, and there was a smudge of flour on the side of her neck that made his thumb itch to rub it away.

It had been too long since she'd been here. No wonder he'd been going crazy.

"Happy Birthday!" She brandished the cake, one of the fancy, sugary confections from Lacey's Cakes, and brushed past him into the house. "Can I just say how weird it is to have a boss who insists I have to ring up my employee purchases through her? I had to go through the most ridiculous song and dance to get a cake that *I baked for you*."

"You don't like working for Lacey?"

"I don't hate it." She made her way to the kitchen, setting down the cake and making herself at home, getting out serving plates and a knife. "Actually, it's pretty great. I just wish I actually had job security. She decided to keep me on after the holidays because I was 'an efficient addition to the business' but she cut my hours back and she keeps reminding me it's only temporary. Sometimes she looks at me and I wonder if she thinks I'm planning some elaborate Cake Coupe D'état. As if I would go to all the trouble of closing Common Grounds just to mess with the competition."

"A baker with a persecution complex?"

"Don't let the icing fool you. It's a cut-throat business." She mimed cutting her throat with the giant cake knife, grinning ear to ear, and then sliced mercilessly into the cake.

"Hey. Don't I get to blow out the candles?"

"I didn't bring candles. And the boy who has everything doesn't get to make additional wishes. That's just greedy."

He wasn't going to get a better opening than that. Max looked into the bottomless depth of her eyes. "I do still have one thing I would wish for—"

Her cell phone buzzed, ruining the moment and breaking the eye contact as she fished it out of a pocket and flicked a thumb across the screen to shut it up—but not before he saw the contact photo of the person calling her. He didn't recognize the name, but the photo was of Parv and a man he didn't know, their faces mashed close together, grinning goofily.

"Who's that?"

Parv looked up and smiled—and his hopes dropped to his stomach before she even said the words. "It's my boyfriend."

Shit.

* * * * *

Parv wasn't prepared for the long beat of silence that met her announcement. She and Max were just friends, right? She hadn't even seen him in almost two months. After the disappearing act he'd pulled, he couldn't expect her to be waiting for him, still pining for him…could he?

He almost looked disappointed. Definitely taken aback. And suddenly she wished she'd asked what he would have wished for. Had it been her?

Tripping on the heels of that thought was the guilty reminder that it didn't matter what Max wanted. She was with Parker now.

"We met online, but he's so different from the others," she said, filling up the space between them with details as a barrier. "He asked me out for jellybeans."

"Jellybeans?"

She blushed, feeling oddly defensive of the little moment that had become part of her and Parker's story. "He said everyone goes out for coffee and we should be different. It was cute."

And it had made her feel like she was special, not just another face in the online crowd. Parker was good at that.

She'd been too hung up on Max. She should be grateful to him for pulling a Houdini on her because if she'd been seeing him every day she may never have let herself give Parker a real chance.

"What's his name?"

"Parker. I know. Parvati and Parker. It's awful how cute it is. Sidney calls him Perfect Parker. I think she's mostly relieved I've found someone and I'll finally stop whining about being alone all the time." She plated up a slice of cake.

"I'm sure that isn't true." He pulled open a drawer, grabbing forks for them both as she sliced another piece.

"I know. I know she's happy for me. But the last person we all dubbed Mr. Perfect didn't really live up to the title so I guess it makes me nervous." The Mr. Perfect on Sidney's season of the reality show had turned out to be far from it.

"What's his last name?"

"For the background check? It's Simmons. And you won't find anything. He's perfectly, boringly normal. That's the best thing about him."

"That he's boring?" Max frowned as they took their cake to the breakfast bar.

"That he's a nice, normal guy. I get enough of an insecurity complex in my family. I don't need it in my relationship." And Parker had understood that. "He's in middle management at a home goods store. And he likes that I just make cakes for a living."

"I like that too," Max mumbled around a mouthful of the cake in question. "This is incredible."

"I don't expect you to get it. You're a super achiever like everyone in my family and you date super models."

"Models, maybe. I haven't reached super level yet."

"My point is I'm dating in my league and I like it."

"That's bullshit." He pointed his fork at her. "You're amazing. Anyone who thinks he's out of your league is a dumbass who doesn't deserve you."

"You don't get it. I can be myself with Parker. I don't have to worry about making a good impression or living up to expectations. From the very first day we met, I was able to just be honest with him. To just be me. You have no idea how freeing that is."

"You can't be yourself with me?"

She rested her hand on his arm. "Of course I can. But you've known me forever and I still sometimes worry that you're going to judge me as a failure. And I'm not trying to date you. When you're in a couple with someone, you reflect on each other more than just friends do. So people are more sensitive to the flaws in their partner."

"Is this guy saying you're flawed?"

"No. That's my point. He likes me just the way I am." She smiled, patting his arm one last time before lifting her hand and picking up her fork. "You don't have to protect me from him, Max."

"I'm still running a background check."

"I would expect nothing less. But don't be surprised when you don't find anything. He's honest with me."

"So you think."

"Why would he lie about being a store manager?"

His dark expression didn't lighten. "People lie for all sorts of reasons. Do you have his fingerprints?"

Parv laughed and leaned over to hug Max from the side, though his muscles remained rigid as she squeezed. "I've missed you, Maximus. Where've you been all this time?"

She didn't know why Max had suddenly decided to reenter her life, but she couldn't deny she was glad he had—even if it did make her relationship with Parker feel a little more complicated. Though it shouldn't. The two things had nothing to do with one another.

"Working," Max replied. "After my father married his twenty-something secretary and she had his baby, I sort of lost my center for a while there. Work was the only thing that made sense."

Parv cocked her head to the side, studying Max's profile over a forkful of cake. "I'm not trying to be a jerk, but why did that hit you so hard? You guys never had what most people would consider a normal relationship with your father."

"You aren't a jerk. I actually asked myself the same question." He shoved his empty plate away, spinning his fork on one tine. "Why was I letting anything he did bother me if I'd always been determined to prove I could succeed without his help?"

"And? Did you figure it out?"

"It's the lying. The hiding. Why couldn't he just tell us? I could accept him being the distant father we only saw a couple times a year. I could accept that my parents weren't really that invested in the idea of parenting from the start. I made my peace with all that a long time ago. But the idea that he's had this secret life and he never saw fit to even mention it to Sidney or me—that just pisses me off. Especially when he's making this big show about how I'm his *legacy* at the separation proceedings. Who does that?"

"Have you talked to him since you found out?"

"No. He calls sometimes, but I don't know what to say to him. I guess I'll see him at Sidney's wedding."

"That's months from now. Do you want this hanging over you that entire time?"

Max stood, gathering up their dishes and carrying them to the sink. "It isn't hanging over me. I'm good."

"Which is why you're working yourself to death?"

"I had lunch with my mother today," Max said, rinsing the plates as Parv moved to put the leftover cake away. "She made me see the error of my overworking ways. I'm here with you, aren't I? You can keep me from working myself into an early grave."

"Then it's a good thing I brought my guaranteed de-stress film masterpiece." She grabbed her oversized purse where she'd dropped it on the island and fished out the DVD. "Inigo Montoya and the Dread Pirate Roberts?"

Max grinned. "Don't you have that movie memorized? You and Sidney must have watched it every weekend in middle school."

"Because it's just that good. And memorization enhances the experience. Come on, birthday boy. I defy you not to be cheered up by *The Princess Bride*."

His gaze went pensive. "How did you know I needed to be cheered up?"

"When are you going to figure it out?" She grinned. "I know you, Max Dewitt."

* * * * *

By the time Westley and Buttercup had ridden off into the sunset on their matching white horses, Parvati was out cold, sprawled out on his couch with her head lolling on his thigh. Max absently rubbed a lock of her hair between his thumb and fingers, turning over in his mind what a bitch timing could be.

He'd missed his window—but maybe he wasn't in love with her after all because he didn't feel heartbroken. He felt...relieved. Relieved that they could be friends again, without the complications of more. This was good. It didn't need to be about sex. He'd missed her, and if sex got involved he would invariably screw it up and then he'd be missing her all over again. This time for good.

No. It was better this way.

He shook her shoulder gently as the credits rolled and she stirred, twisting to blink sleepily up at him. She'd never been much of a night owl. Funny, the things he hadn't even realized he knew about her.

"Early morning at the bakery?" he asked.

She scrubbed at her eyes, grimacing. "Always. Did I miss the Pit of Despair?"

"I think you missed everything from the Fire Swamp on."

She shoved at his thigh, leveraging herself into a sitting position at his side. "Sorry. Not much of a birthday party."

"Best birthday I've had in years. And I have cake for breakfast."

"How do you have abs like yours if you have cake for breakfast?"

"Are you supposed to be noticing my abs? Won't Perfect Parker object?"

"I think a cake-to-ab ratio question is fair game."

Max shrugged. "I work out."

She groaned. "Like it's nothing. Like anyone can eat cake for breakfast and have abs of steel. You know, sometimes I hate you."

"You've said that before. Luckily, I never seem to believe you."

She looked at him—and something of the way he wanted her must have shown on his face because her own open, easy expression shuttered for a moment and she stood. "I should get home."

Max rose, walking her out without protest. When

they got to the door, he held it open for her. "Hey, Parv?"

She paused on the threshold, looking back at him.

"If this Parker ever hurts you, I'll kill him slowly."

She seemed to realize he wasn't joking because her eyes softened as she turned back to face him. "You don't have to worry about that. He would never touch me."

"There are other ways people can be hurt."

"I know. But he isn't like that. Parker will never cheat on me."

"How can you be so sure? You've known this guy, what? A couple months?"

"Only a few weeks actually. But I know." She hesitated, then leaned in confiding, "His last couple girlfriends cheated on him. He knows what it feels like. He's been hurt too badly by women who used him, so I know he would never do that to me. My heart is safe with him, Max. He could really be my guy."

He took a moment to process that one, nodding slowly. "Then I'm happy for you."

And the craziest thing was that he really was happy for her.

CHAPTER TWENTY-FOUR

Parker's background check came back so squeaky clean Max had Candy dig deeper—twice—just to be sure. Not that he wanted to find something. He just needed to know that Parvati was in good hands.

Part of him was relieved that Parker Simmons seemed to be the nice, boring guy that Parv thought he was. But another part—a part he wasn't proud of—couldn't help the bitter spike of frustration that there were no skeletons in his closet that Max could use to drive so-called-Perfect Parker away.

Not that he would have done that.

Okay, yes, he would have done it. But it would have been for Parvati's own good. He was looking out for her. As a friend, damn it.

At least they were back on speaking terms. He may have missed his window, but he hadn't completely screwed up their friendship.

He still wanted to meet this Parker, to get a read on him personally, but Parv didn't seem to be in any hurry to make that happen and he wasn't going to push. But he was going to be ready with an unmarked grave if Perfect Parker ever laid a finger on her.

* * * * *

The letter arrived on a Saturday morning, hand-delivered by her landlady.

"Here it is!" Carolina announced cheerfully as she handed over the envelope. "The official notice."

Parv frowned as she accepted the bulging white packet. "Official notice?"

Carolina's face fell. "Oh no. Antonio said he would call you."

Dread congealed. "Call me about what?"

"We're moving. It started to feel wasteful, keeping the house in Eden when all the kids are in college and we're spending most of the year on the boat anyway. You know better than anyone how rarely we're here."

"I do," Parv admitted numbly, her thoughts racing ahead to the inevitable.

"We hadn't really considered selling until a buyer approached us with a cash offer and it just seemed perfect. I'm so sorry. Antonio was supposed to contact you about this weeks ago."

"The new buyers…"

"Want to use the mother-in-law apartment. I can talk to them about letting you stay on for a month or two — until you can find something else. I'm going to kill Antonio."

Parv muttered something vaguely understanding, barely aware of her surroundings. She hadn't had a formal lease agreement with Carolina and Antonio in years. They were casual and month-to-month — which she'd thought was convenient if she ever got on *Marrying Mister Perfect* or fell madly in love with a tycoon and decided to run away to Monte Carlo with him, but in retrospect just meant she wasn't protected against a situation like this one. "How long do I have?"

"We close in three weeks. You'll need to be out by

March first, unless we can negotiate an extension."

Three weeks.

She started to call Max as soon as Carolina retreated back to the main house, standing in her lovely little apartment with the sobering realization that she would never be able to afford anything half this nice…and she wasn't sure she could meet the income requirements to get an apartment on her own. She might have to sublet a room in someone else's place. At thirty. When her friends were getting married and buying houses, she was reverting back to a college mode of living.

Max picked up on the second ring. "Hey."

She didn't bother with pleasantries. "I'm being evicted."

"What? I thought your landlords loved you."

"They do. But they're selling. I thought month-to-month gave me all this freedom, but it turns out it's also the freedom to be kicked out with three weeks' notice."

"Crap. What are you gonna do?"

"House hunt, I guess. Though I have to admit it's tempting to pull a Max and run off to Thailand and leave all this bullshit behind—maybe the Peace Corps is hiring."

"Hey. You aren't going anywhere. I have a perfectly good guest room with your name on it until you can find something better. You can pay me in baked goods."

"I can't do that, Max."

"Why not? I'm your friend and I want to help you out. So let me. Unless you think Parker would object."

Parv froze. She'd forgotten about Parker. Was that a bad sign? Wasn't she supposed to run to him when these things happened? Though they were still new. She just wasn't in the habit of relying on him yet. Though it hadn't been a hard habit to get into with Max.

"What did he say when you told him?" Max asked.

"I haven't talked to him yet," she admitted. "He has to work today." Though the excuse felt weak. She hadn't even thought of him. Her first instinct had been Max.

"I'm serious about you staying with me." Max's voice was unbearably comforting. And strangely enough it was Parker's presence in her life that made her comfortable answering the way she did.

"I might take you up on that."

* * * * *

Parker rose from their usual booth at the sushi restaurant they'd gotten in the habit of visiting on Saturday nights, smiling a greeting. "Hey, babe. You look great. Good day?"

"Actually it was lousy," Parv admitted, sliding into the booth opposite him, irrationally annoyed that he couldn't tell her day had sucked. "I'm losing my apartment."

Parker went still behind his menu, chin tucked down, only his pale blue eyes moving, evading her gaze. "What are you going to do?" he asked, after a barely noticeable pause.

But she did notice. And though he'd used the same words Max had, they sounded completely different. Perfect Parker almost seemed *scared*. As if he knew the Good Boyfriend would immediately ask her to move in with him and the idea horrified him so much he couldn't face it.

Not that she wanted to move in with him. She knew it was too early for that—and moving in together too soon just because she was desperate sounded like a good way to kill a budding relationship—but the fact that his reaction to the thought seemed to be *fear* didn't exactly inspire confidence.

Of course she would have been the strong, independent woman who said no and stood on her own two feet—or leaned on Max—but she wanted Parker to at least *want* to take care of her.

The last year had been a process of breaking down and stripping away the life she'd had—her friends, her job, now her home. This was just the cherry on top. Her boyfriend hitting the panic button at the idea of something more permanent with her.

"I have a friend who's willing to let me crash in his guest room. At least until I can find something else—since I have so little notice."

Parker visibly brightened. "Good. That's good." Then his brows pulled together. "*His* guest room? Is this that Max? The one you say you hang out with sometimes?"

"Yeah." And then—even though she knew she shouldn't, even though she knew it would be picking a fight, she looked him dead in the eye and challenged, "Is that a problem?"

Parker set down his menu. "Exactly how close are you?"

She knew Parker was insecure about being cheated on, knew he had a tendency to veer toward jealousy at the slightest little hint that she was interested in someone else, but she told herself he had to trust her, that she was justified in pushing this button.

"How close are you and Jenna?"

He flushed at the mention of the female friend who used his place as a landing pad whenever she and her off-again-on-again boyfriend were on the outs—which seemed to be every other weekend. "That isn't the same."

"Because I've never slept with Max and you dated Jenna for two years when you were in college? Is that how it's different?"

"We're just friends."

"And so are Max and I." And if she was a little extra defensive about that, no force on earth would have made her admit it in that moment. "And I'm lucky he has someplace for me to crash." Since Perfect Parker seemed to have no interest in being her white knight. Not that she needed one. But the man sure knew how to wreck a fairy tale fantasy. "Should we order?"

* * * * *

"Are you sure you don't need help moving your stuff into my place?" Max wedged his phone between his ear and shoulder, waving Pretty Boy into his office when he knocked on the open door.

"No. Parker's going to help me. Since your furniture is so much nicer than mine, my crap is all going into a storage unit and we're mostly just bringing over boxes."

"Okay, but give me a call if you need anything. I'm happy to force my employees to do physical labor for you." Pretty Boy made a face. "See you later, Parv."

She would be in his house when he got home that night. He tried not to get too excited by the thought. He was helping out a friend. Nothing more. A taken friend. Who was moving her stuff in *with her boyfriend* as he hung up the phone.

"Parvati's moving in with you?" Pretty Boy asked as he set his phone on his desk. "I always thought she was cute."

"She's off limits."

"Well, of course she is, if she's moving in with you."

"It isn't like that," Max explained.

"No? That why you almost jumped across your desk and throttled me when I said she was cute?" Max glared and Pretty Boy grinned his lazy, easy grin. "Never mind. You do you, Boss. What did you want to see me about?"

"I wanted to ask you about Candy."

Pretty Boy's open expression instantly closed. "What about her?"

"I don't know what's going on with you two and I don't want to. I just wanted to know if you'd noticed her having any problems with clients lately."

"You mean Hank the Hammer."

Max swore under his breath. He'd hoped his gut was wrong, but Pretty Boy hadn't hesitated for a second. "Is he harassing her?"

"Not that she admits," Pretty Boy said. "But I don't think he's calling all the time just because he's worried about darling Cherish."

Max grimaced. The Hammer had called at least half a dozen times trying to get Max to assign Candy as Cherish's full time, live-in bodyguard, refusing to accept his referrals to other close protection services or his insistence that Candy didn't do that kind of work. He'd suspected Hank wasn't leaving it at that, but Candy tended to keep her troubles close to the vest, so he hadn't known for sure.

But if Pretty Boy was worried too, he would take a more active stance. No client—no matter how big a star they thought they were—had the right to try to intimidate one of his people.

"You think she'll talk to you about it?" Max asked.

"I doubt it, but I'll give it a shot if you want."

"Yeah. Thanks."

"You got it, Boss."

CHAPTER TWENTY-FIVE

By the second week of March, Parvati was beginning to wonder if it was possible to overanalyze until she drove herself into a nervous breakdown.

She was still working at Lacey's and submitting resumes for every job she was remotely qualified for so she could stop being dependent on Max—though he didn't seem to mind. But the job quest couldn't take up all her time and every other waking hour seemed to be consumed by obsessing over her possible future—or lack thereof—with Parker.

Maybe she was just the kind of person who created stress in her life, and without Common Grounds to generate stress she would fabricate it with Perfect Parker.

Or maybe he wasn't so perfect and she needed to listen to her instincts and get out before things got any more serious than they already were.

She needed someone she could talk to about her semi-constant relationship panic, but Sidney had been sucked back into her work vortex when *Once Upon a Bride* was renewed for a second season. Parv saw Max all the time, and it was tempting to talk to him, but it felt wrong to badmouth Parker to Max. Like she'd be crossing a line she couldn't come back from.

No. Clear boundaries were better where Max and

Parker were concerned. Friends on one side. Boyfriends on the other.

Maybe that was why she never invited Parker to Max's, always going over to his place instead. It would just be too weird, being with Parker in Max's house. Luckily Parker didn't seem to mind—he always suggested meeting at his place anyway since it saved him the hour plus commute up to Eden.

She walked through the front door of Once Upon a Bride on a Friday night after the shop was officially closed, half-hoping to see Sidney for a few minutes even though it was Tori who'd asked her to drop by. But when the little bell over the door chimed, it was Tori who stepped out from the back room, looking like a high end ad for a maternity magazine.

"Parvati. Thanks for coming. I'd planned to drop by Lacey's to have a word, but then I realized I didn't know your schedule."

"I don't mind coming by. Is Sidney here?"

Tori shook her head, waving Parv over to the cozy seating area where they wooed their prospective clients—not that their clients needed much wooing these days with their sudden fame as wedding planners. "She's got an event of some kind with the network, schmoozing advertisers, but it's best she isn't around since I wanted to talk to you about bachelorette party stuff and Caitlyn thought it'd be fun if it was a surprise."

"*Marrying Mister Perfect* Caitlyn?"

"I know you and I are technically maid and matron of honor, but Caitlyn was so grateful for everything Sidney did for her for her own wedding, she wanted to make the bachelorette party something really special. So we've been talking and we were thinking that the same weekend Josh's buddies are taking him to Vegas, we'd all chip in and get a villa at a resort in Baja California. Sidney's not really a blow-job shots, dildo necklaces and male strippers kind of girl, but sun, sand, and margaritas with the girls?"

"She'd love it," Parv said, weakly. Because Sidney *would* love it. And Parvati couldn't afford it. Especially when she was already spending hundreds she didn't have on bridesmaid dresses and gifts for Sidney's posh bridal shower the following day.

"That's what we thought. It's the perfect place to forget about the stress of planning the Wedding of the Century—which Sidney is convinced her wedding has to be or she'll singlehandedly destroy our brand. She's putting all this pressure on herself, so we are going to make this the most relaxing bachelorette getaway possible. None of us can get away for long—which is why we were thinking Mexico rather than Caribbean, shorter flights for those who are flying and I'll be able to drive down since I'll be in my third trimester and can't fly, but there's this resort Miranda knows near Ensenada where they used to film *Marrying Mister Perfect* dream dates and it sounds *amazing*—"

Tori went on and Parv tuned out, mentally adding up the tally—flights, her share of the villa, taxis, probably parasailing and scuba diving and swimming with dolphins because they'd want the weekend to be special for Sidney. And Parv wanted that too.

She just didn't have the money.

What kind of loser couldn't afford to celebrate her best friend in the whole world's wedding in style? It was the one time—hopefully—that Sidney was ever going to marry the love of her life. Parv would make it work.

Parv tuned back in to find Tori had segued back into talking about the stresses of planning the Wedding of the Century.

"And then Sidney's been completely consumed by this new season of *Once Upon a Bride* so I'm pretty much managing this side of the business by myself and we're busier than ever. Thank God for Madison or I'd be even more behind than I am. I don't suppose you have two more like her hidden somewhere?"

"You need more help?"

"Desperately. Madison is amazing, but she has her classes and we don't want to completely overload her. She's eager to learn and I think when she graduates we might bring her on as a full-time assistant and train her in event planning, but that's not for another year and with all the attention we've been getting from the show, we really need a full-time receptionist we can trust to manage the phone and email inquiries, but I don't even have time to put up an ad, let alone interview candidates—"

"I could do it. I'd still want to work at Lacey's, but she's said she can be flexible with my schedule."

Tori's face lit, but her eyes were hesitant. "Are you sure? I don't want you to feel like you have to bail us out—"

"We'd be bailing each other out." And she couldn't really afford pride right now. Or squeamishness. "How much does it pay?"

She was just grateful it was Tori she was negotiating with. She couldn't have had this conversation with Sidney. Not after twenty years of being on equal footing. She couldn't have gone begging.

"Babe?" Nick's voice carried down the back stairs from the apartment above, accompanied by the sound of his footsteps on the treads. "Dinner'll be ready in ten—oh, sorry to interrupt. I didn't know you were here,

Parvati."

"We were just finishing up," Parv explained as Tori's husband approached the sitting area, looking less like a lawyer and more like a handyman in his ragged jeans and t-shirt.

"Would you like to stay for dinner?" Nick asked after a glance exchanged with his wife. "It's lasagna night—Lore's favorite."

"No, I can't stay. I have plans with Parker. But thanks for the invite."

"Anytime." Nick gave his pregnant wife one last look—a look that somehow felt more intimate than a kiss—and retreated upstairs.

Parv couldn't help the bite of envy. They had it. That elusive thing she was looking for. The connection. The intimacy.

Parker had never looked at her like that—but she'd only known him three months compared to the decades of history Tori and Nick had built up.

"So how is Perfect Parker?" Tori asked, then caught something in Parv's expression and her own fell. "Uh oh. Not so perfect?"

"I don't know. Relationships are about compromise, right?" She looked at Tori, half pleading. "You're married. Things aren't always perfect with Nick, are they?"

Tori snorted. "No. Things are not always perfect. I think the more you love someone, the more they know exactly which buttons to push to make you crazy. The question is—even when you're arguing does the idea of being apart make you even crazier than the thought of staying together?"

"We don't really argue." Not since their little discussion about her moving in with Max. "Not that we don't disagree on things, but with the small things I just…"

Parv blinked, going still with the realization.

She gave him his way. That was why they didn't argue.

Whenever Parker started to get upset and sullen, she would see a choice in front of her clear as day between starting a fight and giving him his way. And she would give him what he wanted—because relationships were about compromise and she needed to prove that she could make it work.

Moving in with Max was the one time she hadn't done that.

"I *want* it to work with him," she admitted to Tori. "I'm just not sure that's the same thing as it actually working. But then I start worrying that I'm being unreasonable and sabotaging the relationship by overthinking every single thing."

"What are you worried about?" Tori asked.

"That he doesn't want to be with me. He just wants someone to fill the Girlfriend Role. That he doesn't actually care about me as much as the idea of me." *That I feel the same way about him.*

It had been such a relief just to be able to tell people that she was seeing someone. To not have to deal with the pitying glances anymore. To be part of the club.

"Those first few dates, I felt so connected to him. He was funny and easy to be with and we had inside jokes about jellybeans, but now sometimes even when I'm sitting right next to him I will feel completely alone. And I don't know if that's me or him or…"

"Or?" Tori prompted gently.

"Please don't tell Sidney, but I wonder if I'm screwing this up because of Max. I hadn't seen him for months when I met Parker and now we're hanging out again and I never feel alone when I'm with him—"

"Max Dewitt?"

"I know. Believe me, I know he's not the kind of guy who stays. And Parker is. Parker will never leave me. But is that reason enough to stay with him? Just for that security of knowing I don't have to worry about being dumped?"

"If that's the only reason you're with him—"

"It isn't. I just—I don't know what I want right now. Is he Perfect-on-Paper Parker or is that my self-sabotaging tendencies talking? Am I a complete relationships failure? Am I expecting too much? Have I read too many romance novels and watched too many seasons of *Marrying Mister Perfect* and completely screwed up my idea of what love should be? Or do I have a right to hold out for a little magic in my life?"

"Just don't expect every moment to be magical."

"I don't. But it would be nice if there were a few sparks."

Her chemistry with Parker had been unimpressive from the start, but she'd told herself that attraction would grow over time. She'd noticed often enough that a Suitor on *Marrying Mister Perfect* who seemed hot at first glance could be ugly by the third episode because he turned out to be such a dick and someone who was sort of odd looking at first could become handsome in her eyes by the end because of his sweet personality.

She didn't need insta-chemistry to fall in love. It would grow as she got to know him.

But the chemistry hadn't gotten better. And the sex continued to be lackluster at best. Perfect-on-Paper Parker was not so perfect in bed. Foreplay and reciprocation seemed to be concepts he hadn't quite grasped and when she tried to gently hint that she might like certain things he would get so upset that he hadn't 'satisfied' her that he'd leave the bedroom—but she told herself it was early in their relationship. They were still learning one another. Maybe he would get better.

Relationships were about compromise. Which, lately, meant Parvati compromising on her need for orgasms.

"There's more to life than sparks," Tori said. "I lucked out and got both, but if he's a good man who cares about you and you care about him…" She trailed off with a shrug.

"I'm keeping you from lasagna night." Parv stood. "And I should get going. I'm going to be late to meet Parker."

Another Friday night of pizza, watching some awful horror movie he'd picked out, and bad sex to look forward to. Well. She'd said she wanted to be in a relationship.

CHAPTER TWENTY-SIX

Her cell phone rang too early Saturday morning for it to be good news.

Parvati rolled over, ignoring Parker's sleepy groaning attempt to drag her back to the center of the mattress and leaned over her nightstandless side of the bed to grab her phone off the floor. Katie's face lit up the screen.

Six seventeen in the morning. Parv's heart rate kicked up and she was fully awake as she swiped her thumb. "Katie? Are you okay?"

"Aunt Parv?" Katie's voice wavered wetly. "I screwed up."

Parv's feet hit the floor and she grabbed her clothes, carrying them with her to the bathroom so she could dress while she talked. "Where are you? What happened?"

She kicked the door shut and elbowed on the light in the bathroom, dumping her stuff on the counter and fishing through the pile to find her underwear.

"I'm at Lolly's." She sniffled. "Oh God, Parv, I screwed up so big."

Cousin Lolly's. Not at home with her fiancé. Had they called off the wedding? They were getting married in a *week*. "Did something happen with Jonah?"

"I don't know!" Then the tears obscured what Katie

was saying and all Parv could make out was *drunk dial* and *mistake*.

"It's okay, hon. Take a deep breath."

Katie did, miraculously managing to bring herself under control enough to explain. "My friends wanted to throw me a bachelorette party on my last weekend of singledom, but none of us have fake IDs so Lolly offered to host us and I thought how much trouble can we get into at Lolly's apartment?"

Famous last words. Parv ignored her cousin's contributing to the delinquency of minors and focused on the immediate issue. "So you were drinking," she prompted.

"God, Parv, I've never been so drunk. I've never really been a party girl and they kept giving me these fruity shots and I thought what's the harm, right? But then there were these guys…"

"Strippers?"

"I don't know. I was so hammered I can't even really remember. I think they were just friends of Lolly's. I remember that guy from her band being there, but most of it's a blur."

"Okay. So there were guys…"

Katie took a deep breath and dropped the next words hard, like a boulder of guilt landing in the middle of the conversation. "I kissed one."

"Is that it?"

"Isn't that enough?" Katie screeched. "I'm getting married in a week and I kissed another man last night. A man whose name I don't even remember."

"Would it be better if you remembered his name?" She couldn't help being relieved. She was standing half-dressed in Parker's bathroom, getting ready to ride to the rescue, and the crisis was a kiss.

"I *betrayed* my fiancé. And when I woke up, my phone showed that I called him last night. What if I told him? What if he called off the wedding?"

"One—you didn't betray him. You kissed another guy at your bachelorette party. I know it feels like a huge deal because you've never kissed anyone but Jonah in your entire life, but you obviously regret it and I'm pretty sure you're never going to do anything like that ever again because of the way you feel right now, so I don't think the betrayal thing is really an issue. And two—don't borrow trouble. Maybe you drunk dialed him last night, but I sincerely doubt you could have said anything to make Jonah call off the wedding. He's *crazy* about you. And even if you did, I'm betting you can fix it. You just have to call him and figure out what you said."

"What if he won't talk to me?"

"What if a meteor hits the earth tomorrow and we all go the way of the dinosaurs? Don't worry about what ifs. Call him. Find out what you're dealing with." Parv caught sight of herself in the mirror and grimaced at the dark circles under her eyes. "Normally I would recommend waiting until a civilized hour to call, but since you're just going to freak out until you talk to him, call now. Rip the band-aid off. And tell him you love him. That usually helps."

"What if this is a sign?"

"A sign of something other than you had too much to drink?"

"It's like all those wedding movies. *27 Dresses, Bride Wars, The Wedding Ringer, The Wedding Date, Something Borrowed, Wedding Crashers, Four Weddings and a Funeral, Made of Honor*—the girl is always marrying the wrong guy. They're so in love with love or so convinced that their life needs to follow a certain path with a certain kind of guy that they never even stop to check to see if they're marrying the right guy."

"Of course not. Otherwise there wouldn't be any drama. Those aren't real life."

"But what if I'm doing that? What if Jonah is the wrong guy and I just want to get married so badly I'm ignoring all the signs?"

Parvati knew irrational panic when she heard it. "Do you want to break up with him?"

"Of course not! I can't imagine my life without him in it."

That didn't sound like the wrong guy to Parv. "Are you more excited about the wedding or about being married to him?"

"Being married to him—but it's a close call, Aunt Parv. I really want the wedding. Is that wrong? I want it to be pretty and perfect. I want it to be the best day of my life."

"Wanting your wedding to be perfect doesn't mean you picked the wrong guy. It just means you're your mother's daughter. Is he your best friend?"

"Of course."

"Do you love him?"

"More than anything in the world."

"Then maybe the only sign we have here is that you've been watching too many wedding movies. Step away from the drama and call your fiancé. Everything's going to be great." And, unlike when she'd used those words for Common Grounds, she really believed them.

Katie sniffled. "Thank you, Aunt Parv. I don't know what I would do without you."

It wasn't until Parv had gotten off the phone with a much calmer Katie that she realized she'd just talked her niece back into marrying Jonah.

That would have been the perfect time to ask Katie if she was sure. To remind her that she was young and she had time and maybe she wasn't ready to spend the rest of her life with one guy if she was still getting drunk and kissing other guys...but she just hadn't been able to do it.

Katie loved Jonah. It was there in her voice every time she talked about him and Parv genuinely believed they would work it out—whatever came at them, those two would be able to face it together. She'd worried that Katie was cutting herself off from experiences by being with Jonah, but the truth was they were lucky. They'd found that love early.

Parv crept back to the bedroom, climbing back into bed beside Parker. He stirred, reaching out an arm to drag her against him. "What was that?" he mumbled sleepily.

"Katie kissed some guy at her bachelorette party last night and was freaking out. She needed someone to talk her down."

Parker's shoulder stiffened beneath her cheek. "Is the wedding off?"

"I hope not. She's talking to Jonah now. I'm sure they'll work it out."

"But she cheated." Parker slid his arm out from under her, shifting away.

"She got drunk and kissed a stranger at a bachelorette party with all her friends egging her on. It's not really the same."

A snort. "I doubt Jonah will see it that way."

The condemnation in his voice made Parv's hackles rise. *No one* was allowed to judge her family. "She's a kid who made a mistake and kissed a guy. She already knows it was a mistake. Sometimes people need to make mistakes in order to learn never to make them again. As mistakes go, this one was pretty minor."

He shifted away from her, putting more distance between them in the bed. "So if you cheat on me, it's just a learning experience?"

Parvati fought to keep her temper in check. This was a trigger for him. She needed to be sensitive to that. But it was starting to make her crazy. The jealousy. The insecurity. How it never let up. "I'm not going to cheat on you, Parker. That isn't who I am."

"I wish I could trust that, but you took her side."

"She's my niece. I love her and I support her. That doesn't mean I'm going to cheat on you. What have I ever done to make you think you can't trust me?"

"Nothing," he snapped, sarcasm eating away at the words like acid. "You would never do anything. You're always right. You're always perfect."

"Parker—"

But he was already turning on his side, giving her his back. Shutting her out.

Her punishment for disagreeing with him.

"Parker."

Nothing.

She could have stayed. A good girlfriend probably would have stayed. Maybe if she'd loved him, she would have stayed. But she didn't want to watch him sleep the sleep of the righteously indignant, waiting for him to wake up and pretend nothing had happened. She didn't want to lie awake for hours stewing and there was no way she'd get back to sleep now—she was normally up at this hour for the bakery anyway and she was too irritated to sleep.

She got out of bed and put on the rest of her clothes,

gathering up her things. She said his name softly, but he ignored her, pretending to be asleep, pretending he was a grown man and not a toddler throwing a tantrum.

She could have stayed. Maybe she should have stayed. But she went home instead. And Parker never said a word.

* * * * *

Max hated the nights Parvati spent at Parker's and he was man enough to admit it. Jealousy had dug its ugly claws into his gut and it twisted them every time he thought about Parv, naked and soft and smiling in the arms of another man. He was hyperaware of her absence—so he noticed the second the security system beeped with the opening of the front door, too early on Saturday morning.

"Hey." He padded barefoot out of the kitchen, carrying the orange juice he'd just poured for himself. "You're back early."

She grimaced, dropping her overnight bag on the floor in the foyer as she kicked off her sparkly flip flops. "Katie called at the crack of dawn with a crisis and I couldn't get back to sleep so I figured I might as well make the drive before the traffic got too bad. I've got Sidney's shower at Elena's place in Malibu later and I didn't want to be too crunched for time."

"Is Katie okay?"

She looked at him like he'd just earned sainthood. "Thank you for asking that. She's fine. She got drunk and kissed someone else at her bachelorette party and then drunk dialed Jonah and when she woke up this morning she was in a regret spiral."

"Which you pulled her out of like the brilliant aunt

you are?"

"I did." She padded past him toward the kitchen and he fell in beside her.

"I don't think of Katie as old enough to drink."

"Legally, she isn't. Lolly decided to contribute to the delinquency of some minors in the name of bachelorette tradition."

Max leaned his hip against the counter, watching her move around his kitchen. Their kitchen, really. She was more comfortable around his appliances than he was. "If Sidney does a Brides Gone Wild at her bachelorette party, I don't want to know about it."

"I think it's going to be pretty tame, but I don't think it's going to be my call."

"Do I detect a note of bitterness?"

Parv grimaced behind her juice. "I'm being edged out of bachelorette party planning by Sidney's MMP friends. And yes, I'm annoyed." She took a long drink, then set down her glass and began pulling ingredients out of the fridge for something that was bound to be delicious. "I never thought of myself as the kind of girl who wanted to be involved in every little detail of wedding planning, but then Sidney moved without me and bought her dress without me and Tori and Elena planned the bridal shower without me and now Caitlyn's planning the bachelorette party without me and the only thing every part of this wedding seems to have in common is that it's happening without me—which is fine, it isn't my wedding, but I always figured when Sidney got married I'd be the one she relied on."

He leaned against the counter, letting her vent, watching her hands as she beat flour into some eggy mixture.

"I had an anxiety dream the other night," she went

on. "I arrived at the wedding wearing the wrong color dress, because I'd had to get it myself because Sidney didn't have time to shop with me, and I'd missed the rehearsal and didn't know where to stand or when to walk and Sidney kept looking at me like she was so disappointed in me because I was ruining her wedding."

"That isn't going to happen."

"I know. But it felt real." She released a sad huff of breath. "It felt really real."

"Have you talked to her?" Max asked, eager to fix the problem.

"I haven't *seen* her in weeks. But I'll see her this afternoon. It's her bridal shower. She has to show up."

"So you'll talk to her. And everything will be fine. You'll see. She took those best friends forever pacts you two made in fourth grade very seriously."

Parv smiled—and Max took that smile as a personal victory. She'd been tense ever since she arrived home and he'd needed that smile almost as much as she had. She may not be his, but when she smiled at him like that he could almost forget the other guy.

CHAPTER TWENTY-SEVEN

Parvati arrived in Malibu early, but neither Tori's nor Sidney's car was parked out front of the address her GPS had led her to, so she circled the block, finding a lookout point about a mile up the road to pull off and wait, deciding she'd rather hide out in her car for fifteen minutes than go inside and mingle with women she barely knew.

She'd been thinking about Parker all day, hating the way she'd left things with him—and hating the way she'd just left. Now that it wasn't six-thirty in the morning and she wasn't glaring at the wall of his back, she wished she'd made a different choice.

She pulled out her cell phone and dialed his number, staring out over the ocean. The phone rang until she was convinced it was going to go to voicemail, but then there was a muted click and a lingering pause before Parker sullenly muttered, "Hey."

"Hey. I was hoping we could talk."

He began speaking almost before she finished her sentence. "I knew this was coming. I knew you were going to do this."

Apparently she was the only one who'd gotten over her earlier irritation. "Look, I'm sorry about this morning—"

"I should have known better. I don't know why I

thought you were different. Women say they want nice guys, but what they really want are men they can walk all over until someone more exciting comes along." Spite saturated the words. "You think I don't know that you were just using me until you worked up the courage to make a play for Max?"

Where the hell was this coming from? "What are you talking about?"

"You're the one who called to break up with me."

"I didn't call to break up with you. I called to patch things up."

"You said we needed to talk."

"And we do. I didn't like how we left things this morning."

"Then you shouldn't have left."

"And maybe you shouldn't have tried to freeze me out," she snapped.

She didn't know how he looked during the long pause on the other end of the line, but she had a feeling it was pretty damn sullen. Perfect-on-Paper Parker never reacted well when she called him on his shit.

She'd been determined to make it work, but was it supposed to be this much work? And was she supposed to be the only one putting in any effort? She was always the one who commuted—which she hadn't minded because his work hours were longer and she didn't really want him in Max's house, but he never even *offered* to put in the hours in the car to get to her. He always picked the movie when they watched one together, because the one time she'd tried to show him one of her favorites he'd spent the entire time bitching about how dumb it was until she couldn't even enjoy it. He picked the restaurant and she went along. He picked everything and she made it work, but she wasn't sure she wanted to anymore.

He wasn't just selfish in bed; he was selfish everywhere else too. She wanted balance. She wanted a partner.

She wanted to break up with him.

He still hadn't spoken, pouting on the other end of the line.

Parv let the words pushing against her tongue come out, "Maybe we should take a break."

"I thought you weren't calling to break up."

"I wasn't, but maybe I should have been. Maybe we've both been trying to force something that was never there."

"I think that's probably for the best. I could never be with someone I couldn't trust."

Then you're going to be alone a long time, buddy. She held back the words. Maybe he'd never really let go of his baggage. Maybe he'd never really given them a chance, but had she?

"I hope you find what you're looking for," she said instead.

He left her with one last sullen silence to remember him by. And then it was over.

A not-quite-three month romance. And the closest she'd ever gotten to feeling like she might really cross the finish line with someone. She'd had longer relationships, but this one had been serious. On paper he'd wanted all the same things she wanted—a family, a home, a future.

Had she done the right thing, breaking up with him? She wasn't getting any younger and the options weren't getting any more plentiful. Had she just given up on her last chance?

It was hard to regret it with that last silence ringing

in her ears. She couldn't imagine bringing him to Katie's wedding next week. Let alone Sidney's in two months.

How long ago had she stopped seeing a future with him? She'd wanted so badly to see it, but wouldn't she be sad now if he'd been the One? She didn't feel heartbroken. She felt relieved.

Though in retrospect, perhaps it hadn't been the best idea to break up with her boyfriend *immediately* before attending an event where everyone would be talking about relationships nonstop.

Parvati tucked her car into the crowded driveway at exactly two o'clock and made her way to the door of the Malibu beach house where one of Sidney's *Marrying Mister Perfect* friends, Elena, now lived with her husband.

The place wasn't much from the street side, but as soon as she stepped into the sunken living room, the three-million-dollar view through the floor-to-ceiling windows smacked her in the face.

"Parvati!" Elena thrust a mimosa into her hand and plucked the present from her grasp before she disappeared to answer the door again.

Sidney was already here—thank God—and so was Tori, but they were surrounded by a gaggle of women Parv had most recently seen on her television screen as Sidney's co-Suitorettes on *Marrying Mister Perfect*, as well as a few faces she vaguely recognized from her high school and college days.

She found a place on one of the pristine white couches, feeling less maid-of-honor and more awkward guest.

"Parvati Jai? I thought that was you! My gosh, it's been years. What *have* you been up to?"

Her relief at being joined by another guest died a

quick death when she realized it was Ally Hopkins—their high school valedictorian—who was currently wearing a rock the size of Gibraltar on her left hand.

She'd been to enough bridal showers to know that they were mostly presents, champagne, wedding gossip and relationship advice—but she'd failed to take one other element into account: everyone catching everyone else up on their fabulous, exciting lives.

Except Parv's life wasn't fabulous and exciting. She'd broken up with her boyfriend fifteen minutes ago. She worked as a receptionist and a bakery slave. Her housing situation could best be described as "mooch."

"Oh," she pasted on a smile. "This and that. What about you? Is that a wedding ring I see?"

Ally beamed. "Guilty! Ally Hopkins-Adalpe, now. And Chris is just the greatest guy. We both do corporate law and we met when both our clients were named in a lawsuit. It was love at first discovery hearing! What about you?" Her eyes flicked down to Parvati's naked hand. "Are you seeing anyone?"

"Oh, no one special."

"What?" Tori chose that exact moment to appear with fruit and cheese skewers. "What about Parker?"

"We broke up."

"When?"

About three minutes ago. Luckily, Elena tapped a fork against her champagne flute to call the shower to order and saved Parvati from having to answer.

Tori shot Parv a look that demanded answers later, but didn't push the subject as the showering commenced.

* * * * *

By the time Sidney opened the cute little spatula set Parvati had given her and set it alongside the designer dishes and high end cookware she'd already opened, everyone in the room had asked Parvati about her employment and relationship status—except Sidney.

Admittedly, Sidney was busy—opening presents, getting unsolicited advice for a happy marriage, and answering questions about how she and Josh fell in love, their plans for the wedding, and when they were going to start a family—but the omission still felt significant somehow.

Sidney had no idea what was going on in her life. It was possible she didn't even know that Parv was living with her brother.

And with her break-up with Parker echoing in her thoughts, Parv couldn't stop thinking about balance. Where was the balance in their friendship? When was the last time Sidney had given a damn?

By the time the last prospective baby name—not for Tori's baby, but for Sidney and Josh's future offspring—had been discussed, Parv had a running tally of Sidney's transgressions playing in her head. Moving without telling her. Not being there for her when Common Grounds closed. The hours of unreturned voicemail messages.

All the things Parvati had told herself didn't bother her until the collective weight of them felt like a piano crashing down on top of her, painfully discordant.

When the party was officially over, she lingered, helping pack the presents into Sidney's shiny new SUV in the hope that she'd catch a moment alone with her friend, a single moment of connection that would make that piano-weight of grievance vanish into smoke.

But then someone else was trying to leave and Parv

needed to move her car and by the time she'd reparked it and come back in to help load again, all the gifts were in and Sidney was hugging Elena and Tori, thanking them for the lovely party, and getting ready to leave.

She turned to Parv with a tired smile and for a moment Parvati forgot her grievances. Sidney had always hated being on display. It was part of why her choice to go on a reality TV show again after *Marrying Mister Perfect* had come as such a surprise to Parv.

"Long day for you," Parv said, with genuine sympathy.

"Long year. Planning a wedding, launching a reality television show—how would anyone have the energy for kids after all this?" Sidney groaned, opening the driver's door. "You headed back to Casa Marquez?"

And there it was. The reminder of how far apart they were now. "Actually, the Marquezes sold their place. I'm staying at Max's now."

That stopped Sidney. She turned in the crook of the open door, frowning at Parv with her eyebrows arched high. "What does Parker think of that?"

"We broke up."

Sidney groaned, the sound heavy with judgment. "Oh God, Parvati."

"Don't look at me like that. It had nothing to do with Max."

"Are you sure about that?"

She wasn't. But she wasn't about to admit it, bristling defensively. "He's my *friend*, Sidney. And I've needed one because you sure as hell haven't been around. Lately I feel like I'm besties with your voicemail."

Sidney rocked back on her heels. "Excuse me?"

"You couldn't take five minutes to drop by Common Grounds when I had to close?"

"I've been a little busy."

"I know! But does that mean you stop giving a crap about me?" Parv heard her voice getting louder and couldn't seem to stop it. "You moved without telling me. You don't even know what's going on with me right now. Am I the thing that gets knocked off your priority list when something has to give?"

"That isn't fair—"

"I understand that you have different priorities now. Your job is important and your fiancé is important and Tori is important and her baby is important, but when did I stop being important? When did I become the deadweight in this friendship?"

Now that she'd started talking she couldn't seem to stop, all her pent-up frustrations from the last few months spilling out in a rush. "I know it isn't going to be like it was. I know we aren't going to be Tuesday nights vegging out and watching *Marrying Mister Perfect* together. I know everything is different and I'm the one who can't keep up. I'm the one who can't find a man. I'm the one who always *wanted* what you and Tori have, but I'm the desperate old spinster and you're living the dream with your perfect life."

Sidney's jaw dropped. "You think my life is perfect? My life is stressful as hell! Do you have any idea how much pressure I'm under? Every week I have to make some insanely deserving couple's wedding dreams come true—cancer survivors, military vets—flawless happy endings *every week.* But no pressure. It's just televised for the entire world to see. And now I have to feel guilty because you're feeling left out?" Sidney gripped the car's doorframe. "I'm sorry you're going through shit. I really am. But I'm going through shit too. And you aren't old. You aren't a spinster. That's just ridiculous." She climbed into the car. "I'm not going to throw you a pity party. I don't have the energy or the time. And I'm sorry if that makes me a bad friend, but I would hope my best friend would cut me a little slack." She reached out to grip the door, ready to pull it closed. "Now I'm sorry, but I have to go. I have twenty-seven things on my to-do list to keep Once Upon a Bride afloat so we can afford to pay our employees. By the way, Tori told me we hired you. Welcome aboard."

The car door slammed shut on the sarcastic words and Parvati fell back to watch the woman who had once been her best friend in the world drive away. She didn't know what they were now.

CHAPTER TWENTY-EIGHT

Max arrived home to find Parvati sitting on the couch in yoga pants and a tank top, staring at a blank television with a full tumbler of scotch in her hand. The corners of her lips pulled down and her free arm was wrapped around her knees, hugging them tight. The sight was so foreign, he found himself creeping up to her cautiously rather than just walking over and throwing himself on the couch like he normally would.

"Parv? You okay?"

She looked up at the sound of his voice, as if she hadn't heard the door slam when he came in from the garage. "I blew up my life today."

She toasted him with the full glass and he nodded to the tumbler. "How many is that?"

"First. I keep forgetting to drink it." She took a long swallow.

So he hadn't caught her mid-bender. That wasn't the origin of her vaguely catatonic state. "What happened?" Was it Parker? Her family?

"Sidney and I had a fight."

Max settled down beside her on the couch, moving carefully. "It can't be the first one."

She shook her head, still staring at the blank television. "We've never fought like this. Even when we argued before it never felt like we were really on

255

opposing sides. Now we're separate. There's this gulf between us that keeps getting wider. I'm losing my best friend, Max. And I know I made it worse today. I shouldn't have blown up like that, but I just got so sick of the lack of balance. Nothing has any balance. I broke up with Parker too."

"What?" The words hit him like a sucker punch—but he'd never been so relieved to be socked in the gut.

"There was no balance." Parv took another lingering swallow of scotch—a big enough gulp that he would have known she'd watered it down even if the pale color hadn't given it away. "Parker. Sidney. I would drop everything to help someone I care about and they know that, they take advantage of it, but do I have anyone in my life I can depend on like that?" She turned her head, looking at him now, her gaze no longer distant. "Except maybe you. You're my rock."

A jolt of something that closely resembled fear but wasn't entirely unpleasant streaked through him. He wasn't sure he wanted to be her rock, though part of him definitely liked the idea even if it scared the shit out of the rest of him.

"I don't complain—at least not to anyone but myself—or you—and I tell myself I'm not keeping score, and I never used to, not when I felt like Sidney actually gave a damn, but now I'm bitter about the lack of balance—but you can't bitch about getting nothing if you don't ask for something. I'm tired of getting nothing, so from now on when I want something, I'm going to ask for it. No more Miss Nice Girl."

"I like Miss Nice Girl."

"I like you too." She looked at him, something serious in her gaze that made him want to squirm.

Danger, Will Robinson. "Parv…"

"I broke up with Parker."

Oh Sweet Christ. "You said."

"He wasn't right for me."

He swallowed, his tongue suddenly thick. "I'm sorry to hear that."

"Are you? Are you sorry?"

Fuck no. His gaze fell to her mouth. That damn mouth he'd fantasized about since he was a horny teenager. The full lower lip. The perfect shape of the upper. It was the mouth of a forties pin-up girl and she had the body to match. All touchable curves.

This was a bad idea. It had always been a bad idea and it still was. She was looking at him with her soul in her eyes, but she was falling today and if he was her friend, he wouldn't take advantage. He would prop her back up on her feet and walk away.

Her glass hit the coffee table. "Max…"

She put her hand on his arm and he felt the touch like a brand through his sleeve. He was shaking his head, but that wasn't stopping her. She was leaning toward him, her gaze dropping to his lips, and all he could think of was that last kiss. The one that hadn't lasted nearly long enough. The one that kept him up nights. The one that he'd relived more times than he cared to count over the last few months.

"Are you sure about this?" Christ, was that his voice? All hoarse and raspy?

"I'm going after what I want," she whispered, so close he could feel her breath on his lips. "And I want you."

The kiss was soft and tasted lightly of scotch, but it wasn't tentative. There was nothing unsure about the way she kissed him. If there had been even a trace of uncertainty, he could have walked away. At least that's what he told himself. But there wasn't. The touch was gentle, but she leaned into it until it was sweeter, deeper, shoving him past his best intentions and into the feel of her.

He didn't know if she moved or if he reached for her. All he knew was that she was sideways across his lap, his hands full of her, the kiss never breaking as her mouth opened and her tongue teased against his. After months of foreplay, he'd expected them to be a short-burning fuse, igniting quickly and taking them into insanity in a frantic rush of flying clothes, but now that he was here, in this moment, with her exactly where he wanted her, he wasn't going to rush this. No matter how she squirmed in his lap, urging him on.

"Max," she gasped impatiently when he finally broke the kiss to move along the side of her neck, one hand smoothing down to grab a handful of her ass and position her more snugly against him.

"Easy," he murmured against her skin.

"What if I don't want easy?"

He blew against the skin of her neck he'd just wetted with his tongue, making her shiver. "You sure you don't want easy?" With one hand around her back, keeping her upright in his lap, he stroked the other from her hip to her ribcage, pausing just below her breast. With just the backs of his fingers, he grazed the full lower curve through her tank top.

"I hate easy," she gasped, arching into his touch. He teased her nipple through her clothes, the touch light enough to make her twist helplessly.

"Is that like when you say you hate me?" he asked with a grin against her neck. "Because I think you really like easy. And me."

She twisted in his arms, biting the side of his neck.

"Ouch."

"Shut up. You liked it."

He grinned. "True. But it's not going to make me hurry. I've been waiting for this for too long not to savor every second of it."

She shivered at the words. "Savoring can be good."

His hand slid back down to her hip. "Oh sweetheart. You have no idea." But she was about to.

* * * * *

After all the fantasies she'd had in her life starring Max Dewitt, the reality really should have been a letdown. There was no human way he should have been able to live up to expectations. But she should have known that when it came to expectations, Max was never satisfied unless he surpassed them.

By the time her first earth-shattering orgasm rolled over her, Parvati had realized that Max was in a whole different league from Parker. By the fourth, she realized they weren't even playing the same game. Not that she thought of Parker. Max consumed every sense and every thought.

She was aware of nothing but him on the couch—and when he carried her to the master bedroom. And the master shower. And the floor.

She was perfectly, blissfully sated when she fell asleep and perfectly, blissfully happy when she woke up. The feeling lasted as she stretched and closed her eyes, reliving every moment of the night before. It lasted right up until she opened her eyes and rolled over to find Max studying her.

There was nothing in his look to pop her happy bubble, but she still felt it deflate a bit when she met his eyes with the morning light streaming through the windows behind him. A moment ago she'd been reveling in the fact that it had *really happened*, but now facing him just felt too real.

"Hey." He smiled, adorably lopsided, his dimple making an appearance on one side, and her heart lurched a little.

"Hey."

"So that happened."

"Repeatedly."

He released a short, startled laugh. "That it did. I'm guessing we should talk."

And there it was. That ugly bitch reality come to ruin her perfectly sated morning.

She reached down deep, but couldn't find a shred of regret. No matter what came next, she was glad they'd done that. And she wasn't ready for it to be over just yet. But they did need to talk about expectations.

Were they friends with benefits? Something more?

This was Max, of the two week attention span. But this was also Max, her rock.

She needed him to know that he would always be the latter, even if he was also always going to be the former. She needed to keep him as her friend. This wasn't a fairy tale, where they lived happily ever after. She knew that. This was the story where Cinderella and Prince Charming enjoyed the ball while it lasted and then went their separate ways. And she needed him to know that she already knew that because she didn't think she could bear listening to him explain it.

But first…

She closed the distance between them and kissed him—quick enough to avoid the horrors of morning breath, but long enough for him to know she meant it as more than a brush off.

"I like you, Max. I even love you, in a way, but don't worry that I don't know what I'm doing. I know you. And maybe this won't be forever, but I refuse to think of it as a mistake—and if it is a mistake I'm making it with my eyes open. I'm choosing this. I'm choosing you. For however long it lasts."

And she wouldn't get in too deep. She wouldn't get hurt because she knew what she was getting into.

* * * * *

She was saying exactly what his fantasy version of her would say—all the affection, all the sex, none of the commitment. So there was no explanation for why Max almost felt a little…*hurt* by the words. Maybe the idea of forever scared the shit out of him. Maybe he was a man who didn't know the first thing about long term relationships, but he still wanted her to want it. He wanted her to give him the benefit of the doubt. To believe that he could do it even when he didn't.

Shit. He wanted her to at least *want* him to love her.

Because he fucking loved her, damn it.

But how could he say that now, with her lying there beside him giving him an out? Would she even believe him? Or would she think that was part of his game—that he told all the women he dated that he loved them in week one and then dumped them in week three?

It wasn't supposed to go like this.

Not that he had any fucking clue how it was supposed to go, but he was used to women coiling around him like clinging vines, not throwing open the gates and telling him to run free.

He didn't like it.

But how did you argue with a woman who was giving you exactly what you always wanted in relationships? What if he talked her into a real relationship and then screwed it up? What if he lost her as his friend?

If he was her rock, she was his. She was his connection to the world. He couldn't lose her.

He reached out, tucking a lock of hair behind her ear. "So we're in this for as long as it lasts. All in."

He needed to be exclusive.

"All in," she agreed. "For as long as it lasts."

"Do I need to wear a suit to Katie's wedding?"

Parvati's big brown eyes flew wide with panic. "You can't come to Katie's wedding. My entire family will start planning ours."

"You'd rather go alone and explain to everyone why you aren't bringing Parker?"

"No." She groaned, burying her head in the pillow. "But we can't go as a couple. Just friends."

"And if I want to kiss you on the dance floor?"

"Restrain yourself." Her grin turned wicked. "I'll make it up to you when we get home."

His smile matched hers. "I think I might want a preview of what this *making it up to me* would entail."

"I believe that could be arranged..." Her hand slid down his chest.

Max closed his eyes, taking a moment before his thoughts blanked out as the blood rushed away from his brain to remind himself to savor every second of this. To burn every last moment into his memory. For as long as he had her. Because all too soon she could be gone.

CHAPTER TWENTY-NINE

Katie's wedding was flawless.

Parv clutched her bouquet at the far end of a long line of bridesmaids, making sure not to lock her knees so she wouldn't pass out, determined not to do anything to mar Katie's big day—though from the light in Katie's eyes every time she looked at Jonah, the chuppah could have come crashing down around their ears and neither of them would have noticed or cared.

The sun shone down on them, a gentle breeze rustling through the vines and keeping the hilltop wedding from getting too hot.

Katie, the baby she'd held, was now marrying the man of her dreams—and if he was still more boy than man, well, they'd grow up together. Parv teared up during the vows and was openly crying by the time Jonah's parents' rabbi pronounced them husband and wife.

She trailed them down the aisle, wobbling a little on the uneven ground, looping her arm through a groomsman's—who didn't look old enough to shave, but had a sort of goofy adorable thing going for him that made the other bridesmaids jealous of Parv for getting to walk with him.

Katie had confessed before the processional that she'd matched up Parvati and Aidan to keep the other bridesmaids from brawling over who got to walk with him. She'd also pulled Parv aside at the rehearsal dinner to whisper her thanks for talking her down the previous weekend. Apparently her drunk dial had consisted of sloppily declaring her love for Jonah over and over—and when she'd confessed her transgression, Jonah had been a saint. Katie's word. He'd told her that some random guy could have the kiss from her bachelorette party. He got all the rest of the kisses for all the rest of their life.

He was a sweetheart, really. And he loved Katie like crazy.

There had been a couple of awkward moments at the rehearsal dinner with family members asking after Parker, but she'd been glad to have Max there as a buffer—and a friend. Word had spread quickly that Parvati and Parker had broken up and several of her family members had come over to express condolences. Parv had made a conscious effort not to be annoyed when everyone assumed that the break-up had been Parker's choice—and almost succeeded.

Luckily, she was too busy being happy for Katie and Jonah to care.

A soft linen handkerchief appeared in front of her face. "You look like you need this."

She plucked the cloth out of Max's hand and dabbed carefully at her eyes. "I never used to be a crier. Now all it takes is one *dearly beloved* and I'm leaking all over the place."

"It was a nice ceremony."

"Yeah." She smiled toward where Angie was trying to wrangle her daughter and new son-in-law toward the best views for the photographer. "I have to stick around for the pictures, but I can catch a ride over to the reception with one of the groomsmen if you want to meet me there."

"I'll wait for you."

But he didn't just wait. He watched. He lingered in the background, his eyes always on her. She knew it was just instinct—he was protective. He was trained to guard people. But she blushed through the photos, her smile feeling different because he was there.

They'd only been together a week, but she felt like she'd packed more keepsake memories into that week than she had in the entire previous year.

She'd started work at Once Upon a Bride, guiltily relieved that Sidney was working outside the office most days and they rarely saw one another. She wasn't eager to rehash their argument. Even working both jobs, she still got home before Max almost every day. The comfortable domestic routine they'd fallen into when she moved into his house hadn't changed much—except now when he came home and found her puttering in the kitchen he pressed a kiss to the side of her neck and distracted her until she nearly burned the ladyfingers she'd been baking.

But it wasn't just the sex that had her grinning giddily to herself whenever she thought about him. It was the way they could talk about anything and everything. The little stories he told her about his day. The way she finally felt like she had a *partner*.

It was a dangerous feeling, she knew. She could get used to it far too easily.

She told herself that she was living in the moment, but the rationalization didn't hold up even in her own mind. She loved him like crazy and that feeling wasn't going to go away—so she might as well throw herself into it and live it to the fullest for as long as it lasted.

And maybe, a little voice inside her whispered, it wouldn't have to end at all.

Max drove them to the reception venue and Parvati nobly resisted the urge to drag him into the Tesla's comfortable back seat and have her way with him. There weren't any handy side streets as they wound down the hill from the vineyard and she didn't want to give her family any reason to be suspicious. The questions about Parker hadn't bothered her—the more she talked about him, the more certain she became that she'd made the right decision—but she had a feeling things wouldn't be so easy to explain away with Max.

They arrived at the reception hall and found their table—as much as Parv adored Katie, she was glad the bridal party had been big enough that there hadn't been room for all of them at the head table so she could spend the evening bumping ankles with Max under the table rather than watching the other bridesmaids vie for Groomsman Aidan's attention.

Angie looked happy—but then she usually was when her orders were being obeyed. Devi and her husband were seated at the same table as Parvati and Max—and she kept frowning at Max as if she couldn't figure him out, but even Devi's permafrown couldn't dampen Parv's mood as the happy couple took the floor for their first dance.

Max tugged his chair closer behind hers on the pretense of getting a better view of the dance floor, and proffered his handkerchief when she started to sniffle sappily. "So we're in favor of marrying off children now?" he murmured, his breath against her neck.

She leaned back until her shoulder rested against his chest. "They found each other. It's beautiful."

"It is."

She glanced over her shoulder at him, meeting his eyes. "And even if they're making a mistake, there are some mistakes you have to make. Otherwise what are you living for?"

Like Max.

When the dancing opened up for other couples, Max scraped back his chair and extended his hand to her, palm up. Parvati placed her hand on top of his and let him tug her onto the floor and into his arms. He was a great dancer. It wasn't a romantic thing. It was just a fact.

Katie and Jonah twirled past, laughing, and Parvati grinned. "They make it look so easy."

"Dancing?"

"Love."

"They aren't carrying a lifetime of baggage and bad habits." He spun her out, reeling her back in—and she managed not to stomp on his toes. Little victories.

"Their lives will be so different, marrying so young. Every decision they make for the rest of their lives, they'll make together. Where to live. What car to buy. When to take a job."

"Do you wish you'd done that?" Max asked as they swayed in time to the beat. "Married young?"

"I never really came close. I was convinced that wasn't what I wanted. But it's both a blessing and curse, I think. One of those bad habits, I guess. Getting used to making every decision without taking someone else into account. Do you think we reach a point where we forget how to be anything but independent?" She hadn't wanted to consider Parker's feelings when she moved in with Max. Had that been the beginning of the end for them?

Max tucked her a little closer. "Personally, I think an

267

old dog can learn new tricks. Especially when it comes to love."

She looked up at him, his words sinking into her skin as the look in his eyes warmed her from the inside out. Was he saying what she thought he was saying? That he could learn new tricks to be with her?

Could Max Dewitt be in love with her?

Her heart rate accelerated until she could feel it thrumming in her throat. Her mouth suddenly dry, she wet her lips, and Max's gaze tracked the glimpse of her tongue. Was he going to kiss her? *Here*? Right in the middle of the dance floor in front of her entire family?

It was a romantic comedy declaration of love. A reality dating show moment. The kind of thing that didn't happen to girls like Parvati. But wasn't it exactly what she wanted? For him to throw caution to the wind and love her?

The song ended—and the moment was gone. Parv's stupid hope gave a protesting scream that faded into oblivion as it died. So much for Big Gestures.

The emcee called for the dancers to clear the floor for the father-daughter dance and Max caught her hand, his grip hard. "Come on."

He tugged her off the floor—not moving too quickly, the picture of casual ease. She never would have known something was up if she hadn't felt the tension in his biceps when she braced her free hand on his arm.

He didn't take her back to their table, weaving instead through the crowd that had formed at the edges of the dance floor until he was at the far end of the reception hall where the caterers were busy clearing away the remains of dinner. He tugged her through the nearest door and into the hallway. Parv looked back over her shoulder, but no one noticed their exit, all eyes on Kateri's dance with her dad.

The hallway was crowded with catering carts and waiters moving with brisk purpose—purpose no doubt inspired by their fear of Angie's wrath. Max moved with similar purpose—and a very different inspiration—down the hall, away from the activity, scanning the doors they passed.

"Where's a freaking coat closet when you need one?"

Parv smothered a laugh behind her hand.

"Here." They rounded a corner and Max yanked open a door, spinning her into a small room that appeared to be a janitor's closet and pinning her to the door as it closed them inside.

"Oooh, mops. Sexy."

"Shush, you. Desperate times." Then his hands framed her face and his mouth was on hers and she forgot everything else. He broke the kiss, resting his forehead against hers with a groan. "God, I've been dying to do that for hours."

"Weddings turn you on?"

"*You* turn me on." His lips sealed hers again, stealing whatever reply she would have made. When he finally let her come up for air, he sank down to his knees in front of her. A draft touched her legs as he raised the long hem of her bridesmaid dress.

"What are you doing?"

"Begging for a quickie in a supply closet." His fingers brushed the backs of her knees as he nibbled the skin he'd exposed on her upper thighs.

Parv let her head fall back to thunk against the door as he moved higher. "I like the way you beg," she gasped.

"Shh. If anyone in your family comes looking for you, we're searching for a safety pin for a wardrobe malfunction."

"Mm-hmm," she mumbled, thrusting her fingers into his hair to keep him exactly where he was.

"Focus. We need to keep our stories straight."

"I am focused." Focused on his fingers, his mouth…

"Parv?" A voice called from the hallway outside and Max froze with Parvati's fingers still clenched in his hair.

"No one saw us come in here," she whispered.

Max straightened, carefully putting Parv's clothing back to rights as the voice came again, this time right outside the door. "Parvati? She has to be out here somewhere."

Devi. And reality intruded.

"They might need me for something for the bridal party," Parv whispered.

"Do you want to go back out?" Max offered, his voice barely audible next to her ear.

Did she *want* to? Hell no. Should she? "Yeah. I should get back."

Parv reached for the doorknob, but Max's hand closed over hers before she could turn it. "Give it a second," he murmured, and she listened, straining her ears for the sound of Devi's footsteps retreating down the hall.

He was warm against her back, tempting her to turn into his arms and forget about the rest of the world—but she didn't want to miss Katie's reception. He lifted his hand and she turned the knob, slipping out into the hallway. It was empty—Devi nowhere in sight—and Parvati let out the breath she'd been holding.

She turned to find Max carefully closing the door behind him, his hair sticking up at all angles. She giggled, reaching up to smooth it down, and he grinned, tidying her hair and adjusting her skirt.

"You're a terrible influence," she told him, still smiling.

"You're blaming this on me? You're the one who looked at me like that when we were dancing."

She stepped closer, pretending she needed to smooth his jacket. "I guess we might both deserve a share of the blame—"

"There you are." Devi appeared around the corner and Parv only managed not to jump away from Max guiltily because his hand tightened on her arm, stilling her reaction. "Mom's been looking for you."

"Wardrobe malfunction." Parv turned to face her sister with a calm smile, trotting out the excuse Max had given her. "I needed a safety pin."

Devi eyed Max and the door behind him skeptically. "Did you find one?"

"Yep." Parv dropped her hand from Max's jacket and sailed down the hall past her sister. "Did we miss much? Or are they still on the dances?"

"Just finishing up," Devi said, falling into step beside her. "Toasts are next."

"Oh good." Parv pushed through the door into the reception hall, pretending nothing had happened for all she was worth, but Devi leaned close as they made their way back to their table.

"I hope you know what you're doing," she murmured under her breath—proving Parv's act hadn't been quite as convincing as she might have hoped.

Parv plucked a champagne flute off a nearby tray and shoved it at Devi. "Better get ready for the toasts."

Devi didn't comment, taking the champagne and returning to her seat next to her husband.

"Everything okay?" Max asked, grabbing two flutes of champagne and handing one to Parvati.

"Of course." She smiled through the shiver of disquiet that tried to creep into her happiness. "Everything's perfect."

Just perfect.

CHAPTER THIRTY

"You look awfully happy."

Max looked up from his cell phone as his sister walked into their mother's sitting room, only realizing after she spoke that he'd been grinning like an idiot. Parvati had texted him a picture of the cake she'd just finished for a bachelorette party—along with a reference to their creative use of cake from a couple night ago.

"I am happy." Really freaking happy. "What does it say about our relationship that you sound annoyed by that?"

"I grew up with you," Sidney said as she perched on the sofa. "I don't trust you when you have that self-satisfied look on your face. You're hiding something."

"What would I be hiding?" He pocketed his phone. "How's the wedding planning going?" he asked in an attempt to distract her from the previous topic. Sidney had always had a weird ability to sniff him out in a lie and he didn't want to be the one to tell her he'd been hooking up with her best friend.

Not that he was ashamed of Parv. He just didn't know what was going on between them and as soon as they introduced Sidney into the equation, things were going to change. And he didn't want things to change. The status quo was pretty damn awesome.

They'd been "together"—whatever that meant—for

three weeks now and life was pretty damn good.

"God, don't ask," Sidney groaned—and luckily their mother appeared then, completing the distraction.

Max thought he was in the clear as they migrated to the dining room—until his mother's chef served the quiche and Sidney frowned across the table at him.

"Why haven't you been flirting with Mom's chefs lately?" she asked suspiciously. "In fact, why haven't I seen pictures of you going to events with any aspiring starlets and models for the last couple months?"

It had been more like six months, but Max wasn't going to help her with the timeline. "I've been busy. Elite Protection has really taken off."

Sidney narrowed her eyes at him, not buying it. "Are you seeing someone in secret?"

"Who has the time to date?" he evaded.

"You should make the time, Maximus," his mother chimed in. "I hate to think of you having nothing in your life but your work."

"I have plenty in my life. I have you," Max said with a saccharine smile that made Sidney roll her eyes.

"What about some of the single women at your wedding, Sidney?" their mother suggested.

"Most of my friends are in relationships," Sidney commented. "Except Parvati."

Max took a bite of his quiche, trying to look innocent—and like he hadn't been doing debauched things to Parvati for half the previous night. They hadn't technically agreed to relationship status, but they were definitely moving in that direction.

He'd been working less, eager to get home to her. He'd never really invested time in a woman he was seeing before. Not like this. But Parvati was different. Even if this was just a glorified fling.

He'd always been a low-hanging fruit kind of guy in the past, going for the girls who were right in front of him—and there had always been plenty of those. Women who flirted with him at parties and made it clear they were interested. He would let nature take its course, exerting enough effort to be charming, to make them feel sexy and appreciated, but never enough to lead them on. Dating had always been easy. Getting laid when you were young, attractive, and wealthy wasn't hard in L.A., but a few months ago he'd just stopped noticing when women were flirting with him. Long before he'd actually started seeing Parvati he'd stopped *seeing* anyone but her. He didn't notice them making eyes at him anymore.

But if he admitted that to Sidney she would definitely know something was up, so he kept his mouth shut and listened to his sister and his mother match-make for him at the former's wedding.

He kept Sidney talking about her wedding—and off of his love life—as they were walking out. His familial duties for the month complete, he climbed into his car and glanced at his watch. Parvati was closing the bakery today and even though they kept shorter hours on weekends it was still half an hour until she would be free.

He never would have considered learning someone else's schedule with any of the other women he'd dated. He would have just texted to see if they were free and shrugged it off if they weren't. Everything was different now. Did Parv know that? Did she see the change?

His phone rang as he was debating going home and sneaking in some work before she was free or going by the bakery's back door and seeing if he could distract her as she closed up. Her grinning face lit up the screen.

"Parv? I thought you weren't off until three."

"Technically, I'm not. Are you still at your mom's?"

"Just leaving. What's up?" Something about the tone of her voice had him straightening in his seat.

"It's probably nothing."

He pushed the button to start the car, fastening his seatbelt one handed, every instinct waking up. "What is?"

"I got a weird feeling, like I wasn't alone, and then I thought I heard someone in the storage room, but when I looked there wasn't anyone there—"

"Don't move. I'm coming."

"That's what she said."

It took him a moment for Parv's nervous joke to penetrate the wall of his concentration. "Ha."

"It's probably nothing."

"I'm five minutes out. Do you hear anything else?" Then he thought of Parvati. "Do *not* go investigating strange sounds." He spun the wheel, whipping the Tesla around a corner and punching the accelerator.

"I'm probably overreacting. The shop is tiny. There isn't exactly anywhere for someone to hide."

"I don't like you being alone there."

"It's a bakery. Who's going to rob us? Cookie Monster?"

The thought of anything happening to her…*anything*… Max sped the entire way to the bakery's back parking lot. The back door was locked—and he didn't bother knocking on it. "I'm here," he told Parvati over the phone and the door opened a moment later. His heart rate didn't slow to normal levels until he saw her—whole, fine, giving him a look like his crazy was showing and he should tuck it away.

"I shouldn't have called you," she said. "It was

probably a cat."

"In your storage room?"

She shrugged. "There's a window."

"Show me." He moved past her, his gaze taking in every corner of the space. It was a bakery kitchen. Innocuous. Utterly nonthreatening. He searched the front display area and the restroom, trying the door on the office, which Parv informed him was always kept locked except when Lacey was doing the books, and then she pointed him toward the storage room.

The window was high, but large enough for a person to squeeze through. And unlocked. Max secured the window lock, directing her attention to the stores. "Does anything look like it's missing?"

"I shouldn't have called you. It was nothing."

"Keep this locked." He pointed to the window.

She nodded—and then her lips twitched. "It's kind of fun to see you in full on Guard Mode."

Parvati wasn't the kind to cry wolf—and Max fully intended to examine the area outside this window to see if there were any signs of someone using it to gain access. And he was glad she'd called. He didn't want her too embarrassed to call him again. He needed to make this something she wouldn't hesitate to repeat.

He caged her between his arms, bending down to kiss her neck. "You know you can see me in Full Guard Mode whenever you want."

She flushed, leaning into the caress. "I really did think I heard something. I didn't just call—"

"Parvati." He shut up her explanations with a kiss.

* * * * *

Parvati's embarrassment over the way she'd overreacted

lasted approximately three seconds after Max sealed his lips to hers. Then the relief—that he was here, that she was safe, that he would always come when she called— melded seamlessly with the rush of lust he never failed to inspire in her.

"We can't have sex here," she whispered, pinned against the wall of the storeroom some time later.

"Okay," Max agreed, though he didn't stop touching her or kissing her or…

Parv lost her train of thought and had to drag coherency back by her fingernails. "It isn't my place," she explained breathlessly. "And it isn't sanitary. We prepare food here."

"In the storeroom?"

Okay, so they didn't prepare food in the dry storage room and her ability to argue was severely compromised by what he was doing with his hands, but Parv still somehow managed to have the presence of mind to remind him, "I work here. Lacey will fire me."

"Does she have cameras in here?"

"I don't think so."

"She should. For security. I'll install some tonight. And some on the exterior. So next time I'll be able to check the feeds from wherever I am and know whether someone is here with you."

"How are you still able to form full sentences?" She felt like all her powers of logic—and resistance—were being drained into a pool of weak-kneed willingness.

"Different part of my brain. The part of me that protects you will never shut off."

Jesus, that was hot. She'd always wanted a partner, someone who was in it with her, someone she could rely on—and all of that was Max. He would always be there for her. Making her feel safe.

After that her resistance was token at best.

"I am officially a terrible employee," she declared, quite a while later, sprawled against him on the storeroom floor. They were still mostly clothed, but what they'd just done was definitely grounds for termination. Max stretched his neck back, studying the walls around them. "What are you doing?"

"Looking for cameras."

"A little late for that, isn't it?"

"I was distracted earlier." He relaxed back down onto the concrete slab—which really was extremely uncomfortable. Parv figured they had about ten more seconds of post-coital cuddling before her joints started to protest the location. "I don't see any, but if Lacey did hide some in here... Well. This would certainly be one way to come out as a couple."

Parv suddenly forgot about the uncomfortable floor. "A couple?"

"Sidney kept asking me at lunch today if I was seeing anyone."

Nerves tumbled through her stomach and Parv sat up. She didn't want Max to have to lie to Sidney, but the idea of her knowing the truth didn't sit well either. "What did you tell her?"

"I didn't lie to her outright." He sat up as well, putting his clothing to rights. "I mostly evaded the question."

"Did she seem suspicious?"

"Not of the evasion—that's pretty much how I've always responded to any personal questions—but she's definitely starting to wonder why I seem to have given up my man-whoring ways. It really seemed to bug her that I wasn't flirting with my mother's chef."

"You could," Parvati said, hating the words even as

they came out of her mouth. "We don't have any rules—"

"Are you seeing someone else?" His voice was sharp, his gaze sharper. "I thought we agreed we weren't doing that. All in for as long as it lasts."

"I am all in, but we didn't really define this—"

"How do you want to define it?" His voice was brusque, businesslike—and made her heart rate quadruple.

He was going to make her say it. She was going to have to walk out on that limb and tell him what she wanted. They were temporary. She *knew* they were temporary. But what she really wanted was something else entirely. Only one thought saved her from being a complete nervous wreck.

He'd called them a couple.

She swallowed, carefully choosing her words. "We're together. Exclusive. I guess I'd call you my boyfriend." *I guess I'm totally in love with you.*

She watched his face, ready for him to bolt at the word. Max didn't do girlfriends. He had dates. But he just nodded. Calm. All business as he gathered up the condom wrapper. While Parv was quietly having a nervous breakdown.

"Good." He helped her up from the floor.

Good. Like it was easy. Like it was simple.

The word boyfriend made it real. It made this thing between them something they couldn't hide anymore. "We need to tell Sidney."

Max nodded, opening the door into the rear of the bakery for her. "I'll tell her."

"You don't think it would be better coming from me?" Parvati glanced behind her, checking for evidence of the fact that they'd just had a quickie in the storeroom, but it looked totally normal. Though she was definitely going to guilt-mop that floor later.

"We could tell her together. What more do you need to do to close up here?"

"Just finish restocking the displays—and disinfect the storeroom floor. I was almost done when I thought I heard someone back here."

Max nodded. "Do you have a number for Lacey? I need to get her permission if I'm going to install cameras on site, but I have some in my car and it'll only take a few minutes. I can do that while you finish up."

Parvati pointed him toward Lacey's cell phone number on the bulletin board next to the office. "Don't you think it will be weird if we tell her together?" At his blank look, she clarified, "Sidney. I don't want her to feel like she's being ganged up on."

"I think you're over-thinking this."

"I just think it's going to be weird enough for her without us sitting her down and telling her we're together the same way a tween's parents might sit them down and explain they're getting a divorce. I'm her best friend—and you never talk to her about your love life anyway. I should be the one to tell her."

"Okay."

She glared at him. "Sometimes I hate how blasé you are about things."

He slanted her a glance as he punched Lacey's number into his phone. "You realize you make things more difficult than they have to be by worrying about how people will react before they do. Don't borrow trouble."

"It's not borrowing trouble. It's being mentally prepared. You are constantly thinking ahead and trying to predict reactions in your business," she reminded him. "Why not do it in your personal life?"

Max frowned. "I'm going to call Lacey."

Parvati glared after him after he unlocked the back door and slipped into the back parking lot—still running away from the real moments.

Then she went to disinfect the storeroom floor.

* * * * *

Max leaned against the back of the bakery after he got off the phone with Lacey, taking a moment before he went to get the cameras out of his trunk, Parvati's words still working their way through his system like a slow-acting drug.

He didn't look ahead in his personal life, didn't try to anticipate or predict the way he would in his professional world, in part because he'd never really had a personal life. At least not the way Parv was talking about—maneuvering the emotions and reactions of the people he cared about.

He'd breezed through his personal life, never taking anything too seriously. Never taking anything to heart. Because what was the point? He'd never been able to change anything that upset him in his personal life so he'd learned not to care.

He had power in business, the power to control his own fate, but he'd always felt helpless to change the people around him. His parents. His sister. They had fixed ideas of who he was. He couldn't seem to crack the already established concrete of his relationships with them and he'd hated the helpless feeling, so he'd shrugged it off. He'd learned not to try.

And he'd done the same thing with women. When things got complicated, he shrugged them off. He went for the easy get. Never expending effort. Never putting himself out there—especially not emotionally. Max Dewitt didn't put his heart on the line.

But Parvati *always* did.

She lived her life caring what other people thought, worrying about making them happy. Because she had those connections he lacked.

He'd worried about her being too open. About her vulnerability. But he was the one who was broken. He was the one whose default setting seemed to be careless indifference. How was he ever going to be what she needed?

He pushed away from the exterior wall, moving to his car to get the surveillance gear. He may not ever be enough for her, but he would keep her safe.

CHAPTER THIRTY-ONE

Parvati arrived at Once Upon a Bride on Monday morning determined to find the perfect moment to explain to Sidney that she was seeing Max. She'd practiced a couple oh-so-subtle segues to introduce the idea—only resisting the urge to make Max rehearse with her because she didn't want to hear him talk any more about borrowing trouble or psyching herself out.

The phones began ringing early on Monday, but Parv kept one eye on the door, watching for Sidney to come in as she did what they paid her for. The work at Once Upon a Bride wasn't hard—keeping up with scheduling and fielding basic questions from prospective brides who had heard about them through the television show, referring the brides who wanted to be on the show to the production company's website—but it did keep her busy, making the hours fly by.

It was lunchtime before she realized it—and Sidney still hadn't been in. Parvati set the answering machine to take over during her lunch break and wandered over to Tori's office, poking her head through the open doorway.

"Hey. Do you know if Sid's going to be in today?"

Tori looked up from her computer, a frown pulling between her brows. "What's today?"

"Monday."

Tori nodded absently. "Filming all day. Sorry. I should have mentioned it earlier. Pregnancy brain. Have people been calling for her?"

"No more than usual. I was just hoping to talk to her about something. I'll catch her tomorrow."

Tori nodded, her attention already back on her computer, and Parvati retreated—feeling a little guilty for the depth of her relief that she'd been granted a twenty-four hour reprieve.

Max would tell her she should just rip the band-aid off, but when it came to stuff like this, Parv was perfectly happy to ease into it as slowly as possible. Sidney would find out soon enough. And she couldn't escape the fear that when she did, everything would change.

* * * * *

"Your sister's here to see you."

Max looked up from his computer at Candy's words, experiencing an uncharacteristic stab of dread at the mention of his little sister.

Sidney never came to his office.

Parvati must have told her.

And no matter how many times he'd told Parvati that everything was okay and she shouldn't borrow trouble, he felt an unexpected surge of nervousness at the thought of facing Sidney now. He didn't think she would have come all the way down here to see him just to tell him how happy she was for them.

But regardless of what she said to him, it wasn't going to change anything. He and Parvati were together. Sidney was just going to have to get used to it.

"Thanks. Will you send her in?"

"Sure thing, Boss."

Max watched Candy retreat—distracting himself by wondering if she seemed a little more subdued than usual. Elite Protection had discontinued doing business with Hank the Hammer and Max had encouraged Candy to file a restraining order if he kept bothering her, but he wasn't her keeper, he was her employer and there was only so much he could do.

Then his sister walked in, ruining his attempt to forget about her arrival. "Hey, big brother."

"Sidney. Hi." He barely stopped himself before asking to what he owed the honor of her presence. He didn't want to hurry her into chewing him out for dating her best friend. He stood, rounding his desk, and met her halfway across his office. "How's the wedding stuff going?"

She made a face. "I am so sick of people asking that. I love weddings. *Love* them. Weddings are my life. And for the first time I'm starting to wish I did something else for a living. *Anything* else. It's all anyone can talk to me about anymore."

"I promise I don't really care how your wedding crap is going. I was just trying to be polite."

She snorted a laugh. "I appreciate that. Thanks. I'm actually here about something else," she said as she perched on the edge of one of the chairs facing the desk.

Max retreated back behind the big slab of wood, stalling for time to figure out what he was going to say to Sidney about Parv—and understanding for the first time why Parv was so nervous about telling Sidney. Talking about it with her made it real in an indelible way.

He looked up, forcing himself to meet Sidney's gaze without flinching. "I guess you're here to talk about me and Parv."

Max's first clue that he'd royally screwed up was the slow upward creep of Sidney's left eyebrow. "Excuse me?"

Shit. Double shit. He'd agreed Parvati should be the one to tell her and then he'd gone and spilled it the first chance he got. "Why did you say you'd come by?"

Sidney wasn't so easily distracted. "What do you mean *you and Parv*?"

"Hmm?" Max played dumb, but Sidney's expression said she wasn't buying.

"What about you and Parv, Max?"

"It's nothing," he said—and then immediately regretted the words. "Or not nothing. It's something. But not a big deal." That was wrong too. It was a huge deal. "No reason to make a thing of it. We're just hanging out." Jesus. He was making a mess of this.

"'Hanging out'?"

"Seeing each other."

Sidney's eyes narrowed. "And what exactly does that mean?"

"She's my—we're a couple." The word girlfriend stuck on its way out in a way it hadn't when he'd said it to Parvati. It had been so easy then.

"Jesus, Max." Sidney looked like she would have thrown something at him if there'd been any projectiles in range. "She's my best friend."

"I'm aware of that."

"And it didn't occur to you that maybe you should keep your hands off her?"

"I like her." Which was the height of understatement, but he didn't think Sidney would believe him if he tried to express how he really felt. Not that he was capable of expressing it.

"Yeah? Well, so do I. And I don't want you taking advantage of her just because she's right there in front of you as an easy target."

"I'm not—"

Sidney talked over him. "I know you won't do it on purpose. You probably won't even realize you're leading her on, but she's going to read into things because she's been in love with you since we were teenagers."

"In love?" He'd known she had a crush on him— she'd told him that herself—but he hadn't considered that it could have been more serious than a little infatuation.

Sidney groaned. "Great. Now you're going to run for the hills and I'm going to be the bad guy."

"I'm not running anywhere." And the idea of Parvati being in love with him certainly wasn't going to spook him. Part of him liked it. More than he was ready to admit.

It felt a little strange though, the idea that she could have loved him for all that time. Like it gave more weight to the way he felt about her now, dragging the fledgling feeling into reality.

"Anyone else," Sidney groaned. "You could have dated any woman in Southern California."

"I'm dating Parvati. That isn't going to change just because you don't like it." She opened her mouth to argue and he played his trump card. "Do you really want to be the one responsible for breaking us up? I thought you didn't want to be the bad guy."

"Are you together enough to be broken up? I thought you were just *hanging out*."

"What we're doing is none of your business."

"If you were dating anyone else, that may be the

case, but you made it my business when you went after my best friend."

"I didn't go after her."

"Of course not. The great Maximus is never at fault."

Max stood up, having taken enough shit for one afternoon. "Was there a reason you dropped by? Or was it just to give me shit?"

"I was filming in the area and wanted to ask you about Dad. He's refusing to come to the wedding unless I extend a personal invitation to his new wife—but I don't want to piss off Mom by having her there even if this Claudine would really want to travel halfway around the world with a six month old."

He sank back down onto his chair. "Shit."

"My sentiments exactly. It's so much easier when it's someone else's family drama I'm having to referee on their wedding day."

"I'm not sure Mom would be bothered by Claudine. She seems awfully okay with the whole thing."

"*I'm* bothered by it," Sidney snapped before cringing and pinching the bridge of her nose. "Sorry. He was just such a dick when he met Josh and now he wants me to kowtow to his trophy wife. Josh is being a prince. Down the road, he doesn't want me to regret not having my father at my wedding because I'm mad at him in the moment, but it's so tempting to just tell him not to bother."

Max shrugged, useless when it came to the emotional stuff. "If that's what you want."

"I *wanted* him to actually be there for me for once in my life. I wanted to know it mattered to him to be there. But since he's pulling this shit, part of me just wants him to stay away." She looked him in the eye then. "Can you talk to him? I'm not asking you to mediate, but if you could just get a read on the situation...I don't know. Maybe it would help."

"I'll try," Max promised.

"And regardless of what he says, FI wanted to ask for one other thing."

"Anything." As long as it wasn't leaving Parvati alone.

"Would you walk me down the aisle?"

Max froze, the words hitting him with unexpected force. "Are you sure?"

Sidney wet her lips. "He can come to the wedding, but he doesn't have the right to give me away. He was never there, Max. You were. Even if I give you shit about being unreliable, when it matters you're always there. So will you be there when I get married?"

He cleared his throat roughly. "I'd be honored."

Her shoulders lowered with relief. "Good. Now if we can just get our father to stop being a selfish dick, everything will be perfect."

Max grimaced. "I'll do what I can." He rose, coming around his desk. "I know we don't really do the mushy crap, but I'm proud of you, Sid. I always envied the way you went your own way."

"Are you kidding? I envied *you*. You were good at everything."

"Not everything."

"No." She met his eyes and he could see her wanting to resurrect the argument about Parvati. "Not everything."

"I'll call Dad. Maybe he'll be reasonable."

"Maybe," Sidney agreed.

But as soon as she left, it wasn't his father he called.

* * * * *

"I screwed up."

"Max?" Parv shifted her cell phone, wedging it between her shoulder and ear as she juggled her bag and tried to unlock her car. She'd just finished her hours at Once Upon a Bride and was looking forward to enjoying a rare afternoon off from Lacey's Cakes when Max had called. "What did you screw up?"

"I didn't mean to tell her. I thought you'd already talked to her or I never would have said anything, but when she showed up here—I just blurted it out."

She didn't need to ask who, dread kicking in at his first sentence. She finally got the door open and slumped into the driver's side, dropping her bag on the passenger seat beside her. "What exactly did you say?"

"I said we were together. I think. I wasn't exactly smooth."

"How did she take it?"

"Honestly? She was pretty pissed. But I think it was all directed at me, so you should be okay."

Parv frowned, confused. "She was mad at you?"

"She seems to think I'm taking advantage of you. She accused me of going after an easy mark because you've been in love with me for a decade."

"She told you that?" Parv had gushed about her feelings for Max when they were younger, but Sidney was her best friend and that was in confidence. For her to tell him like that—it felt like a betrayal. Like her best friend was actively trying to sabotage things with Max. Things that weren't exactly rock-solid to begin with.

"In her defense, you'd already told me something similar," Max reminded her.

"She didn't know that." Parv hadn't talked to Sidney about the way things were developing with Max at all—

in part because every time she started to Sidney would roll her eyes at the very idea. "I have to go," she said into the phone, shoving her keys into the ignition. "I need to talk to her."

"Babe, I'm sorry I told her. It just slipped out."

"It's okay." She wasn't sure it would have made a difference how it came out. Sidney had been against it from day one. "I'll see you tonight, Max."

She tossed the phone on the passenger seat when the call disconnected, only realizing when she'd started the car and gripped the steering wheel that she had no idea where to find Sidney. She wanted to have this conversation in person. She could feel the force of everything she wanted to say pressing against the back of her throat and she didn't want to do this over the phone, but Sidney was filming today and could be anywhere.

Parv kept the car in park and reached for her phone. She expected to get Sidney's voicemail, especially if they were filming—but her friend picked up on the first ring, answering with, "What the hell were you thinking?"

Of course she picked up now. Sidney could make time for Parv when she wanted to chew her out. Bitterness twisted around the hurt caused by the oh-so-supportive greeting.

What had she expected? Congratulations? A champagne toast? She'd known Sidney disapproved. But she wasn't going on the defensive today. She hadn't done anything wrong.

"Did you tell Max that I was in love with him when we were teenagers?" she demanded instead.

There was a beat of silence as Sidney changed gears. Then, "Yes, I said that, but—"

"And it didn't occur to you that maybe that would be

a huge violation of my confidence? That I trusted you not to throw me under the bus with your brother but you were too busy being right to stop and think maybe you shouldn't say something like that?"

"Don't blame me if he broke up with you because of something I said—"

"God, you just can't believe it, can you? You can't imagine a world in which Max might actually want me. You're supposed to be my friend."

"Friends look out for one another," Sidney snapped, sounding far from friendly. "Max never sticks with anyone—you've seen the women he normally dates. Models and aspiring actresses—"

"So you're saying I'm not good enough for him."

"Of course not! Stop putting words—"

"Who am I good enough for, Sidney?" Parv interrupted, rolling now. "Who *should* I be with if I'm out of my league with Max?"

"Parker seemed like a nice guy."

"All two times you met him."

Sidney groaned. "Oh my God. Please tell me you didn't sabotage a perfectly good relationship with Parker to be with my brother."

The words hit a little close to home and Parvati wasn't in the mood to hear them. This wasn't about Parker. Or even Max. This was about Sidney.

"Is it so hard for you to support me? I brought you to audition for *Marrying Mister Perfect* with me. You knew I wanted it, but when you got it instead, I supported you. When you needed a pep talk to go on the show, I was there. And when you walked away from the show in the middle of the process, spitting in the face of the dream I hadn't been allowed to have, I didn't say a freaking word. I supported you. And then again when you fell in love with Josh—the host I'd begged you to introduce me to because I had such a crush on him—God, you probably told him that too, didn't you?" She could see it so clearly—Sidney and Josh laughing together at poor little Parvati and her crushes. "You got everything I'd ever wanted and yes, I was envious. Of course I was. But I supported you. I was happy for you. Because that's what friends do. But you can't even be happy for me when I'm going on a few harmless little dates with Max?"

It was more than that with Max. So much more. But Parvati couldn't talk to Sidney about her hopes and fears—not with her so-called best friend determined to disapprove.

"I refuse to be the one to pick up the pieces when this falls apart," Sidney said, unapologetic—and Parv felt her spirits sink. She hadn't gotten through to her at all.

"What if it doesn't?" she asked softly. "What if we can just be happy? Don't you want that for us?"

"You want me to be happy to sit by and watch the train wreck I can see coming a mile away? I know you both too well. You're going to fall for him and he's going to break your heart."

"It isn't your choice, Sidney. It's mine. It's my life and I love him and you can either get on board or…" She trailed off, unable to finish the ultimatum. What was happening? Was Sidney really going to make her choose between her and Max?

"Just don't come crying to me when he pulls a Max. You know I'm right or you wouldn't be so defensive."

"I'm not defensive, Sidney," Parvati said, her voice low and sad. "And he isn't the one who's hurting me."

CHAPTER THIRTY-TWO

She was waiting on the couch when Max got home that night, wearing comfort clothes and nursing a glass of scotch in what she was coming to think of as her post-fight ritual where Sidney was concerned.

"Hey," Max said as he tossed his keys into the dish and crossed the open-concept room to her side, a wealth of concern in the single syllable.

"Sidney and I talked," she explained, lifting the scotch to take a sip. "Or screamed at one another. Same difference."

Max cringed. "I'm sorry I told—"

"It wasn't anything you did." She set down her scotch with a clink and crawled across the distance separating them—finding more comfort when his arms closed around her than she had in the drink. She slipped her arms around his midsection and hugged him close. "She thinks she's protecting me, but it feels like she's making me choose."

"I don't want to come between—"

"I know. It isn't you, Max. I just hate this." Her voice broke on the word hate and the tears she'd been holding back began to sneak out.

"Hey." He held her close, kissing the top of her head in a way that she would have thought would be patronizing, but with Max it was all comfort.

She and Sidney had argued in the past, but she'd never felt like their relationship was truly threatened before. But after the way they'd left things on the phone, she felt that way now. The cold stretches of angry silence. Sidney stubbornly refusing to admit she might not be in the right.

It wasn't about Max—though he'd obviously been the catalyst. This had been building up for months. Months of unreturned voicemails and being shoved down the priority list.

She knew Sidney was stressed. Knew she was dealing with a lot of new shit and things were going to change. But didn't Parvati have the right to expect at least a feigned *I'm happy for you*? Because Sidney wasn't happy. She was too busy thinking Parvati the Perennially Single was about to have her heart broken again.

Her tears drying, Parvati leaned back in Max's arms until she could meet his eyes. "Whatever happens between us, I don't blame you for any of this."

"You can't absolve me of guilt, Parv. I played a part."

"Maybe so, but I'm glad you did. I'm never going to regret this, Max."

He met her gaze, his own unwavering. "Neither am I."

* * * * *

Her first shift on Tuesday morning was at Lacey's Cakes—which was a relief because it meant she didn't have to face anyone at Once Upon a Bride. She didn't know what the tone was going to be there. She and Sidney weren't really on speaking terms after the way they'd left things and she wasn't sure Victoria would want Parvati working there if the atmosphere was going to make the Cold War look warm and fuzzy.

Whether she was about to be fired from Once Upon a Bride or not, she was relieved to have the reprieve, keeping her hands busy laying fondant on what would become a four-tier wedding cake.

She tried to channel the Dalai Lama and think Zen thoughts, but she was still having a hard time getting past Sidney's utter lack of anything resembling supportiveness when the chime over the shop door rang and she set aside the fondant she'd been rolling out, heading out front to greet the customer.

But her greeting died on her lips when she saw that her visitor was Josh Pendleton—former host of *Marrying Mister Perfect*, current co-host of Sidney's wedding planning show, and Sidney's fiancé.

He had a face for television and his charming smile had once been the primary reason Parvati tuned in to *Marrying Mister Perfect* every Tuesday night, but now she just glared at him as he stood in front of the cupcake display.

"Parvati."

"Josh." She didn't say anything else, staring him down. He'd come to her. He could broach the awkwardness.

"Sidney was awfully upset last night."

"That's funny. So was I."

"She's under a lot of pressure. The wedding—"

"Josh," Parvati interrupted. "I understand that Sidney is making herself nuts trying to have the perfect wedding—I've seen firsthand her anxiety over trying to be what she thinks she should more times than I can count over the last twenty-odd years. I get it. Her life is hard. But mine isn't exactly peaches and cream right now. And friends are supposed to be there for each other. It goes both ways. You want me to cut her some slack? Why don't you talk to her about doing the same for me? Now, unless you're buying something, I'm going to have to ask you not to loiter."

Josh retreated without further argument.

Half an hour later, the chime rang again and Parvati returned to the front—where Tori was waiting to tag in on the gang-up-on-Parvati team.

Parvati folded her arms defensively. "I guess you heard what happened."

"Only that you had a fight." Tori's smooth brow pinched with concern. "What's going on, Parv?"

"I'm dating Max."

Tori didn't blink. "I can't say I'm surprised. I've wondered if you guys would ever get around to dating."

"Then maybe you can talk to Sidney. She seems to see me dating Max as a personal attack on her."

"I'm sure she doesn't—"

"I'm sorry, Tori, I really don't want to listen to you defend her when you don't know what she said. If you really want to help, maybe you should try telling Sidney to get her head out of her ass and be a friend for a change."

Tori blinked then, nodding slowly. "Okay."

"I'm sorry." Parv swallowed, regretting snapping at the one person who had almost seemed to be onboard with the whole Max thing. "Do you still want me to come in this afternoon for my shift at Once Upon a Bride? I'll understand if you don't want the tension in your shop."

"Are you still going to be able to do your job?"

"Of course."

"Then I don't see a problem. Sidney's only there a

few hours a week these days anyway. And neither of you is the type to make scenes in front of clients."

"No," Parv agreed.

Tori nodded. "Okay then. I'll see you at two."

Parv hoped that would be it, but the Universe wasn't done piling on just yet.

Lacey arrived at one-thirty to take over manning the bakery for the afternoon—and she was already wearing her most disapproving glower.

She's found out about the sex in the storeroom, Parvati's guilty conscience immediately supplied as an explanation for the glower. But then Lacey spoke.

"What's this I hear about you feuding with Sidney Dewitt?"

Her stomach dropped. "We aren't feuding." *Not exactly*. "Where did you hear that?"

"It's all over town." Lacey's frown grew even more ominous. "I can't afford a Hatfields and McCoys feud with the premiere wedding planner in town, Parvati. You're a good worker, but I'm going to have to let you go if you threaten the bakery's relationship with Once Upon a Bride."

Parvati's irritation that Sidney was apparently spreading their personal business all over town was drowned in the nervous awareness that Lacey could fire her on the spot.

Sure, Lacey was almost universally grumpy and she tended to micromanage everything Parvati did and examine her timecard as if she was suspicious that Parvati was trying to bill her for extra seconds, but Parv *liked* working at Lacey's Cakes. She found the work inherently therapeutic, baking the one thing that could always sap away her stress, and she was actually learning a surprising amount from her grouchy boss.

Lacey didn't like to stray from the way she'd always done things, but often the way she'd always done things was classic and delicious. There was a reason she was the go-to baker in Eden.

"I'm still working at Once Upon a Bride—I'm on my way there now," Parv explained. "Everything's fine."

Lacey frowned. "Just as long as it stays that way."

Nothing like the threat of unemployment to encourage her to make up with Sidney. But somehow she felt even more stubbornly reluctant to bridge the gap than she had been when she woke up that morning.

She wasn't going to apologize for being with Max. Sidney needed to apologize to *her*. Until that happened she would just wait it out. Sidney would come to her senses. This entire mess would be a memory by the weekend.

But Sidney didn't call. She didn't apologize.

The weekend came and went without a word passing between them. As the second week of the Cold War stretched on, she began to suspect that Sidney was checking her schedule and intentionally avoiding her during her hours at Once Upon a Bride.

Things were good with Max, but it was hard to ignore the deep freeze from Sidney hanging over them. The awareness of the friction with Sidney added a constant hum of tension, like static in the back of her mind every time she was with Max.

She didn't ask if they were still speaking, but she got the sense from stray comments from Max that he had seen his sister though they didn't discuss it.

The wedding was approaching—a fact that was reinforced when the bridal boutique called to inform her that her bridesmaid dress had arrived and to schedule her fitting. It felt wrong, somehow, to be fitted for a dress for Sidney's wedding when she wasn't even sure she was still invited. She didn't know if she should even have the dress, but she went in and stood for the seamstress, letting her poke and pin.

The bachelorette party was only a week away and Parvati wasn't even sure she was going. She'd scraped together enough to pay for her share of the vacation rental, but would Sidney even want her there? Every day that went by without the two of them speaking to one another only made the gulf between them seem even more impassable until it seemed like an impossible breach.

CHAPTER THIRTY-THREE

Max pulled up in front of the modest ranch in Culver City.

He was just here to talk. He wasn't going to kick the living shit out of the man who'd appeared on the surveillance feeds, lurking around Lacey's Cakes. Parvati wouldn't thank him if he was brought up on assault charges and he wasn't sure he'd be able to convince her to file a restraining order, so he was going to talk.

No matter how much he wanted to put his fist through Perfect Parker's face.

Parvati had plans that didn't involve him tonight— her niece was back from her honeymoon and Parv had promised she'd have dinner with the newlyweds—so Max was on his own, a sensation that felt surprisingly foreign. Especially considering he'd been solo his entire life.

He'd stayed late at the office, catching up on a few things and reviewing the feeds he'd set up around Lacey's Cakes. That was when he'd noticed the man testing the locks he'd installed on the storeroom window.

Perfect Parker. Apparently even less perfect than they'd suspected.

Max let some of his anger out on the front door,

pounding his fist against the wood until it shook in the frame. Max would have hesitated if someone that pissed had rattled his door, but Parker apparently lacked self-preservation instincts. As soon as the door opened, Max threw his first question, not giving Parker a chance to take control of the interaction.

"Hi, Parker. Would you care to explain why you're stalking Parvati?"

He expected a guilty flush, an attempt to run—what he got was a petulant scowl and a stubborn set of Parker's jaw. "I'm not."

"So you're claiming you didn't try to break into Lacey's Cakes while she was alone there? And before you answer you might want to keep in mind that we have you on the surveillance feed."

Now Parker did flush, but he didn't look away—the man didn't look guilty, which was really starting to piss Max off.

"I wasn't trying to break in," he insisted. "I just wanted to make sure she was all right. I knew they were closed, but I knew she was alone there sometimes and I was in the area so I thought I'd make sure everything was secure."

"So you climbed through the storeroom window?"

"I didn't! I was just testing to make sure it was locked, but then it came open all of a sudden and I knocked over some tin or something. It clattered and I freaked because I didn't think Parv would understand what I was doing there—"

"Gee, I wonder why."

"So I closed the window and ran, but that was it. I haven't gone back."

"Now I know you're lying. I have you on camera, dumbass. And running when you think you're going to be discovered isn't exactly the behavior of an innocent man."

"I'm not stalking her, okay?" Parker snapped, more irritable than defensive—which had the annoying effect of convincing Max that he might be telling the truth. "I went back one more time, just to make sure things were secure, and the window was locked that time. But I swear I'm only trying to look out for her. We had a fight and she overreacted, but she needs me."

"No, she doesn't. Looking out for her isn't your job anymore. I've got that covered."

"Sure you do." Parker snorted. "But for how long? You think you're hot shit, but I know guys like you. Girls come easy to you, but you tire of your toys quickly. Parvati told me all about you. You'll dump her soon enough and I'm going to be right there, ready and waiting when you do. She'll realize that I'm the kind of guy she wants forever. You're just a distraction."

Max marveled at Parker's complete lack of survival instincts, though he managed not to put his fist through his face, thanks to years of discipline.

"Let's get something straight," he bit out. "Regardless of what happens between Parvati and me, you're going to stay the fuck away from her. She's made her choice and that was to leave you." This asshole obviously thought Parvati still belonged to him—an idea which made Max see red. "She isn't yours to watch over and she isn't going to be. Not ever again. Understand?"

"You just keep telling yourself that, buddy," Parker sneered. "You may be flashy, but I'm the good guy here. And nice guys don't always finish last. Not if we're patient. Assholes like you break girls' hearts and then they realize they need guys like me. You could never be what she needs. You don't know how."

Max ignored the flicker of unease stirred up by the words. "Just stay away from Parvati. Stay away from Lacey's Cakes. Stay out of her life." He didn't bother to add an *or else*. It wasn't necessary.

He pointed his car north, driving too aggressively, but he couldn't seem to stop thinking about Parker's last words. The man was an ass and an idiot. He'd never deserved Parvati—but was he right about that one thing? Did Max not deserve her either?

His agitation chased him up the coast, getting worse with every mile instead of better. He couldn't imagine tiring of Parvati, but what if he did? How badly would he hurt her? Was it better to end things now before they got too serious? They'd said they were all in for as long as it lasted, but how long was that?

He'd never had a long term relationship. What if he wasn't capable of it? Was the best thing for her for him to get out of her life? Did she really belong with someone else? Not Parker. That was *not* happening, but someone who would treat her like a goddess and give her everything she'd ever dreamed of?

A tiny voice inside Max insisted he could be that guy, he could do that, but what if he failed? What if he hurt her instead?

He didn't know what to do. He'd always been good at trusting his instincts, but they were pulling him in two different directions this time. The only thing he knew was that there was one situation he refused to let stand. He punched a button to activate his car's voice feature.

"Call Sidney."

Two rings later, his sister picked up. "Max?"

"You have to talk to Parvati."

"And here I thought you were calling to tell me

you'd finally talked to Dad about the wedding crap."

Max muttered a curse and checked the clock on his dash as he zipped through traffic. Almost eight at night put it at not quite five in the morning in Switzerland. "The time zones have been killing me. What's your excuse?"

"Butt out, Max." Sidney's voice came through his speakers, loud and clear. Max kept his answer just as clear.

"No." He braked hard as a bus cut him off, then swerved around it. "This is ridiculous. It's been weeks. You're upsetting her and that isn't okay with me. I don't like being pissed at you. It upsets the natural order of things." The order in which Max kept things copacetic and breezed through life without drama.

And tired of his toys quickly? Was he really that guy? Did he have to be?

"See? This is why you shouldn't be dating her. It complicates everything. You're messing with the separation of church and state."

"This isn't about you, Sidney."

"If you were serious about her, it would be different."

Everyone was so freaking sure he was going to hurt her. It was starting to piss him off. "What makes you so sure I'm not?"

"Years of experience," came the dry response.

He couldn't argue with his history. "If it's me you have a problem with, why is it Parvati you won't talk to?"

Sidney sighed. "Look, I hate it too, okay?

"So talk to her."

"You think she'd actually listen? I know I shouldn't have freaked about you two dating, but when I did she made her opinions very clear. Apparently, I've been disappointing her ever since I was picked to go on *Marrying Mister Perfect* instead of her."

He jolted to a stop at a red light. "That isn't fair."

"I'll talk to her, okay?"

"When?"

"We'll see each other at the bachelorette party this weekend."

"Will you? You might want to confirm that with her. She isn't sure you still want her there."

"Of course I do." Sidney went on before Max could argue his point. "I'll make sure she knows. I've just been dreading talking to her. I know I put my foot in my mouth, but I still think you're both being idiots and I'm afraid I'm going to make things worse by trying to make them better."

"I'm not going to hurt her, Sidney. That's the last thing I want."

"You don't have to set out to hurt someone for it to happen."

"Maybe you can give us the benefit of the doubt that we know what we're doing? And I'll call Dad for you again when I get home. He'll probably be waking up soon anyway."

"Thanks. And Max?"

"Yeah?"

"Please don't break her heart."

"I won't," he promised—and wondered if it was a promise he could keep. He didn't *want* to hurt her, but was he really capable of protecting her heart?

She was still out when he got home, dining with the newlyweds. Max tossed his keys in the dish and pulled out his phone, dialing the string of numbers for the call to Switzerland on his father's private line.

His father picked up immediately, startling him with the crisp, alert response so early in the morning. "*Halo*?"

"Dad. It's Max."

"Maximus. Your timing is excellent. I was just about to call you."

"You were?" Max could count on one hand the number of times his father had called him in the last five years.

"I have a proposition for you. An opportunity."

CHAPTER THIRTY-FOUR

Parvati came home to the sound of OneRepublic blasting from the master bedroom. "Max?"

She followed the sound, finding the bedroom empty, but the bed strewn with threadbare screen t-shirts, ratty cargo shorts, hiking boots, and a battered green backpack that looked like it had been around the world three times and dragged through at least six muddy rivers.

"Parv. Hey. I didn't hear you come home."

"I'm not surprised," she shouted over the music declaring *I lived* in a power anthem.

Max took the hint and turned the music down en route to the bed with another armful of clothing from his run-away-to-Thailand phase, his movements brisk.

"Are you going somewhere?"

"Hmm?" Max chucked a poncho that had long since ceased being waterproof onto a pile that looked to be trash and glanced at her, his expression barely shifting as his gaze traced her face. "Oh. No. I just hadn't looked at this stuff in a while. Spring cleaning."

"Uh huh." Except it didn't look like spring cleaning. It looked like Max was having some kind of nervous fit that somehow involved all of his old backpacking gear. "Are you okay?"

"Great. Talked to my father. Sidney wanted me to

confront him about his dickishness regarding her wedding."

"How'd that go?"

"He wants me to run Titacorp."

Parv blinked, thrown by the non sequitur. "What?"

"His company. Titacorp."

"I know what it is."

"Apparently his new wife has convinced him that his relationships with his children are broken and she doesn't want the same thing to happen to her kid, so she's insisting he retire—or at least cut back. She wants to patch up his relationship with me by bringing me on as his successor. And apparently she's also the reason he's been such a dick to Sidney. She encouraged him to be more 'parental' toward her—which he translated as going after her fiancé with a metaphorical shotgun. And he's insisting Sidney invite her to the wedding because she wants us all to be one happy family. Not sure how she sees my mother fitting into that picture." Max frowned at a broken belt as if it had personally offended him by cracking. "I'm not sure if she has him totally whipped or if I just never had the first idea who he was. Maybe both. I thought they'd have to pry his business from his cold dead hands. Queen Elizabeth seems less attached to the throne of England than he is to Titacorp."

"Do you want it?"

His chin jerked. "It never seemed like a possibility. The idea of wanting Titacorp is so foreign I can't even process it."

Which wasn't a no. And Titacorp was headquartered in Switzerland. Thousands of miles away.

"You already have a business," she reminded him.

"I know. That's what I told him." Max paused to study a hat, a slight grin tipping his lips before he tossed it onto the bed with the other items she assumed were part of the keeper pile. "He said he knows someone who has been wanting to buy out Elite Protection for a while. Some British company that specializes in political sector close protection in Europe and wants to expand into the celebrity side of things as well as the U.S. market. It could be a smart move. Always good to sell while you're hot. When you *need* to sell is when you're gonna get screwed."

"Why do you have to sell at all?"

He didn't answer, frowning at a perfectly good shirt and chucking it onto the trash pile with a grunt.

"Max?" He was obviously intrigued by the idea of selling Elite Protection—far too intrigued for Parvati's comfort. Had he even thought of her once as he wrestled with the decision? "Are you going to take over Titacorp?"

"No. The one thing I know is that I don't want to be my father. And as nice as the idea of being one big happy family is to my step-mother—who's younger than me, by the way—I don't live my life trying to make him proud anymore."

It sounded like he was lying to himself, but Parv kept her opinion to herself. "What are you going to do?"

"Just because I sell Elite Protection doesn't mean I have to work for him. I could just get away. There's nothing like the perspective you get when you're traveling. You never know yourself better than when you're outside your comfort zone. It's tempting. To just take off. Hit the reset button."

She didn't want the reset button. She liked where they were—but if she was the only one in this relationship who liked it, that wasn't worth much. It was obvious he wasn't taking her into account, which really

311

drove home the fact that they weren't a couple, no matter what they called themselves. He had one foot out the door—on a plane to Thailand.

"I'm always judged by him," Max said, his focus far away—and on the items he was sorting. "No one would have paid attention to the sale of my first business or really cared much about Elite Protection if not for who my father is. Forbes wouldn't have given a shit about me if not for my father, but Titus Dewitt's son gets a feature. And all anyone ever wants to say is how alike we are. How I'm a chip off the old block. But I never wanted that. I never wanted to be him—and here I keep turning into him anyway. All work. No balance."

"You're nothing like your father. You've built a family at Elite Protection—it's more than just a business."

He didn't seem to hear her. "For once it would be nice to be my own man, but I'm never going to escape the connection. Not unless I change my name and move to Guam."

"So you're going to Guam?"

He looked at her, finally seeming to see how his words were hitting her. "I'm not going anywhere."

"But you want to."

"Part of me is always going to want to, Parvati. That doesn't mean it's going to happen."

But he wanted it. And that scared the crap out of her. She was never going to be able to love him enough to make him want to stay.

Was Sidney right? Was she walking into a tornado with a stupid smile on her face?

"Running away doesn't solve anything—"

Max's head snapped toward her, with a frown darker than any other she'd seen on his face. "I'm not running.

That isn't what this is."

It was just what it looked like…

He shook his head, as if he'd heard the words she didn't say, and swiped up his gym bag from the chair beside the bed. "I'm gonna go workout."

And he said he wasn't running. "Max. Don't go. Talk to me."

He was already across the room. "I need to think."

Parvati watched him vanish out the door with a sense of ominous foreshadowing. Was this her future? Watching him disconnect and walk away?

Her phone buzzed and she fished it out—he couldn't be any farther than the bottom of the driveway, but she wanted it to be Max, just something silly to reassure her that they were still good. But instead the name on the screen was Sidney's.

I'm sorry. I hope you're still coming to my bachelorette party. It wouldn't be right without you.

Unexpected tears pressed against the backs of her eyes.

Thank God.

She needed her friend back. Her thumbs raced over the screen, composing her reply.

I'm sorry too. I wouldn't miss it for the world.

* * * * *

The bachelorette weekend festivities began on Thursday afternoon. All the local attendees were meeting at Once Upon a Bride where an SUV limo would pick them up to drive them down to Ensenada to meet up with the women flying in from across the country, since Tori was too far along to get on a plane.

Parvati was the first one there, her little roller bag

propped against her ankle as she waited in the small parking lot behind the shop. She hadn't worked today, Thursday being one of Madison's regular days, and as tempting as it was to peek inside to see how her former employee was liking Once Upon a Bride, she didn't want to disturb her while she was working.

And she was preoccupied anyway. Busy worrying about how things would go with Sidney and all of her new reality television friends. Busy worrying about Max.

She'd fallen asleep on the couch waiting for him the other night and woken up beside him in bed the next morning. She would have regretted that she'd missed him carrying her to the bedroom, if she hadn't been so worried about his sudden outbreak of wanderlust.

The backpacking gear had been nowhere in sight, all of it tucked back away into a far corner of his closet, and Max had rolled over and kissed her shoulder when his alarm went off and asked her if she wanted a quick omelet before work. As if nothing had happened. As if all her fears were just her own paranoia.

And maybe they were. But that didn't make them feel any less real.

"Well, I'll be damned. What's up, boss lady?"

Parvati turned at the familiar voice, a smile already tugging up her lips when she saw her former barista, her row of earrings glittering in the late afternoon sun. "Anna! What a great surprise. How've you been?"

"Can't complain." She raked a hand through her short hair, revealing a new tattoo on the underside of her arm. "That internship thing has been amazing. They've already offered me a job for when I graduate in two weeks."

"Oh my goodness, I forgot it's May. You're

graduating." She teared up like a proud parent and Anna just shrugged.

"The ceremony's on the fifteenth. It'd be cool if you came. It kinda sucked that we stopped hanging out after Common Grounds went down "

"It did suck. I've been hoping we'd bump into one another around town, but I guess without a job here you don't have any reason to come to Eden." Parv frowned. "What are you doing here?"

"I'm here to pick up Madison." She hooked a thumb toward the back door of Once Upon a Bride.

Parv blinked. "Madison?"

"She didn't tell you? We've been together for, I don't know, two months now?"

"Together. Like together together?" Though Parv didn't know another interpretation for the word. "I thought you weren't interested?"

"I wasn't. And I was kind of a dick about it. But she called me a few weeks after Common Grounds closed—right as the new term was beginning—and gave me this lecture about judging people, about how I was poisoning myself with my misconceptions about her, telling myself these stories about who she was until that was all I could see."

"And you started dating?"

"Nah, I was still a dick. But I kept hearing what she said over and over in my head. It was like she was haunting me. Then a couple months later, I bumped into her on campus and she was with another chick. Like hardcore sucking face 'with'. And my mind just exploded. That level of PDA went against everything I knew about her. She was breaking my preconceived notion of her and I was *pissed*. Which might have also had something to do with the fact that I have never been so jealous in my life as I was in that moment." Anna grinned, as if the memory of her jealous rage was a fond one. "I marched over there and started shouting at her in the middle of the student union. And she told me I was just jealous because I'd missed my shot at something amazing because I'd had my head too far up my ass to see it—and of course she was right, but I was too busy losing my shit to hear it. She walked off with that girl—I don't know why I expected her to break up with her on the spot because I was having a tantrum—but then two weeks later she texts me and asks if I'd like to get coffee. So we got coffee. And it was crazy. It was like we were two completely different people than I'd always thought we were. Our vibe was totally different. I don't know. I'd been so busy telling myself I knew who she was that I'd completely missed her. And when I finally saw her, everything changed. She told me she wasn't with that girl anymore and we've been seeing each other ever since."

"Wow. That's fantastic. I'm so happy for you." And she was, but she couldn't seem to stop thinking about Madison's words, as relayed through Anna. *Poisoning herself with her own misconceptions.* She could feel the echoes of those words in her own life, but couldn't quite put her finger on where.

"It's pretty great," Anna agreed. She hooked her thumb toward Once Upon a Bride again. "You going in?"

Parvati shook her head. "I'm going to wait out here. We're congregating for Sidney's bachelorette weekend."

"Right. Maddy mentioned that. T-minus nine days until the Wedding of the Century, huh?"

"Yeah." But it still didn't feel real. Sidney was getting married. And Parv was losing her.

316

"I should go let Maddy know I'm here." Anna gave her a hug and started toward the door. "Have fun on your trip. Don't do anything I wouldn't do."

"That definitely leaves room for going wild."

"Damn right it does." Anna grinned. "Good to see you, boss lady. Don't be such a stranger, okay?"

"I won't," Parvati promised—wondering if she would ever be as confident and self-composed as Anna. At twenty-two she seemed to have more figured out than Parv had managed with almost another decade of life experience.

Anna knew who she was. She knew what she wanted. And even when she was wrong—as she apparently had been about Madison—she grinned when she told the story, completely comfortable with her own mistakes.

If only Parv could be Anna when she grew up.

The back door to Once Upon a Bride opened again within a minute of Anna disappearing inside and Tori poked her head out. "There you are! Everyone's already here. Come inside, you're missing the kick-off toast."

Parvati gathered up her roller bag, feeling more nerves than excitement as she went to join the party, apparently already in progress.

CHAPTER THIRTY-FIVE

Of the eight women attending Sidney's bachelorette party, only two of them were flying down to meet them in Ensenada, so six of them climbed into the party limo for the five and a half hour drive to the resort—which turned into a nearly eight hour drive thanks to Victoria's baby pressing on her bladder at frequent intervals and the vagaries of Los Angeles traffic.

Parvati had heard Sidney talk about all the women before, but she hadn't actually met most of them—though she'd seen several on Sidney's season of *Marrying Mister Perfect*.

Elena was the notorious Bad Girl of the season—and the sexy Latina was just as outspoken and unrestrained as she'd seemed on television, visibly more relaxed than she'd been at the shower, speaking enthusiastically about her new anti-slut-shaming book and the charity organization she and another member of their group were establishing to help women facing sex tapes and vengeance porn.

Elena's partner in that endeavor was the former producer of *Marrying Mister Perfect* and current producer of *Once Upon a Bride*, Miranda Pierce—a frighteningly efficient woman with a way of looking at people like she was slicing away all their defenses and peering at the exposed core.

Another producer from *Once Upon a Bride*, Erica Yumata, had a loud voice and a laugh that seemed to echo inside the limo, the sound startling coming from such a tiny woman. She couldn't be more than five feet tall, but her personality rivaled Elena's for flamboyance and she shared Miranda's definitive way of declaring her opinions as if the idea of contradicting her was ludicrous.

Tori, Sidney and Parv rounded out the group in the limo since Caitlyn and Samantha—another two Suitorettes from *Marrying Mister Perfect*—would meet them in Mexico.

All in all, an intimidating group.

And it quickly became apparent that every single one of them was married or seriously seeing someone— except Erica, who definitively declared that she had zero desire to have a relationship and would have kicked out any lover who tried to trap her into one. The high-decibel, high-speed clatter of conversation centered almost entirely around husbands and boyfriends— which pretty much edged Parvati out of it, since she couldn't exactly gossip about Max's sexual prowess in front of Sidney, even if she'd been inclined to.

She sat quietly, sipping the pre-party margarita Elena had thrust at her, and felt like she was drowning in a sea of giant personalities. Maybe Max was right. Maybe she would have been lousy at *Marrying Mister Perfect*. There would have been a lot of limo rides like this one, with loudly chattering, confident women who made her feel small and insignificant.

Sidney was smiling—not joining in the conversation, but clearly comfortable in it. Caitlyn and Samantha had seemed more tame on television, and Parvati found herself hoping the two of them would tone things down when they were added to the mix—then she felt guilty for the wish. This was Sidney's bachelorette party. It was supposed to be a party. But Parv couldn't seem to get into the party spirit.

She kept thinking about what Anna had said.

Poisoning her own mind with bitterness. Had she been doing that?

She'd gotten into the habit of telling herself stories about how Sidney didn't care, didn't have time for her, dwelling on the evidence of friendly neglect, reinforcing the negative beliefs until her mental bitching became a self-fulfilling prophecy. She'd fallen into a pattern of self-pity, but Sidney hadn't been trying to hurt her. She'd just needed a little slack.

How differently would things have gone if Parvati had focused on the good rather than on her hurt feelings and the stories that validated her feeling of being wronged?

Sidney laughed with her new friends in the limo—but she wasn't trying to evict Parvati as her best friend. Parv was doing a good enough job of kicking herself out of the post by fixating on the distance between them rather than trying to cross it.

But deciding to focus on positivity didn't magically eliminate that distance. She still didn't know how to make things like they were before.

It was hours after dark when they arrived at the villa, but the exterior lighting illuminated the tropical landscaping and three story stucco house as they piled out of the limo in the driveway. The front door popped open and a woman Parvati recognized as Samantha rushed out to greet them.

"You're here! We have to wake Caitlyn up. She took a nap as soon as we realized we'd beat you. Apparently any second without the baby is a second she can be sleeping and she wasn't going to waste the opportunity."

The next few minutes were a rush of unloading, amid hugs of greeting and laughing inquiries whether the strippers had arrived yet.

Parvati stepped into the foyer of the gorgeous villa and felt a distinct sense of disorientation as everyone rushed past her to claim their rooms.

She and Sidney must have talked about her wedding a hundred times over the years. They'd always just assumed that Parv would be the maid of honor. And that she would plan the bachelorette party. They'd talked about what Sidney would and wouldn't want. Classy, but fun. Festive, but tasteful. No strippers, but definitely a spa trip.

This was exactly what Sidney had described— supersized to *Marrying Mister Perfect* proportions. The only thing missing was Parvati's role in it. She'd always thought she would be the one going early to make sure everything was set up. Hanging the decorations by hand. Picking out the novelty champagne flutes with little rings on the stems. But the resort's staff had done all that for them. Everything had been taken care of, flawlessly, and Parvati was unnecessary.

She caught herself starting to slide into that same poisonous bitterness and fished herself out again, slapping a smile on her face and heading off to find her room.

The only one left was the smallest, with no balcony and no private bathroom, but since Parvati hadn't been able to chip in as much as the others, she didn't mind the little closet of a room with a curtain rather than a door. She tossed her things onto the bed and returned to the villa's kitchen where everyone else was gathering and margaritas were already being poured.

Caitlyn had joined the group and was raising a glass in a toast to two-days without breastfeeding as she sipped her first drink in over a year. Everyone cooed over Tori's belly, asking about names for the baby girl who was due in just over three weeks. Elena admitted she and Adam had been considering trying for one of their own. Miranda declared that she'd had her tubes tied since she and Bennett were definitely *not* in the market for offspring. And Samantha declared she wouldn't be drinking this weekend—which set off another round of squeals.

Apparently it was very new and they weren't telling anyone yet, but the second-runner-up from Sidney's season was definitely glowing. And Parv could only drain her margarita as she was surrounded by happily-ever-afters in progress.

She probably should have taken things a little slower on the alcohol, considering she hadn't had much to eat when they stopped for dinner, but she found she had a sudden empathy for the girls who got rip-roaring drunk on the first night of *Marrying Mister Perfect*, when they were at a cocktail party surrounded by dozens of perfect women.

When she had a drink in her hand and a pleasant level of margarita sloshing in her stomach, it was so much easier to smile and pretend she wasn't freaking out about how she and Max would never be one of those sappy-happy couples.

Maybe that was why she was so jealous of the other women planning Sidney's bachelorette party. Because she needed it to be perfect for Sidney because she was living vicariously through her. Parvati had stopped believing she would ever have a bachelorette party and a marriage of her own.

Awfully young to be so jaded. She could almost hear Max's voice in her mind—which somehow only made things worse.

The others had excused themselves one by one earlier to go check in with their husbands and boyfriends. Nothing was stopping her from doing the same.

She just needed to hear his voice. To know that they were still together, for now, even if he had one foot out the door.

But when she stood on the balcony with the warm, salt breeze pressing against her skin, her phone bleeped a lack-of-service message, reminding her that she was in Mexico and her cut-rate plan didn't include foreign roaming.

Parvati pocketed her phone and leaned against the balcony, looking out toward an ocean she could hear but not see.

"Mind if I join you?"

Parv twisted toward the sound of Sidney's voice, hating the hesitation she'd helped put there. "I'm sorry."

Sidney's face screwed up. "What for?"

"For the last few months? Can it just be a blanket apology?"

Sidney rushed forward, all her hesitation gone. "I'm sorry too. I've been a total bridezilla. So completely focused on myself and what was going on with me that I completely failed you as a friend. When you said I was treating you like you weren't a priority anymore, you were totally right. I was horrible—"

"You weren't horrible. I should have given you a break—"

"I took you for granted. You've just always been

there so it didn't occur to me that I couldn't just ignore you until I had time to be a friend again. I didn't realize I was doing it, but when I look back now—"

"No. I should have cut you some slack. I was just so jealous."

"It isn't all sunshine and roses over here," Sidney insisted. "I've been freaking out nonstop. You'd think that I'd be good at this, that I'd be calm and collected because I've seen this a hundred times before, but all I can think about is how everyone is going to be watching this wedding because of who Josh and I are. Because we've built a brand around being the best at weddings *everyone* is going to judge us. I keep having these awful anxiety dreams about the show being canceled and Once Upon a Bride going under because one of my centerpieces doesn't match."

"It's going to be great—whether the centerpieces match or not."

"I know. Because I'm marrying Josh and *that's* the dream, not the centerpieces. I've said those words to a thousand brides, but I never realized how completely inadequate they are to stem the panic."

Parvati offered her glass to Sidney. "Margarita? I hear they're pretty good for panic too."

Sidney laughed briefly. "If only I could just be buzzed for the next two weeks."

"Who says you can't?"

Sidney stared out over the blackness where the water would be in the morning. "The brides I work with on the show—they've all been through hell. Some of them have this incredible perspective, this ability to not sweat the small stuff, because, hey, they beat cancer, right? But others get so wound up making the moment perfect, because they *need* it to be perfect as a reward for all the shit they went through, that it can be hard to get them to enjoy their own wedding."

"What do you tell them when they're freaking out?"

"That they deserve the happiest day of their lives—and that no one will care if the centerpieces are perfect if they're happy." Sidney swallowed hard, her mouth pinching.

"Hey," Parv slid her arm around Sidney. "You deserve it too. You deserve a happily ever after as much as anyone."

"Do I? People keep asking us when we're going to have kids. I feel like I just found Josh and everyone is rushing us toward being a family unit. And then I see Caitlyn—who looks like she hasn't slept in a month—and all I can think is that I'm *so tired* all the time and that's without children. I'm just trying to have a job and plan a wedding. That's it. And I want to lie down and sleep for a year. How can people even think I would want a kid right now?" She gripped the rail in a white-knuckle grasp. "I mean, I've always wanted kids in a sort of theoretical way. I just sort of assumed that it would happen. Eventually. But now that eventually is now, I kind of want to run screaming in the other direction."

"You don't have to—"

"Josh wants them. He thinks once the wedding pressure is over I'll be ready. But what if I'm never ready? Or what if I get pregnant and blow up like a balloon and he leaves me?"

Suddenly a lot of things made sense. Sidney had been bigger when she was younger. She'd lost a ton of weight in college, but the fear that she wasn't good enough if she wasn't skinny had stuck around. "Josh loves *you*. He isn't going to leave you."

"You can't guarantee that. No one can. What if I suck at marriage? I haven't exactly had good examples. My parents just got divorced and I'm not sure either of them would have noticed if my father hadn't decided that his mid-life crisis was going to come with a new wife younger than me and a baby."

"You aren't going to suck at marriage. You and Josh will figure it out. You're smart. You're compassionate. You love each other. You can do this."

"Can I? Because I'm a little amazed he hasn't left me already with the way I've become a complete basket case leading up to this wedding. I don't know how anyone does it. Everyone should elope."

"That might have a negative impact on your business."

"It feels like my life has become a freight train and I'm just strapped to the front, trying to hang on and avoid getting crushed on the rails. They say it's all about the bride, but that's bullshit. It's about everyone else driving the bride toward insanity one choice at a time. One of Josh's friends changes his mind about bringing a date after he RSVPs no and *I'm* the bad guy because the seating chart was already finalized. So I do backflips to rearrange *everything* and then he changes his mind again. And I start to hate Josh's friends before I even meet all of them because they are making my life suck when it's supposed to be the happiest day of my freaking life."

"Can I help?"

"Can you make me a version of the seating chart where I get to seat my father's new bride at the kids' table?"

Parvati snorted. "That might not go over so well."

"No. But it's a nice fantasy." Sidney sighed, tipping

her head back to take in the stars. "I never realized how much I relied on the status quo in my family until everything changed. I think I hate change. I never knew that about myself. It just feels like everything's happening at once and I can't catch my breath. My parents are divorced, I have to have the perfect wedding or I'll destroy my career and Josh's, everyone wants me to have a baby...all of it. It's just so much."

"I'm sorry I made it worse by getting mad at you."

"No. You didn't," Sidney insisted. "You were right to call me out. I just hate to think of you getting hurt and we both know Max isn't a good bet."

Parv gripped her margarita glass more tightly. Sidney wasn't wrong. She knew better than to get carried away thinking of Max in terms of forever. And she wanted forever. But it was so hard to walk away from someone you loved. And she did love him. More every day.

"I told myself I wouldn't get in too deep," she admitted. "That I wouldn't get hurt because I knew what I was doing. Famous last words."

Sidney's shoulder bumped hers gently. "I thought you two were doing okay?"

"That's what I keep telling myself. Then yesterday I'm listening to the radio in my car and *Angel of the Morning* comes on and suddenly I'm bawling at a stoplight. Then when I turn on my car to drive home, *Sometimes Love Just Ain't Enough* is playing. And when I change the channel I get *I Can't Make You Love Me*. It was like my fears were stalking me through my radio."

"Maybe you should stop listening to the radio."

"I did. And I'm still scared." Parv angled a look at Sidney's profile. "And I felt like I couldn't admit that before because you would just say you told me so. I'm scared you're right. That I'm just setting myself up for a broken heart. That I need to stop living in fantasyland and accept reality."

"Did something happen?"

"He'd probably say no. The other night he freaked out about something your dad said and before I knew it he was planning a trip around the world—then he goes to the gym, just walks out, and when he came back it was like it had never happened, but I've been nervous ever since and he's been different. Distracted. Like half of him is already gone. He says he's my boyfriend, but he told me himself that part of him would always want to run away. How is that not supposed to mess with my mind?"

"I'm not sure I've ever really understood why Max does what he does, but I do think he cares about you."

"I know." She'd never doubted that. But she wanted what Sidney had. A man who wanted to spend his life with her. Telling Sidney had made it real—and exposed all the cracks she'd wanted to ignore. "I just wish that were enough."

"Maybe it will be." But she didn't sound like she believed her own words and if Sidney, who knew them both so well, didn't think they would make it…

Parv couldn't escape the thought that maybe she was fooling herself. Maybe this had all been a dream and it was time to wake up and acknowledge the writing on the wall.

CHAPTER THIRTY-SIX

He missed her.

Max had started looking at this weekend as a preview of what his life would be like when he lost Parvati—because he was starting to feel like it was an inevitable certainty that he would lose her. When enough people told you that you were constitutionally incapable of commitment, it was hard to ignore all those voices.

He went into the office on Saturday for the first time in weeks. He'd worked from home a few Saturdays while Parvati was putting in hours at Lacey's Cakes or Once Upon a Bride, but he'd gotten out of the habit of spending seven days a week practically living at EP.

He arrived just as Candy and Dylan were finishing up one of the new Elite Self Defense classes. The class series hadn't been as popular as he'd anticipated and Max felt a flicker of guilt that perhaps he hadn't done enough to promote the new feature. Too preoccupied with Parvati.

Was this why his father wanted to retire? Were Dewitt men all or nothing when it came to business or relationships? Was one of the two bound to suffer?

Maybe he should sell. Maybe that was the only way he would be able to keep Parv.

He waited until the class was over, observing Dylan's

329

easy rapport with the students and Candy's smug grin every time she got to throw him to the mat—a grin that was mirrored on a couple of the actresses' faces when they succeeded in mimicking the move.

They were good teachers. Confident. In their element. And either one of them would be capable of taking over the administrative side if he decided not to stay on after he sold. Elite Protection would be fine, whatever he decided.

"Hey, Boss." Candy joined him when the class ended and the actresses filed out—several pausing to flutter their extended lashes at Dylan, though he didn't seem to notice the attention. "Coming by to check up on us?"

Adam Dylan joined them as the last actress wandered out to the secure parking lot. "He's bored because Parvati is off at Sidney's bachelorette weekend."

"Ah." Candy nodded as if that explained everything.

"I forgot Elena was going too." Adam's wife was one of Sidney's closest friends from her season of *Marrying Mister Perfect*—which explained why the bodyguard hadn't bitched about being double scheduled this weekend. "How's she doing?"

"Still determined to conquer the world. She's doing a lot of press for her book now—when she isn't auditioning."

"Do you think she'd be willing to mention the self defense classes in some of that press? I was just thinking we could use some more word of mouth."

Dylan snorted. "She'd probably love to. I've never seen anyone train as hard as she does. She's determined to get her black belt by the end of the year and claims she won't be satisfied until she can kick my ass. Her new mission is to make the women of America badass, so I'm sure she'd love to pimp the classes."

"Good. That'll be good."

Candy frowned, reading something on his face. "Is everything okay, Boss? We don't *need* the classes to be a success, do we? I thought we were doing well."

"We are. Busier than ever. I only want to make sure everything's taken care of. That you guys would be good if I wasn't here anymore."

Candy shot him a stricken look. "Are you dying?"

"No. God, nothing like that. I just got an offer to sell and it's a good offer, so I'm considering all the options. Trying to figure out what would be best for EP."

Dylan stared at him, hard and expressionless—but then he never revealed much when he didn't want to. "Are you serious?"

"It's worth considering."

"None of us will stay," Candy declared.

"It wouldn't change anything—"

"Would you stay on to run things?" she demanded.

"Maybe. Probably not," Max admitted.

Candy glared at him. "Then it would change things. It would change everything."

"None of you would lose your jobs. And if you wanted to move on, you'd be able to write your own ticket—"

"That isn't the point," Candy snapped. "But if you really think this is just a job, maybe you should sell."

Max frowned after her as she stalked away, disappearing up the stairs. "What was that?"

Dylan looked at him like he was particularly dim. "Do you remember when I first came to work here? How guarded I was because my team at the Secret Service had thrown me under the bus? How I didn't want to ask for help from anyone?"

"I do. You've changed a lot."

"I know. And a lot of that was Elena, but a lot of it was you, Max. When Elena was in trouble, you bent over backwards to help us. Who else would have done that? What other boss would piss off a powerful client like Hank the Hammer just because he was looking at Candy wrong? Who else would look out for us? Or give Elia a chance? You take us in when other people throw us out and you make us feel elite, so we're elite for you. But do you really think this place would be the same if you sold it and walked away? You *are* Elite Protection. Do you really think nothing would change?"

Of all his bodyguards, Adam Dylan was the least likely to speak, but when he did Max had found it was smart to listen. Now he stared after him as he jerked a goodbye nod and wandered over to put away the mats they'd used in the class. Was Adam right? Was he Elite Protection? He'd always seen himself as the boss, running the show but undeniably replaceable.

He'd objected when Parvati called him an island—but he had thought of himself that way. No connections. But had the connections been there all the time and he'd never seen them? Connections to his employees. To Sidney.

To Parvati.

Maybe he could do forever. Maybe Perfect Parker was full of shit and he *was* good enough for her.

Maybe this was what being part of something felt like—not ensnared or tied up, but comfortable with the knowledge that he had a place. A role. Boss. Brother. Lover. Friend.

Maybe he wasn't his father's son after all.

* * * * *

When the party limo dropped them off at Once Upon a Bride on Sunday evening, Parvati hugged each of the women in turn, a little sad that the weekend was over already. After that first rocky night, she'd discovered she had more in common with them than she'd suspected. When she'd stopped focusing on all the things they had that she didn't—like men who actually wanted to spend the rest of their lives with them—they'd bonded over Cards Against Humanity and kamikaze shooters.

Now, as Parvati drove toward Max's place, she found herself strangely reluctant to go.

What if he wasn't there? What if—while she'd been agonizing over how hard it would be to break up with him, even though she knew it was the right thing to do—he'd been packing a bag and booking a flight to Bangkok?

She didn't know if he was going to be there when she got to the house. If she stayed with him, would she always have that feeling when she came home from a trip? Or if he was a little late coming home from work? She couldn't *make* him want the same things she wanted, and as long as he didn't, she'd always wonder when the other shoe was going to drop.

She didn't want that.

But she couldn't break up with him before the wedding. She wouldn't do that to Sidney.

But neither could she go home and pretend everything was the same.

She kept going, past the turn-off to Max's house, all the way to Santa Barbara, until she landed on Angie's doorstep. She listened through the door to the stately chime of the doorbell and for the familiar sound of her sister's heels clacking over the marble tiles in the foyer. The sound was so Angie—pearls and heels even in her own home on a Sunday night. It had always sounded like perfection to Parvati before, but maybe that was more of the poisoning her own mind that Anna had mentioned.

She'd spent her childhood—hell, her entire life—trying to be good enough for her family. It had made her into the pleaser she was—the one who had almost convinced herself to stay with Perfect-on-Paper Parker. She didn't know how to be around her sisters without feeling like she needed to be doing everything she could to earn their affection—but was that them? Or was it her? She'd always worried that she wasn't good enough and tried to please everyone so no one would notice, but in the last few years the weight of that had gotten too heavy and she'd started to resent it. And the only thing she could think of to get herself to stop feeling bitter about trying to earn their love all the time was to just be honest, like Anna had been, even when it didn't paint her in a particularly flattering light.

The door opened without a squeak. "Parvati." Surprise coated her sister's voice.

"Hey, Angie. Can we talk?"

Angie looked startled by the request, but she only hesitated a moment before opening the door all the way. "Of course."

She led the way into the front sitting room, waving Parvati to one of the designer love seats before perching on the edge of an armchair. "Can I get you anything to drink? Tea? Coffee?"

"No. I'm good. Thanks." Parvati twisted her hands in her lap, suddenly wondering if this was such a good idea after all. She'd wanted to do something to shake up the pattern she'd fallen into with Angie, but what if they just couldn't change? What if the old awkwardness was too ingrained? "I have a favor to ask, actually. I was wondering if I could stay here next week."

Angie blinked. "Oh."

"I'm going to need a new apartment," Parvati explained. "I'm going to ask Mom and Dad to cosign with me, since I'm pretty broke right now—Common Grounds pretty much drained all my savings before it went under."

Angie's eyes widened and she repeated, "Oh."

"Yeah. Turns out I pretty much suck at business. Who knew? Well. I knew. But I tried to hide it from everyone else. It felt too much like admitting I was the defective daughter. The one who couldn't be successful. But I want you guys to know *me*. Not the person I'm trying to pretend to be. So I'm going with honesty. And the honest truth is I need someplace to stay next week because I'm going to break up with the man I love and I can't live in his house anymore after I do."

Angie blinked and this time Parvati was tempted to say it with her, "Oh."

"So can I stay here?"

Angie paused a beat, the moment stretching before she shook herself and her businesslike approach fell back into place. "Of course. You can have Katie's room. What are you going to do?"

"The same thing I've been doing, actually. I'll just be living somewhere else."

Angie frowned and Parvati tried not to shrink in the face of the judgment that kindled in her eyes. "Is that really what you want? Icing cakes and answering phones forever? If you need help starting a new business, Kevin and I could—"

"No. I don't want help. And yes. That is what I really want. I think maybe my definition of success isn't going to be about achievement. I'm still figuring out what it is, but I think what really matters to me are the people in my life. So my friends and loved ones being able to depend on me will be my success. I think I want to be *that* girl. And maybe I'll always be a little broke, but I think I won't mind that so much as long as I know what really matters to me. My friends. And you guys."

Angie pursed her lips for a long moment and Parvati braced herself, but the words, when they came, were the last ones she'd expected. "I wish I could be more like you."

"Seriously?"

"You wouldn't believe how many times Katie yelled at me when we were planning her wedding. All I could think about was how it had to be perfect and be what people expected, but Katie would have been happy going to City Hall."

"No, she wouldn't. She wanted the big wedding too."

"I guess. I just wish I'd worried less about what people thought."

"I worry about that too," Parv confessed. "Why do you think I hid the fact that my business was failing for years? I didn't want you guys to think I was the loser sister who couldn't live up to the Jai family name."

"Are you kidding? Everyone loves you. They think I'm a bossy annoying bitch."

"Well, you are bossy."

Angie glared at her. "Shut up. Brat."

Parvati grinned, her sister matching it before she sobered. "So you're in love?"

Parv groaned. "With Max."

"Devi ratted you out after Katie's wedding."

"Yeah. I thought she might."

"And you're ending it?"

Parv was impressed that Angie didn't call her an idiot. She just implied it with her tone.

"He doesn't do commitment. He's my best friend and I'm head over heels for him, but if I stayed I would always be wondering when he was going to get bored, sell everything and run off to Asia for a year."

Angie nodded, but her expression stayed guarded.

"What?" Parvati prompted—not quite snapping, though it was a close call.

"What if he doesn't?"

"*You're* telling me to make a decision with my heart instead of my head? Are you feeling okay?"

"I don't know. Sometimes people surprise you. I never would have predicted that you would come here and tell me anything about your life, let alone ask for help and advice."

"I didn't technically ask for advice."

Angie shrugged. "You're getting it anyway. I'm your big sister. It's my job to steer you."

"I'm not a horse."

"No, you're a mule. Stubborn as one. I'm just saying maybe you should give this guy a chance. I would have known you were nuts about him even if Asha hadn't told me. I've never seen you look at anyone the way you look at him."

"Which is why it's going to kill me when he walks away."

"And if he wouldn't?"

"That's easy for you to say. You've been married for twenty years."

"You think being married for twenty years means I always know he loves me? You think I never wonder if he's going to decide I'm too much of a pain in the ass and finally come to his senses and leave me?"

"Angie. Kevin's crazy about you."

"I know. And I wonder every day how that happened. Who made a mistake and made someone that great fall for someone as anal and high strung as me? I constantly nag at him and I see myself doing it and I *can't stop*. I just can't. Does it matter if he leaves dirty socks underneath the couch? No. Do I want to kill him when he does it no matter how many times I ask him to be a civilized human being and put them in the goddamn hamper? So much. Marriage isn't easy, Parv. It isn't a guarantee. Do you know how much I envy you sometimes? That you got to spend your twenties without anyone hanging off you with snot running down their nose asking when dinner was?"

"I always thought your life was perfect."

"Everyone's life is perfect from the outside." She waved around her flawless sitting room. "Welcome to imperfection."

Parvati looked from the curtains to the perfectly coordinated rug. "I think I like imperfection better." She met her sister's eyes. "It's nice to meet you, Angie."

Her sister smiled. "Nice to meet you, Parv."

* * * * *

Max called as she was driving home.

"Hey. Where are you? I thought you guys were getting in hours ago."

"We were. We did, actually. Sorry. I should have called. I went to go see Angie."

"In Santa Barbara?"

"Yeah. I'm on my way back now. Will you still be awake in half an hour?"

"I haven't seen you in days. I wasn't planning to sleep anytime soon."

"Good." Because neither was she. They had an expiration date now. After the wedding, she was going to end things. But between now and then she was going to live every second like it was their last.

Because all too soon, it would be.

CHAPTER THIRTY-SEVEN

It was a horrible day for a wedding.

The wind started at dawn, blowing over the decorations that had already been set up. The first rain shower came through around mid-morning, drenching everything that hadn't been blown loose.

Sidney had been in dictator mode all week, directing the last minute preparations with an iron fist and a barely concealed note of panic in her voice, so Parvati braced herself to witness full-on Bridezilla when she arrived at the resort where the wedding was being held on Saturday morning to get ready. But when she walked into the suite where the bridal party was gathering, she found Sidney gazing out the window at the torrential downpour with a serene expression.

Parv would have suspected Tori had slipped her a valium, but Tori was watching Sidney like a zookeeper watching a feral tiger who just happened to be sleeping peacefully. Parvati set down the bag with her bridesmaid dress and shoes and crept over to stand beside Tori, careful not to draw the attention of the tiger.

"How is she?" she whispered.

"She seems good," Tori murmured back, a note of wonder in her voice. "One of the floral arrangements flew across the back lawn like a javelin and stabbed into the side of the tent protecting the altar and she actually laughed."

Not the reaction Parvati would have expected from the Wedding Martinet, but Sidney was actually smiling as she gazed out at the freak storm. She tried a careful, "Hey, Sid."

Sidney turned away from the window with a grin. "Hi, Parv. Isn't it wonderful?"

"Wonderful?"

Sidney beamed. "We're going to the rain plan—which is perfectly lovely in its own way—but everyone knew we were planning it outdoors, so instead of me worrying about everyone judging every single one of my choices, everyone is going to be marveling at this crazy storm and how prepared we were that we had a complete back-up plan for rain even though it's Eden and it almost never rains like this. It's like God wanted me to relax on my wedding day so he sent a flood."

Parv wasn't going to argue with that. Her main wish for Sidney today was that she was actually able to relax enough to enjoy her own wedding. If the storm could do that, more power to it.

As if to emphasize the point, the wind rattled the window panes and Sidney giggled. "Come on. Time for manicures."

The pampering ritual took hours. Mani-pedis, hair, makeup. By the time they were all primped, powdered, and dressed there was only an hour until the guests were scheduled to begin arriving, just enough time for a few bridal-party-only pictures. Parvati found herself wondering if the elaborate grooming rituals were designed to keep the bride so busy she couldn't freak out. It echoed the henna rituals in Indian ceremonies—did every culture have a way to distract the bride before the big moment?

Then Sidney was in her dress—a gorgeous fit and flare with a long train for Parvati to maneuver, since Tori couldn't bend down far enough to help adjust it—and Max was there in his charcoal tails, looking entirely too handsome as he got ready to walk Sidney down the aisle, and suddenly everything was moving at warp speed.

She blinked and the processional music was starting.

A heartbeat later Max was handing Sidney over to Josh.

They were saying their vows and there wasn't a dry eye in the house when Sidney choked up on hers—but Parv didn't cry, she felt like she didn't have time. The moment was already past her.

The recessional. More pictures. Dinner. Toasts—she'd rehearsed hers, and the words all came out in the right order, but that feeling refused to go away, like the evening was rushing past her and she couldn't get a grip on any single moment.

Then they were dancing—the first dance, *Shout* and *YMCA, As Time Goes By* and *At Last*. Max was there, pulling her onto the floor, as smooth as silk—

And suddenly the world slowed down. His hand in hers, the swell of violins, the shuffle of feet across the dance floor, the muscle of his shoulder beneath her palm…the moment stretched out and she wanted to hold onto it, terrified of letting it go.

"You didn't cry at this one," Max commented as they swayed. "I had my pocket square all ready, but you didn't even sniffle."

"I guess I've changed," she replied, realizing the truth in the words. She felt different somehow. More mature. Like all her dreams of the perfect man and the perfect relationship were finally ready to cede to reality.

"And here I thought you'd always be a romantic."

"I am. But maybe I'm a more realistic one now."

She'd focused on the wedding for the last week, putting everything but Sidney out of her mind. It had been easy to do—there had been a million details to see to—but maybe it was time to face reality now.

The reality that she needed to break up with Max if she was ever going to find the kind of love she wanted.

She needed to move on with her life. With someone who would let her be his partner.

She looked up at his perfect face. "Can I talk to you for a minute?"

His eyebrows arched. "Of course."

Parvati stopped dancing, catching Max's hand and tugging him off the dance floor and toward the balcony before she remembered the storm outside and changed direction toward the stairs up to the interior balcony looking over the rest of the ballroom.

The cake had already been cut. The reception was officially winding down. She didn't have any more excuses for putting it off—and she needed to get out of the habit of putting off the big things when she knew they were coming. She needed to end it now.

* * * * *

Max half-jogged to keep up with Parvati, biting back a grin until he realized they weren't sneaking off for illicit coatroom sex. She pulled him up the stairs and halfway around the balcony until they were able to look down on the reception below, but the music wasn't so loud that they couldn't talk easily.

"What's up?" he asked when she dropped his hand and pivoted to face him, something oddly tight about her expression. "You okay?"

"I know I said I wasn't expecting forever, but I deserve forever. I deserve someone who wants it as badly as I do."

The world slid sideways for half a moment before it stabilized—and when it did everything had shifted into an alignment more perfect than he could have predicted. They couldn't be more on the same page. "I couldn't agree more."

For the last few days all he'd been able to think about was forever—and how he wanted Parvati in his, no matter what it took. All day people had been repeatedly asking him when it was going to be his turn, when he was finally going to settle down, and he'd had to bite back the urge to tell them all he was ready now. He could get married tomorrow.

He'd been at weddings before where people asked him when he was going to get married—they seemed to love asking single men that question—and he'd always joked that guys like him didn't get romantic at weddings, but now…with Parvati…

He kept wanting to propose. He'd bought a little something on Wednesday when Sidney had asked him to pick up the wedding bands for her at the jeweler.

The ring had been too perfect to pass up. Delicate white gold curls around a brilliant stone. It was Parvati's ring. He'd known as soon as he saw it in the display case. So he bought it and figured he would just hold onto it for a few months until they were ready for that. He didn't have it in his pocket—which was possibly the only thing keeping him from dropping to one knee. But it was locked in the glove compartment of his car. It would only take him a minute to get it.

He probably would have proposed already, right

there in the middle of the dance floor, if he hadn't been trying to avoid stealing Sidney's thunder on her wedding day. But this was perfect. Private, but still a place and a moment they would remember forever.

"I know I'm changing the rules," Parvati went on as if she hadn't heard him. "I know that isn't fair. I never want to ask you to change. I don't think that's what love is."

"I don't want that either." He didn't want to change a thing about her.

Parvati nodded, as if some conclusion had been reached. "Okay. So I guess that's it. We're breaking up."

"Exact—Wait. What?" Max backtracked through the conversation, trying to figure out what had just happened. "That wasn't what I was talking about."

"I know things are good between us, but we want different things and ultimately isn't it better to break up now rather than wait until we're both even more invested?"

"Who says we have to break up at all?" He'd been planning to propose. It hadn't occurred to him that she wouldn't say yes, let alone that she'd been planning their break-up.

Parvati's face closed off. "Max."

"What?"

"You didn't talk to me when you got the offer to buy out Elite Protection."

What the fuck did that have to do with anything? "I told you about it. I told you right away."

"Yeah. Right after you started doing inventory in case you wanted to escape. But did you even think to ask what I thought? Or consider what you leaving would mean to me?"

What was happening? How had this conversation

gone so far off the rails? "You'd come with me. You'd love Thailand."

"You didn't invite me, Max. You didn't ask. You just went off to think and then came back as if nothing had happened. What was I supposed to think?"

"Okay, I screwed up. One time." That hadn't been his finest moment, but he was new to this relationship thing. Wasn't he allowed to have a learning curve?

"One time." She breathed out a soft, disbelieving laugh. "Do you remember Katie's engagement party?"

"You think I forgot the first time we kissed?"

Her smile turned sharp. "Well, you did pretend it didn't happen for weeks afterward, but that wasn't my point."

"Fine. What's the point?" And what the hell did it have to do with this?

"Why didn't you tell Sidney you were going to the party with me?"

"What?" He was supposed to remember what he'd said to Sidney in *November*? "I don't know. That was months ago."

Parvati folded her arms—less like a pissy girlfriend and more like a woman holding herself together. "Sidney invited you to dinner with her and Josh and you said you couldn't go, but you wouldn't tell her why. Why didn't you just tell her you were with me?"

"I don't know. And I can't imagine why it matters. We weren't even dating yet."

"You keep people at a distance, Max," she insisted.

"She didn't need to know where I was. I can't believe you're bringing this up now." How long had she been holding onto this, waiting to bring it up when they were fighting? It was such a freaking relationship cliché.

"But why not tell her?"

"I wasn't ashamed of being with you, if that's what you're trying to imply."

She shook her head. "I wondered at the time, but now I think it's just habit for you. You don't explain yourself to anyone. If you don't tell her *why* you're missing dinner with her, she can't argue with you. You don't have to justify anything. You don't have to make yourself vulnerable in front of anyone or let them really know you or have a say in your life. You're an island."

"Stop saying that. I'm not an island."

"No? Then who are you responsible to? Not responsible for, but responsible *to*. Who do you explain yourself to? Who really knows you? Because I don't think it's me, and I can't be an afterthought. I just can't, Max."

"You aren't an afterthought. How can you think that? *You* know me. I explain myself to you."

"Do you? When?"

He knew there were examples. A thousand examples. A million. But he couldn't think of one. A hive of angry bees were taking up all the space in his brain. "I don't know, but I'm not an island. I'm not unreliable or isolated. How can you not see that? How can you think that I'm pushing you away? Because I'm not the one running this time, Parv. I'm not the one who's scared."

She shook her head again, backing away. "I'm sorry, Max. Maybe I am scared. I love you. I really do. But I can't do this anymore."

"Parvati." He hadn't been prepared for her to bolt. She didn't run away from the tough stuff. She hung on—sometimes for months after she knew something was a lost cause, but she was already ten yards away now. Fleeing down the steps. Running. "Parvati!"

His shout got lost in the sound of Beyonce's "Single

Ladies" blaring through the ballroom. She didn't stop. Not when she reached the bottom of the steps and had to shove her way through a knot of women gathered there. Not even when the bouquet came flying through the air and smacked her in the face.

"Parvati!" Max chased after her, jogging down the steps as she caught the flowers against her face and forced a smile for the cameras. He was still too far away to see the real expression in her eyes as she ducked through the spectators gathered along the edge of the dance floor and rushed toward the side door.

She was leaving him.

No.

The reaction was visceral. Primitive. The most basic part of him objecting to losing her.

She was wrong. He wasn't an island. He was a freaking peninsula and she was his connection to the rest of the world. He *needed* her. And he needed her to see that need.

If she wanted to walk away after that, fine—well, not fine, but he would make himself let her go if that was what she really wanted, but he wasn't giving up without a fight.

"Max! You're single, buddy. Get your ass over there."

Max shook off someone trying to herd him toward the cluster of men waiting for the garter toss and cut through the crowd. She'd been moving toward the west doors—

"Maximus! Just the man I was looking for."

"Sorry, Dad. Not a good time." He started to weave around, but his father blocked his path.

"Nonsense. You have five minutes for your father. Especially when I'm about to be your new boss."

"Not now, I don't." He tried to dodge again, but his father grabbed his arm and he whirled, shaking off the grip, fists clenched. "What? What is so fucking important?"

Titus puffed up, swollen with his own importance. "There's no need to take that tone—"

"You don't even have anything to talk to me about, do you? You just want to pat yourself on the back for your fucking *legacy*, regardless of what I want. But that isn't going to happen. You don't get to dictate my life. You aren't the boss here. And you aren't going to be mine. I'm not coming to work at Titacorp and I'm not selling Elite Protection."

His father's mouth tightened, unaccustomed to the sour taste of rejection. "Don't be ridiculous. The timing is perfect—"

"I don't care. It's more than just a business to me. I've built something pretty damn amazing and I'm going to continue to grow it."

To his father's credit, he adjusted quickly. His demeanor took a one-eighty and he clapped Max on the shoulder, nodding proudly as if Max keeping Elite Protection had been his idea. "Good for you. You always were just like me."

"No," Max shrugged off his hand. "I'm not. For years I wanted to be. I was so messed up by being the great Titus Dewitt's kid—always pushing for more, trying to be the best, trying to be enough, never satisfied, never happy, so fucking caught up with success that I almost missed seeing what I'd created in Elite Protection. A family. Which is something you know nothing about."

Indignation made Titus seem to inflate. "That isn't fair. I'm still your father."

"You are. The only one I'll ever have. And we both

have to live with that." Suddenly Parvati's words echoed in his mind. *You aren't accountable to anyone.* "Why didn't you tell us your mistress was pregnant? Why didn't you let us know you were getting married? Why let your children find out from a tabloid?"

"I wanted to tell you after the divorce was final—I didn't want you hating Claudine, thinking she had broken your mother and I up, so I chose to wait. Claudine argued for telling you, but I thought it was better to keep the divorce and my new marriage separate, so you wouldn't apply your emotions about one to the other. But then when I came out to tell you, you didn't join Sidney and me for dinner. So I decided the time wasn't right."

"And after that?"

He shrugged. "The time wasn't right. I still think Sidney is overreacting. Refusing to let me walk my own daughter down the aisle—"

"You told her she shouldn't marry Josh."

"She could do so much better. He's insubstantial. And she's a Dewitt. Though lately she seems determined to become a Kardashian."

Max shook his head. "You don't know us at all, do you? But why would you? You're an island."

He started to push past his father, determined to track down Parvati, but his father caught his shoulder. "Max. Please. Claudine wants us to have a relationship. It's important to her."

"Yeah, well. We wanted a father who gave a shit for the first thirty years of our lives. We can't always get what we want."

Later he might relent, but right now Max wove through the crowd, moving quickly, looking for Parvati, though he couldn't stop thinking about the conversation with his father and the disconnect between who he was and what people seemed to see when they looked at him.

His father saw a chip off the old block. Parvati saw someone who would never commit. He knew he'd done a lot to perpetuate those ideas of who he was, but he wasn't that guy anymore. But could he ever overcome those ideas of him? His father might be a lost cause, but how could he make Parvati see him differently? See him as a man who could be her forever?

He found the bride and groom before he found the love of his life.

"Max!" Sidney flung her arms around him in a rustle of tulle. "How's the best big brother on the planet?"

He wasn't sure if she was drunk or just that happy, but he didn't want to burst her bubble so he kept his answer vague. "I'm actually looking for Parvati. Have you seen her?"

"Not since she caught the bouquet with her face." Sidney's dizzy-happy expression faded into concern. "Is everything okay?"

His instinct was to say yes, everything was fine, and solve the problem on his own—but he wasn't his father, damn it. And it was time for him to prove it.

"Actually, I could use your help."

CHAPTER THIRTY-EIGHT

Running out of a wedding reception into the rain, carrying a bouquet and sobbing, she'd probably terrified the parking attendant, but by that point Parvati had given up on any pretext of dignity or caring what other people thought of her.

When they delivered her car, she managed to keep it together long enough to get out of the parking lot before pulling over less than a mile down the road to bawl.

Breaking up with Max was nothing like breaking up with Parker had been.

She was wrecked. Destroyed.

Max had teased her about not crying at Sidney's wedding? Well she was crying now, damn it.

The second thoughts began almost immediately.

Had she ever given him the benefit of the doubt? Or had the stories she told herself about him been designed to remind her that he couldn't commit? Had she ever really committed to the idea of them either? Or had she always had one foot out the door because she was afraid he was the same way? Had her fears been a self-fulfilling prophecy? Was that fair to him? Had she been too guarded with her heart? Had she made a huge mistake?

She hadn't even said goodbye to Sidney, running out the side door. The happy couple would be headed off to their honeymoon by now. Would Sidney wonder why

Parv wasn't there to wave them off? She would never get that moment back—but right now all she could think of was Max and the way he'd looked at her when she'd told him it was over.

She made it to Angie's house in one piece, but was still such a basket case when she got there that her sister took one look at her and groaned, "Dear God, you're a mess," with the perfect amount of disgust to snap Parv out of her urge to bawl for another two hours.

Angie wrapped her in a towel to keep her from marring the furniture and put Parvati in her sitting room again—the one part of the house that was completely Angie's, not overrun by Kevin and the kids—and thrust a glass of water into her hands with a command to hydrate. Then she leaned against the arm of the loveseat across from Parvati's chair, folded her arms, and glowered.

"I think you're being an idiot, by the way."

"I know." Parvati sniffled and sipped her water.

"What happened?"

"We broke up." Parvati didn't elaborate. There really wasn't anything else to say.

"For a reason? Or just because you care about him more than you've ever cared about anyone and that terrifies you?"

"Is this supposed to be helpful?" Parvati glowered as Angie glanced at her phone, her thumb moving across the screen. "Who are you texting in the middle of my emotional crisis?"

"Katie. She thinks you're being ridiculous too. I thought you believed love conquered all. What happened to that?"

"Well maybe I'm afraid he will never love me as much as I love him. Did you think of that? That maybe love only conquers all when you both love one another, not when one of you has had an unhealthy crush since she was fourteen that she really needs to get over."

"So that's all this was? A crush? The realization of a fantasy?"

"Of course not. I just…I was always going to be that girl to him. The one who was obsessed with him. The one who would take whatever scraps of affection he wanted to give her."

Angie cocked her head to the side, considering that. "That may be where you started, but relationships change all the time. What makes you think yours wouldn't?"

"He doesn't let people in, Angie," she explained. "I probably know him better than just about anyone and his first instinct is still to shut me out. I bet no one we know would even know we'd broken up if I didn't tell them. Max doesn't share his feelings. He doesn't share himself."

Angie eyed her phone again. "People change."

"Not that much. And I can't ask him to change who he is."

"What if he could show you that he wanted to change? That he was already changing? Would that make a difference?"

"That isn't going to happen, Angie."

"Hypothetically." Her thumb moved over her cell phone screen.

Parvati narrowed her eyes. "Are you still texting Katie?"

"And Devi. And Asha. Ranee's at a conference in Atlanta and I think she's already asleep or we'd definitely patch her in."

"I'm glad to know my crisis can bring the family

closer together."

Angie rolled her eyes. "Don't be sarcastic. We love you. We want to help you fix this."

"I know this might go against your worldview, Angie, but not everything can be fixed. Not even with a color-coded to-do list."

"I don't accept that." Her oldest sister looked at her with militant determination.

"I know if you could give me a happy life through sheer force of will you would—and I love you for it. But sometimes you have to accept that things aren't going to work out the way you want them to and move on with your life before you become so tangled up in trying to force a fairy tale that you make yourself miserable."

"I agree. But what if this isn't one of those times? What if this is just the time where Prince Charming is a little slow on the uptake but he really loves you like crazy?"

"That is a fairy tale—but the sad thing about fairy tales is that they aren't real." The doorbell rang and Parvati frowned in the direction of the front door. "Did you invite someone over?"

Angie glanced at her phone. "It's probably Katie. Sit tight."

Her sister vanished to go answer the door and Parvati stared fixedly at the curtains, wondering exactly how long it would take her to get over this gaping, empty feeling, as if her emotions had been scooped out by a melon baller.

She'd read somewhere that it took half as long to get over a relationship as the length of the relationship—but did that mean half of the three months they'd been together or half of the fifteen-plus years she'd loved him?

The scuff of a footstep in the doorway drew her attention off the diamond pattern on the rug—but it wasn't Angie who hesitated on the threshold.

Max stood between the propped-open French doors, still wearing his wedding tux and looking like something out of a bridal magazine, though his expression was more tentative than would have been allowed to grace the pages of *The Vow* or *Modern Bride*. "Can we talk?"

Parvati stood, needing to not be looking up at him— at least not so much. "What are you doing here?"

"I needed to see you. You ran off before I got to my rebuttal."

"But how did you know I was here?"

"I asked Sidney where she thought you would have gone and she suggested Katie's, so I called Katie, but she hadn't seen you so she texted Angie and Angie told us you were planning to stay here and then updated us when you showed up at the door, but by then we were already headed this way." He took a half step into the room and she took a step back, which made him stop. "I must have broken every speed limit on my way up here."

"I can't believe Angie ratted me out to you." Though frankly she could. It was so freaking Angie to think she knew best and act accordingly.

"Don't be mad at Angie. It was either this or have Tori call you and pretend to be in labor. She offered— which was really very sweet—but I thought you might kill me if we did that to you." Another half step and this time she forced herself not to retreat, even when he was only three feet away. Close enough to reach out and touch her. "Your friends were pretty determined to help me get you back. Don't you think you should at least listen to what I have to say?"

Something about what he'd said caught at her brain. "Did you tell them we'd broken up?"

"I was telling anyone I thought might know how to help me get you back. I know you don't think I'm capable of admitting weakness or asking for help—and a few months ago, you may have been right, but I have changed, Parvati. And not because you asked me to, but because you changed me. You opened my eyes. I'm not sure I ever would have realized how empty my life was without you. You're my link to everything. You're my heart. I'm not even sure I knew I had one before I gave it to you. So please. Give us a shot. Break up with me if you don't love me. Or if I hurt you. But not because you think I can't love you enough. Because if there is one thing I know I will always do, it's love you."

She couldn't seem to speak. The space where all her emotions had been scooped out was full again— bursting, so full she couldn't find room for words. "Max…"

"If I have to beg my sister for help or even *your* sisters, I will. You show me how to let people in, how to connect. You teach me that I need to be responsible *to* you—even if I suck at it sometimes because I don't know what I'm doing. I don't know anything about healthy relationships, Parv, but I *love* you and I will always keep trying. Please just give me the chance to prove I'm not a freaking island. I'm a peninsula. Because of you. Okay? You're my isthmus. Which sounded much more romantic in my head."

"That was quite a speech," she managed to whisper around the bursting well of feels.

"I practiced it on the drive. Did it work? Because if it didn't Sidney and Josh are waiting outside to vouch for me. And I've still got Tori ready to fake going into labor so I can rush her to the hospital and be a hero—thus proving how reliable I am. I mobilized the troops—"

"Max," she cut him off gently, putting a hand on his shoulder and going up on her toes. "It worked."

He didn't need any more encouragement to close the last of the distance between them. His arms slid around her, his lips settled on hers, and Parvati was home. God, how was it possible she'd missed him so much in just a matter of hours? One minute she'd been running out of the wedding reception, feeling like she'd broken her own heart on the rocks and the next—

"Hang on—" She broke the kiss, leaning back in his arms. "Aren't Sidney and Josh supposed to be leaving for their honeymoon right now?"

"They decided to take a later flight. She said she owed us."

Parvati teared up at the gesture—her best friend giving her blessing by helping Max and putting her own life on hold to do it—but gestures could be expensive with flight change fees. "We should tell them they can go the airport. Maybe they can still catch their original flight."

"Good idea," Max murmured, but his eyes were on her lips and he was lowering his head—

"You guys!" A rustle of tulle announced the arrival of Sidney, still in her wedding dress. "Glad to see everything's working out, but can we wrap this up? Tori's water just broke."

Max laughed. "We're good, Sid. We don't need the fake labor plan," he explained—not seeming to notice the tight strain in Sidney's voice, or the fact that Sid had never been that good an actor.

"Good for you," Sidney said. "But Tori's water really

did break in Angie's driveway. So come on, Romeo. Your car is the fastest."

* * * * *

"So this is what it means to be connected to people, huh? Everyone bossing you around and appropriating your car and making you sit around for hours in an uncomfortable tux waiting for the arrival of a very slow baby?" Max griped good-naturedly.

"Shut up." Parvati grabbed his arm and wrapped it around her shoulders, leaning into his side. "You know you love it."

He looked at her, the weight of the moment in his eyes. "I do."

They'd been at the hospital for nearly seven hours now, joined by the entire bridal party and Lorelei. They were all still in their formal wear because it seemed like every time one of them would feint toward going home and collecting jeans or yoga pants, Nick would rush into the waiting room with an update and everyone would forget that they were currently dressed to the bridal nines.

Then Nick rushed in with one last update—his eyes glazed with wonder. "Lorelei, come meet your little brother."

There were tears, cheers, questions after the mother (who was wonderful), the name (Jordan Neil), when they could see him. Parvati hugged everyone—grateful for Max's pocket square when she became a sappy mess. But if ever there was a day she was allowed to be a sappy mess, it was this one.

"Jordan Neil."

He was perfect. It was over an hour later when he

was put in the nursery and they were finally able to see him en masse. Parvati looked through the glass, Max standing behind her with his arms looped around her waist as he peered over her shoulder.

His voice rumbled through his chest at her back. "I was thinking we could get married."

Parvati twisted—trust Max to find the one thing that could distract her from Jordan in that moment. "What did you just say?"

"You did catch the bouquet. It's tradition."

"Don't you think that's a little fast?"

"I've known you since you were six years old. You're my best friend. You're the only one who calls me on my bullshit and drags me kicking and screaming into the human race. I need you, Parvati. And I love you like crazy. Let's make it legal."

Wow. When the universe decided to give her her dreams, it didn't play around. It was fast. It was so fast. But it felt like she'd been waiting all her life for something to feel this right. She wet her lips. "You're supposed to ask me, remember? Not just dictate the way things are."

He grinned, sheepish, that dimple flashing. "I'm afraid you'll say no."

She turned fully in his arms. "Ask, Max. I won't say no."

Then the love of her life smiled. He dropped his arms, reached into his pocket, pulled out a box and sank down onto one knee in the hallway in front of a nursery full of babies only a few hours old.

"Parvati Jai. Will you marry me?"

ABOUT THE AUTHOR

Award-winning contemporary romance author Lizzie Shane lives in Alaska where she uses the long winter months to cook up happily-ever-afters (and indulge her fascination with the world of reality television). She also writes paranormal romance under the pen name Vivi Andrews. Find more about Lizzie or sign up to receive her newsletter for updates on upcoming releases at www.lizzieshane.com.

WANT MORE LIZZIE SHANE?

MARRYING MISTER PERFECT
(Reality Romance, Book 1)

ROMANCING MISS RIGHT
(Reality Romance, Book 2)

FALLING FOR MISTER WRONG
(Reality Romance, Book 3)

PLANNING ON PRINCE CHARMING
(Reality Romance, Book 4)

COURTING TROUBLE
(Reality Romance, Book 5)

And look for Candy's story, LITTLE WHITE LIES,
coming in 2017.

LITTLE WHITE LIES

It all started with one harmless little fib...

Candy Raines has made a damn fine life for herself in California as the resident tech specialist for Elite Protection—far away from her high profile DC family. She may have told a few harmless little lies to keep her parents off her back, but as long as she keeps her two lives separate, no one has to know the truth.

Only now her sister is getting married and to keep her entire family from descending on Malibu and blowing up her perfect California life, Candy is forced to agree to come home for the splashy society wedding— and bring her husband with her. There's just one tiny problem. She isn't actually married.

Ren "Pretty Boy" Xiao owes Candy big, but flying to DC and pretending to be her husband for a week of glitzy events isn't exactly how he pictured repaying her. However, it may be the perfect chance to pin her down to something more than their on-again-off-again friends-with-benefits relationship.

Surrounded by her family, maybe that one little lie can finally reveal the truth he's been trying to make her see for years: that his heart was made for her.

Printed in Great Britain
by Amazon

57521718R00215